A BREACH IN TIME
COEUR DE LION BOOK I

First Published in Great Britain 2019 by Mirador Publishing

First edition: 2019

A copy of this work is available through the British Library.

ISBN: 978-1-913264-15-4

Mirador Publishing
10 Greenbrook Terrace
Taunton
Somerset
UK
TA1 1UT

A Breach in Time

Coeur de Lion Book I

Pamela Todd-Hunter

~ *Acknowledgements* ~

For Elyse and Rowan
A huge thank you to Chis O. who first helped me craft this book. I also want to
thank Kay C., Karen P., and Julie H. who fine-tuned it. I'd also like to thank
my husband for his unwavering support.

~ *Chapter 1* ~

THE AIR CRACKLED AND PULSED with electricity that raised the hair on Alix Evans's arms. She blinked and focused. The starburst behind her eyes faded, and her vision returned to normal. A canopy of dense trees towered above her, the scent of wet earth and decaying foliage thick in the air. Instead of sitting on the stone bench in the gardens at Nottingham Faire outside of Austin, she now lay on the ground in a pile of damp leaves.

Alix sat up. Her head spun and she closed her eyes, taking slow, deep breaths to calm her roiling stomach. Air gusted into her lungs and the dizziness passed. The stench of wet leaves and earth filled her nostrils. She glanced around the dense enclosure of trees. A hum assaulted her ears followed by the same electric charge she felt when she held the brooch.

The brooch. A warm sensation along with an eerie glow emanated from between her clenched fingers. She opened her hand to find that traces of blood had marked her palm with the insignia of the mounted knight. Her skin tingled as the powerful connection to the piece surged through her, but she forced herself to drop the bit of metal before something else strange happened.

The air stilled, and the glow dissipated. The brooch lay amongst red and golden leaves. Bloodstained or not, she would return it to the shopkeeper, that strange old crone who'd conned her friend Thomas into purchasing it for her in the first place.

Sunlight broke through the branches of the cedar, beech, and poplar trees, not the pine and oak trees characteristic of central Texas. The alcove she'd entered at Nottingham Faire had vanished. The bright sun dimmed as a cloud floated by, and Alix shivered. The temperature had dropped in a matter of minutes and she rubbed her arms for warmth. Other than the wind whispering through the foliage, silence suffocated her.

Somehow, she'd been transported into a true forest, not the carefully cultivated garden she'd enjoyed only seconds ago.

Did I fall asleep? Is this a dream?

Her stomach clenched, and her staccato breaths thundered like drumbeats in the quiet. Where were the Faire patrons? The silence struck her again. She was alone.

Her phone. If she could only find it and get a signal, she could text her friends. Going down on hands and knees, she swept through the rotting leaves. A moldy smell surrounded her as she brushed debris aside. "Where is it?" she muttered. She brushed her bangs out of her eyes and scrutinized the ground. The tightening in her chest told her the phone had disappeared along with the walking path and the bench.

The only familiar items were her Medieval costume and the leather pouch secured to her waist. She ripped it from her belt and peered inside, thinking she might have stashed the phone there, but no such luck. The pouch only contained a small wooden pot of lip balm, a glass vial of perfume, and the mirrored compact she'd dropped in it that morning.

A ray of sun glinted off the gold rim of the brooch. Using the hem of her skirt so she wouldn't have to touch it again, Alix picked it up and placed it in her pouch.

She stood and brushed off bits of leaves and sodden earth. Her muddy hands smeared dirt in long streaks down her dank skirt. Her best friend Cara had spent weeks hand-stitching the dress and now it was filthy. "Great, I look like I've been rolling around in a pigsty." A few steps away, a dirt road lay before her. Alix peered in both directions, seeing nothing familiar. Where were Cara and her cousin, Thomas?

She sighed and ran her hand through her hair. "Where am I?" Behind her the faint clumping of horses' hooves followed by voices echoed under the wooded canopy. She turned and squinted.

Men on horseback? Could they be from the Faire?

Alix walked a few steps closer to the road and then froze. Nothing looked familiar. The one thing she hoped to hear—the comforting laughter of visitors and the sounds of minstrels and hawkers was eerily absent. Her scalp prickled in warning. What if these strangers weren't from the Faire? She spun around and searched for the nearest object that could provide cover. A huge tree a few yards from the dirt road would do.

The jagged bark pricked her back, but she pressed closer to her means of protection. The jangle of metal and voices came closer. Her chest rose and fell with each rapid breath. If there was any hope of finding out where she was, she had to take a chance that these riders might offer a clue. Her heart beating in her throat, she peeked out to see men on horseback, dressed in Medieval armor. A lone man rode in front of the group, taking no part in the laughing and talking of those behind him.

Careful to remain hidden she craned her neck enough to study their garb. From pictures she'd studied in her doctoral courses in European history, their well-worn hauberks—shirts of mail protecting their bodies—looked to be from the twelfth century. Their manner of dress didn't match those of the patrons she'd been with at the Faire. Where did they get those amazing costumes?

She strained to listen as they rode close enough for her to hear.

"I wonder if that wench with the generous bosom is working tonight," one rider declared. "I've slept on the ground far too many nights and would like something much softer to lie down upon."

Alix's fingers convulsed on the tree bark until bits clumped under her nails. Her head swam and her mouth dried. The man spoke French. She'd spent a year studying in Paris and was fairly fluent in the language but this seemed to be an archaic dialect. How was she able to understand it?

"For certes, it's not a bed he wants to rest his head on," another man joked. "Fortunately for you, I know the girl and she is very accommodating."

Loud laughter filled the air and they continued to banter about the ladies that would be theirs for the taking when they reached the next town. She watched them for a few more seconds, again noticing their authentic armor, their posture, and even their strange accents.

Alix maneuvered around behind the tree, hiding and yet keeping them in sight while they rode by. Inching forward, her foot caught on a root. Pinwheeling her arms to keep her balance, she crashed through the underbrush and stumbled onto the road. The last rider turned and cried out, *"Domaisèla!"*

The procession came to a halt. The knight in the lead turned and rode back toward her. His beast loomed large as he drew it up a few feet away.

"I'm s-sorry," Alix stuttered, steadying herself. "I didn't mean…"

The knight cocked his head. "Miss, what are you doing so far from town?" He spoke to her in French, with the same odd dialect as the others, but in a more formal tone. "It's not safe for anyone to travel alone in this forest."

She looked up. Even seated on the horse, he appeared taller and more muscular than the others. His golden hair with its reddish undertones shone in the filtered sunlight. His blue-gray eyes fixed steadily on her, causing her breath to catch and her heart to hammer. He was gorgeous. His unwavering gaze held hers. Their surroundings faded and she focused on his angular cheekbones, strong, clean-shaven jaw, and his well-formed lips. His broad chest and muscular arms flexed as he shortened the reins to control his restless steed.

The man, clearly the group's leader, exuded power and danger. She drew a shaky breath and dragged her thoughts back to her situation with much effort. Until she could figure out where she was, she would stay in character, speak French, and hopefully keep safe.

"My lord, I was out taking a walk, but I fear I have gotten lost. Could you please give me directions back?"

He raised a brow. "You came out here to take a stroll? The town is five miles from here."

She looked down to one end of the road and then the other. All she could see in either direction was the packed-dirt path framed by a tunnel of trees, and nothing looked familiar. "You must be mistaken, sir. I'm certain I haven't walked that far."

"This is *my* realm, and I know it very well." His lips thinned. "You have traveled a much farther distance than you realize."

Two of the men mounted nearby snickered. She glanced sharply at them. "It's possible that I've ventured out farther than I thought, so would you please direct me how to get back?" Her instinct for survival kicked in. She swallowed to mask the tremor in her voice and pressed her trembling hands in fists against her skirt.

The man's jaw tightened. "Being delayed from wine and a soft bed by this slip of a girl is becoming a nuisance," he muttered behind clenched teeth to one of his men who'd ridden to his side. "Walk north on this road. Eventually, you will reach the outer gates."

Her chest constricted. Maybe once she reached the town she could figure out what was happening. She raised her shaking hand and pointed. "North is this direction, the way you travel?"

He gave her one curt nod.

"Your help has been truly invaluable. What little of it you gave." She uttered the last part under her breath. Who were these men? As a historian, she couldn't refute what she was seeing, but her rational mind rejected it. It was crazy to even consider the idea.

He lingered a bit longer, as if he considered saying something more, then turned. "Carry on, then." He spurred his horse and rode ahead of his men. He was heading the way she needed to go and hadn't even offered her a ride. The rest of his knights followed, except for the young, dark-haired man whom she'd startled earlier.

"The town truly is quite some distance away. Will you be safe by yourself?" Concern filled his amber eyes.

Alix peered down the seemingly endless dirt road and couldn't see any evidence of a town in the distance. She regretted her earlier snitty outburst but her pride refused to let her ask for help. She forced a smile. "Yes, but you must be running late. I don't want to keep you any longer."

"Are you sure you won't allow the Duke to escort you?"

"I can manage. You'd best go."

The young man nodded to her one last time and rode after the others.

As the hoof beats receded in the distance, she listened to the sounds of the forest return. Birds warbled in the trees and small animals rustled through the bushes. Alix filled her lungs with the clean crisp air and let out a big sigh. "Well, north it is." Five miles could take her up to two hours to walk and from the position of the sun's rays, it would be nightfall before she arrived. She took another deep breath and set off toward the nearest town, whatever it was.

She trudged along the dirt path, her stomach churning. Shadows from the forest lengthened, stretching like gnarled fingers as the sun arced toward the horizon.

The air chilled and she rubbed her upper arms, quickening her pace into a jog. To be caught at night in this forest terrified her.

Her nerves jangled as the creeping darkness brought back the memory of the worst night of her life. The man demanded her purse, a long, serrated knife in his hand, the blade shining blood-red as it reflected the sun sinking low in the sky. When she'd screamed and resisted, he'd struck her. After the assault, it had taken several weeks before she'd felt brave enough to leave the sanctuary of her apartment and feel safe again.

Alix fingered the two-inch scar hidden beneath her hair. Thomas had been there for her during the weeks after the attack. The self-defense classes he'd encouraged her to take had helped her develop an inner strength. She worked hard to stay in shape, and she could put up quite a fight.

"Get a grip, Alix. You can do this." Although her voice sounded small amongst the vast expanse of forest, the pep talk gave her a sense of calm as she continued on the well-traveled path. Her heart jumped at every sound and rustle from invisible hunters that prowled amongst the tangle of trees. Cold sweat broke out over her body and congealed on her icy skin as the scream from an animal, predator or prey, shattered the silence and her courage.

~~*

Night birds called out in the gathering dusk as the Duke held his steed to a trot. He breathed deeply of the cooling air and once again, his thoughts returned to the comely young woman they'd met. A bemused smile crossed his lips as he recalled her standing in front of him. Long copper-colored hair fell over her shoulders, but it was cut short in an unusual fashion over her brow, framing her hazel eyes and delicate features. Her manner of speaking was also quite different from the women in this region. He'd been surprised and intrigued by the brazenness with which she'd addressed him, but he'd sensed fear lurking beneath her bravado.

The Duke was accustomed to people recognizing him and attempting to curry favor, but this woman apparently had no idea who he was. What was she doing so far from town? At the rate she was walking it would be dark before she reached her destination. A gust of cold air rattled the skeletal branches and his breath misted in the air. The thin dress she wore would offer no protection in the autumn night. Not to mention what predators she might disturb in the dark. No longer could he ignore the guilt that had gnawed at him since they'd ridden on. He tightened the reins, slowed his horse, and wheeled around. He couldn't leave her alone in the forest.

~~*

After Alix had walked about half an hour, several small dark objects began to take shape in the distance. She recognized the men she had happened upon earlier. Although she hadn't forgotten the Duke's dismissive attitude, her heart hammered, and adrenaline snaked through her as he rode closer. She exhaled and then took slow breaths. The excitement that strummed in her blood could only be relief that he'd returned. She dashed to the side of the road to prevent being trampled under heavy hooves. The Duke reined in his horse a scant five feet from her.

"You will accompany us." His tone firm, and his jaw set, she knew there would be no arguing with him. That didn't mean she wouldn't try. This man needed to know she was not one to be ordered around.

"No, thank you. I can get to town myself." There was no need to add more problems to her current situation by traveling with men she didn't know to some unknown location. She had no hope of defending herself against them if they had dishonorable intentions. Every fiber in her body screamed *no way.*

"That was not a request." His gruff voice echoed under the dome of tangled branches.

She flinched. His order came from someone used to being in charge. She shook her head, trying to wrap her mind around her new reality and gain her bearings.

Alix focused on the path in front of her. "Miss, we need to ride on." His voice tensed, and his watchful gaze focused on the dark, impenetrable wall of thick trees. "There could be routiers wandering about. We don't have enough men to fend off an attack of that sort."

Her stomach clenched. *Routiers,* mercenary soldiers used during wartime in the mid-eleven hundreds? No. She wasn't in Austin anymore.

She shook her head. "I'm not going anywhere with you. I don't even know who you are."

The man arched his brow and his lips twitched as if he was amused by her query. "I am the Duke of Aquitaine."

Her equilibrium shifted and her mouth hung open. Instead of bedtime stories, her mother had filled her only daughter's head with tales of infamous kings and queens, starting her lifelong love of history. Richard the First had been the Duke of Aquitaine in the eleven hundreds before becoming the King of England. It couldn't possibly be him, the man she'd been fascinated with since she was a little girl. *Could it?* She'd spent countless months studying Richard, the subject of her dissertation, a man who had been vilified in history for his cruelty toward his subjects during his reign. The knight mounted before her looked eerily similar to drawings of the English king she'd seen. If he was Richard, somehow, she was in twelfth century France.

~ *Chapter 2* ~

HOW COULD SHE EVEN entertain an idea so ludicrous? This had to be a dream. Alix pressed her lips together to stop them from trembling. She was used to solving problems quickly, but her reasoning was as blurred as the amorphous shadows that threatened to engulf her. That brooch. It must have been poisoned or dipped in some hallucinogenic drug.

The snap of a large branch from the woods behind her decided the matter. Even in a dream she couldn't stay out here by herself.

"Very well," she said. "I'll go with you. I don't see an extra horse..."

"You will ride with my squire." He motioned toward the young man who had shown concern for her safety earlier. "Make haste." The command filled the air with authority. "I don't relish the idea of tarrying here in the coming darkness."

The sun sank below the horizon and the last golden rays cast long shadows from the forest on the road. It had only been late morning when she'd entered the gardens at the Faire, but it was getting inexplicably darker. And fast. She bowed her head. "Thank you. I do appreciate your generosity. My name is Alixandra."

"You are most welcome." He turned his horse and returned to the front of the group.

"Alixandra, let me help you up." The young squire dismounted quickly.

"Thank you. I didn't catch your name..."

"I'm Rob." He nodded to her and clasped his hands together to give her a boost. Alix fumbled about as she mounted the horse, trying to figure out what to do with her skirt. Alix's heart thudded. She'd worn thick cotton leggings under her costume since October in the Texas Hill Country could be chilly. Although she was glad that she wasn't about to give the young man an eyeful, women didn't wear leggings or any type of leg covering in Medieval time. She lifted her skirts and threw her leg over the saddle, hoping he wouldn't notice the modern garment. His eyes widened, and he glanced away nervously.

"They're called leggings, Rob. Haven't you seen a woman wear them before?"

"No, miss, I have not."

"They're common where I'm from." She smiled at him.

"And where might that be?"

Her smile faltered. "Excuse me? What do you mean?"

"Although you speak well, your accent is markedly different, as is your manner of speech."

Rushing blood filled her ears and her heart lurched. Alix struggled to come up with a plausible answer. "I'm from… the north of England." She prayed Rob bought her lie. The less information she offered, the less chance there was to make a mistake. She needed to keep things vague until she figured out where she was. "The Duke is waiting," she whispered, trying to change the subject as Richard's impatient scowl fell on them.

Rob sprang up behind her.

"Don't let me fall, Rob." Alix had ridden horses before, but Rob's steed was much larger than she was used to.

"I will keep you safe. You have my word."

"I'll hold you to that."

Alix needed time to think. Thank heavens Rob didn't say anything else. The foliage and natural forest along the road weren't native to the Texas Hill Country. She was no longer anywhere near Austin. That much was obvious. Where was she and how had she gone so far astray?

The longer she studied the men's manner of dress and speech, the more they seemed like true historical figures, and not of her time. Their armor was different, their hauberks dull and scuffed, not as highly polished as those of the Faire actors. Even the Duke's hauberk looked worn and repaired as if it had seen many battles. Her heart beat faster as she tried to reason out the facts. Although she knew what all this looked like, it didn't make sense. The brooch smeared with her blood rushed into her mind.

"How long have you served the Duke?" She both hoped and feared that her attempt to draw Rob into conversation would help solidify and confirm her suspicion, however wild and impossible it seemed.

"Six years. I was fourteen when I first became his squire."

Alix mulled over Rob's words. "Do these men often travel with him?"

"Yes. There are many disgruntled barons and lords in the Duke's realm that would wish him harm."

"I imagine it must be a difficult task keeping the peace over such a large region."

Rob laughed. "You're correct, but the Duke is a great military leader, and has been victorious in many battles. No man would dare oppose his rule."

"Will you remain in his household in order to become a knight?"

"Yes. It's an honor to be in his service." She felt his posture straighten. "He helped lead an army against his father when he was but sixteen." Admiration and a touch of envy filled his voice. "His bravery on the battlefield is legendary and many have said he has the heart of a lion. I know his skill as a commander is unparalleled. Now, at only five and twenty, he is one of the most renowned soldiers in all of France."

Alix's heart hammered so hard, it threatened to beat right out of her rib cage. Rob confirmed her suspicion. If what he told her was true, this particular Richard was the son of King Henry the Second, and although French born, would one day become the King of England. "No, no it can't be. That's impossible." Her whisper, muffled by the wind, would never find an ear. Her vision blurred, and she gripped the pommel of the saddle, her knuckles whitening.

Knowing Richard's date of birth, she quickly calculated it must be the year 1182 and she was in Medieval France, in the presence of the future ruler of England.

Their horse skittered as a bird flew out of a nearby tree. Already tense, Alix cried out. Rob put his arm around her to steady her but removed it quickly. "I apologize, miss, did I scratch you with my hauberk?"

Frustrated, confused and scared, Alix turned on him. "No! I am lost. I can't find my friends, and you people aren't helping at all!"

"Could you please repeat that?" Rob furrowed his brow. "I don't speak English."

Fear congealed in Alix's veins. How could he not understand English? It was spoken world-wide. This was further proof that she wasn't in Austin, or her time.

Richard turned back toward them at Alix's outburst. "Is there a problem?"

"What town are we going to?" she asked, making sure she spoke in French. "I don't even know where I am!"

"We are headed to the town of Poitiers, where I'm sure you will be able to sort yourself out."

"I highly doubt that," she whispered.

Richard stopped his horse until Rob and his steed came alongside. "What did you say?"

She sensed his growing annoyance as his eyes bored into hers. Richard was known to be a cruel ruler. If this was the true Duke of Aquitaine, she'd better stay in line, lest she end up in a dungeon or in the stocks. She gave him a shaky smile. "I appreciate your help." He stared at her a moment longer then turned his mount and rode ahead.

The thick foliage that bordered the dirt road began to thin, grading into an undulating grass plain. They rounded a bend, the dust tossed in the air by the horses' hooves creating a mystical feeling as they came up to two huge, wooden gates. Thick stone walls flanked either side of the road, towering above it. Richard cantered ahead and called out to the sentry perched atop the catwalk. The soldier's crossbow lowered when he recognized the Duke and motioned to the men below to allow the knights entry.

The gate and guardhouse looked nothing like the props used at Nottingham Faire. Alix scanned her surroundings, hoping to see something familiar. Instead, small wooden houses and stalls lined the dirt street. Merchants weren't hawking their wares to passers-by. Minstrels weren't trying to coax patrons to come to their shows, and the townspeople were dressed in simple, twelfth century fashion, unlike the fancy dresses and costumes of the Faire's patrons. Above the town in the distance, the battlements of a structure rose high, the rest of the building hidden by houses built on the rise.

"We've arrived." Rob dismounted and offered his hand.

Alix tried to hide her growing panic and swung her leg over the saddle as Rob helped her down. His cheeks flushed again at the sight of the leggings. She straightened her long tunic and noted that Richard had ridden over to the sentry to speak with him.

She stared at the ancient buildings. Her knees turned to water and she bit her lips to stifle a desperate sob.

Somehow, she had been transported to twelfth century France, with no friends, no money, nowhere to stay, and no idea how to return home. She had nothing, and these knights, the only people she'd had contact with, would soon leave. The temperature had continued to drop as the sun disappeared below the horizon, and she wrapped her arms around herself, shivering in the thin cotton tunic that covered her long dress. If she didn't find somewhere to stay for the night, she would certainly freeze.

"I trust you will be fine now, Alixandra?" Richard asked, when he rejoined the group several minutes later.

"Is there an inn where I can find a room for the night?" Women rarely traveled alone and staying at an inn without a chaperone was unheard of, but she had little choice but to ask outright for help.

Richard's brow arched. "Yes, follow this road for about three hundred yards. There is a tavern called the *Stag's Head* on the left. It's one of the more reputable ones in town, and I believe they might rent rooms."

He turned his horse away, and she tightened her arms around herself, nails digging into her upper arms, trying to curb her desire to run after him and beg him to take her with him.

"Farewell, Alixandra. I hope you find your friends." Rob bid her adieu.

"Thank you, I'm sure I will." She watched the knights spur their horses and gallop up the path toward the castle.

Finding a place to stay was paramount. She needed a warm haven where she could figure out what had happened and what to do next. She shivered again as the evening chill bit at her cheeks and numbed her hands. She exhaled a shaky sigh, the condensation of her breath drifting past her like a white cloud as she trudged toward the tavern. Her stomach knotted with fear and she rubbed her hands briskly then cupped them to her lips to blow warm air on them.

She didn't belong here.

~ *Chapter 3* ~

ALIX STOOD IN FRONT of the dreary looking tavern and breathed deeply. Hopefully, the owners would have a vacant room for the night and she could attempt to sort things out. Brushing the dried dirt from her skirt, she prayed she wouldn't be taken for a vagrant.

The heavy tavern door creaked as she pulled it open and stepped inside. All eyes turned toward her. She glanced around the dim, smoky room ignoring the men's stares, but one particular man caught her eye. He'd spoken to Richard at the town's gate and was now appraising her. She turned away, knowing her best hope was to find a serving girl who might help her.

Alix spied a plump, older woman with sandy-brown hair and approached her. The woman looked at her suspiciously and wiped her hands on a cloth.

"May I please have a cup of water? I've been traveling for quite some time and I'm very thirsty." The woman regarded her in silence. "I have..." Alix started to offer, but her voice trailed off when she realized she had no money. Tired and thirsty, the strange events of the day caught up with her. Tears rolled down her cheeks.

The woman's disposition changed instantly. "Oh, *chérie*." She hurried to Alix's side and put her arm around her. "There, there, don't worry. Come with me. Gerard!" she called out. "Bring me some water and food. Sit here, dearie." The portly woman led Alix to a table and moments later, Gerard, a mountain of a man with red hair and a full beard, placed a heaping plate of stew in front of her.

Alix looked gratefully up at him. "*Mercés*." She turned her attention to the woman. "I was told you might have a room for the night? I'm not from here and I don't have any place to stay."

"*Mon dieu*, you're traveling alone? How did you get here?"

That was a good question, and one Alix wished she had an answer to. She tore a chunk of bread in half. "I was lost in the forest. Some knights found me and brought me here."

"And then they just left you?"

"The man in charge did his duty by escorting me, and I have no complaints."

"I'm Petronilla. My husband, Gerard, and I own this tavern. You'll be safe here, so you needn't worry. I have a storeroom in the kitchen. It's not much, but you won't have to share it, and it will keep you out of the cold."

Alix's stomach churned at the thought of being turned out. She needed a safe place to stay until she could figure out exactly where she was and how she was going to get home. "I don't have any money, but I would like to repay you. Do you have need of a serving girl?" Alix's voice shook a bit and she hoped her desperation wasn't too obvious.

Petronilla studied her.

"I've worked in a tavern before. I can wash cups, help cook... do whatever needs to be done."

"Actually, I do require some help."

Alix smiled in relief. "Thank you. Again, I really do appreciate this. My name is Alixandra, but I am called Alix."

"Finish your dinner and then I will show you where you may sleep." Petronilla rose and returned to her tasks. Tendrils of steam wafted up from the stew and Alix dug in. She had no idea what meat it was made from, but she was so hungry it didn't matter. It tasted incredible.

Richard and his men galloped along the dirt road that graded slowly upward to where his residence perched as sentinel over the town. He hardly noticed the frigid air that seeped through his hauberk. The early fall chill was a normal part of traveling throughout his realm. The palace courtyard was empty as he reined his steed to a halt, but as his men entered behind him, stable boys hurried out to take care of the horses.

"Rob, I'm expecting the gatekeeper. Instruct the guards to send him to my chambers upon his arrival," Richard ordered. Without waiting for a response, he turned and strode toward the palace. He had arrived in Poitiers later than he desired. Although Alixandra's outspokenness had exasperated him, she'd also piqued his curiosity. As the Duke of Aquitaine his subjects treated him with deference and wouldn't dare stand up to him, yet this unknown girl had openly defied him. He wanted to learn more about her. A squire rushed forward to open the heavy wooden door.

"I require a hot bath and wine."

"Certainly, Your Grace."

Two hours later, Richard reclined in a large, ornately carved chair, in his chambers. One lean leg was flung over the arm as he listened to his knights and squires discussing the building of his latest castle, Clairvaux. Richly-colored tapestries depicting hunting scenes hung on the stone walls of the large airy chamber, while a crackling fire warmed and lit the room with an amber glow. Banter and laughter echoed from the camaraderie between the men, seated at various tables, playing chess and card games, their bets laid out on the smooth wood between them. Some relaxed on the settees, while others stood before the fire, taking advantage of the heat. Servants hovered, ready to refill cups with sweet wine.

A sharp knock sounded on the door, and at Richard's quick nod, a servant opened it. When the gatekeeper entered, Richard motioned him to approach. "Tell me what news you have, Stephen."

Stephen bowed. "The girl went to the tavern, as you expected, and spoke to the owner. I couldn't hear their conversation, but she began to cry."

Cry? She didn't seem to be that type of woman. "What happened then?" Richard demanded, raking his hand through his hair.

"The owner brought her food, and when she was finished, led her into the back. I didn't see her afterward."

Richard hadn't been able to forget the brave front she'd affected when he and his men left her, or the relief in her eyes when he'd returned. Usually chance meetings with women were of little consequence, but something about Alixandra captivated him. "I believe a visit to the tavern could prove very interesting," Richard mused. "Have a drink, Stephen. Well done."

* ~ * ~ *

Petronilla showed Alix to a small, dark storeroom that smelled faintly of stale beer and sour wine.

"Please, is there a privy I can use?" Alix asked.

"Certainly, it's outside to the left in a circle of trees. You can reach it through the kitchen. Take this lantern, for you'll have need of it."

The frigid outside air shocked Alix. Shaking from the cold, she waited for her eyes to adjust to the darkness. The babbling sound of water flowing over rocks and a small copse of trees silhouetted against the dark indigo sky indicated where the toilet was located. Alix walked over, eyes on the ground to avoid roots and stones. A wooden seat with a carved hole was placed just above a deep hollow in the earth. Her nose wrinkled but needing to relieve herself, she had no other choice than to use it. She lifted her skirts, and feeling very exposed, finished quickly. Alix scrubbed her hands in the icy water upstream until they were numb, then rushed back to the tavern.

Petronilla had left a tallow candle for her in the storeroom, which smoked and emitted a foul scent, but Alix prayed it would never go out as she settled down on the grimy pallet and looked with distaste at the threadbare blanket that would serve as her only cover. She exhaled heavily and chided herself for feeling ungrateful. She now knew where and when she was but had no idea how she got there or how to get home. This was not Nottingham Faire, nor was it Austin. Her world had been turned upside down and she had no idea how to right it.

She shifted uncomfortably on the pallet and winced as the wound on her hand scraped against the rough blanket. She held up her hand and looked at the small puncture. When she'd examined the brooch in the gardens at the Faire, she'd accidentally pricked herself. Then, she'd awoken here. Somehow the brooch Thomas bought had transported her to this place, but how and why?

Her pouch still hung from the belt around her waist. It appeared as though the items on her physical body had remained with her. She wished she hadn't placed her phone beside her on the bench in the Faire's garden. Then again, there wasn't cell service, electricity, or indoor plumbing in 1182. All the creature comforts she'd taken for granted had vanished with her trip to the past.

She grabbed the pouch, opened it, and carefully pushed aside the contents until she found the brooch. Alix took it out. Her heart raced, and adrenaline shot through her. The strange connection she'd felt when she'd first seen the piece of jewelry in the shop surged again. She turned it over in her hands, her soul connecting anew with the piece. She knew this image of an engraved knight on horseback well. It was Richard the First's great seal.

The wizened shopkeeper had told her it was authentic but that was impossible. If it was a priceless antique, it would be under lock and key in a museum, not in a shop at a renaissance fair in twenty-first century Texas. Alix frowned and scraped remnants of her dried blood off the brooch with her fingernail to uncover the engraving. It was a plain piece of jewelry, so why did she feel so drawn to it?

The woman's prediction echoed in her ears. After wrapping up the brooch and handing it to Alix, the shopkeeper had pointed to Thomas with a gnarled index finger. "He's not the man for you. You're meant for another. The path you are on remains unwritten, but you can decide your fate, and his."

At the time, Alix had scoffed at her words. The woman probably read tarot cards and tea leaves and was adept at delivering cryptic messages. But was it possible the brooch had the power to move her through time? She shook her head at the idea. Witches and spells only existed in fairy tales, yet somehow, she'd landed in the twelfth century and she was able to converse in an ancient dialect. She studied the brooch, turning it this way and that, willing it to do something, anything, but it only reflected the dim light from the candle as any normal piece of jewelry would.

Panic's icy fingers crept up her spine. Her breath came quick and the walls of the small room closed in on her. She forced herself to pull in deep, calming breaths, but it took only one exhale to extinguish the fragile candle flame. The squeaking and scurrying of rodents were easy to detect now that the lack of light provided cover for their nocturnal travels. She could strangle Thomas for buying the brooch for her. If he hadn't, she'd be with him and Cara now, enjoying the shows at the renaissance festival, instead of sitting in a dingy storeroom wondering how and if she was ever going to find a way home.

"What am I going to do?" she whispered into the darkness.

* ~ * ~ *

The tiny room echoed with the sound of a light knocking on the door. "Wake up. It's time for work," Petronilla called out. "I've left a basin with some water in case you'd like to wash up."

"God, Mom," Alix muttered, rolling over on the pallet. Then, with a jerk, she bolted upright, remembering where she was. "Okay, I'm getting up." Dust motes swirled in the narrow shafts of sunlight that streamed through small cracks in the walls. Alix shivered in the cool morning air that had drifted in. She padded to the door, opened it, and saw a small wooden basin filled with water and a cloth. She hesitated. Where did the water come from? She hoped it wasn't from the stream the privy was adjacent to. Just in case, she only used the water to wash her arms. Dirt streaked down when she sluiced the water over them and she scrubbed them briskly with the towel.

Opening her pouch, she took out her compact and gazed into it. Fortunately, her eyes weren't as bloodshot as she had expected. She searched for the lip balm and applied it. Such a simple thing here was a luxury. As she smoothed the salve on, the familiar act calmed her, and she leaned back against the wall, a touch less anxious than when she'd first stepped into the tiny room. She spritzed some perfume on her wrists, pinched her pale cheeks to bring the blood to the surface and finger-combed her hair. Ready to face the day, whatever it may hold, she took a deep breath. The scent of wood smoke mixed with the aroma of cooking wafted through the air and caused her stomach to rumble.

She found Petronilla in the kitchen. "Good morrow, Petronilla, and thank you again for your generosity."

"You're most welcome, *chérie*. Can I get you something to eat?" Petronilla wiped her hands on the apron that protected her plain home-spun dress.

"Yes, whatever you've cooked smells incredible and coffee would be wonderful."

"Coffee? What is coffee?"

She sighed. She'd forgotten that coffee hadn't even been discovered yet. "Cider then, if you have it?"

Petronilla brightened. "Yes, I have that. Go sit."

Alix took a seat at one of the long, trestle tables, darkened with age and use. Now that she was in a better frame of mind, she looked curiously around the room. The only window in the tavern was cut into the wall near the door. A thin animal hide covered it, which allowed watery sunshine into the room. Tallow candles as well as lanterns provided light for most of the room. The kitchen, although small, was the food and drink preparation area. Alix found it strange that the traditional bar she'd imagined in every alehouse was absent. Instead, Alix surmised the large wooden casks stacked in a corner near the kitchen were filled with the wine and ale.

Petronilla emerged from the kitchen and put a plate on the table in front of Alix, filled with crusty bread and butter and a slab of thick, salted pork.

"Thank you, Petronilla, but you don't even know me. What made you decide to take me in?"

"You looked desperate. Gerard and I were never able to have children, but I can imagine how I would feel if my daughter was in trouble. I would hope someone would help her out."

"I am pretty desperate," Alix joked, trying to lighten the severity of her situation with laughter.

"You can stay as long as you need. Now, finish your breakfast. We open soon, and I have some chores for you." Petronilla pointed to cups and wooden trenchers piled high on the table next to a large, wooden bucket.

The rest of the morning passed in a blur. Alix was kept busy serving patrons and didn't have a minute to herself. By the time the tavern closed, her feet hurt and her arms were sore from carrying heavy trays. She massaged her aching shoulders and guessed it had to be at least eight o'clock, perhaps later, but without her cell phone or even a watch, she had no way of knowing. She mentally thanked God she'd worn simple flats to Nottingham Faire instead of the heeled boots she had originally planned on. At the thought of the Faire, her stomach knotted and beads of sweat broke out on her brow. Were her friends and family aware she was missing? How would she return to them? While working, she had been able to forget her situation, but here, in the quiet of the empty tavern, reality came crashing down on her.

"You did very well today, Alix; much better than other girls I've hired." Petronilla's compliment was coupled with smiling eyes.

"Thank you. I truly had nowhere else to go." Alix lowered her gaze before Petronilla could observe the spur of panic in her eyes. The older woman patted her on the shoulder before turning away to sort cups.

The hours passed quickly. While the two washed the dishes and wiped down the wooden tables, Petronilla told stories of opening the tavern and the mistakes and missteps made while learning the business. The tavern owner was very outgoing, and if she noticed Alix did not reciprocate in kind, she didn't mention it.

After bidding Petronilla good night, Alix retreated to the storeroom with a tallow candle and sank onto her pallet. She wrapped her arms around her knees and watched the candle flame flicker, throwing menacing shadows on the walls.

Time travel was impossible, of course. It was the stuff of fantasy and fiction, and yet somehow here she was. While reading Medieval history, she'd imagined the difficulties of living in the Middle Ages, with no electricity, running water, or modern conveniences, but experiencing them was entirely different.

She took out the brooch again and studied it, tracing the edges, but it remained unchanged. If she wasn't able to return home soon, she wondered if she ever could.

* ~ * ~ *

By the following afternoon, Alix was beginning to learn the routine at the tavern. Delivering drinks and cleaning tables wasn't too difficult a task, and she felt confident that soon she would be able to master the job. This tangible skill might keep a roof over her head. That is, if Petronilla allowed her stay.

"There are only a few patrons left. Why don't you fix a plate of food for yourself and take a rest? I'll manage things out here." Petronilla's offer couldn't come soon enough. Alix helped her carry drinks to one of the few occupied tables.

"Thanks. I didn't realize how hungry I was until you mentioned food."

Petronilla laughed. "You have worked quite hard today. You deserve to get off your feet for a while."

Alix went to the kitchen and sliced a chunk of dark bread. She looked at the meat, swimming in a gelatinous brown sauce. Unsure of its origin, she decided to pass and instead added some turnips and carrots to her plate. After learning that the water used for cooking and cleaning came from the town well, Alix felt that it was safe to drink. She poured a cup and took her lunch outside.

She leaned against a tree and inhaled deeply, the cool, crisp air filling her lungs. The front of the wooden tavern faced the main road, and the small copse of birch trees bordered the back. The nearby stream murmured soothingly as it wound its way through the countryside. Golden chords of sunlight streamed through the leaves, creating undulating designs on the soft, green grass. The sky was a more vivid blue than any she'd ever seen in Texas, contrasting sharply with the gold and red leaves. It was so beautiful here. Perhaps she could manage this after all, for a while at least. She refused to let herself dwell on the possibility of never seeing her home and family again.

Opening her pouch, she removed the brooch and rubbed her fingers over the engraving, focusing on returning to the Faire and her friends. Once again, its appearance remained unchanged, and she let out a sigh before putting it back. She finished her meal and clambered to her feet, brushing dust and leaves from her skirt.

Soon after she entered the kitchen, Gerard called out to her. "Alix, deliver these mugs to the men in the corner and when you are done, clear the rest of the tables."

Alix leaned over a long table, pulled soiled mugs toward her, and placed them on a tray. She took a wet rag and wiped down pools of spilled ale and burgundy wine discoloring the wood even more than it already was. Once done, she glanced around to check if other tables required her attention. A man sitting in the shadows motioned to her with his cup. She picked up the tray, balancing the empty mugs and maneuvered to avoid men who tried to grope her.

"Wine or ale, sir?" she queried as she drew near.

"Wine." The man's eyes met hers and her heart fluttered. Somehow, he seemed familiar, although his face was in shadow.

She took his proffered cup and returned a few minutes later with the drink. As she turned to leave, he grabbed her hand.

An electric shock snaked through her body at his touch. "Let go of me!" she hissed through clenched teeth.

"Obviously you've persuaded someone else to help you. You appear to have a talent for that."

She knew the deep baritone voice.

"Come now, no witty riposte?"

She rubbed her fingers to erase the feel of his warm hand. "Ri— uh, Your Grace? What are you doing here? I would have thought you had better things to do than spend your coin in a tavern. Don't you have a duchy to run?" Her annoyance at his rudeness the day he'd rescued her colored her tone, and her reply came out tart.

"I had misgivings about leaving you and wanted to see how you were faring, but I believe I have wasted my time."

"I daresay you have." She turned away, her words belying the fact that she was thrilled this legendary man had even remembered her, let alone was interested in her welfare. She whirled to face him again. "Why did you really come here? You couldn't possibly have felt guilty about abandoning me."

"You didn't seem like the type of woman to work in a tavern."

"Well, it's only been a couple of days." She crossed her arms. "I'm still learning."

"I meant that you carry yourself well, Alixandra, and your manner of speech indicates you're better educated than most women who work in taverns. I came to offer you a position."

"Oh. What sort of position, may I ask, is appropriate if I'm well educated?"

"I imagine you are aware that my mother has been—" Richard paused, a flash of fury in his eyes, "— confined— for many years, and I am overseeing her domiciles. Currently, I am in residence at her palace here in Poitiers. Since her imprisonment, many of the household servants have sought out other employment. My duties as the Duke of Aquitaine have brought me here more often, and I've found I require more help with the upkeep of the palace, if you are amenable?" He drank deeply of his wine, awaiting her response.

She shifted the wooden tray to reposition the weight, and a tingle of excitement crept up her spine for the first time since she'd landed in this upside-down world. This was a golden opportunity to be close to the legendary subject of her dissertation. Being able to include a first-hand account of surviving in the Middle Ages would make her library research pale in comparison.

She stood back and took a long account of the Duke. His steady blue-gray gaze held hers, and even seated, his strength and magnetism were impossible to ignore. She wasn't quite ready to acknowledge it but being close to him stirred something in her.

Serving in his household would most likely be similar to working at the tavern, but in this unfamiliar place, a position in his household would undoubtedly give her more options, and she needed as much help as she could get until she could sort things out. Petronilla and Gerard had been very kind to take her in, even though they didn't have the means to give her more than food and a place to sleep. She needed money to survive, and Richard was in a better position to provide that.

"Why are you so willing to help me now, when it appeared as though you couldn't wait to get rid of me only a few days past?" She set the heavy tray down on the table.

"I thought we might be beneficial to each other, but I'm beginning to believe otherwise." His cool reply intrigued her.

"I accept your offer," she blurted out before he had the chance to rescind it. Alix picked up the tray again. "Let me tell the owners. They've been generous to me. I would be grateful if you gave them some money for their trouble." She smiled brightly at him, turned, and walked over to Petronilla.

"Petronilla, I was offered a... um, position..." Alix fumbled for words, feeling guilty about leaving the tavern owner so abruptly after being shown such kindness. She looked down at the floor, trying to find the words as to why she was leaving, when Richard unexpectedly saved her.

"Thank you for taking Alixandra in and giving her a place to stay, but she is leaving with me."

Petronilla looked at him with suspicion, then at Alix. "Are you sure about this, *chérie*? You don't know this man, do you?"

"Actually, I do. He's the one who brought me here."

"You mean he's the one that left you?" Petronilla glared at him.

Richard's lips twisted at the accusation. "A situation I am currently remedying."

Petronilla looked at him carefully, then curtsied. "Oh! Your Grace, I didn't recognize you. Forgive me for being so bold."

"I appreciate what you did for Alixandra." He turned to steer Alix to the door, but she stopped and looked at Petronilla.

Richard stared at her, lifting his shoulders in question. She touched her pouch then glanced again at Petronilla.

"Ah." He smiled wryly.

Alix sensed he was controlling his tone with difficulty, but he put enough coins in Petronilla's hand to run the tavern for at least two months. "For your trouble."

Petronilla gasped in shock. "You are too generous, Your Grace." Richard nodded curtly and left.

Alix gave Petronilla an impulsive hug. "Thank you again for your kindness and thank Gerard for me too."

"You are most welcome, and you could do much worse than the Duke. I've heard he is a fair man."

Based on what Alix knew of Richard, she wasn't at all sure of that assessment, but she hugged Petronilla again and whispered in her ear, "I pray you're right."

~ *Chapter 4* ~

ALIX PULLED THE HEAVY, tavern door open, as Richard led his horse toward her. She eyed the huge animal and Richard smiled at her. "Allow me, Alixandra." He clasped his hands together and she gathered her skirt up and straddled the horse. His eyes widened as he took notice of her leggings, and then leapt up behind her. "Easy." He laid a calming hand against the horse's neck as the animal shifted restlessly beneath them. He put his well-muscled arm around Alix to hold her steady and she covered it with her own. Richard spurred his steed forward and she rocked back, feeling his warmth behind her. They cantered up the road to the palace, and she was all too aware of his arm around her waist as they moved together with the horse's long stride. Richard's breath caressed her neck and his thighs lightly brushed against hers.

An ache burned low in her stomach and warmth flowed through her body, the strength of the urge catching her by surprise. After all, she'd spent years fascinated by, yet despising the very man who now held her in his arms. She concentrated on the scenery and tried to ignore her desire. However misplaced, she didn't fully trust this man.

They passed small but tidy houses, leaving the town behind. As they rounded a curve, the palace of Poitiers appeared in all its glory.

"My God," she breathed. "It's beautiful. I've never seen anything that rivals it." Her honest statement surprised even her as she stared in awe at the structure, which had stood in various incarnations since the ninth century. Numerous vendors had parked their carts outside the gates to sell produce, meat, and other necessities to the inhabitants. Richard wove his way through the mass of people and nodded to the guardsmen as they entered the gates. The tall, rectangular keep, constructed with light-gray stones, gleamed in the bright sun. Four smaller towers projected from each corner.

"The architecture is amazing! If there is a garden here, I would love to see it! And the dining hall, it must be immense. Do you have a chapel, as well?" Alix couldn't keep the excitement from her voice and turned around in his arms to look at him.

"Alixandra, you're going to be here quite a while. You will have much time to explore." The low rumble of his laughter vibrated against her back, sending goose bumps down her arms.

She wasn't sure how long she would be here before the brooch decided to whisk her back to the present, but she was going to do her very best to make the most of the time she had. When they reached the courtyard, Richard jumped down and then turned to help Alix. He gripped her waist as she held on to his shoulders and slid her leg off the horse. She had to look up to thank him. Blue-gray eyes caught hers. Blood pounded in her ears and her mind went blank. She swallowed, lowering her gaze to his neck where his pulse beat strong and quick. His warm hands squeezed her waist ever so softly. Had she imagined that, or did he just indicate interest in her?

A groom reached for the reins, breaking their moment. Richard released her. Placing his hand on the small of her back, he guided her to the large, wooden door of the palace. The hinges grated as a servant opened it and the click of their shoes echoed off the high-ceilinged entryway. Through a stone archway to the left, a vast hall, measured at least fifty feet in length. Long wooden trestle tables and benches filled it, no doubt to accommodate the large number of residents and guests. A short flight of steps, which spanned the width of the room, led to a dais where another trestle table flanked an immense fireplace located along the wall. Arched windows stood high above the stone floor and lanterns hung from the heavy, wooden beams, which supported the ceiling. Ahead of her, a set of stairs led upward, and to her right was a closed door.

He followed her gaze. "Obviously, the dining hall is to the left. The stairs ahead lead to the royal apartments, and the door to the right leads to more guest quarters and the kitchen." He stood aside to let her ascend first, and they climbed the steps to a long hallway flanked by windows on one side. Through the glass, the tops of trees swayed in the breeze, and as she moved closer, she found that they overlooked the gardens.

She gasped at the sweeping expanse of land with its neatly trimmed shrubs and hedges as well as sculpted trees. "Your gardens are incredible! You must enjoy spending time in them."

Richard's lips curved and he shrugged. "I haven't had much cause to frequent them." He led her down the hallway while she furtively glanced into open doorways as they passed.

"This is where the servants reside." They reached a door at the end of the hall. At his knock, a very young girl with blonde ringlets opened the door.

"Good evening, Your Grace." She curtsied dutifully.

"Is Lady Melisende within?"

The girl stood aside to let them in. A woman in her mid-fifties with graying hair and stern features hurried to greet them.

"How can I be of service, Your Grace?"

"This is Alixandra. She is now a member of your staff." Richard put his hand on Alix's shoulder and pushed her forward.

Alix looked around the room with interest. It was very spacious with several windows on the far wall. Tapestries hung from the ceilings and Alix surmised they cordoned off the sleeping and bathing areas. Rushes covered the stone floor to help ward off the chill, and she tried to hide her horror, aware of what vermin lived within. approached.

"Certainly." Melisende's eyes widened in surprise. "She is most welcome. Sybilla, please come here." A curvaceous brunette girl a few years younger than Alix had been watching the exchange closely. At Melisende's request she rushed over.

"Sybilla, find a place for Alixandra to sleep and put her belongings," Melisende requested quietly, kindness shining from her brown eyes.

Alix's cheeks reddened. In this world, she was a pauper, void of any possessions, money or status. "I don't have..." she began to say, but Richard held up his hand, silencing her.

"Provide Alixandra with everything she requires."

Melisende understood immediately. "I'll take care of her, Your Grace."

"I trust you will." And with that, the conversation was over. Richard nodded at Alix and turned, his large frame leaving the expansive doorway vacant as he strode purposefully down the corridor, his footsteps echoing behind him.

A pretty, blonde, buxom girl appeared from within one of the doorways Alix and Richard had passed. The girl sashayed over to him and leaned in. Whispering in his ear, she batted her eyelashes and pouted out her bottom lip. Alix raised a brow. She had a good idea of what the girl offered. In this age, a single, incredibly handsome man had his choice of bedmates, and this girl's boldness indicated a familiarity between them. Alix imagined that a nobleman would prefer a bird in the hand as opposed to finding a woman in town, and many a servant girl had warmed royal beds.

Her face warmed and her jaw tightened. A stab of disappointment as well as jealousy shot through her, but she quickly pushed the feelings deep down so her catty emotions wouldn't show. No need to start off looking like a jealous brat. She would need the trust and friendship of the women in this room to survive.

As the blonde tart stroked Richard's arm, he turned, and his eyes met Alix's disapproving look. A light flush colored his high cheekbones. Looking down his nose at the girl, he shook his head and moved on.

"Tell me what you have need of." Alix heard Melisende's kind voice and turned from the scene before her.

"A bath, please." Alix rubbed her hand over her skirt. "And I'd like to launder my clothes, if possible."

"Sybilla will assist you with both of those things."

"Thank you very much. I appreciate it." Alix gave the older woman a fleeting smile.

Melisende hurried off and left Alix with Sybilla. "Who was that fair woman talking to the Duke?" Alix asked as nonchalantly as possible.

"That's Beatrice, one of his preferred women. It looks like she'll be sleeping here tonight." Before covering her mouth with her hand, Sybilla giggled, deep dimples appearing in her round cheeks. "Come on. Let's ready you for supper."

She led Alix behind one of the curtains where a medium-sized wooden tub stood empty next to several metal buckets filled with water. Alix grimaced. The water was ice cold. In a deep recess in the corner of the room, a wooden bench caught her eye. With difficulty, she swallowed down her disgust as she recognized the toilet, but at least it was indoors.

"I'll heat the water for you. We always keep the buckets full since the well is some distance away." Sybilla busied herself with the extensive task of preparing Alix's bath. A fire burned in the fireplace in the main chamber, and soon hot water filled the tub, the steam curling and disappearing into the cool air above.

Sybilla pointed to glass bottles on a shelf next to the tub. "We have scented oils, rose, lilac, and lavender. Here's some soap and a cloth for you to dry off with, Alixandra."

"You can call me Alix, and thank you, I can manage now." Sybilla smiled, then left her alone to bathe in peace.

Alix picked up the oils and sniffed each one, deciding on lilac. She added the scent and inhaled the heady aroma. As the sun set, the room began to darken, and she undressed quickly. She faced the wooden tub and wrinkled her nose. It looked like it hadn't been scrubbed in some time, so she steeled herself before she stepped into the bath. When she did, she was surprised that the lukewarm water was heavenly. She lathered the gritty cake of soap in her hands and scoured her skin thoroughly. The water began to chill and she washed her hair before it became too cold. The 'towel' was coarse against her sensitive skin, but she rubbed herself vigorously to get as clean and dry as possible.

She padded to the curtain and called out tentatively, "Sybilla?"

"Yes, what do you need?"

"I don't have anything to wear."

"Oh." Sybilla entered the room. "Melisende has taken your clothes to be laundered. You can borrow one of my dresses. You're a bit taller than I am and more slender, but the skirt can be lengthened, and we can adjust the bodice using the laces. If you would like, I can also help you with your hair. It's the most beautiful chestnut color, but I've never seen the sun cause streaks in the hair like yours." Sybilla ran her fingers gingerly over Alix's wet tresses.

Alix forced herself not to laugh. Of course, highlighting your hair wouldn't be invented for centuries. She wondered how much her copper streaks would have grown out by the time she returned home. If she could return home. "Why do you cut your hair like this?" Sybilla asked, pointing to Alix's forehead.

Alix fluffed her damp bangs. "These are called bangs, or fringe, depending on where you're from."

"Your hairstyle is quite unusual, but if you're from another country..." Sybilla pursed her lips. "Now we need to find a veil for you to wear."

"Don't bother. I'll wear it loose."

Sybilla looked shocked. "Alixandra, you must wear a veil, since you're not married. Or, are you?"

Alix pulled her lips between her teeth to keep from laughing aloud. Well-bred women in this time wore veils so upstanding men wouldn't be enticed by the sight of the beauty of their hair. She hated wearing anything on her head but she knew she had to blend in. "No, I'm not, so, you're correct. I'll wear a veil."

"Good. I have one you can borrow," Sybilla stated, no doubt relieved that Alix was going to adhere to the proper attire and she wouldn't be scolded for letting Alix out inappropriately dressed. "Now for the dress." She handed Alix a white chemise followed by a simple brown tunic.

Sybilla altered the bodice by tightening the laces and it fit well enough. The skirt was a little short, but the bell sleeves were long and weren't noticeably ill-fitting.

She stood back and eyed Alix. "You look very pretty. I'm sure the Duke and his knights won't be able to keep their eyes off you." A touch of wistfulness laced her tone.

The same girlish envy appeared to transcend centuries. "Thank you for the compliment, but I'm certain no one will be interested in me." The other girl turned away and Alix opened her compact to examine her fresh-faced appearance. She never went outside without mascara and a touch of eyeliner and she felt naked and self-conscious. The little make-up she had on when she arrived was gone, so she pinched her cheeks and bit her lips to bring some color into her pale complexion. She spritzed some perfume on the inside of her wrists, and replaced the small, glass vial in her pouch, feeling more confident.

As they entered the dining hall, Alix hung back, amazed at how many people already occupied the benches. A warm fire roared in the enormous fireplace at the end of the room and Alix wondered how close she could get to it, as the cavernous hall was quite chilly. The long tables were set with trenchers, cups, and platters of food. Well-dressed nobles took their places at tables below a raised dais, while knights, squires and pages sat further down. Kitchen servants hovered attentively, refilling cups and flagons, minding their code of silence in the presence of the nobles.

"Is that where the royals sit?" Alix nodded toward the dais. She knew that's where Richard would be, but her pretense of being a curious, new servant would serve her well for some time as she adjusted to her new life. Upon close inspection of the room, she was disappointed to find him absent.

"Yes. The Duke's household servants' tables are over there. Follow me." Sybilla pointed toward the opposite end of the hall, far from the roaring fire.

Several other servants, already seated at the table, chattered, and stole glances at the knights. Alix took her place, gazing around and taking in everything when Sybilla pulled her to her feet. "The Duke will arrive soon. We must stand and curtsy, as we're in his service. There he is."

Richard entered, deep in conversation with a dark-haired, well-dressed older man. Alix's breath caught in her throat. The strands of red in his golden hair reflected in the light from the fire and his close-fitting tunic accentuated his muscular chest while his chausses encased his long legs. No one could mistake him for one of his knights. He exuded royalty.

As soon as he passed by, the girls at the table were free to sit. Their babble started at once.

"Isn't he handsome?"

"I wish he would notice me."

"Beatrice is indeed fortunate to warm his bed." At that comment, she was taken aback by another stab of jealousy. This man seemed to bring out feelings in her she had not felt in, well, ever, and it caught her off guard every time they flared. The disdain she had developed for Richard over years of studying him mixed with a warm feeling in her chest. She rebuked herself. He hadn't even glanced in her direction.

Servants appeared, carrying trays and platters of meats and boiled vegetables.

"What type of food is served here?" Alix was adventurous and enjoyed trying a wide variety of cuisines but was certain she wouldn't recognize any dishes placed before her this evening.

"We have the usual vegetables, rabbit, and fish. The night before Christ's Mass, we'll have a veritable feast, with venison, goose, duck, desserts, mulled wine, and mead."

"Christ's Mass?" Alix repeated in a dazed voice.

"It's only two months away, but it's my favorite of the Holy Days." Sybilla smiled and put a bite into her mouth.

Alix's insides quaked at the thought of spending Christmas here. She had to figure out how to get home before then. As unbelievable as this was, the opportunity of a lifetime, she had responsibilities. She'd spent over a year researching and writing her dissertation, and if she didn't meet her deadline, all her hard work would have been for naught. She could kiss her teaching career goodbye.

Besides, her friends and family must know by now that she was missing and be worried sick about her. Her hand shook as she grasped her goblet and she took a gulp of wine to cover her rising panic. She grimaced. The drink was overly spiced and too sweet, not like the wine to which she was accustomed. She motioned to one of the servants and asked for water. A look of bewilderment spread over the girl's pixie-like features.

"Water?" she asked in surprise. "Yes. I will fetch you a flagon from the kitchens."

If most people in modern-day drank wine with every meal, they'd be constantly drunk or have a permanent hangover, herself included. How did these people do it? Waiting for her water, she looked at the platters in front of her but couldn't identify the meats. She took bread, boiled rutabagas, and beans, but skipped the fish since it still had the head on. She scooped up her food with the chunks of bread and managed to eat her meal without the luxury of utensils.

At last, supper was finished and the plates and platters cleared. Alix picked up the flagon of water that the girl had brought and poured it into her cup. The minstrels began to play and people rose to dance. Alix found that she enjoyed the music, although she didn't know the songs or the steps. As she looked around the room, she spied the young squire who'd been concerned about her welfare in the forest. He passed by the table and stopped when he recognized her.

"Alixandra! How is it that you are here?" Rob's enthusiastic question and huge smile turned a few of the servants' heads in her direction.

"Hello, Rob!" Alix was genuinely pleased to recognize a friendly face. "Apparently, the Duke felt guilty about leaving me on my own, so he offered me a position as one of his household servants."

"This is indeed good news!" The music started again and Rob smiled and gave her a small bow. Holding out his hand he asked, "Would you care to dance?"

Sybilla looked none too pleased with this exchange, nor did Richard, who had left his table and was approaching them at a quickened pace.

"I'm unfamiliar with the steps, but I'm sure Sybilla would be pleased to accompany you." Alix's quick response changed the look on Sybilla's face from jealousy to joy. Alix nudged her toward him. "You two go ahead."

Rob offered his arm to Sybilla. "My lady."

Sybilla glanced at Alix, her eyes shining and eager. She stood and took Rob's arm as he led her to where the other dancers twirled in time to the music.

"Well played, Alixandra," a deep voice spoke behind her.

Alix turned, startled. When she had seen Richard descending from the dais, never did she imagine that he was coming to speak to her. "I didn't hear you come over, Your Grace, or my Lord Duke, or Your Highness." She let out an exasperated sigh. "What is it that I call you, now that I work for you?"

"I'm only a duke, not a king," he replied disparagingly.

"Not yet," she muttered under her breath.

"What did you say?" He gave her a sharp look.

"Nothing, I said nothing."

"You will call me 'Your Grace'." He cleared his throat. "May I have this dance?" He held out his hand.

She shook her head. "Regretfully, I wasn't being untruthful about not knowing these dances."

"Come now, don't be shy."

"No, the dances where I'm from are quite different." She thought of her clubbing days and the mixture of disco, hip-hop, and the questionable twerking that was popular back home.

"There has to be at least one you know, or perhaps I'm not to your liking?" He arched an eyebrow.

Flustered, Alix began to stammer. "No, no, it isn't that…"

"Well then," he challenged, extending his hand. "Teach me."

She took a deep breath. Her immediate safety in this unfamiliar world was dependent on the duke, and how she conducted herself could cost her much. "Come, I will show you the waltz. It's a slow dance but it could work with this music. I'll teach you the formal version." She let him lead her to the dance floor and faced him, aware of numerous eyes upon them. "Place your hand here." She took his hand and guided it to her waist. "I put my hand on your shoulder." Richard seemed pleasantly surprised by the closeness of this dance. "Now we hold hands and let me lead." Nervous and excited, she hoped he couldn't feel her pulse quicken as he held her hand in his. Richard was a quick study. She showed him the steps, and within a few minutes, he had it down. "That's the waltz." She stopped as the music ended.

He chuckled. "If that's formal, what is the informal dance like?"

"Pretty much the same," she lied. She didn't want to get any closer to Richard than she had to and couldn't imagine putting her arms around his neck and her cheek on his shoulder as they slow danced. The mere touch of his warm hand on her waist had sent shivers up her spine already.

"You are nervous, Alixandra?" He grinned and moved closer to her.

She gazed up at him and took a steadying breath. She wasn't going to squander this opportunity to dance with this legendary man. "I'll show you the more common way of dancing." She moved toward him until they were almost touching. Taking his hands once more, she placed them on her waist then reached up and put her arms around his neck. Alix was fairly tall, but Richard towered over her by a good seven inches. He pulled her closer and she gasped, her gaze captured by his. Dark lashes fringed his blue-gray eyes. Flustered, she looked down to his well-formed lips, immediately regretting the decision. God, she could really fall for him.

Richard bent down toward her, his lips dangerously close, and breathed in the spicy scent that lingered on her warm skin. "I'm not familiar with the particular oil you're wearing. It's exotic." His lips grazed her neck and all of her nerve endings tingled. "It suits you."

A hot blush crept up Alix's neck as Richard guided them off the dance floor to a shadowy recess of the hall. He stared at her with darkened eyes and caressed her cheek. Moving his thumb, he gently brushed her full, bottom lip, then bent down, leaned toward her and pinned her against the cold, stone wall. His audacity sent a rush of adrenaline through her and she stood on tiptoe, her hands on his chest, readying herself for his kiss. Electric shocks rippled through her as Richard's warm breath caressed her skin. He cupped her face in his hands and paused, their lips almost touching. Desire burned in her belly as she craved the touch of his mouth.

He lightly brushed his lips over hers. Beneath her hands his body tensed as he caught her lower lip in between his and swept his tongue over it. She gripped his shoulders as her knees weakened. Her tongue met his and the flavor of spiced wine was an unexpected aphrodisiac. Her breath quickened as she crushed her lips against his. The heat of his body burned through her clothes as his hands moved to her waist to pull her even closer. She ran her hands up his muscled back and the thought of what he would feel like in bed, his weight upon her, her legs wrapped around him, sent an ache into her very core.

"Your Grace. Ahem, Your Grace." One of his knights coughed behind them.

Richard slowly drew back, his eyes never leaving Alix's. "What is it?" His husky voice was tinged with annoyance at the interruption.

"Begging your pardon, Your Grace. A courier has just ridden in. He has news."

In an instant, Richard spun around, his demeanor changed. "Escort him to my chambers immediately. Send my men up as well."

Alix stood, forgotten in the dark corner against the cold wall. Her gaze focused on the floor, and her face flamed with embarrassment at the man's witness of her wanton response to Richard's kiss.

Richard turned back toward her, placed a finger under her chin, and tilted her head up. He kissed her lips lightly. "This isn't finished." The gravelly tone of his voice and the hunger in his eyes confirmed his words. Seconds later, he turned and stalked out of the dining hall.

Alix floated back to the table, her reddened lips evidence of their encounter. As she passed Beatrice, the hatred that raged behind the blonde's eyes chilled the heat that burned inside moments before. Unmistakable whispering followed her as she continued to her seat. She could little afford to alienate anyone, especially the girls with whom she would be working and living. She sat down next to a beaming Sybilla.

"Oh, Alix, Rob is a marvelous dancer! I felt as if I were floating while he had me in his arms. He's quite comely don't you think?" Her lips curved upward as she reminisced.

"I agree, and very chivalrous as well." Alix smiled at Sybilla's starry-eyed look.

"He is, and so gallant. After our dance ended, he bowed and pressed a kiss in the palm of my hand. I thought my heart was going to jump out of my chest at his touch."

Alix nodded, having experienced the very same feelings for Richard. She sighed as the stress of the last couple of days finally caught up with her. She excused herself, ready for her first good night's sleep since finding herself there.

When she reached the second floor, angry voices echoed from the end of the hall opposite the servants' room, but she was unable to make out any words. She padded quietly to her chamber door and slipped inside. Many of the girls already there talked in groups of two or three, and she smiled at them as she passed. Beatrice's absence was a relief. She headed to her pallet to find a small wooden clothes coffer at the foot of her bed. Covering it was a blanket and a neatly folded shift. She mentally thanked whomever had supplied it.

"How was your supper, dear?"

"Hello, Melisende. It was very welcome." She motioned to the garment on the pallet. "Was it you who supplied this?" At Melisende's nod, Alix smiled. "I appreciate it, and thank you again for taking me in."

"You have the Duke to thank for that. Now, to bed with you. We have Mass in the morning and you must be tired." She picked up the blanket, shook it out, and Alix helped spread it over the thin pallet. "There we are. Good night, Alix."

"Good night Melisende." Under cover of darkness, Alix changed into the clean shift, then lay down on her hard pallet, and pulled up the blanket. She couldn't erase the feel of Richard's warm lips against her own. She'd never held Richard as king in high esteem, but the man himself intrigued her. She wanted to know more and decided in that moment that her prior knowledge of his history didn't matter. In the flesh he was mysterious, handsome, and regal and his parting words excited her in a way she'd never experienced before. The flutter in her chest at the chance for another rendezvous with him sealed her fate. She searched her feelings and came to only one conclusion.

She wanted him to pursue her, and she would let him.

~ *Chapter 5* ~

"WHAT NEWS?" RICHARD'S DEMAND echoed throughout his chambers as he stormed in.

"Your Grace." The courier addressed Richard nervously. "Your man in Limoges bade me tell you that your brother, the Young King, has been meeting secretly with vassals and barons from your own realm. The regions of Poitou and Limousin in particular."

Richard's lips twisted in derision at the mention of his older brother. Named after his father Henry, his elder brother had been referred to as Hal since birth so as to avoid confusion. Richard turned to his cousin, André de Chauvigny and clenched his fist. "God's blood! I'm sure Hal has been lending those malcontents a sympathetic ear and has promised to right their supposed grievances in return for their support against me."

Richard paced the length of the chamber, his heavy footsteps muted by the rushes that covered the floor. "Would that I could rid myself of him! This is Father's doing. Anointing Hal as king to rule alongside him allows Hal to play king without actually making any decisions, while Father pulls at his strings like a puppet to rule in his name." Richard paused and stroked his chin. "Father's empty promises to me, and my brothers Geoffrey and John do nothing to forge a peaceful empire or family. I wonder which side Geoffrey will choose. He won't wait much longer to decide, I'll wager."

"What more could Geoffrey want?" André's light, brown eyes narrowed. The older man was Richard's closest confidant, and one of his most trusted household knights. "He is already Duke of Brittany."

"You're aware that Father had long coveted the Duchy of Brittany since it was independent from France and he desired to control his French territories. Once he attacked and deposed the former Duke of Brittany and claimed the

~ 42 ~

duchy on behalf of the Duke's young daughter, Constance, he then betrothed the girl to Geoffrey. This agreement brought Brittany into Father's clutches."

André nodded. "Ah, yes, your father still controls two of the wealthier cities in Brittany, which by right should belong to Geoffrey. I'm certain Constance reminds Geoffrey of that at every turn, which would make any man bitter."

Richard stopped at the table and refilled his goblet with wine. "Hal wants my duchy in order to prove to Father he can best me and rule in my stead. I daresay Geoffrey sees Hal bringing my vassals and barons to his side as an opportunity to claim Aquitaine lands for himself and show that he is at the end of his tether waiting for what he feels he is owed." Richard sneered before drinking deeply of his cup. "Let them come and try to take my duchy."

* ~ * ~ *

The following morning chatter and laughter filled the servants' chamber as everyone dressed to attend Sunday Mass. Alix pushed her blankets aside, shivering at the chill in the large room. Sometime during the night, the fire had gone out and stone walls provided poor insulation.

"Hurry, Alixandra. You need to ready for Mass." Sybilla pulled on a simple dress of green wool, while tugging at Alix's sleeve to get her motivated.

"Do you think I can wear the dress from last night since mine hasn't been returned yet?" Alix dreaded putting her feet on the sharp rushes covering the icy floor but had no choice if she was going to get dressed.

"Yes. Maud can easily lengthen the dress for you, if you need further use of it." Sybilla gave Alix a soft smile. "You can borrow one of my cloaks, and you mustn't forget your veil."

"Whatever would I do without my veil?" Alix laughed. "Which one is Maud? I will need to thank her."

"She's the young, blonde girl down on the left." Sybilla motioned toward a petite girl who was as slender as a reed and looked to be no older than twelve. Alix recognized her as the girl who had opened the door when Richard had taken her to meet Melisende.

"She's only a child! How long has she been working here?"

"At least two years. Her mother was a favorite lady of Queen Eleanor's and when her mother died, Maud was given a position. I have no doubt the Queen will make sure Maud finds a good husband as well."

This kindness to the young girl proved to Alix that Eleanor was a generous woman. Alix recalled a story in which William Marshal, a famous knight renowned for his bravery, was captured in a skirmish. After spending some time in captivity, Eleanor, apparently impressed by his heroic tales, paid his ransom. In turn, he served her husband, Henry II, and her sons Richard as well as John.

Sybilla glanced around and lowered her voice. "I'm sure you've heard of her imprisonment by King Henry. It's been almost ten years since her own husband made her his prisoner. I can't imagine living that kind of life."

Alix knew that it was the rebellion between Eleanor and her sons against the King of England, and subsequent defeat, which led to her imprisonment. "The King couldn't very well allow her leniency. He had to exact his punishment swiftly, lest his subjects question his competence as ruler. He did what he had to in his position."

Sybilla nodded. "I agree, but it's been years. Hasn't she suffered enough?"

Alix found herself saved from answering by Melisende gathering the servants. They left the chamber by means of a back staircase, of which Alix had been unaware. Once outside, she breathed in the fresh, cold air. The sun was about to peek over the horizon and pink and orange streaks colored the cloudless sky, promising a beautiful day. The gravel path ran the periphery of the building and bordered the gardens, opening onto the courtyard, which the servants' quarters overlooked.

Sybilla strolled beside Alix. "Everyone attends Sunday Mass here together, even the Duke and his knights. For daily Matins, the Duke and his men take their prayers in the small chapel inside the palace walls."

Alix wasn't religious, but she loved old churches for their aesthetic beauty, and the Église Notre Dame, near the palace, was no exception. The Romanesque chapel was small compared to the soaring cathedrals she'd seen in Europe. It didn't have high, vaulted ceilings, but instead a curved barrel vault. The interior of the chapel was comprised of a central nave with aisles, and radiating chapels developed around the church. Multi-colored stained-glass windows depicted saints in various poses and a plain wooden cross hung over the altar.

Marveling at the simple beauty of the building, Alix was unaware that noblemen and the Duke had entered, followed by the priest. Sybilla elbowed her, and she nodded her head. The priest began prayers in Latin and Alix let her mind wander.

She was no closer to figuring out how she was going to get back home, but this was an incredible opportunity to find out how true the history books were. Best of all, she was close to Richard. Historians had long maligned his morals and character but being in his household could allow her to discover if their accounts were true. It was ironic, really. When she had first arrived, all she had wanted was to return home, but now, even despite the difficult living conditions, she couldn't imagine leaving yet. There was still too much to discover.

Another elbow from Sybilla sent Alix to her knees to pray.

She bowed her head and sent out a plea into the unknown. *Please, please let me stay longer.* She hoped that whatever force had brought her there would comply.

The priest droned on, and Alix's feet began to ache from standing on the hard stone floor. She shifted her position and wished for a pew to sit on, but they didn't exist in this time. Unfamiliar with the service, she looked around at the simple stained-glass windows and tried to not to think of her discomfort. After what seemed like an eternity, it was over and Alix sighed thankfully.

"Alix," murmured Sybilla.

"What now? Isn't this over?"

"Yes, but we must curtsy when the Duke leaves."

"Of course, we must." Alix turned, and found herself staring at Richard's chest. She curtsied and glanced upward. "Your Grace."

"Alixandra. I hope you enjoyed the sermon."

"Yes, I did, the words were very… melodic."

"I've never heard anyone describe Mass quite in that way before. I take it you don't understand Latin?" Richard frowned.

"I understand a little of it."

"We'll have to remedy that." He pivoted on his heel and strode out of the church.

"Oh, please don't." Her whisper went unheard and she fought to hide her grin at the fact that he'd spoken to her, although language lessons weren't quite the topic of conversation she was hoping for. She moved forward, but Beatrice brushed by, almost knocking her over.

Sybilla leaned close to Alix, keeping her voice low as she adjusted her cloak. "Watch out for her. She's accustomed to getting what she wants and if she considers you a rival, she'll make life very unpleasant for you."

"Duly noted." Slowly, they made their way back to the palace, the day warming in the bright sun. The girls discussed possible chores they might be required to do as they entered the dining hall for breakfast. As they took their seats, Alix wished for a cup of coffee or tea, unable to stomach the idea of drinking wine with breakfast. The servants brought out bread, butter and different types of boiled meat.

The same serving girl who had brought Alix water at dinner, again offered her wine.

"May I please have water instead?"

The girl looked at her in bewilderment but turned to fetch her a flagon. The heavy meal lasted about an hour, and Alix was relieved when Richard and his company rose and left, allowing everyone else to vacate the hall.

Melisende stopped Alix at the bottom of the stairwell. "We need to determine what chores you are able to do. Follow me, please." She led her into a study containing a large desk flanked by chairs. A lantern stood at one end with ledgers neatly stacked beside it. A chair sat by the small fireplace and two rectangular windows let in the bright, morning sunshine.

"The Duke didn't tell me anything about you. What exactly is your background?" Melisende took a seat at the table and motioned for Alix to do the same.

Vague, unprovable information would be the best solution. "I'm from England originally, but several years ago my mother and I moved to France. We fell on hard times, and as I am unmarried, I needed to find work. I applied as a governess to a family outside of Poitiers. Unfortunately, the master of the house insisted I become his mistress. When I refused, he put me out with only the clothes on my back. I was returning home when the Duke found me and took me under his protection."

Melisende's brows arched upward. The concocted story had more holes in it than a sieve, but she appeared to accept it. "When the Duke visits, he rarely stays long, so he doesn't require too many servants. The girls handle a multitude of tasks from making candles and polishing lanterns, to dusting and sweeping the floors. I employ laundresses to wash linens and clothes when the Duke and his men are in residence, but when they leave, that chore falls upon us. I assume you embroider or sew?"

Alix shook her head. Her stomach churned and her mouth went dry. If she were unable to do the simplest of chores, Melisende would undoubtedly tell Richard. She could very well find herself emptying chamber pots or out on the street.

"You can cook at least?"

"If opening a box and putting it in the microwave counts," Alix muttered under her breath. Again, she shook her head helplessly at Melisende.

"Pardon me?"

"I can tend gardens. I am very familiar with medicinal herbs and their use. I enjoy teaching children, although I haven't seen any around. I can help with the household chores. I'll do anything. Please, let me stay?" she begged. Knowledge of herbs and medicine was a highly sought skill in this time period. She prayed it was enough to convince Melisende to let her stay.

"The Duke has requested that I find a position for you, so I will figure out something for you to do." Melisende's stiff reply could only mean that Alix had none of the skills needed to serve in a household like this.

"Whatever chores you choose for me will be fine. I will do my very best to accomplish them. It must be extremely difficult to manage a large household, but yours runs smoothly. How did you come to work here, if you don't mind my asking?"

Melisende smiled, seemingly pleased with the compliment. "I was in Queen Eleanor's service for fourteen years, until she was captured and imprisoned by that man she married." The anger in her voice was almost endearing as she spoke of her queen.

"I can't imagine being held prisoner, let alone by my own husband. She must be a very strong woman."

"Indeed. She is one of the most formidable women I have ever met. I despise King Henry for taking away what matters most to her."

Alix tilted her head.

"Aquitaine, of course. It was Eleanor's birthright. Even though Richard now rules in her stead, being imprisoned in England and forced to stay away from her homeland is one of the cruelest things Henry could have done."

Alix knew that Eleanor would gain her freedom and tried to convey hope to the older woman. "Keep praying. I'm sure your beloved queen will be released."

"I pray for that every day." Melisende gave Alix a hopeful smile. "Now come, we have much to do."

The servant girls spent the day polishing serving platters, bronze candlesticks and other odds and ends. Alix's arms ached and her hands were red and chafed from the gritty polish. She was surprised when she finally looked up from her tasks to see that it was nearly dark outside. Her task done for the day, the headache that had been coming on from inhaling the strong odor of the polish took root and she shuffled to her bed and lay down.

It seemed as if she had been in Poitiers for weeks, but only days had passed since she had found herself lost in the forest. Alix rolled over, feeling homesick and sorry for herself, missing her easy twenty-first century life. She was fortunate that Richard had taken her in. Living amongst royalty was certainly preferable to life as a commoner. So far, she had managed to fit in, but she wondered if she would be able to continue to pretend to be something she wasn't. Thinking of Richard, she felt a mix of excitement and disenchantment.

She admired his intelligence and wit, and enjoyed bantering with him, but was unable to ignore how the history books portrayed him. He had treated his subjects poorly. In the aftermath of battles, he had taken his defeated enemies' wives and daughters for his own pleasure, then gave them to his soldiers when he was done with them. This was an atrocity that all historians made note of, and those facts troubled her.

When she opened her eyes, moonlight streamed in through the window. She must have slept through supper. The other girls in the room slept soundly, save for soft crying coming from the direction of Maud's pallet. The rushes crackled under her bare feet as Alix tip-toed over to where Maud was curled up in a ball, her fist pressed against her lips to muffle her sobs.

"Maud," she whispered, not wanting to scare the girl. Maud sniffled but didn't respond. "What's wrong, why are you crying?"

"I miss my mother." Maud dissolved into fresh tears.

"Come here." Alix joined her on the pallet and put her arms around the girl. Maud's thin frame shook with sobs. "Come with me." She led the young girl to the back stairway so they could sit and talk privately.

"I miss my mother, too," Alix confided, trying to comfort her.

"You do? But your mother didn't die, did she?" Maud sniffed, and wiped her eyes.

"No, but she's far away. I miss not being able to talk to her and I'm so afraid we can't spend the holidays together."

"What holidays do you mean? Christ's Mass?"

"Yes, and Halloween."

"What's Halloween?"

She mentally chastised herself again for using modern terminology, but decided to explain, hoping it would cheer up the girl. "It's a holiday we celebrate where I'm from. The children dress in costumes, knock on neighbors' doors and ask for candy. We also hang scary decorations like bats and ghosts outside our houses, and we carve jack-o-lanterns."

"What's a jack-o-lantern?" Maud gave her a questioning look.

"They are pumpkins or big gourds that we clean out, carve scary faces on, and put candles inside to light them."

"That sounds like fun. I wish we celebrated that holiday."

"Maybe Melisende will let us carve some pumpkins, or gourds since I don't know if pumpkins even grow here."

"What do you do for Christ's Mass?"

Alix's eyes filled with warmth as she recalled childhood memories of driving with her family to a Christmas tree farm outside of Austin. Dirt paths lined with fir trees stretched out before them, their sharp, pine-like fragrance permeating the air. Alix remembered the hours spent, carefully inspecting all of the trees for *the* one. "We would go out to the forest and cut down the most perfect fir tree we could find. Afterward, we'd spend the evening decorating it with beautiful ornaments, lights and garlands strung along the branches."

"Lights?" The curiosity on Maud's face made Alix giggle.

"I mean candles. We put candles on the tree, but we make sure they don't catch fire." Another little white lie about how she celebrated Christmas, but she couldn't very well explain electricity. "When my brother, James and I were younger, around your age, we would gather around the tree, and my mother would tell us the Christmas story, then we would all go to bed. The next morning we'd race downstairs to see what gifts Santa Claus brought us to celebrate the birth of Jesus."

"The story?" Maud's interest brightened her face as she looked up at Alix with red, puffy eyes.

"Yes, the Nativity story."

"Then who is Santa Claus?"

"You've heard of Saint Nicholas, the bishop who helped the needy by giving them gifts?" Maud nodded. "Well, Santa Claus is based on that history. He is a portly man with a great, bushy white beard who brings presents to the good girls and boys, but if he finds out you have been naughty he brings you a lump of coal."

Maud laughed, delighted. "I think I like Santa. We do that too, you know. We give each other gifts, one for each of the twelve days of Christmastide."

"That sounds like a nice tradition."

"Would you tell the Nativity?"

"Certainly, I can but would you truly like to hear it?"

"Yes, oh yes, please!"

"Very well, when Christmastide arrives, I will tell you the Nativity story. Now off to bed with you, it's late."

Alix remained sitting on the stairs long after Maud had left. Reliving her holidays reminded her of her situation. Her stomach tightened from fear and she pressed the heels of her palms to her eyes to stifle the tears that burned and threatened to fall. Isolation pressed in on her. Frustration had worn her nerves raw. She rubbed her arms as cold air seeped into the stairwell from chinks between the stone wall and the wooden door below. Her safety depended on one man; a man she wasn't sure she should entrust her well-being to, but she had no choice. Should she let her circumstances weigh on her or make the best of what she had been given? Wiping her eyes, she rose and headed for bed.

~ *Chapter 6* ~

THE FOLLOWING MORNING MELISENDE rounded up the girls for Matins. The last thing Alix wanted to do right now was face the palace's residents. The decision she'd made in the small hours of the morning to make the best of her situation didn't erase the homesickness that tugged at her heart and the uneasiness that nagged at her as she worried about her future. She desperately needed time alone to regain her courage. When Melisende reached her pallet to prod her to join the other girls, Alix pled a headache. Avoiding the chapel and the people within would be a small blessing this morning.

"I'm sorry you're feeling poorly." Melisende felt Alix's forehead with the back of her hand and looked in her eyes. "You don't feel warm, so that's good. I noticed you've not eaten anything since yesterday's breakfast."

"That's probably why I have a headache. I'll get something from the kitchen. I'm sure after I've eaten, I'll be fine and can manage my chores."

"I hope so. We have much to do today."

The servants' voices faded as they disappeared down the back stairs. Grateful to be alone, Alix decided a bath was essential. The wooden bucket still held some water from an earlier trip to the outside well. She added tinder to the embers in the fireplace until the fire crackled and warmth filled the room. After heating the water, she took her time rinsing off until the water cooled enough to make the bath unpleasant. Clothed again in Sybilla's borrowed dress, Alix made her way down the hall, sparing a glance toward Richard's apartments before descending the stairs.

Unfamiliar with the layout of the palace, she took several wrong turns before finding the kitchen. She opened the door to a huge room. An immense fireplace, large enough for at least ten men to stand in, was built into one wall. Overhead, pots and pans hung suspended from wooden beams.

The servants were busy preparing food and Alix waited for a moment, deciding which of them to approach. She recognized the servant girl with the pixie face who had brought her water and beckoned to her.

"Excuse me, may I have some bread or cheese? I missed supper last night and I'm too hungry to wait for breakfast."

The girl smiled. "I noticed you were absent last night. I will get you something to eat."

"Thank you. I'm Alix. What's your name?"

The girl's eyes widened and her mouth went slack. "I'm Emma."

"Is there a problem?"

"No." Emma shifted, noticeably uncomfortable. "Begging your pardon, miss, but I'm surprised you're speaking to me."

"Why shouldn't I speak to you? We're both servants in the Duke's household."

Emma stared at her. "Miss, you work upstairs in the palace. I work in the kitchens." She curtsied and turned to leave, returning with bread, butter, and cheese, wrapped in a cloth.

Alix knew that servants were classified by their station, but her modern ideals rebelled against this archaic practice. She swallowed the denial that hovered on her lips, nodded to Emma, and left her to her work, hoping she hadn't offended or alienated the girl by her words.

"Damnation!" Alix's voice echoed off the stone walls as she finally stumbled upon the courtyard after many wrong turns. She looked up into the crystal-blue sky and inhaled deeply. The nervous tension that had taken up residence in her muscles since her arrival began to fade and she relaxed as the simple beauty of nature soothed her.

The air was cool against her skin, the sun warm on her face, and she had no desire to go back inside to eat her meal. Her stomach growled as the scent of warm bread wafted from under the cloth and she chose to follow a path that led away from the palace to find a comfortable area to enjoy her breakfast. As she rounded a corner, the dirt path led to a low hill on which a copse of poplar trees grew. She strolled toward the trees, the trilling of birds accompanying her, and paused to admire the view. The town spread out in front of her, neat houses lining the dirt streets and the spires of a church visible in the distance.

Beyond Poitiers, green hills gently rolled to where the sky met the land, and checker-board patches of tilled fields bordered small structures, but no other villages were visible. There was little evidence of human habitation, but she wasn't surprised. The population of twelfth century France in the Middle Ages was only about twelve million.

Settling under one of the leafy poplars, she ate her bread and cheese, relishing the flavors and the peace and quiet. Satisfied, she laid back, closed her eyes, and was almost asleep when voices rang out in the distance. She jumped up, hoping she would remain unseen by the groups of people streaming back from the chapel. The last thing she wanted was for Melisende to return from prayer and catch her playing hooky. She rushed back down, skidding on the fallen leaves and chose to take the footpath to the left, hoping it would lead to the back of the palace. She rounded the other side, but the twists and turns in the path took much longer to navigate than she anticipated.

Slowing to catch her breath, she pressed her hand against a stitch in her side. Movement in an upper window on the second floor caught her eye. Richard moved past, gesturing with his hands, his focus on an unseen person. She continued, optimistic she could escape his notice, but then she risked another glance upward.

He was standing at the window now, frowning down at her. She gulped and continued her trek at a hasty pace. What had started out as a potentially good day quickly deteriorated.

* ~ * ~ *

"What was that you asked?" Richard frowned at the empty grounds outside of his window where Alix had stood only moments ago.

"When do you plan to return to Clairvaux to complete your latest castle?" André asked.

Richard turned away from the window. "In a few days' time. I must see to some things here, first."

André nodded. Even though he appeared satisfied with the answer, there was something in the older man's eyes that bothered Richard. "What is it?"

"Richard, you have seemed distracted of late. I assume that Hal's plotting is weighing heavily on your mind? It wasn't too long ago the two of you were on the same side, leading a rebellion against your father, so I could understand the distraction. But I also wonder if there's another reason for the diversion of your attention." André paused to take a drink of wine, his eyes narrowing as Richard remained silent.

"The other night at supper, I was surprised to see an unfamiliar young woman sitting with the servants. Rob told me you came across her in the forest. Is there any particular reason she is here?" A knowing curve tilted up the corner of his mouth.

Richard had always appreciated André's candidness. There was no other that could see through Richard like his cousin did. André's eyebrow raised, as he seemed to know exactly what was on Richard's mind.

Richard shrugged and rested one hip on the edge of the table while he poured himself a drink. Although not first born, he was still the son of a king, and accustomed to having women of all classes throw themselves at him. All women except for Alixandra. She intrigued him with her openness and ease, but he sensed a distance within her.

A surge of lust pulsed within him at the memory of how her soft, feminine curves had fit perfectly against his body when he pressed her against the wall and the eagerness and skill with which she returned his kisses. He drained his cup in an attempt to dampen his sudden desire. "Lady Melisende mentioned needing help and I thought Alixandra would be amenable to the offer."

"You know nothing of this woman. Can you trust that she wasn't put in your path by one of your brothers? It would be a clever move. Few men would suspect a woman of being a spy."

"Your point is duly noted, but in ruling my realm, I've become quite adept at reading a person's character. This young woman is in no man's pocket."

"I'm aware that Poitiers doesn't provide the..." André sighed and gave Richard a lopsided grin, "...variety of entertainment you desire, but was it necessary to find her a position if you simply wish to entice her into your bed?"

Richard laughed. "You know me too well, cousin. Yes, Poitiers is rather dull and Alixandra could prove to be a welcome distraction for the time being." If her kisses were any indication of the passion that lay within her, Jesu, he would have her in his bed this very night.

"The fact that she is very comely surely has not escaped your notice?" André laughed.

"For certes, it hasn't." Richard smiled.

~~*

Melisende entered the servants' rooms and immediately found Alix. "Are you feeling better? Did you get something to eat?" Alix nodded. "Good, I require your help then."

The rest of the day flew by. Alix kept busy as she heated water for baths, helped the other girls brush their long hair, and folded clothes that the laundresses had brought upstairs.

Alix missed her closet of comfortable clothes back home. Wearing different and clean outfits every day seemed like such a luxury now. Even royal women only possessed three or four dresses, and commoners owned less. She looked down in disgust at her soiled dress and was relieved that her freshly laundered Faire costume lay on her pallet. Sybilla was readying for supper, and as Alix picked up her modern made Faire garment, she looked at it with uncertainty.

"Sybilla, do you think my dress is suitable?"

"Certainly, it's very nice."

"It's a lovely garment, fit for a peasant. Too bad no one will notice you in it." The jealousy in Beatrice's voice almost made Alix laugh, but Beatrice was right. Alix's dress didn't compare to the beautiful, royal blue woolen dress she wore.

Alix glared at Beatrice's retreating figure. "I know I should be charitable. I don't even know her, but I have to admit, I don't like her very much." *Especially since she's been with the Duke.*

"Alix, are you jealous?"

"No!" Alix knew there was a bite to her response and Sybilla didn't deserve that. Her reply needed to be logical, matter-of-fact and smart. If she were to have a chance to truly get close to Richard, she needed to build her reputation as a woman unlike any other. "Any woman who shares a man's bed has the potential to wield her influence over him. I worry that Beatrice might have power over the Duke, and with her obvious feelings toward me…who knows what she's said to him."

"I don't think you have anything to fear, Alix. Everyone watched you dance with the Duke. Since your arrival, Beatrice has spent every night here." Sybilla smiled knowingly. "Hurry and get ready."

Alix turned to hide her smile from Sybilla and picked up her dress.

Melisende approached her. "Alix, why don't you wear this instead?" Melisende held a beautiful, unrefined cotton, forest-green gown, more elegant than either the borrowed dress or her Faire costume.

"Oh, my goodness, it's incredible. Wherever did this come from?" Alix asked in shock.

"It's from the Duke. Who else could have done this?" Sybilla eyed the gown, awestruck.

Refusing the gift would be an insult, but what would be the consequences of accepting it? "But, Melisende, he hardly knows me. Why would he have gone to the trouble?"

"Accept the gift, Alixandra and wear it tonight." Melisende's stern tone told her to tread carefully. "Tomorrow we can figure out how to get some fabric to make you clothes. With winter coming, your light cotton dress won't provide any warmth."

An anxious flush ran through her at the thought of being there for months, of not being able to return home. She swallowed hard, forcing the tension down and took the dress from Melisende, marveling at the exquisite stitching and rich color. She pulled it on and Sybilla tightened her laces in the back.

"You need a veil, Alix." Sybilla looked around for the borrowed one.

"Well-bred women might always wear veils in public, but tonight, I'm wearing my hair loose. I think it will look better with the dress."

"I wouldn't advise it." Sybilla shook her head and walked off.

As the other girls readied themselves, Alix opened her pouch, took out the glass vial of perfume, and dabbed the amber scent on her wrists. She replaced the perfume and froze as her fingers brushed the cold metal of the brooch. Surprised that she had forgotten about it for several days, Alix jerked her hand away, afraid of what might happen if her touch lingered on it. One thing she was sure of, if the metal didn't feel warm, then she must be safe, at least for now. She stashed the pouch back in her coffer.

The girls entered the dining hall, casually conversing and giggling. A quick glance toward the dais confirmed the Duke's absence. The mixture of relief and disappointment that he wasn't there made for a confusing emotional state, and Alix sighed. As she made her way to their usual table, a rich baritone voice came from behind her.

"Thank you for deigning to grace us with your presence this evening."

Richard. She would know his voice anywhere.

She turned to face him. "You are most welcome."

Richard gazed openly at her, starting at her feet and moving his eyes upward. The dress he'd gifted her hugged her slender figure perfectly. His eyes lingered on her lips, making her heart flutter, wondering if he was remembering the heated kisses they'd shared. He met her widened eyes and reached out to caress one of the loose coppery waves that hung past her shoulders, brushing the back of his hand along her collarbone as he rubbed her silken hair between his fingers. Her breath hitched as his gentle touch scorched her skin.

"That dress looks quite becoming on you, Alixandra." His enticing smile revealed a dimple in his cheek she hadn't noticed before.

"Thank you." Alix felt her cheeks grow warmer. "The dress is beautiful. I don't know how to repay you."

"I'm sure I can think of something."

We're playing that game, are we? "You look quite handsome yourself, Your Grace." Richard wore a long tunic in rich reds and blues.

Richard inclined his head in acknowledgement and leaned toward her. "The other night ended all too soon. I would welcome the chance to continue our interlude. Without interruption." His rich, deep voice was almost a caress.

Her heart skipped a beat and she gave him a coy smile, then she turned away before being dismissed. Surely, no servant or even noblewoman had ever turned their back on the Duke before. Peeking over her shoulder, he stood slack mouthed, gazing after her. She took note that not only did he not scold her feistiness, he seemed drawn to it.

Making her way to the table where Maud and Sybilla conversed, she groaned at the sight of Beatrice. Alix was determined not to let the snitty blonde ruin this night. The future King of England, by his own admission, wished to spend more time with her and nothing could dampen Alix's excitement, not even the hostility from the girl whom Richard had favored…before.

She ignored Beatrice as best she could while servants brought in platters of food. Alix helped herself to beef stew and vegetables, but again abstained from any dishes she was unable to identify. There were two flagons in front of her. She lifted one and peered into it. Clear. How thoughtful of Emma to remember she preferred to drink water with her meals. The other one she assumed to be wine. She poured some wine into her cup, lifted it, sent a mental toast to her mother and brother, and lifted the cup to her lips.

She raised her eyebrows in surprise. "The wine is really good tonight. What did they do to it?"

"Occasionally we are allowed to drink the same wine as the royals." Sybilla held out her cup for a toast.

"I could actually drink this every day, but maybe not for breakfast."

Sybilla grinned at Alix, then looked at the table where the knights sat. Following her gaze, Alix enquired, "Have you spoken to Rob since you danced?"

"No, but he has smiled at me often."

"I would say that's a sign that he's interested."

"I do hope so. I'm becoming quite fond of him."

Servants moved around the tables clearing dishes and trenchers. The minstrels took their places in the middle of the cavernous room and soon the cheerful tones of lutes and harps filled the air. Once the dancing started, Rob came over and asked Sybilla to accompany him.

"Sybilla is so lucky to have such a handsome squire to dance with. Alix, if someone, such as the Duke, asks you to dance, you must." Maud gazed wistfully at the twirling dancers. She was too young, but her time would come.

Alix shook her head at Maud's innocent boldness. "Oh, I will, but I'm not holding my breath. Besides, I like hanging out with you."

"Hanging out? You say the strangest things sometimes."

Alix bit her lip, reminding herself to watch her words.

The dancers moved around the hall falling in step with each other gracefully. Before the dance concluded, Rob led Sybilla away from the others. "At least one of us is with the man of her dreams tonight," she mumbled into her cup of wine. She turned and looked at Richard's table, startled to find him watching her. A genuine radiant smile bubbled up from within, surprising even her.

She'd had boyfriends in high school and off and on through her undergraduate years at university, but she'd never felt this strong an attraction to any other man. After the night she'd been robbed at knifepoint, she'd worried that she might have sublimated her fears into her studies, and she would never find passion in her life. Richard's kisses had laid those worries to rest.

"Thank you for talking to me last night." Maud's soft comment pulled her attention back to the table. "I hope I didn't ruin your sleep?"

"Not at all. I wasn't really tired anyway."

"Good." Maud paused and rather shyly met Alix's eyes with her own. "I'm very glad the Duke brought you here."

"Me too, Maud." Alix patted the girl on the hand fondly.

The musicians' melodies floated to Alix's ears and she shuddered to think where she might be right now if Richard and his men hadn't found her in the forest. Despite its hardships, she had grown strangely fond of everyday life in this Medieval world, and as she looked about the room, she marveled at finding herself surrounded by the actual people she'd long studied.

She lifted her cup of wine and let the spicy, sweet bouquet wash over her tongue. Yes, the luxuries of palace life were true blessings. The fabric of the gown that Richard had given her was like heaven against her skin compared to the rough material of the borrowed dress she'd spent the last few days in, and she moved her hand in long strokes over her skirt, feeling the softness. The music of the harp and lutes changed and the minstrel began singing a beautiful, albeit haunting melody.

Alix closed her eyes, enjoying the atmosphere, until a familiar, yet unwelcome, voice cut through her reverie.

"I'm sure Richard will ask me to join him in his chambers tonight. We haven't been together in some time. He's a strong man and he doesn't often sleep alone. I should know."

Alix's eyes opened slowly and she gazed upon Beatrice with indifference.

Beatrice let out a snide laugh. "Although he will never be king, he is a duke. He'll take care of me. He always does." She looked Alix in the eye, but her attempt to intimidate was flimsy. Alix knew that only time and opportunity separated her from Richard's bed.

Just then, Sybilla came back, flushed and breathless.

"Oh, Alix!" she burst out. "Rob took me into the alcove and kissed me. I must confess, I'm quite smitten."

"Good for you." Alix grasped her friend's hand and looked around. "Where did he go?"

"The Duke requested his presence." Sybilla motioned to where the men stood, her face still glowing with warmth for the young squire.

Alix chatted with the girls, as the dancing and music continued, but soon Maud tried to stifle a yawn. "Let's go to our room, Maud before you fall asleep." Alix took her under the arm and led her away from the table.

"It's been a long day." Maud yawned again.

"Sybilla, we're going upstairs. I assume you wish to bid Rob a good-night?"

"Yes, I would like to stay a bit longer." Sybilla looked to where Rob still conversed with Richard. "I hope he returns soon."

The conversation looked to be wrapping up between Richard and his men. Maybe Sybilla wouldn't have to wait to spend time with Rob again, after all. The Duke beckoned to one of his other squires, spoke to him briefly, and left the hall. Alix found this strange, for he usually stayed until well after most of his men left. As Alix turned to go, Beatrice rose, smiled triumphantly at her, and followed Richard.

Alix sighed. It looked like Beatrice had won. "Let's head upstairs, Maud."

As they were leaving, Sybilla grasped her arm. "Are you going to the room already?"

"Yes, I have a headache," Alix lied.

"Oh, you're not joining the Duke tonight, then?" Sybilla sounded surprised.

"I'm not sure what you mean."

"He didn't request your presence in his chambers when you spoke earlier?"

"No, he most certainly did not."

Sybilla looked at her sorrowfully. "I'm so sorry. I thought for sure he would have asked you."

"Sybilla, he gave me a dress. Don't read too much into it." Alix knew full well what Richard intended, just as Sybilla did, but that didn't mean she needed to let on that she was looking forward to whatever might happen. She had only just arrived and the last thing she wanted was to be thought of as an easy conquest. She turned and trailed Maud out of the hall.

The two girls entered their chambers and worked together to light a fire to ward off the chill. Some of the other girls had come upstairs and were preparing for bed. As they settled down, Alix watched the fire burn, the logs collapsing in showers of red-hot embers. She added more wood, and then extinguished the various lanterns around her, leaving only one lit as she waited for her eyes to adjust in the dark.

Pale moonlight streamed through the windows, illuminating a path on the floor. She followed it and looked out over the courtyard, bathed in moonlight. It was beautiful outside. With the rest of the girls in bed, Alix was now wide awake and knew sleep wouldn't come easily. She headed to her coffer and took out her borrowed cloak, pausing as she spied her pouch that lay beneath.

Alix carefully lifted the small bag and carried it gingerly to the back stairs. Slowly opening the bag, she drew out the brooch and held it warily in her hand, expecting it to glow or begin to warm, but nothing happened. She exhaled, frustrated. What had caused it to glow in Austin but not here?

She pinned the brooch to her dress, wrapped the cloak around her and descended the uneven stone steps. Breathing deeply of the fresh, cold night air she looked up at the dark, velvety sky filled with more stars than she had ever seen before. She waited but the brooch remained unchanged.

A funny sense of relief crept into her chest. As much as she wanted to return home, the thought of leaving Richard tore at her. Brushing her fingers lightly over her lips, she remembered the warmth of his mouth on hers. What would his hands feel like skimming down her body? An aching need throbbed at her core as she imagined his hard length pressed against her. God, she wanted this man.

She ambled down the path and didn't realize where she was until she looked up and noticed Richard's suite of rooms.

Firelight flickered in the window, setting the perfect mood for seduction. "At least someone is enjoying their night," she whispered, then tried in vain to banish the unpleasant thought.

A few moments more on the stone walk and the drop in temperature, forced her inside. She quickly wound around the castle and as she pushed open the heavy door, laughter and music spilled out from the dining hall. She hoped Sybilla was enjoying herself and Rob was giving her the romantic interlude she so desired. She climbed the main stairs, looking forward to warming her hands in front of the fire in her chamber.

As she reached the landing, the squire standing outside Richard's door cleared his throat. Alix paid him no attention and continued down the hall to the servants' chamber, but a deep grumble echoed in the hall again. "Miss, a word please?" he called out quietly, gesturing to her.

She approached and stopped. "What is it?"

"The Duke requests your presence."

"Excuse me?" In her shock, her retort was louder than she expected. The boy looked startled and Alix relented. "Sorry, I didn't mean to yell, but how many women does he need in one night? Are there more lined up after me?"

"No. You are the only one." The boy's eyes were wide with shock at her outburst.

"What do you mean? I saw Lady Beatrice leave the hall earlier. Isn't she with the Duke?"

"She turned up uninvited." He smirked. "He sent her away."

"He did?" Alix smiled. "Good."

"He asked me to deliver the message to you in the dining hall this evening, but you had already left. He has been waiting." The young squire squirmed as he stood. "He doesn't like to be kept waiting. I was afraid I would miss you altogether this evening. My punishment will most likely follow on the morrow if you don't meet with him."

Surely, her not visiting with the Duke didn't warrant disciplinary measures? She considered making Richard wait all night, but she was honestly curious about what lay behind the door, and she certainly couldn't have an innocent boy punished on her account. It was true, she didn't wish to be labelled as the Duke's bedmate, but there was no denying her attraction to him. Adrenaline rushed through her body and heated her desire, confirming this was a once in a lifetime chance.

She wouldn't waste it.

~ *Chapter 7* ~

ALIX TOOK A DEEP breath and knocked on the wooden door. After a few seconds of tense silence, straining for any sound from within, she rapped louder.

"Enter!" Richard called out.

Alix's throat tightened, but she opened the door and stepped inside, her blood pounding in her ears, fearful of his potential ire. "Your Grace." She wasn't sure her timid greeting reached him until he turned.

"Alixandra, I am surprised that you changed your mind." There was no mistaking the icy tone of his voice.

"You heard me speaking in the hall?" He stared at her intensely. "That was just a... I misunderstood the situation." She laced her fingers together as his face darkened.

"What situation?" he demanded.

"It's not important."

That was obviously the wrong thing to say, as Richard glared at her. She would need to explain herself, however embarrassing.

"I watched you leave the dining hall. Beatrice left soon afterward so... I assumed you were with her and..." She looked at the floor, her cheeks burning.

"You thought I had invited multiple women to my chambers for the evening?"

She nodded, forcing her head up to meet his eyes.

A ghost of a smile played on his lips, then he burst out laughing. "Jesu, I found someone who is more suspicious than myself!"

"It was possible." Alix's retort came out more sarcastic than she liked. "Beatrice is your bedmate is she not?"

He crossed his arms. "No, she is not. Would I have invited you here if she were?"

She shrugged and toed the rushes on the floor. "I don't know. Perhaps."

"Alixandra, you are the only one I invited."

Her heart skipped a beat at his words. The squire helped remove her cloak, hung it on a chair, and at Richard's sharp dismissive hand motion, the young man hurried out and closed the door behind him.

Alix took in the rich trappings of the chamber. Richard had good taste. Fine tapestries depicting hunting scenes covered the walls. A fire crackled in the fireplace and on the far wall was a closed door, which she assumed led to the bedroom. A row of tall, rectangular windows stood in front of her, and in the middle of the room was a large, heavy, wooden table, strewn with maps, with four ornately-carved chairs arranged around it. A settee sat next to the fireplace. A charming window seat beckoned her. She went, knelt on it, and peered out into the inky darkness.

"Would you care for some wine?"

"Yes, please."

He handed her a goblet, and set down a plate of sliced oranges, figs, and nuts beside her.

"You shouldn't have gone to all this trouble! Where did you find oranges?"

"I have my methods."

"You do appear to be very resourceful." She picked up her cup and her eyes widened as the spicy sweet flavor exploded over her taste buds. She recognized it as being the same that she had at supper. "Now, this is good wine! I wish it was offered every day."

"I assume you drink wine at meals. Do you not like it? Aquitaine produces some of the best wine in France."

She shook her head. "I find it too sweet, too spiced."

"I do not find it so."

"You drink better wine than your servants, Your Grace."

"What do you drink then, ale?" Richard's lip curled in distaste.

"No, water."

"Alixandra, you can't rely on the water. Even though we have our own water source here, we never know if it's tainted or not."

"You do have a point. I will ask Emma to boil it early in the morning so it's ready to drink by breakfast."

"Who is Emma?"

"One of your kitchen servants. Don't you even know who works here?"

"Lady Melisende manages those in my employ. I have no need to take an interest."

"And you're overseeing this palace? You really ought to make more of an effort," Alix teased.

"Well, as you said at the tavern, I have more pressing matters."

"I understand. Your realm is vast and you spend much of your time traveling from one town to another, dealing with your enemies." She raised her cup to her lips. The smooth flavor rolled over her tongue, and she let out a little sigh of appreciation.

She moistened her lips with her tongue. Richard inhaled sharply and his eyes darkened. Her body tightened in response, but she forced herself not to think of his lips and hands on her skin. Instead, she reached for an orange section. "Did the courier arrive with unwelcome news, Your Grace?"

He studied her, as if trying to decide how much to tell, if anything at all. "My brother Hal has liaised with my barons in an attempt to turn them to his side."

"I assume the counts of Limoges and Perigord are among them?"

"Why do you say that?" His tone was suspicious.

Her mind ran through the history of his rule in Aquitaine and she came up with an acceptable answer. "Didn't Viscount Aimar of Limoges and Count Elie of Perigord rebel several years ago before and you subdued them? It only makes sense that they would align themselves with your brother."

He nodded. "Yes. Those miscreants, amongst others, are negotiating with him."

"I imagine you'll have to leave soon to quash their rebellion."

"The timing is uncertain, but my spies keep me informed. When the time does come, they will get a fight they never expected." He took a fig and leaned back. "I seldom meet a woman truly interested in matters of state, but I don't wish to discuss my malcontent barons any longer. I want to know about you."

"Me?" Her glance slid away from him. "There's not much to tell." There was really nothing to tell since she couldn't very well divulge the truth.

"And don't give me the fabricated story you gave Melisende," he warned her.

"I have no idea what you're talking about." Of course, Melisende had told him, making Alix wish she was a better liar.

"Come now, a blind man could have seen through that."

"So why am I still here, then? If you knew I lied about my background, why did you let me stay?"

He looked at her thoughtfully. "I'm an excellent judge of character."

She grinned. "And modest as well."

"That, too." He laughed. "Simply put, you needed help and I could provide it."

She leaned forward and put her hand on his. "I do appreciate it. You have no idea."

He looked down at her hand and she drew back, a nervous smile pulling up one side of her mouth.

"More wine?"

She nodded and he rose gracefully to fetch the flagon. Her gaze lingered on his long, muscular legs and broad expanse of back. She swallowed at the thought of caressing his skin and enjoying the play of his muscles under her hands.

"I don't know what to tell you…" She sipped the refilled cup he handed her. "I have an older brother, James, who is married, and has a little girl named Erin." She stopped, unsure of what to say next. Her parents were divorced, but that was unacceptable in the Middle Ages.

"What of your parents? They are still living?"

Alix nodded, considering her words carefully. "Yes. I'm close to my mother, but my father and I have had a difficult relationship. There was a time when he was unfaithful to my mother." She stopped suddenly, surprised she had shared such personal information with a relative stranger.

"I am familiar with that scenario."

"Your father was with someone besides Queen Eleanor, wasn't he?" she asked carefully.

"Yes, more than one, but he was most taken with a beauty named Rosamund Clifford." His voice was flat as he stared off into the distance. "My mother never forgave him for his public displays."

"I'm sure it was hard for her. Was that the reason she…" Alix broke off abruptly, sure he didn't want to talk about the rebellion which had provoked Henry into imprisoning his wife. Historians had hotly disputed the reasons behind the rebellion of 1173. What motive would make a queen, along with her three teenage sons, plot a revolt against her own husband? Alix had always wondered what the catalyst was and hoped Richard would provide insight.

"You were going to ask about the rebellion, I assume?"

"I apologize, I've overstepped."

"No, it's a valid question." He picked up an orange section and offered it to her. "Rosamund was the main reason Mother and Father became estranged. He hurt and humiliated her by being so open with his infidelity, but that's not why she sided against him."

"Then why?"

"It was my mother's political views that caused her to rebel against Father. As Duchess of Aquitaine, she inherited the claim to Toulouse. Count Raymond of Toulouse was embroiled in a quarrel with the King of Aragon and feared an attack upon his lands. He determined it was in his best interest to have the support of my father's army. He paid homage first to my father as the King of England, then Hal as the anointed king, followed lastly to me as Duke of Aquitaine."

This was an insight into Eleanor that Alix hadn't considered. "Oh. Did she feel that King Henry saw her only as his wife and not the ruler of Aquitaine?" Richard shifted, but did not answer. "When the Count paid homage to your father instead of to her as his rightful ruler, she probably felt slighted and took that as a sign that her realm would be subordinate to his."

Richard gave her an appraising look. "Yes, I believe that's the main reason she conspired against him. After inheriting Aquitaine from her father, my mother became one of the wealthiest and most powerful women in France. She was not one to accept being overlooked."

Queen Eleanor had been a formidable woman, and more progressive than her contemporaries. Hearing about her character firsthand from Eleanor's own son thrilled Alix.

"In his infinite wisdom," Richard sneered, "Father crowned Hal as king alongside him, but Hal had no true power and became more resentful. Hal is easily influenced, and Father's enemies encouraged him to revolt."

Alix nodded. "So, your mother allied herself with Hal, and you and your younger brother Geoffrey joined the rebellion in her support." She knew well where his loyalties lay. "That would be a difficult decision for me." At Richard's raised eyebrow, she hurried to explain. "On one hand, it must have infuriated her to know that, although marriage to your father brought him the great duchy of Aquitaine, he still considered it secondary to his own realm. On the other hand, I don't think I could have supported my sons going to war, and against their own father, at such a young age. I would have been afraid I would lose them in battle."

"My mother is a very strong woman, that's true. I think she truly believed we would win. We had the support of her Aquitaine lords as well as the King of France, who happens to be Hal's father-in-law. By all accounts, we should have won, but instead all of our attacks failed." A distant look entered his eyes and Alix surmised he was reliving the defeats. "Father enacted a truce with the King of France, Hal and Geoffrey. I lost the support of the French king and the rebellion was over."

Alix knew that Henry's main priority had been to sign a truce with the French king, but Richard continued his fight against his father, which delayed the meeting. At last, the two kings agreed to a truce, leaving Henry able to focus on subduing his rebellious son. Alix's heart ached for the sixteen-year-old Richard whom Henry excluded from the peace talks. She'd read accounts of how he'd met with his father at Poitiers, and humbly asked for forgiveness. She couldn't imagine the anguish Richard felt when he learned his father forgave his brothers but not him, or his mother.

"Father was furious with Mother's part in the rebellion and she ended up his prisoner."

The painful emotions behind his hard eyes chilled Alix.

Eleanor had many allies and supporters in France, so to avoid jailer sympathy and those who might try to rescue her, Henry housed her in his various castles in England.

"How is it that you know all this about my family?"

"Your history is legendary, Your Grace." Alix hoped her Cheshire smile would distract him, while she remained careful about concealing how much of his history she knew.

"Is it now?" He smiled back, clearly pleased.

"People relish stories of intrigue within royal families, especially when sons challenge their father for lands and power."

"Is that so? Tell me, Alixandra, what intrigue are you aware of in my family? I would truly like for you to regale me with your seemingly vast knowledge."

She gripped her cup, her hands trembling as she raced through Richard's history in her mind up until the current date. She mustn't slip in a tale of future events. What a catastrophe that could cause. Instead she would recount how the historians described the character of his family members in lieu of its history. "It is said that Hal is the golden one. A Young King, who holds essentially an empty title, since your father still rules. He has no true lands of his own and is kept under Henry's thumb, so to speak, but one day will become King of England, Normandy, and Count of Anjou. He is popular with his peers, and renowned as a skilled jouster in tournaments. Geoffrey is viewed as an intellectual. Reputedly, he has a silver tongue with which he can garner political allies, such as his nobles in Brittany."

She stopped and glanced at him. Richard was silent as he digested this information.

He cocked a questioning brow. "Anything else?"

"As for you, I've heard tales of your exploits. As a brilliant military leader, you put down rebellions at the age of sixteen, and were given the name 'Lionheart' for your bravery and prowess on the battlefield."

He inclined his head. "What they say is quite true, but surely the chroniclers attest to how Aquitaine has flourished and become even more powerful under my rule?"

"Indeed, but is that story not still being written?" She skirted the issue gracefully. One of the main reasons Richard was always in contention with his nobles was his heavy-handed ruling of them. He leaned back, his lips curving into a satisfied grin.

She hid her smile, amused at his reaction, and finished her wine. "Thank you so much for this. It was wonderful, but I suppose I should go." She stood.

He stood as well and moved closer to her. "Stay."

"No, I really..."

She wanted to stay but knew where that would inevitably lead. Was she ready to be intimate with him or willing to risk her reputation? Their kiss the other night told her that he desired her. The idea of being with him made her heart pound, but Richard was dangerous. The stories of his cruelty to his subjects proved that, and her well-being depended upon him. This wasn't a man who could be toyed with and put aside.

If she gave in to her desire, he would have a unique power over her, one she would have to give him until he ended their affair. And what of her heart? The fluttering inside her chest told her she was in fear of falling for him. Before her stood a man, who was virile, strong, and decisive. This was the kind of man she'd dreamed about; longed for, even. How ironic that he was the man she'd studied for years and learned to despise; a disdain, she was realizing, that was crumbling at her feet the more she got to know him.

As he placed his warm hands on her waist, she wondered if she could ever recover from their inevitable separation. She looked into his eyes and saw a man she could love. And if she were to love him, would the inevitability of their parting matter?

No, she would embrace this time with him and hold onto it with both hands.

He raised his hand and caressed her cheek, trailing soft strokes with rough fingers from her jaw to her ear. His stormy, blue-gray eyes searched hers intently. What was he looking for? He bent down, lightly brushing her lips with his, as he pulled her closer. Her nerves tingled at the touch of his lips and her breath caught as his tongue touched hers. She pressed against his chest, needing to feel his body against her. His hands tangled in her hair, his kiss becoming urgent as their tongues met, tasting the tang of wine and desire the other had to offer. He stroked her neck then moved his hand down her collarbone to brush the swell of her breast.

Boldly cupping her breast, he rubbed his thumb against the nipple until it peaked. She ached for the touch of his lips and the feel of his hands on her skin. He trailed light kisses down her jawline. This was the moment; the moment she would decide to give herself to him. She tilted her head back offering him easy access. He trailed hot, moist kisses along her throat down to her collarbone. A deep moan vibrated up from Alix's throat, as Richard pushed the top of her tunic down to capture her full breast in his mouth. His hot tongue swirled around her nipple and she cried out as he sucked it gently. Wantonly, she pulled his hips closer to her, feeling his heat through her clothes. When he finally moved back, Alix's erratic, labored breaths mimicked Richard's.

"Do you still want to leave?" His voice sounded husky with raw need.

She shook her head and moved into him, initiating a forceful, passionate kiss. She ran her hands down his body, reveling in the feel of the hard planes and muscles underneath. Alix pushed up his shirt and pressed her lips to his chest, crisp hair tickling her cheek. He inhaled, his body rigid under her hands, and she stepped back, thrown by her forwardness.

"My apologies, I forgot myself."

He smiled. "I don't mind at all."

"I do. I just met you, and I don't want you to think that I... that I'm..." she stuttered, embarrassed by the intensity of her passion.

Richard laughed, "Alixandra, I never thought you were like that. I'm not going to force my attentions upon you. I give you my word."

"Thank you, but I really must leave."

Frustration flashed in his eyes then he nodded. "I wouldn't want your reputation sullied by gossip. Go, before I change my mind." His lips lifted in a half smile. "This has been one of the most enjoyable nights I have spent in a long time, Alix."

She raised her brow at the nickname. "For me too." She walked to the door and turned to face him. "By the way, only my friends call me Alix."

"Are we friends then?" He crossed his arms in jest.

"I'll let you know." She turned and opened the door, his low laughter filling the room as she left.

Alix crept down the shadowy hallway, her footfalls whispering on the moonlit streaked stone floor. She paused outside the closed door to the study. It would be impossible to enter the servants' quarters without waking some of them. Testing the door handle and finding it unlocked, she entered and waited for her eyes to adjust to the darkness. A small settee stood near the fireplace. The room was cold, but it was preferable to announcing her nocturnal activities to the girls. She lay down and wrapped her arms around herself, wishing she could have stayed with Richard, but relieved she'd made the right decision.

* ~ * ~ *

Pale sunbeams inched across the floor, banishing the darkness. Alix clenched her eyes tighter against the unwelcome light. The room brightened until the possibility of sleep was as elusive as the hazy half-remembered snippets of her dreams last night. She sat up and stretched, her muscles tight from sleeping on the cramped settee. Exiting the room, she almost ran into Melisende.

"Alixandra! You slept here last night?" Melisende asked, astonished.

"Yes, I was restless and didn't want to bother anyone so I came in here and I must have fallen asleep. I hope it didn't inconvenience you?"

"No, I thought that you... I mean I was sure that... oh never mind." Melisende feigned a laugh. "Hurry now, we must ready for Matins."

Alix went to her pallet, finger combing her hair to make it presentable.

Sybilla rushed over. "Alix, where were you last night? Were you with the Duke?"

Alix looked behind her, putting her finger to her lips. "I'll tell you on the way to Matins." They ambled downstairs, letting the others go ahead.

"Tell me! What happened last night?"

"Whatever do you mean?" Alix knew her demure tone wouldn't fool Sybilla.

"Alix, don't keep me in suspense."

Alix turned to her, keeping her voice low, "I was invited to his chambers, and actually enjoyed myself. We had a real conversation, instead of flirting and bantering as we normally do. He isn't what I expected."

"What did you expect?"

"I don't know exactly." Alix knew she had to be careful in her explanation. "Being the Duke of Aquitaine and a king's son, I imagined he would be egotistical and self-absorbed. True, he has his pride, but he was genuine, easy to talk to, and he honestly seemed interested in what I had to say."

"Did anything else happen?" Sybilla's eyes were wide with curiosity.

Alix's stomach clenched in desire as she relived his touch and kisses, then she remembered how close she had come to losing control. And wanting to. God, what must he think of her? She met Sybilla's expectant gaze. "No, he was the perfect gentleman."

Conveniently, Beatrice just happened to flounce by at that moment. "Oh Alix," she sighed with fake pity, "playing the chaste woman won't get you anywhere with Richard. He's going to tire of you and find someone else who knows what he really wants."

After last night's fiery kisses, Alix knew Richard desired her and Beatrice's snide remark was insignificant. "Richard strikes me as the kind of man who enjoys the thrill of the hunt." Alix looked at her pointedly. "Instead of easy prey." A quiet snarl accompanied Beatrice's heated glare before she huffed and stalked off. "Sorry, Sybilla. She just makes me so angry."

"She makes everyone angry, but you need to be careful. She can make your life miserable."

"In what way?"

Sybilla glanced around and lowered her voice. "She initiates gossip and isn't above spreading lies, especially when it serves her own needs. You don't want to antagonize her. She's been with the Duke for some time now and isn't one to accept being cast aside." Sybilla's warning was duly noted as they entered the dimly-lit chapel and took their places quickly. Their tardy entrance caused the priest to glower at them.

The service began, and the priest droned on. Alix was beginning to enjoy this free time to ponder her life. Some days her thoughts were filled with excitement about the things she saw or experienced, other days homesickness would wrap around her like an icy blanket and she wondered if she would ever be able to return to her own time.

Every chance she had to hold the brooch, it remained unchanged. A simple piece of jewelry, lifeless in her hand. The weather was turning colder and soon winter would hold France in its unrelenting grasp. Her Faire costume was too thin for the frigid weather, the dress Richard had given her was too finely detailed for daily wear, and she couldn't continue to borrow Sybilla's clothes. She chafed at her lack of independence. She resolved to find a way where she didn't have to live off of charity.

The service over, Alix and Sybilla, slowly followed the long line of people filing out of the chapel door. "The Duke pays us monetarily, doesn't he?" Alix blinked against the bright sunlight that poured through the open door, replacing the gloom of the chapel.

"Not much. He mainly provides lodging and food."

Alix's tone was hushed as they walked the path from the chapel to the castle. "How do you get fabric for clothes and other essentials?"

"Melisende will give you money if you require it. Why?" Alix paused as the horde of bodies around them entered the dining hall for breakfast and took their usual seats.

"I can't continue to borrow your clothes. I wonder if he would pay me early so I can purchase my own items."

Sybilla tilted her head. "You might ask. I'm sure he could arrange something."

Alix chewed her bread slowly, mulling over the best time to approach Richard, when a hand reached down and picked up her cup.

"What the...?" She turned and looked up at Richard. "Must you skulk around like a thief in the night?"

He laughed. "Well, I did have much practice during my youth." He leaned down and whispered in her ear. "I used to hide and spy on my brothers to learn useful information in order to blackmail them later."

Alix stared down at her empty plate. "You are quite good at it, Your Grace. I ought to put a bell around your neck."

He smiled, lifted her cup to his lips and grimaced.

She chuckled at the look on his face. "I assume you don't care for water," Alix chided him.

"Not particularly." He bent down to replace the tumbler and brushed her ear with his lips. "I would like you to come to my chambers tonight after compline. We can take a late supper." His warm breath moved the hairs on her neck and she shivered.

"I think I can clear my schedule."

Richard paused at her unfamiliar words. "I choose to believe that means yes, and I will look forward to it." He stood triumphantly and paced to his table.

Their morning meal finished, the girls attended to their chores. For Alix, this was the most tedious day she had spent since finding herself in France. Melisende, not knowing what Alix was capable of, gave her some embroidery samples to work on. Sybilla showed her how to make the most commonly used stitches, but she finally gave up after Alix had destroyed the piece of fabric.

"I can't do this!" Alix exclaimed, throwing the wrecked sample on the table in front of her. "I won't have to ask Richard for any help, since Melisende will get rid of me before supper."

"Try this one."

Sybilla handed her another sample, this one showing a design already drawn on it with marks indicating which stitch to make. Alix took it, raising her brows.

"This type of sample is used for, well, children to learn how to embroider. It might help." However, four hours later, there was little improvement in Alix's technique. While she sucked on her finger, which she had repeatedly pricked with the needle, Sybilla ripped out every stitch.

"If I had learned how to sew instead of taking martial arts, I could at least fake proficiency," Alix muttered under her breath, then said louder, "I should have stayed at the tavern. It's much easier serving beer and wine to drunken men than trying to learn this useless endeavor."

Sybilla chuckled at Alix's frustration. "We'll work on this. You will succeed... eventually. It's almost time for supper, anyway. I daresay you're done for the day." Alix fought the urge to roll her eyes when Sybilla gave up and tossed the ruined fabric aside.

As the girls dressed for the evening meal, Alix fixed her gaze on the fireplace and tried to contain her excitement about her rendezvous with Richard later that evening. Lost in thought as she flipped through safe discussion topics in her mind, she jumped as Melisende spoke from behind her.

"I hear the embroidery was a complete failure."

"I told you sewing and I don't mesh well. I will try harder tomorrow, I promise."

"That won't be necessary." Alix shot her a panicked look. "I only meant that we need to find another chore that you would be more suited for. Now, let's go downstairs. Try not to worry about it, dear."

"Melisende, Alix is having dinner with the Duke tonight!" Maud had snuck up behind them and was beaming with the news.

"However did you know that?" Alix was sure that she and Richard had kept the volume of their short interlude that morning low enough as to not be overheard.

Melisende laughed. "Maud has an uncanny way of eavesdropping, don't you, my child?" Maud looked away bashfully. "Well, good, I think you and the Duke might have a lot to talk about."

"I don't. He's royalty and I'm not. He knows what he wants out of life. I'm floating through it like an uncharted boat on the high seas."

"That could very well be exactly what he needs."

The room emptied and the girls' footsteps and chatter faded. Alix's stomach grumbled and she hoped Richard would have appetizing offerings to feast on, unlike the heavy, sometimes unrecognizable fare served in the main hall. She drifted over to the window and gazed out as dusk crept in, stealing the last remnants of the sun's golden rays. The stars began to emerge from their daytime prison and the moon rose over the horizon. Out of habit, she searched for her cell phone to check the time. Sighing, she wondered how people ever knew what time it was there. Bells rang out in the distance, beckoning the town to the compline service after supper. She admired the beautiful view a while longer, then made her way down the hallway toward Richard's chamber.

* ~ * ~ *

The same squire stood watch in front of the heavy, wooden door of Richard's chambers. "Good evening."

"Good evening." Alix looked at the door, then back toward the boy, not sure what to ask. "Earlier, the Duke mentioned the possibility of granting me an audience."

"Yes, miss, he's expecting you."

She gave him a small smile and knocked on the door.

"Enter!"

She pushed open the door and gasped in awe. The spread before her far exceeded her hope for a feast. Embers sparked in the fireplace and the room was warm and fragrant with the scent of wood smoke. Platters of meats and vegetables as well as several flagons covered the table. "You shouldn't have gone to so much trouble. This looks incredible."

"I wasn't sure what you liked, so I asked for everything."

"I think you are going to spoil me." The fire crackled warmly and she focused on the dancing, orange flames, unable to think of anything intelligent to say. He strode across the rushes that covered the stone floor to stand behind her and she leaned back into him as he embraced her.

"Thank you for inviting me this evening." All too aware of his closeness, Alix hoped her anxiety couldn't be detected in her voice.

"I'm glad you were able to... what were your words, 'clear your schedule'?"

Alix laughed, her nervousness calming at his joke. She gazed at the fire, reveling in the feel of his warmth behind her. His heady scent of leather and soap surrounded her. He broke the mood and moved to the table, motioning for her to join him. She took her seat and eyed the multitude of choices before her.

"I don't know what most of these dishes are."

"You must have had these before. They are quite common in this region."

She looked at him, shaking her head. "Sorry, I'm not familiar with most of it."

"There is chicken, venison, hare." He pointed to the various platters of meat. "You must recognize the vegetables."

"I know what the vegetables are, but I wasn't sure about the meats. I'll take some chicken, please."

"Would you care for venison or hare?" He gave her a perturbed look as she shook her head and wrinkled her nose. "Have you ever tried them before?"

She shook her head again. She was an adventurous eater, but back home, no one in her family ate wild game. He put some on her plate and placed it in front of her. Once he fixed his own plate and filled their cups with excellent Aquitaine wine, he waited for her to eat. She took a small piece of venison, frowned at it, and put it in her mouth. She chewed slowly, prepared to gulp her wine to wash it down, but the flavor was not as she expected.

"This is really quite good."

"Try some of the hare. You might like that as well."

"Oh no," she said, laughing. "One new dish a night is all I can manage." They ate in silence while she deliberated how to discuss her daily necessities.

He eyed her as she concentrated on tearing a chunk of bread into small pieces. "What preoccupies you, Alix?"

"Is it that obvious?" She sighed. "I talked with Sybilla today. I was curious as to when and how we get paid." He stared at her in confusion. "You know, monetary compensation for services rendered?"

"I am well aware of what the term means. I pay my employees at the beginning of the month. Why do you ask?"

"I have nothing of my own. I've borrowed dresses and veils from two of the girls, but I'm not used to depending upon others." She reached her hand out to touch his. "I appreciate everything you have done but this isn't my life. I don't belong here."

"Then tell me what your life is like? I wish to know." His request seemed sincere.

You couldn't possibly accept the fact that I am from a time period 800 years in the future, from a country that hasn't even been discovered. "I'm sorry, I can't say more. I know you went to all this trouble and I'm spoiling everything."

"You haven't spoiled anything. I can and will provide you with whatever you require. I told you I will protect you."

"That's very generous of you, while I'm here." She focused upon a piece of chicken on her trencher, trying to hide her disappointment at how true her words were. If she never made it home, she would have nothing if she chose to leave Poitiers, or if she was forced to.

"Alix, you are part of my household now. *I* alone decide whether those in my employ stay or leave."

"Now, yes." She smiled, imagining how his future wife would like the girls he employed, particularly the comely ones. "At least until you marry."

"Is that your concern? My betrothal to Princess Alys?"

"No, I actually hadn't considered that, but I'm surprised you haven't married yet, especially since your brothers have taken wives."

"Father keeps delaying it, unwilling to give another of his sons to the French court."

Alix understood immediately. "Hal's wife is the late French king's daughter."

Narrowing his eyes, he reached for his cup. "I told you the other night that Hal was convinced by King Louis to rebel against Father." Alix nodded. "Upon Louis's death, his son Philippe, who happens to be Alys's brother, was crowned. I'm sure my father is loath for me to marry her and be in proximity to the French court. Truth be told, I have no interest in marrying her."

"The way Henry plays all of you, you're unlikely to be married for many years." She took a sip of wine, aware that marriage would never actually take place.

Richard studied her. "You certainly have an uncanny ability to grasp the nuances of the relationships within my family, don't you?"

Alix stilled at his seemingly innocuous statement. "It's merely speculation on my part, and most likely incorrect."

Richard laughed. "You are more correct than you know. My betrothal, as well as Hal's to Marguerite, was arranged by Father for political reasons. My father and Louis have always been at odds but uniting the two realms through marriage forced peace between them. The heirs born of those unions can forge stronger alliances since they will have both English and French royal blood."

"I was told that Hal's son died soon after birth. I can't imagine how painful that must have been. I wouldn't imagine one would ever recover from that."

"Having a son myself, I am very aware of how fleeting life can be." Richard's voice vibrated with warmth and protectiveness, leaving little doubt that he cared greatly for his child.

"You have a son? Where does he live?" Alix tried to act surprised at this revelation. Richard would be involved in his son's life and would one day arrange his marriage to a wealthy heiress.

"Philip is currently with his mother in Mirebeau. Although he is illegitimate, he is a duke's son and as such, will be raised a nobleman." He leaned back in his chair, his face neutral, but Alix sensed he was judging her based on her response.

"You must visit them occasionally. Was... is she important to you?" She clutched her wine cup, suddenly jealous of a woman he might still care for.

"I'm very interested in the education of my son and what I can offer him when he reaches manhood, but I have no lingering feelings for his mother other than concern for her well-being." He paused once again, as if waiting. She looked down into the depths of the burgundy liquid, hiding her relief at his words.

"Alix, I'm surprised at your silence. I was certain you would have an opinion on the subject."

"I am not going to criticize you for your countless hookups." He frowned in confusion. "I beg your forgiveness. Choosing the correct vocabulary is proving difficult. I'm new to your dialect, after all." If she was going to keep messing up, she thought giving a reason might ease any suspicions he might have now or in the future. "I'm referring to your many liaisons. I'm aware that many royals and noblemen have illegitimate children. Your father has several, does he not?"

His deep chuckle reverberated in the room. "Your choice of words is charming, and yes, he has two baseborn sons, Geoff and William." He rose and walked to the door to call his squire to clear the dishes. Alix picked up her cup, relieved that she had apparently passed the test, and went to sit on the settee. Richard rubbed his shoulder as he joined her.

She put her cup down on the floor. "Turn around."

"What?"

"Just do as I say."

"And here I thought women were supposed to be the weaker sex."

"Oh, of course, and you do know that behind every great man is a great woman."

"I have experience with that."

She rubbed his shoulders, kneading and working his muscles, feeling him slowly relax under her skilled fingers. She worked on a particularly tight area and he winced. "My apologies, Your Grace. I'm sure it's painful. You're very tense."

"Your touch is soothing. Where did you learn to do this?"

"An old acquaintance enjoyed massages, so I dabbled in the study of various techniques."

"You must thank him for me."

"I will." She couldn't decide if it was a blessing or an insult that he was unconcerned with her past liaisons. Leaning back against the arm of the settee, she rested her arms across his chest as he reclined against her. Soon, his deep even breathing told her that he either had fallen asleep or was close to it.

"Richard." She nudged him. "Let's get you to bed."

"I apologize. I'm not being a very good host." He stood, stretched, and began to extinguish the lanterns. When the firelight was the only illumination left in the room, he approached her, took her hand in his, and began to lead her to the bedroom.

She hesitated. "I really should leave but thank you for tonight. It was incredible."

"Everyone is likely asleep and you'll disturb them if you go back to your room." His excuse for her to stay was flimsy and they both knew it, but he did have a point.

"True, and I would hate to wake them all." She looked at him, excited and apprehensive about sharing the same sleeping chambers with this legendary man. "I'll stay, but only if I'm not intruding."

"You're more than welcome to stay. I'll show you where you will sleep."

She already had a good idea of where that would be. She glanced down at her dress. "I can't sleep in this. Do you have a shirt I can borrow?"

"You want to wear one of my shirts?" He furrowed his brow.

"Yes, if you don't mind. I don't want to rumple the dress by sleeping in it."

He went into the adjoining chamber.

As the hours had crept closer to morning, cool air slowly permeated the room from the chinks and gaps surrounding the large windows, and Alix moved to stand before the fireplace to ward off the chill. At the click of his heel on the stone floor, she pivoted toward him. He handed the shirt to her. "Thank you, this is perfect. Can you please untie my laces?" She began to turn around, but then the piece of jewelry on her bodice glinted in the firelight. He reached out his hand to stop her. He tilted the brooch to get a better look at it, curiosity filling his eyes. "Where did you get this? An engraving of a mounted knight is an unusual choice for a woman."

Alix froze the moment he touched it, expecting the worst. After a moment, nothing happened and her hand flew to the brooch to cover it. Her anxiety faded as she felt its coolness beneath her fingertips. "I found it in a shop and I couldn't resist buying it." She couldn't very well tell him that it would become his royal seal, however tempting. "May I use your room to change?" she asked quickly, to distract his attention. He untied her laces as requested, then motioned toward the chamber and she made her escape.

The soft illumination that flooded the room was supplied by lanterns hanging from hooks forged into the stone walls. The wind whistled down the unlit chimney and she shivered in the coolness. The lanterns closest to the fireplace swayed in the light gusts of wind and threw undulating patterns against the walls. A large curtained bed covered with thick, fur blankets dominated the room. She smiled, pleased to note that tonight she would sleep on a soft bed instead of the hard, thin pallet she had yet to grow accustomed to. As she struggled to get out of her dress, she couldn't fathom how women did this on a regular basis. She put on Richard's shirt and rolled up the sleeves. The garment hung past her knees, and would be very comfortable to sleep in. Although tired and eager to find warmth under the heavy pelts, she wasn't ready to end her night with Richard quite yet.

Her stomach clenched as she imagined the sly innuendos and looks that the other girls might direct at her in the morning, but she forced down those thoughts, wanting to enjoy this moment without distraction. This was the man she'd been fascinated with since she was a young girl. She didn't know how long this opportunity to be in his time would last and she wasn't going to waste it. She took one of the smaller pelts from the bed and wrapped it around her. The strange shape of the fur meant that it wouldn't cover her legs, but it did help ward off the chill. She padded out of the bedchamber and into the main living quarters.

Richard's gaze turned lustful at the sight of her. "I must admit, I've never seen a woman wear my clothes before. You look very desirable."

"It's much better for sleeping than the dress, even though it's a bit long." She joined him on the settee, curling her legs underneath her. Her pulse raced at the look of desire in his eyes. He pulled her into his arms crushing his lips against hers. She kissed him back, reaching for the hem of his tunic, her cool hands grazing his skin as she slowly pushed it up. He shuddered under her touch as she removed his shirt. Firelight cast dancing shadows over his body and she gazed admiringly at his well-muscled chest covered lightly with dark, golden hair, then frowned at the sight of scars on his torso. She traced them lightly with her fingertips. "Are these from many battles or just one?"

"Many." She caressed his chest, tracing circles over the scarred skin. He dragged her onto his lap, his hands tangling in her hair as he claimed her lips again. The heat from his body seared her skin through the soft, cotton shirt and the ache that had been growing all night turned into a throbbing between her legs. She pressed her hips against him, desperate to feel him. Richard roughly grasped her breast, then skimmed his hand down to her waist. He caressed her hips moving ever closer to the soft skin of her inner thigh.

Alix whimpered with desire. His fingers grazed the top of her thigh then brushed the curls between her legs. She froze, rational thought replacing the haze of desire that clouded her mind. This was too much, too soon. She placed her hands on his chest and gently pushed him back. "I'm sorry... I can't... perhaps I ought to go."

He stared at her, his eyes dark with lust, his breathing ragged in the silence. She tensed as he reached forward, wondering if he would heed her plea. Richard pulled his shirt back onto her shoulders. "Alix, please stay the night. Your... virtue is safe." He gave her a cocky grin.

"Are you questioning my innocence?" Alix feigned outrage, as she tried to dampen her desire.

Richard pulled her closer and looked steadily into her eyes, caressing her lower lip with his thumb. "No chaste maiden knows how to kiss a man so thoroughly, leaving him wanting—and needing more."

A lump formed in her throat at his words. Women were defined by their marital status. They were either virgins, wives, or widows. If a woman wasn't a virgin, and couldn't produce a marriage license, there was only one other category she fit into. "I'm not a prostitute." Humiliation brought a hot blush to her face as she wrapped her arms protectively around herself and stared at the floor.

"That never crossed my mind. I must ask however, is there a jealous man who might take exception, should he find you in my bed?"

Unable to speak, she shook her head.

"That's all I need to know." He caressed her cheek. She exhaled in relief, unaware she had been holding her breath.

"I suggest we retire for the night else I will be unable to keep my earlier vow."

She gave him a small smile and followed him to the bedroom but stopped when she heard voices and laughter outside the door. "Do your squires sleep here as well?" Alix looked at him in alarm.

"Yes, in the main chamber."

"I'm not comfortable with that."

"Pardon?"

"I'm not staying here with them in the next room." She crossed her arms, firm in her statement.

His eyes narrowed. "They always sleep here. I'm not going to send them away for your benefit."

"Fine. They can stay. Let me change and I'll get out of your way." She padded into his room to collect her dress.

* ~ * ~ *

His icy glare followed her. No woman, with the exception of his mother, and few men, had ever dared to speak to him in such a way. Most women in his social circle were pliable and pampered, or conniving, creating intrigue where there was none. He relied on his ability to assess a person's character immediately since political alliances were intrinsic to his ruling Aquitaine, but Alix perplexed him. Her speech had a strange cadence, but she appeared educated and was well versed in his family's history. She illustrated a keen interest in politics as befitted a noblewoman but seemed ignorant of court life. He strode into the room as she was beginning to undress.

"Alixandra, does the idea of my men sleeping in the next room truly bother you?"

"Yes, it does." She stopped in the process of pulling off his shirt.

"Why? It's a very common practice in court life."

"That's the problem. I'm not used to 'court life', as you put it. At home, I'm not constantly surrounded by masses of people twenty-four seven. Sleeping with a dozen men in the next room makes me feel very uncomfortable."

Richard stared at her, confusion in his eyes. "What in God's name does that mean?"

"Turn around please so I can change."

"I don't understand you, Alixandra. I'm trying to, but you make it impossible."

"I'm making it impossible?" She turned around half dressed and walked slowly toward him. "I'm in a world that I don't understand. I've been tasked to do chores that I've never done before and I'm expected to behave in a way that seems foreign to me. I understand the concept of these things, but the execution has been a difficult adjustment. Don't tell me I'm making it impossible. I'm doing my best, here!" Tears welled in her eyes and she turned away, swiping at them.

He put his hands on her shoulders, feeling an uncharacteristic surge of protection for this young woman standing before him. The realization that he didn't want her to leave surprised him. "Alixandra, I'm sorry. I assumed you were familiar with this life."

She wiped her eyes. "You have no need to apologize. I spoke out of turn. It's one thing to know what I'm supposed to do, but another thing to actually do it."

"Would you stay the night if I sent them away?"

"That's unnecessary. I don't want you to change your routine. I will leave."

He left and soon, the lower tones of Richard followed by louder, angrier voices of the squires and pageboys filled the outer room. Then silence.

"They are going to hate me, aren't they? What did you tell them?" she asked when he re-entered the room.

"I told them we were going to bed and I didn't want our passion to keep them awake so I suggested they find other accommodations."

She gasped in horror. "You didn't!"

A mischievous grin spread across Richard's face. "No, but I assure you they won't hate you."

He turned the furs back, and she nestled beneath them. Wearing only mid-thigh cotton braies, he got in next to her and drew her to him so she was lying halfway on his chest.

"I know you aren't familiar with this life, Alixandra, but I will help you. You are under my protection."

"I'll hold you to that." She sighed. "I've never been so dependent on one single person in my entire life. I've always been able to make my own way. Your Grace, my life is in your hands."

"Shh, everything will be fine." This woman's strength confounded him and excited him at the same time. How could one woman possess so much inner light, so much strength and still be so soft and vulnerable?

He leaned down and brushed her lips in a light kiss. "Go to sleep now."

Alix cuddled closer, her curves fitting perfectly against him. As her hip tucked next to his, he imagined caressing her warm soft skin and kissing her most intimate parts. His body on fire, he prayed that morning would come soon, and surmised from Alix's rigid posture, that she too found sleep elusive.

~ *Chapter 8* ~

ALIX SQUINTED AGAINST THE sun as it streamed in through the window. "Turn it off," she grumbled, burying her head under the covers. Unabated laughter filled the room. She uncovered her head and narrowed her eyes at Richard's obvious amusement.

"Good morrow, Alix."

"How can it be morning so soon?" She bolted upright. "Oh, my God, what time is it?"

"We are too late for Matins, and by the time you are dressed for breakfast, you will have missed that as well."

"Are you suggesting that it takes me a long time to get ready?"

"In my experience with women, I find that it always takes your gender much longer to do anything than mine."

"I don't know what women you choose to be with, but I don't fall into that category."

He raised his hands in mock apology. "That remains to be seen, does it not? Now what would you like for breakfast?"

"I would kill for a cup of coffee." She hung her head and trudged toward the chair where her dress hung.

He stared at her in bemusement. "You do say the strangest things. No wonder I find the English to be so foreign." He grinned at her and went to the main chamber to give her privacy. Approximately ten minutes later, she followed.

"Jesu, if all women readied themselves so quickly, men wouldn't be left to their own devices."

"You don't have to sound so shocked." She sashayed over to him and turned so he could tie her laces. "The one thing I just can't seem to do by myself here."

He cinched her up and gestured to the table. "Go ahead and eat. I will be there momentarily." He unrolled a map on the table and placed small weights on each corner. She was surprised to see it was a blueprint.

"Are you thinking of building this?"

"It's already built. I need to return to make sure all is going as planned."

"Oh, you're leaving." The thought saddened her, to her surprise.

"Yes. Originally, I was only planning to stay a couple of days here in Poitiers before returning to Clairvaux, but I found a very intriguing reason to tarry longer." He slipped his hand under her hair and drew her near for a gentle kiss. "I'm glad I stayed."

Alix gave him a coy look, then she peered down at the drawing. "Where is Clairvaux?"

"It lies to the north between Chatellerault and Mirebeau." He drew his finger from Poitiers to a point west of Chatellerault. Alix's stomach clenched at how close Mirebeau, and Richard's son, were to his destination. She was sure that Richard would wish to visit Philip. Although Richard said he had no feelings for the boy's mother, they shared a child, and at one time, they must have cared for each other.

She forced her unwelcome thoughts away as he continued. "The Viscounts of Chatellerault control the important trade route from Tours to Poitiers. They have grown very wealthy from questionable practices concerning traveling merchants. I wish to remind them that they are my subjects and I will oversee their doings."

"But that region borders Hal's lands, does it not? I'm sure that didn't escape your notice."

He shrugged, seemingly unconcerned about being so near to Hal's holdings.

"Your brother is most likely to view a fortified castle as a direct threat, especially if he is allying himself with your nobles. Aquitaine is a wealthy realm and you have the means to raise an army, but Hal is dependent on your father.

"Why are you defending Hal?" His angry voice echoed in the room.

"I'm not, but I'm sure he fears that, should you attack, reinforcements wouldn't arrive in time. He would be defeated. You have to know that he's going to approach your father about this perceived intimidation toward him."

"You're correct in that assumption. Hal will run to Father." Richard studied her. "You said you weren't politically knowledgeable, but I believe you underestimate yourself, Alix."

"Richard, are you doing this to anger Hal, knowing he will retaliate?" She placed her hands on the table.

"The main reason is to control the trade route and protect the merchants who provide necessary income to the towns. Hal, however, has crossed the line by meeting with my nobles. If he attempts to take my duchy…" He tapped his finger on the map.

"I fear you are not going to like the outcome of this endeavor." Alix moved away from the table, knowing that she couldn't warn him of his father's plans for the castle. "I must go, else Melisende will be furious with me. If I don't see you before you leave, have a safe journey."

"You will join me tonight, if that is acceptable to you?" Richard stated this plainly, but Alix could see the hope in his eyes. "I am leaving on the morrow."

"Certainly. That's acceptable."

He bent down to kiss her, his lips firm on hers, sending her equilibrium spinning. She placed her hands on his lean hips, trembling with the need to touch him. Tension emanated from him as he pulled her closer, only releasing her after he'd passionately and thoroughly kissed her. "I told you your virtue was safe but know this," his warm breath caressed her lips as she stared up at him, "even though I am a patient man, Alix, I have my limits." He brushed his lips lightly over hers again. "Until tonight."

~ *Chapter 9* ~

ALIX'S MIND SPUN AS she hastened down the hallway, her shoes clicking on the stone floor. Knowing what was on Richard's mind sent a surge of warmth rushing through her as she thought of his hands caressing her body, his moist kisses against her heated skin and the feel of him in her arms. This might be her only chance to be with him. He was leaving tomorrow, and she didn't know if she would be there when he returned.

Nearing the chamber door, her steps faltered. When she had first arrived, her focus had been on trying to get home, but living with the girls and getting to know Richard, the man behind the legend, had taken priority. She hadn't even considered what effect her unexpected presence could have in this time. She had been careful not to refer to the future, and had watched her words closely, but she didn't belong there. What if, inadvertently, she changed history?

Her heart lurched and her stomach quivered at the thought, but she shook off the feeling. So far, she was confident she hadn't done or said anything that would make a difference. Surely, one night with Richard couldn't do any harm, could it? She entered the servants' chamber and hurried to Melisende. "I'm so sorry I'm late. I lost track of time."

Melisende sent her a knowing look, the hint of a smile curving her lips. "Did you enjoy yourself last night?"

"I did, very much. I wish there was more time to get to know him, but he's departing tomorrow."

Melisende patted Alix's shoulder. "I'm sorry he's leaving so soon, but that's his way. He sweeps in, turns everything upside down, then leaves for months at a time."

"At least I'll see him before he goes. He invited me to his chambers again tonight. I'm sure he probably has women in every town and city from here to Rouen. But I never thought a man like him would be interested in me."

"I've watched the Duke grow from a headstrong child into an ambitious, authoritative young man. Yes, he's taken women to his bed, but I've never seen him so preoccupied by anyone. He's very interested."

"Well then, I hope he makes tonight memorable." Alix smiled as adrenaline sparked through her.

"Come. I believe sewing is not your forte, so you have a lot of lanterns to polish."

"Too true. Where are they?"

"They're in the kitchen. You will have to work down there today."

"That's fine. I know Emma already, so I have someone to talk to."

Melisende gave her a shocked look. "Alix, we don't associate with the kitchen staff unless it's absolutely necessary. They are beneath our station."

"I don't understand why. We all work for the Duke, so aren't we all servants in some capacity?"

"Our positions are different. We are household servants, which rank higher than the kitchen staff. How we conduct ourselves reflects upon the Duke. The sooner you learn that, the better. Now go downstairs, we have wasted enough time."

Alix hurried back to her room to change into her Faire costume, since polishing lanterns could be quite messy and she would feel guilty if she ruined Sybilla's borrowed dress. As she ran down the stairs to the hallway, she reminded herself that a person's station was extremely important in the Middle Ages. She couldn't ignore the fact that even in her time, however unfairly, people were treated differently depending on their wealth and background. As she entered the kitchen, a few of the servants turned to look at her.

"I was sent down here to polish the lanterns." Alix looked around for the items in question.

A plump, matronly woman with pink cheeks and brown hair tucked in an unkempt bun under her cap, pointed to the corner. "They're over there, with the rags and polish."

"Thank you. I will try to stay out of your way. I know you all are extremely busy." She took a seat at the table, ready to begin a day of monotonous work.

"Alix, what are you doing here?"

"Oh, hello, Emma." Alix gestured toward the brass lanterns. "Melisende doesn't know what to do with me. My attempt at embroidery was disastrous, so she sent me down here to do this. If I detest one chore, it's polishing brass. The polish gets under my nails and takes forever to get out."

"You hate the work, but you don't mind being down here?"

"No, not at all! It smells wonderful in here and it's warm. Upstairs, it's always so cold."

"You are very different from the other servants." Emma's comment was both comforting and disconcerting. "They treat us like dirt, especially that blonde who is always fawning over the Duke."

"You must mean Beatrice. I have heard she and the Duke are together." Alix baited the girl to see what she knew.

Emma laughed. "I would have to say he doesn't seem to agree."

"What do you mean?"

Emma looked around, making sure the others weren't listening, and leaned in. "It's no secret that she was one of his favorites, but it is said that she hasn't been with him in months. Perhaps he has tired of her."

"How do you know all of this?"

Emma simply shrugged. "I hear things here and there."

Of course. The servants were practically invisible to the nobles. They witnessed all manner of gossip and intrigue as they served the lords and ladies. Since they were so far beneath them, they were scarcely considered human, let alone of any importance.

"I'd better get back to work."

Alix nodded. "Me too. Unfortunately, these lanterns won't clean themselves."

The next several hours passed as Alix listened to the other women talking about the various dishes they were preparing for supper and how their children and families were doing. Emma worked near Alix, so they were able to converse as well. When the lanterns gleamed, she stood up, unsure what to do next.

Alix walked over to one of the women who deboned a chicken. "Excuse me, do you know what I should do with these lanterns?"

"They need to be hung in the dining room. Emma and Jeanne can help you." She beckoned to a short, dark-haired girl who hastily wiped her hands on her apron as she hurried over.

It took several trips, but at last all the lanterns were in the dining hall.

"How do we get these up there?" Alix looked at hooks hanging from the soot-darkened rafters soaring above her.

"Stand on the tables and use this, it's the only way." Emma handed Alix a long staff with a curved metal end.

Alix took a lantern and stretched as far as she could. Her tight dress constricted her motion, and she barely managed to hang it from a hook in the rafter. "This is not going to be very fun." Alix laughed and jumped down from the table. "If only I were about three inches taller."

"I'm shorter than you, so I'm absolutely useless for this task." Jeanne watched Alix climb the next table and hook a lantern on the staff.

"What are you doing, Alix?" Richard's deep voice boomed throughout the empty dining hall. "Why aren't you upstairs?"

Alix whirled around and almost fell off the table's edge but managed to catch her balance and save the lantern.

"Hanging lanterns. Isn't it obvious?"

"I can see that."

"Well, Melisende didn't know what to do with me, since I'm not suited to embroidery and sewing. She had me polish lanterns and now we're attempting to hang them."

"I will discuss this with her. You shouldn't be down here." His tone actually made Alix feel afraid for Melisende.

The other two girls followed their discussion avidly.

"Please don't. I like being down here. It's a nice change of scenery. I'll be back up as soon as we finish." She turned around and reached up to try and hang the lantern again. "Damn it." As much as she wanted to finish this chore, she realized she needed about one more inch of height to reach the rafter. She jumped up lightly and hung the lantern.

"Careful, Alix! Let me help you, lest you fall and break something."

"How generous of you to worry about my safety, kind sir." She batted her eyelashes, teasing him.

"I was thinking more along the lines of you breaking a lantern." He winked at her and climbed on the table. He took the staff from Alix, easily hanging the lantern on the hook. "I can't imagine how I get coerced into doing your chores for you."

"My undeniable charm?"

"You are undeniably something, but charming is not what comes to mind."

"I'll work on that. Will you help with the rest of the lanterns?"

"Absolutely. I wouldn't want an injury to keep you from joining me tonight."

He jumped down then offered his hand to help her. "Thank you." She responded as professionally as she could, while trying to get back into the role of employee for the benefit of Emma and Jeanne.

Richard helped hang the rest of the lanterns, and as soon as he departed, Emma ran over to Alix.

"It's you! You're the one he's taken with."

"You're mistaken. The Duke is just being chivalrous. It wouldn't do if one of us were to get injured in his service."

Emma rolled her eyes. "Alix, anyone watching you two can tell that he is drawn to you."

Alix didn't want to fan the flames of gossip. "Nonsense. Nothing has happened between us."

"Well, I must say I've never seen him act this way around Beatrice. You two seem… comfortable together."

"It's always wise to be on good terms with your employer. Now, I'm going upstairs and you two need to get back to work. I won't be held responsible if you get into trouble."

When she opened the door to her quarters, the girls' chattering stopped, and all eyes turned toward her. "What? What have I done?" She crossed the room, fighting a frustrated sigh and eye roll, then stopped abruptly and stared. Bolts of fabric covered her bed. Beige linen, fine wool in hues of russet brown and indigo blue, and charcoal gray silk. She knelt and smoothed her hand over the various materials. She stopped at the silk with a gasp, watching it shimmer in the sunlight. Sitting neatly beside the bolts in a tidy row were also four different colored slippers that matched the fabrics.

Sybilla and Melisende approached. "I believe this should be more than adequate for your needs." Melisende motioned to the fabrics.

"The Duke did this?" Alix's whisper conveyed the shock she felt inside.

Melisende nodded. "I am aware of your lack of sewing skills, but one of the girls will be able to help you."

"I will help, and Maud, too," Sybilla offered. "She's an excellent seamstress."

"Really? Thank you! I can't wait to start designing the dresses!" Alix felt truly overwhelmed, with not only Richard's extravagant generosity, but also the quick benevolence of her friends. "I think he went a bit far. Not that I'm complaining, mind you, but I fear I'm falling deeper and deeper into his debt. I must thank him before he departs."

Sybilla nodded and returned to sit on her pallet. The excitement on her face over Alix's gifts quickly faded, melancholy replacing her happy grin.

"What's wrong?" Alix came and sat beside her. "You seem sad."

"Rob is leaving tomorrow with Richard to oversee the building of some worthless castle. I don't know when he will return." She looked desperately at Alix. "Do you think he'll come back to me or find another girl?"

"Another girl? That's absurd. It's perfectly obvious he's besotted with you. You have nothing to worry about."

"The Duke often stays a month or so before leaving again. I thought we would have more time together."

"I'm sure they'll come back soon. This is Queen Eleanor's palace, after all. The Duke wouldn't want to leave it unprotected for long."

Sybilla sniffed and wiped away her tears. "I'm going to miss Rob." She managed a grin at Alix. "His presence has made Mass bearable, and I've looked forward to supper when we could spend time together."

Alix put her arm around her. "I know how you feel, but at least you have a real chance with him. You have to make tonight count. I'm filthy from polishing and hanging lanterns, but after I bathe, I'm going to help you get ready. Rob will be speechless when he sees you."

Once Alix had changed into the green dress, she sat next to Sybilla on her pallet. She applied her tinted lip balm to redden Sybilla's lips, pinched her cheeks to suffuse them with color, and brushed her brunette hair so it hung like silk down her back, beneath her veil. Sybilla gazed into Alix's mirror and smiled. "I hardly recognize myself."

"You are beautiful. Rob is a very lucky man."

Alix placed the bolts of fabric and shoes in her coffer, smoothing her hand over the gray silk one last time, and then hurried to catch up with Sybilla, who had almost reached the door.

Beatrice stepped in front of her, and a sly look entered her eyes. "I hope you take advantage of Richard's last night here, Alix, because I daresay once he reaches his castle, there will be a new girl in his bed before nightfall."

"I'm sure you're right," Alix conceded. "But at least I can console myself knowing it won't be you." Alix lifted the corners of her mouth.

She had to stifle a laugh at the shock that befell Beatrice's face, but Beatrice recovered quickly. "Well, if I can offer insight into Richard's appetites, don't hesitate to ask. I'm an expert."

"Thank you for the offer, but since that hasn't turned out so well for you, I think I will decline. I have my own methods of pleasing Richard, and I assure you they're nothing like anything he's ever experienced before."

"Girls, stop!" Sybilla hissed, motioning to Melisende who was watching the interaction. Beatrice glared at her but left before Melisende could come over. Sybilla stomped her foot, folded her arms across her chest, and then turned on her heel to head downstairs. Alix ran to catch up, apologizing the entire way, not wanting to ruin Sybilla's night.

The cook had outdone herself with the bountiful meal before them. A last grand supper for the Duke. The mood in the hall was a mix of excitement and solemnity this night. Richard and his retinue must provide a welcome respite from the monotony of daily life for the palace's inhabitants. There was to be no entertainment after dinner since they would depart early the next morning and too many evening distractions made for weary travelers the following day. When Rob came over to sit next to Sybilla, Alix went to look for Maud. Stolen moments like this were rare and she didn't want to intrude on Sybilla's last hours with her love.

~~*

"Alix, a word please."

"Yes, Your Grace?"

"Will you accompany me upstairs?"

She looked around, flustered. "Why are you asking me so publicly?" she responded in a low voice. "I thought we were being discreet."

"Look around you. No one is surprised. This is court life. Everyone knows everyone else's business." He laughed. The many faces of Alix fascinated him, even this stricken expression. Alas, he relented. "This truly bothers you? I'm the Duke. Obviously who I am with is noted."

"I'm aware of that, but I'm not accustomed to my activities being monitored." She spun away from him and headed toward the doorway. He watched her walk away, surprised by her words. He had always accepted the fact that every movement and choice he made was scrutinized, but she hadn't grown up at court. He hastened out of the hall and caught up with her on the stairway.

"I know that you are unfamiliar with this way of life, that you don't understand that rumors permeate every court from here to England."

"Richard, I don't like living under a microscope. Spending time with you doesn't help."

Richard frowned and gave her a hard look. "A micro...?"

"I meant, if you were just Richard instead of the Duke of Aquitaine, the things you do would be of little interest to most. It's not your fault. You can't choose your station, just like you can't choose your family."

"I'm glad someone besides me recognizes that."

She laughed, but then sighed. "It's all on me I'm afraid. I either have to learn to deal with court life or give it up."

"I told you, I will help you. It's not as overwhelming as you make it sound."

"You're leaving tomorrow. You won't be here to help me. I will be left to navigate the gossip and the fallout of our relationship alone." Taking a step back, she leaned against the wall and sighed.

"I don't plan to stay away too long. Upon my return, I will see to it you will be instructed in everything you need to know."

"Everything?" Alix looked up at him through her lashes. "I know quite a few things already."

The corner of her mouth lifted in a teasing, yet seductive smile. His hands trembled with the need to touch her and his pulse raced at the thought of her in his bed. He moved closer to her, inhaling her exotic, spicy perfume. Her brunette hair hung loose over her shoulders and he coiled the strands around his hand, gently pulling it down to tilt her head up. She stood on her tiptoes to kiss his jaw, then brushed his lips with hers. His groin tightened with need. Alix intrigued him with her openness and ease around him. She awakened feelings in him that he'd never felt for a woman before– protectiveness, anticipation, and admiration. His blood heated as her tongue touched his tentatively. He wanted her in his bed, but in this moment, he didn't care where he took his pleasure.

He pressed her against the wall, his hand cupping the back of her head protectively from the hard stone. His kiss deepened and he roughly caressed her breast, his thumb circling her nipple. She moaned and pulled his hips closer, her desire inflaming his own. He ached to push the top of her dress down and kissed the swell of her breast. His hands moved to her laces, desperate to divest her of her cumbersome dress, but rational thought and lilting voices and laughter in the hall below, prevailed. He broke off the kiss with reluctance and took measured breaths, struggling for composure. If he didn't stop now, the gossip concerning their affair would be more lascivious than either of them had planned.

Her eyes were heavy with desire as she stared at him, her breath coming in gasps. "Alix, you don't know the effect you have on me. We'd best continue this in my chambers. The stairs are no place to experience the skills you have teased me with, ones that I hope to learn tonight."

Her hand shook as she placed it on his proffered arm. He smiled at the knowledge that he affected her as well.

* ~ * ~ *

Once inside his rooms, she stood transfixed. It looked as though a tornado had struck. Clothes were strewn about in haphazard piles, maps littered the table and coffers rested against the walls, some packed but most still empty.

"You are more disorganized than I am. I pity your squires trying to make order out of this chaos."

Richard looked around ruefully. "I don't know how long we're going to be gone, so I need to be prepared for anything."

"Good luck with that. Would you like some help?"

"No, that's not necessary." Two squires entered the room. Alix tried to stay out of the way as he directed them as to what went where. Finally, the room was in order, or at least the clothes on the floor were now on chairs or in coffers, resulting in a marked improvement.

"That will be all for now." Richard's order spurred the men to leave, and when they were gone, he poured wine for himself and Alix.

"I guess you must get used to living out of a suitcase?"

"A 'suitcase'? I imagine this is another term English people are so fond of using?"

Since Richard spoke no English, even though he would become king of that country, she would have to tread carefully, so as not to make him feel belittled. "I meant that you probably never really unpack since you don't stay in one place very long."

"One of the inconveniences of having too many castles and too many rebellions to put down. One learns to travel light."

"You call this light?" she teased him.

"Yes. You should see my brothers' households when they travel. Their wives bring their ladies-in-waiting, and everything they would possibly need or want. It's quite a feat they manage to get anywhere."

"One of the advantages of single life."

"Yes, one of the advantages." Long strides brought him next to her. He took her cup and placed it on the table, reaching back to graze her cheek with his hand, roughened from years of mastering swords. His blue-gray eyes caught hers and she shivered at his simple touch.

Richard threaded his fingers through her coppery, streaked hair, his sweet, wine-scented breath igniting her lust as his lips hovered above hers. He lingered there with a mere inch between them, staring into her eyes. Her heart raced in anticipation of what was to come next.

Her blood hummed as he caressed her lower lip with his tongue. She opened her mouth, a soft moan escaping as she tasted him, trembling as his hands slowly moved down to her waist. His embrace was loose and gentle.

She fingered the edges of the soft fabric of his shirt and lifted it, letting her hands play over his taut stomach and muscular chest. His breath hitched and he pulled her closer. Her body responded, her core moistening, as his heat radiated through the fabric of her dress. He tore off his shirt and she caressed his chest down to his stomach. The stormy blue irises of his eyes darkened with desire.

"Jesu, Alix." His whisper came out husky and he shuddered as her hands played with the ties of his pants. An unexpected stab of doubt about what would happen next stopped her. She took a step back, devastated by his quick look of frustration followed by disappointment.

"I'm not going to force you."

"I believe you," she whispered and glanced toward the door.

At her glance he drew a ragged breath and turned to lean heavily on the table.

As she moved away from him, turmoil raged within her. Why did she feel so unsure? She wasn't naïve in the bedroom, but her past boyfriends hadn't been future kings of England. Her heart leapt each time she saw Richard and when they were together, she felt a connection between them that had grown deeper. She cared about this man and would lose her heart to him if she stayed.

The possibility of her own pain didn't concern her. But what if she disappointed him?

Backing away, she reached the door and pushed down on the handle, cracking it, still uncertain.

Could she walk away from Richard? And did she want to?

~ *Chapter 10* ~

HE FOCUSED ON THE wood grain of the smoothly-hewn table in front of him. He couldn't bear to watch Alix walk out, not again. The heavy wooden door opened and closed. He took a deep drink of wine, trying to dampen the raging desire that burned in him and banged the cup down on the table. No woman had ever refused his advances or made him want her so desperately. "God's legs," he cursed aloud. *What have you done to me, Alix*?

His eyes closed and he concentrated on the sounds of the room to help ease the tension knotting in his stomach and lust burning in his blood. Surely, this woman couldn't have affected him to this degree in the few short weeks he had known her?

The door lock clicked into place, then the swish of skirts danced across the floor. Richard's eyes opened and he turned to find Alix standing next to him, a wanton look of desire blazing in her eyes.

"You came back."

"Yes. I need you, Richard. Now."

"You're certain? You will not leave again?" He reached, aching to touch her.

She nodded. "I've never been more certain of anything before in my life."

He picked her up in his arms and strode to his bedroom, kicking open the door with a vigor and anticipation that he'd never felt before. Setting her on her feet, he moved behind her. As he loosened the laces of her dress, he kissed each inch of her skin as it was revealed, caressing her shoulders and trailing hot, wet kisses along the curve of her neck, then slowly pulled the dress down, until the material grazed her breasts.

As he turned her to face him, she grabbed at the falling fabric, seeming reluctant to reveal all so quickly. He tugged to release the heavy fabric that pooled at her feet. He stared at her unblemished skin, admiring her pale, slender beauty. He placed his hands on her waist, touching her smooth, warm skin, and drew her close, needing to feel her softness against him. He kissed her neck, tasting her with his tongue then exhaled, cooling the wet area, causing her to shiver and goosebumps to cascade down her arms.

She swayed against him, her heart racing under the hand he rested at the base of her throat. He lightly licked her collarbone and she sighed, then cried out as he bent down and captured her breast in his mouth, teasing the nipple. She pulled his head up, her hands tangled in his hair, and her lips met his again, their tongues sparring. He finally broke the kiss, staring into her hazel eyes, now gone deep green with desire. Her lips were swollen and red from his kisses.

He swept her into his arms again and laid her on the bed, the flickering light from the lanterns bathing her body in a golden hue. "You are so beautiful, Alix." His throat felt raw with need; his lust fueled by the thought that she would be his at last.

She blushed and turned her face to hide her embarrassment. He hadn't witnessed this characteristic in any woman he'd lain with before. Most who shared his bed had been well-schooled in how to please a man. The others were blurred, drunken nights, the women equally uninhibited.

She leaned forward to kiss him and drew him into the bed alongside her, pushing him back against the pillows. Her lips trailed down his neck to the hollow in his throat where his pulse beat wildly. She took her time, exploring his body as she skimmed his skin with her fingertips, caressing the hard muscles of his arms then moving to his chest. His length hardened painfully as she grazed his nipples. She smiled at his sharp intake of breath and then moved downward. He tried to maintain control, his muscles clenched under her soft lips and roaming hands. After the last few nights of foreplay, he was more than ready for her. When she reached his chausses and began untying them, he was surprised but pleased. Her earlier embarrassment conflicted with her current brazenness, but his musings stopped short at the light touch of her tongue on his stomach.

She removed his remaining clothes and continued her explorations with her lips and tongue. He surrendered to her, pleasure tingling his skin and building, coursing through his muscles unlike anything he'd ever felt before. His breathing quickened and one hand tangled in her hair while the other tightened upon her shoulder as he hovered on the edge of the ultimate pleasure from her kissing and fondling alone. "Alix, if you want this night to last longer, come here."

She shifted her position and crawled up his body, her lips making a wet trail from his stomach as they searched for his. She laid next to him, her hands never leaving his skin. He ran a hand up her inner thigh and as he touched her, she cried out. He continued to tease her, but her soft, escalating moans threatened to break his barely-restrained control.

"I need you now, Alix," he rasped, and started to roll over when she pushed him back against the soft bed and straddled his hips. Most women preferred the man on top, but Alix apparently had no such inclination. He placed his hands on her waist to guide her. She slowly sat on his length and his pride swelled at the look of pure pleasure on her face.

She gave a small moan and began to move of her own volition, creating the perfect rhythm, her breasts bouncing in the dim light. He grasped her hips tightly as her speed picked up and soon she cried out and threw her head back as her body tensed around him. It wasn't often that a woman reached the pinnacle while in his bed, not for lack of his attempts. They were usually so focused on pleasing him that their own pleasure was an afterthought, but as Alix moved faster above him, she cried out again, louder this time, as she rocked against his hardness, her body shuddering, her eyes shut tightly with indulgent satisfaction.

As her breathing slowed, she looked down at him, leaned forward and kissed him as she began moving again. He embraced her, pulling her closer with the urge to feel the soft press of her body against his.

Alix rolled over, dragging him on top of her. Her boldness and authoritative move excited him, causing his length to grow and harden painfully. He thrust into her, burying himself deep inside her heat, losing the last vestige of control. His thoughts fractured, pleasure bringing a cool sweat to his skin, the tension in his groin increasing with every movement. He experienced a rare moment of clarity as he peaked, then his climax utterly consumed him and he cried out, tightening his arms around her.

She held him as aftershocks rippled through his body, and pressed her lips to his, their breath mingling, arms wrapped tightly around each other. This was the place he wanted to stay forever, but he was afraid his heavy weight might crush her. He rolled to his back and she laid her head on his chest, her soft curves fitting perfectly against his muscular body as their damp, heated skin cooled in the chilled room.

As they lay embracing, one thought surfaced, startling him. He wanted her to remain with him. He usually took his pleasure quickly and cared little whether the women stayed or left. But Alix was experienced like no other woman he'd bedded. Just the thought of the raw pleasure they had both found in his bed was enough to arouse him again. She shifted position and the chilly air shocked his skin where her warmth had covered it, pulling a sharp gasp from his throat, and raising goosebumps on his chest.

"Sorry." She smiled as she reached to draw up the covers to warm them. "Hmmm." She traced his gooseflesh with her hands. "I think we can figure out a better way to warm you up." She raised an eyebrow and looked up at him with a wicked gleam in her eye.

He huffed and trailed his lips down her throat as his hands caressed her breasts. He moved lower, feeling renewed desire as she writhed underneath him. He kissed her stomach, lightly touching her with his tongue and she kneaded his shoulders as he pressed his lips to her inner thigh, moving ever so slowly upward. He tasted her and she convulsed. Her cries of pleasure increased as his tongue swirled around her sensitive core and he buried his fingers in her wet warmth. He teased and tormented until her hips jerked and her inner muscles contracted around his fingers. Her screams escalated until she tensed and arched toward him before collapsing back against the pillow again, her body still shaking.

A woman climaxing once was uncommon enough, but twice in one night; his ego was truly bolstered. This woman and he were a perfect sexual match. The thought unnerved him. He kissed her; his blood heated with rekindled desire. She reached down and stroked him, almost causing his tenuous mastery over his body to fail.

"No, not yet," he whispered, as he brushed her tousled hair from her flushed face. He positioned himself between her thighs and slowly entered her, watching her eyes widen then flutter close as he moved. The feel of her heat surrounding him ignited his need. She matched his thrusts, and his body clenched in almost painful desire.

This feeling wasn't purely physical. He'd heard men speak of an emotional connection with their woman, but he'd never before experienced how much that feeling heightened the pure pleasure of the body. He moved faster until his world spun and he gripped her tightly as he climaxed again, then collapsed in her embrace, completely and utterly sated.

She held him, stroking his hair. His body calmed. Exhaustion replaced his earlier lust. He raised himself on one arm, kissed her, and drew her into his arms. She moved closer, one arm over his chest and her leg tucked intimately between his.

He couldn't recall any other time he'd found true peace and contentment in a woman's arms.

* ~ * ~ *

Alix woke before dawn and stretched, warmth filling her heart remembering the passionate night they had shared. She had never felt such need for any man, or lost control so completely. She turned and gazed upon Richard's face. In sleep, he looked much younger than twenty-five, and she pictured the sixteen-year-old boy who'd led an army against his father. She laid back and played his history in her mind, still in shock and disbelief that this was the same man lying next to her.

Richard stirred and reached out to pull her to him, hugging her.

"I didn't mean to disturb you," she said as a strange worry took hold in her mind. Would Richard's interest in her cool, now that he had gotten what he wanted?

"You didn't. I've been watching you for some time. Why are you so pensive?"

"I was just um, wondering..." She played with the covers. "Really, just thinking about... oh never mind."

"I can only assume, since you can't seem to put a sentence together, that you are questioning last night?"

She nodded, holding her breath, expecting to hear the worst.

"Well..." he continued as she rested her head in the crook of his arm. "—I believe that we will probably both go to hell if we don't confess our carnal sins."

Her eyes flew to his, but when the corner of his mouth turned up, she sighed, relieved.

"I don't want your soul to be in jeopardy, so should we not re-visit last night? What say you?"

He pulled her on top of him. "No woman has ever pleased me like you have. I would gladly risk my soul to have multiple repetitions of last night."

"Richard, you shouldn't say things like that." Shifting her position, she was very aware of the direction of his thoughts, and she smiled. "However, I'm not that concerned with my soul, so let me be the one responsible. That way you will be blameless."

She leaned down and kissed his cheek, then neck, then chest. As her soft caresses and kisses shifted south, his muscles tightened and clenched underneath her. She slowly trailed her lips across his stomach, her fingers lightly caressing his thighs. His breathing quickened as she moved closer to his groin, then backed away. She kissed his inner thigh, her tongue lightly touching his heated skin and a low moan escaped his throat. Alix continued to tease him as she moved upward, and when she grazed his erection, his hips jerked.

"Alix, please…" The unmistakable growl of desire in his voice sent tendrils of excited adrenaline through her veins, thrilled for him to have such a response to her touch. She glanced up to see stark need in his eyes as he watched her fondle him. Focusing again, she caressed him with her tongue. He moaned low and long as she slid her lips down his length, tasting him completely. Richard's muscles stiffened and his body shuddered as she increased the pressure of her mouth around him, combined with quick movements of her hand. He cried out, spilling his seed, his body shaking in response. She swirled her tongue over him until his shudders calmed, then shifted position to lie in his embrace and gently kissed his neck and shoulder while his breathing slowed. She propped her head on one hand and let her fingers play over his chest, smiling at his stunned expression.

"My God, woman, where did you learn that?"

She laughed softly. "Have you never experienced it before?"

He shook his head.

"Good. Something to remember me by."

He glanced around the rumpled covers. "I must ask… did you do what I think you did?"

Alix giggled. "Yes." She smoothed her hand over his stubbly cheek and gazed into his eyes. "It's the ultimate gesture, really. Was it not pleasurable?"

He let out a breathy moan and cupped her face in his hands, returning her gaze. "Will you do it again?"

"Now?"

"When I return. Promise me."

"I promise. Now you had better get up. You still need to finish packing and ready your men for departure."

"Regrettably. I'm not looking forward to traveling and after last night and this morning you are not likely to be forgotten." He rose from the bed to attend to his morning ablutions while Alix found her dress, put it on, and managed to tie it clumsily. She wandered into the main chamber to wait for him. A knock on the door startled her, and she unlocked and opened the door. Rob looked at her in surprise, then smiled.

"Alix. So, it is true!" he exclaimed as he entered. "Sybilla told me that you and Richard seemed to be...er..." He cocked his brow at her.

"You must be the only one here who didn't know. According to Richard, it's common knowledge."

He laughed. "Alix, Richard was jesting. Not everyone knows, but you won't be able to hide it much longer."

"What makes you say that?" She knew Rob didn't deserve the sharp tone that laced her voice.

"I've seen the way you look at him."

"You won't say anything will you?"

"For certes not, I will keep your confidence." Although his offer was gallant, she knew he wouldn't be the only one with knowledge of this secret. "Alix, I never got the chance to thank you for suggesting a dance with Sybilla."

"You look so happy together, I know she will miss you when you leave."

"Will you look out for her?"

"I'll keep her so busy she won't have time to long for you."

Richard entered the main chamber.

"Rob." Gone was the soft and tender Richard from moments ago. The Duke had business to conduct and his voice rang of authority. "Send in squires to finish packing."

Rob nodded his head as he backed out of the room. "Certainly, Your Grace."

Alix turned and headed toward the door as well.

"Are you leaving?"

"You're going to be busy supervising. I don't want to be in the way. When do you think you will leave?"

"Not for several hours. I still have much to do, because someone demanded my time this morning."

"I didn't hear you complaining." She drifted back over to him, stopping only a breath from his face.

"I had nothing to complain about." He put his arms around her.

Alix kissed him softly. "I might not get a chance to say goodbye when you leave, so have a safe journey."

"I'm sure you'll see me before we depart."

"But I might not be able to talk to you." He nodded, acknowledging that possibility. Hearing voices outside, she kissed him once more. The mood was broken as the squires entered the chambers. Ignoring their stares, Alix made a quick exit and returned to her quarters.

As she opened the door, she noted that most of the servants were awake and dressing for the day so she tiptoed toward the back stairway and slumped down on the first step. So much had happened in the last few days that her mind was reeling.

Melisende's assessment was correct. Richard had arrived at Poitiers Palace, turned everything upside down, and would soon be off again. She already missed him and he hadn't even left yet, but she knew they'd said their goodbyes. He'd mentioned being gone for a month or so, then she remembered that this was the year Henry would ask all his sons to attend his Christmas court in Caen so they could try to mend the rifts in the tenuous fabric holding the family together.

There was a real possibility that Richard wouldn't return until late in the New Year, and with the rebellions, he could be away even longer. A bereft and melancholy feeling sank into her soul.

This might very well be the last time she would see him. Who knew when she would return to the twenty-first century and leave all this behind?

Her heart filled with pain. How could she have come to care about him so fast? Her view of him had changed so drastically that the historical figure she'd studied and the man she now cared for didn't even seem like the same person. She'd gotten to know Richard the man, not the legend, and found him to be kind, generous, and in possession of a wicked sense of humor.

Maybe it would be best if she made a clean break and returned home while he was away. After all, he had his life to live and history to make. She didn't fit into that equation.

Hearing laughter and chatter, she climbed up the stairs and went back into the chamber. Being part of this history, for however long she was here, would define her life from this point forward.

~ *Chapter 11* ~

SYBILLA WAS UP AND dressed, but her red, watery eyes gave away her sorrow. Alix put her arms around her, commiserating silently. Sybilla attempted a half-hearted smile and put on a brave front.

"Do you feel up to going to the service this morning?" Alix asked.

Sybilla nodded. "I'm sure Rob will be there. The men will want to pray for a safe journey."

They walked to the chapel in silence, each lost in her own morose thoughts. When they entered, most of the household knights were there. Richard stood with André and Rob at the solemn Mass, while the dour priest droned on in sepulchral tones. For once, it was exactly what Alix needed, as it mirrored her own emotions.

Even the men appeared affected by the dismal sermon. She glanced at Richard, hoping to catch a glimpse of affection in his blue-gray eyes, or share a secretive look remembering the passion of last night. He stared at the floor, his attention occupied elsewhere. A few short hours from now, he would ride away, maybe out of her life forever. Her heart plummeted in her chest.

The sound of jangling metal shattered the silence as they neared the palace. Grooms bridled and saddled horses, and the shouts of knights and squires readying themselves to depart filled the air.

Sybilla grabbed Alix's hand. "I don't want Rob to leave!"

"I'm sure he's not looking forward to it either. He asked me to look out for you and when he returns, you will see that he still cares about you. Let's go. I'm sure you wish to say goodbye."

The bailey teemed with knights and soldiers calming their restless horses while squires and pages rushed around tending to last minute tasks. Alix pointed Sybilla toward Rob and he quickly caught her up in his arms and held her close.

Alix's breath hitched as a lump rose in her throat. She wished she could show her affection for Richard as openly as her friend could for Rob, but she had to remember her station. She sought out Melisende.

Melisende raised her brow. "Did you get a chance to say goodbye?"

"Yes, we did, earlier."

"I think that we will use today as a day of leisure. I fear many of the girls won't be able to focus on their chores, anyway."

Alix nodded, searching the crowd of knights and squires for Richard. He stood with André, laughing as if he hadn't a care in the world.

Richard glanced around the courtyard and met her stare. This is what she'd longed for in chapel this morning. His blue gaze sent an electric surge throughout her body.

His eyes never left hers as he approached. Carefully keeping his distance, he addressed Melisende as to the basic upkeep of his property in his absence, then he turned to Alix.

"I trust you will help Melisende with the daily chores and any other issues that arise?"

"Certainly, Your Grace, I will do what is required of me."

Melisende made her goodbyes and left them alone. Alix curbed her desire to throw her arms around him and beg him to stay.

"Alix, please don't get into any trouble while I'm gone."

"What makes you say that?"

"I know you better than you think. Without me here, you need to guard what you say and how you conduct yourself."

"I'm sure I can manage that."

Her heart tightened with sadness, so she curtsied, as this was the only dignified way she could think to break eye contact with him and hide her face. He reached out his hand to help her up. "I will return, and I expect you to be here when I do."

"Well, since you asked so nicely..." She grinned at him.

He smiled down at her. "For certes, I am going to miss you."

"And I you."

He nodded to her once more, then turned and went to his horse. The knights were traveling light, wearing only their hauberks. Since none wore armor, they mounted their steeds easily. This was the moment she had been dreading. In a matter of minutes, they were on their way, riding out of the courtyard. A lone, rogue tear streaked down her face, which she quickly swiped away.

Sybilla joined Alix to watch the men depart. They stood looking into the empty space in front of them.

"Come, girls." Melisende came up behind them, putting one hand on each of their shoulders. "Let's go to breakfast and then I'll check what needs to be done today, if anything."

Breakfast was more somber than the chapel service and the silence weighed on Alix. Emma brought her a flagon of water, smiled, and escaped back to the kitchen. Alix encouraged Sybilla to eat but was unable to manage more than one or two bites herself. After what seemed like an interminably long time, they went back upstairs to their rooms. Some of the servants who had had little flirtations with the knights were still weeping and Alix wanted nothing more than to follow suit, but she refused to show her sorrow.

She went to her pallet, and then remembered all the fabrics that Richard had given her. She pulled them out of her coffer and began to lay out the various pieces. Alix hoped that Sybilla might show some interest, as putting these dresses together would be a welcome distraction from the quiet and emptiness of the palace.

Her plan worked and soon both Sybilla and Maud were helping to organize. Alix separated the indigo blue and russet brown wool from the beige linen, which would be useful for the warmer months. She smiled to herself as she put the linen aside, wondering if Richard expected her to stay well into the coming year. She had no idea where she would have occasion to wear the dark, gray silk, so she folded it carefully and put it in the coffer along with the linen, which she wouldn't need for months.

"We have two bolts of wool. Now what do we do?" Alix asked, staring blankly at the other girls.

"We need to measure you and decide what style of dress you want." Sybilla pulled a cloth measuring tape from her sewing basket.

"What do you think would work? I like the dresses I have been wearing, can we use those as a pattern?"

"Certainly, we can. If you like, we could embellish them so they'll be more elaborate."

"Don't bother. I can't imagine I would need a decorated dress for any reason."

"I'm sure the Duke will hold his Christ's Mass court here. You would have occasion to wear it then." Maud smiled brightly, obviously eager to make the adornments.

Aware that Richard would spend Christmas with his father, Alix shook her head. "Please, let's not go to the trouble now. We can add to it at a later time."

Sybilla picked up the measuring tape and some chalk. The girls discussed possible designs while Sybilla took accurate measurements of Alix's form and wrote each one down on a piece of parchment.

"I would like to alter the sleeves. The ones I've been wearing are too long and they get in the way. Could we shorten them but keep the bell shape? I would also like the bodice to fit more snugly. Would that be appropriate?"

"That would be simple to do." Sybilla spoke as she pulled and twisted the tape around Alix's body.

Alix glanced at the fabrics thoughtfully. "I wonder if it would be possible to have side laces which would make it easier to put the dress on by myself. I can't reach the ties in the back and have had the worst time trying to get in and out of these dresses."

Maud drew her brows together and tucked a blonde ringlet behind her ear. "I've never seen a dress like that, but I could easily do it. Just think, Alix, you could create a new style!"

Alix's mouth fell open at the thought of changing fashion. "Oh, I'm not comfortable with that. Maybe we should just put the laces in the back."

"You could say that it's fashionable in your country, and no one could prove you wrong," Sybilla pointed out.

"True enough," Alix agreed. "But let me consider it." She was wary of anyone perceiving her as different, but it was vital that she not alter history. Creating side laces on a dress seemed too small a detail to effect change, but she didn't want to risk it.

Long shadows slanted across the floor as the hours flew by, the distraction of making her dresses helping her and Sybilla through the interminable day.

"Ladies, it's supper time. Come now, make haste." Melisende's tone was soft and gentle. It reminded Alix of a mother comforting her children and she appreciated the gesture of sympathy.

Enthusiastic chatter filled the hall as the girls went downstairs, but when they entered the dining hall, the mood dropped.

Alix stared at Richard's empty table. She attempted to engage Sybilla in conversation but gave up when she realized Sybilla was just as gloomy. With Richard and his men gone, supper was over quickly. Alix already missed the sound of lutes and the excitement in the air the post-meal festivities brought. She needed a distraction.

"Maud, what do we do now?"

"Whatever do you mean?"

"I was spending my evenings with the Duke, but now…" Alix trailed off.

"Oh, I see. Some girls embroider. Several are accomplished in music and singing."

These activities were quite mundane in comparison to her time with Richard. What she really wanted was a bath and a cup of wine. *Damn you, Richard, now I'm going to turn into a lush to get you out of my head.*

Alix left early to return to the servants' quarters to take advantage of the vacant bathing room. Since the pages had departed with Richard, Alix had the unenviable task of hauling the cumbersome buckets of cold water upstairs herself. Once again, she was reminded of how hard life was in this age, even in a royal household.

Maud looked in. "Do you want any help with your hair after you are done?"

Alix wanted to be alone with her thoughts, but she appreciated the concern and sympathy in the younger girl's eyes and nodded. Maud skipped away and Alix turned to stoke the fire. She undressed and sank into the warm, rose-oil infused water. She inhaled, filling her lungs to their depths, but instead of relaxing, unpleasant thoughts intruded.

Anywhere knights traveled, women followed in the guise of laundresses or cooks, but in reality, they were nothing more than prostitutes. Richard probably wouldn't sleep alone for very long and she tried in vain to banish the stab of jealousy that thought caused. She allowed herself a few moments of self-pity, only one tear escaping down her cheek before she regained control. She sniffed and looked around for a tissue, but of course there weren't any in the Middle Ages. She stepped out of the cooling water, dried off and put on her shift, then went to the curtain and called out to Maud.

"You have beautiful hair, Alix. I like the way the coppery glints catch the light." Envy tinged Maud's voice as she carefully brushed Alix's hair until it hung neatly past her shoulders.

"I wish I had hair the exact shade of gold as yours, Maud. I used to drench my hair in lemon juice and sit in the sun for hours to lighten it. Unfortunately, it turned more red."

Maud's pale cheeks pinked at her praise, and Alix sensed that Maud hadn't received many compliments in her young life. After braiding Alix's hair into two long plaits, they went into the main room where a few of the girls were playing lutes. Alix shared her pallet with Maud and they listened to the music.

It was quite pretty but she couldn't seem to separate her own melancholy from the haunting tone of the notes as they floated through the air. Other girls bunched in groups, chitchatted or braided each other's hair. Life in this room was like living in a never-ending slumber party.

She missed her friend Cara and the late-night girl talks they had, gossiping about co-workers, dishing on boyfriends, and telling each other their hopes and dreams of the future. As she listened to the girls talking and laughing, Alix realized that this was exactly what she wanted, friends to confide in and share secrets, although she would need to choose her friends carefully, lest she slip and divulge something about her past or something Richard told her in confidence. She needed to become better acquainted with the customs and decorum expected of her since she had no idea when or if she would ever return to her own time. With the distraction of Richard removed, she could now concentrate on the task of blending in.

Alix chose to begin with Maud. Although she was young and innocent, she seemed to have a discernment about her that was mature beyond her years.

"I couldn't help but notice that you didn't sleep in our room last night, Alix. Did you spend the night with the Duke?" Maud looked sideways at her; her lips curved in a smile.

Alix's eyes widened and she felt a slight flush on her cheeks. "I have no idea what you are suggesting, Maud. What do you…?"

Their conversation halted when Beatrice approached. "I'm so sorry you have to put up with us instead of spending your nights elsewhere, but you ought to get used to it. At least you have your memories, for that's all you will ever have." Beatrice turned up her nose and looked down over her shoulder. Alix couldn't help but chuckle while Maud's eyes widened.

"It's been some time since you were invited to Richard's chambers, hasn't it? How are your memories, Beatrice? Are the details beginning to fade?"

Beatrice flushed and she took a step toward Alix.

"Ahem. Beatrice, to bed with you." Melisende's order was given under the guise of blowing out the candles, signaling bedtime, but Alix knew she had just diffused a sticky situation.

Beatrice's lip curled and she turned away. Alix exhaled slowly, aware of how close she had come to an argument. Despite Alix's disdain for the other girl, she needed to guard her tongue if she wanted to establish a good reputation within court, especially with Richard gone.

~ *Chapter 12* ~

THE FOLLOWING DAYS WERE monotonous, filled with daily Matins, breakfast, chores and supper, followed by idle talk and music, then bed. It was little wonder ladies made up stories about each other and created intrigue where there was none. They were bored out of their minds! Alix, used to passing her time with work, books and television, wasn't prepared to sit and do nothing, day after day.

After the initial embroidery disaster, Sybilla had sat down and taught Alix several basic stitches, which she was able to copy. She embroidered to pass the time and Sybilla worked diligently on Alix's new dresses. The woolen garments in indigo blue and russet brown were coming together quite nicely. Alix had opted for the ties on the side of the bodice and prayed she wouldn't create too much scandal. She hoped that if she were ever able to go into town, she could locate a shop to buy some colored laces to match her dresses.

The overall depression that lingered after Richard and his knights left began to fade, and after a couple of weeks, the atmosphere in the palace lightened. The younger girls enjoyed experimenting with their long hair, trying out intricate new ways of braiding and weaving. Melisende gave Alix the daunting task of combing and styling their hair after they had bathed. To her surprise, as well as everyone else's, she actually had a talent for braiding, and her new chore kept her busy most of the evenings.

Weeks passed, and although autumn still hung on and the trees were glowing with leaves in hues of gold, orange, and fiery reds, winter nipped in the air, reminding everyone that cold, harsh days were ahead. Alix began to enjoy her time in the castle. The thought of home rarely entered her mind, as she became more comfortable with her new life.

On the way to Matins, Alix inhaled the scent of chimney smoke from the houses below, which lingered in the cold air. Bright sunlight shimmered through the leaves above her and dappled the ground in ever-changing patterns.

"I love this time of year. The colors of the leaves are so beautiful. I've never seen such vibrant reds before."

Maud scrunched her brows. "Alix, the leaves always change color in autumn. You ought to be used to it by now."

"No. Where I'm from, we have an abundance of evergreens. The few species of trees we have which turn color, only change to yellow or brown, and then the leaves fall off. We never get a true autumn, as it's too warm. This is truly beautiful."

For the first time since Richard left, Alix didn't feel the familiar ache when she looked around the half-empty chapel. Was she getting over him? Maybe the old adage 'out of sight, out of mind' was true. She hoped not, but with Richard gone, her life was easier. She stayed on Melisende's good side and, was never absent or tardy with her chores.

Alix also wasn't the center of gossip any longer, which she appreciated. Another good side effect of Richard's absence was Beatrice's silent mouth. Her malicious comments dwindled only a few weeks after his departure, and as of late, had ceased all together. They would never be friends but now they shared a quiet existence of ignoring each other.

After breakfast, Melisende approached Alix. "Do you mind polishing lanterns again? I have trouble getting the other girls to go to the kitchen to do them, and you did such an excellent job last time."

Alix nodded, happy to have a different chore to occupy her time. She went down to the kitchen where, by now, the servants were used to her presence.

"Good morrow, Alix," said Marie the cook, a jolly portly woman, with whom Alix had become friends. Alix returned the greeting, then Marie turned back to stir a pot in the immense fireplace. The fire warmed the kitchens and provided some light in the windowless room. A large stone propped open the side door to allow the heat to escape and let in sunlight.

"Alix! Are you polishing lanterns again?" Emma bounced into the room, a smile pulling up the corners of her mouth.

"Yes, apparently it's one of my few talents." Alix laughed, plopped down at the table and picked up a cloth.

Emma hurried to Alix and whispered in her ear. "Do you think the Duke will come back soon?"

Alix looked up, startled at the unexpected question. "I don't know.

Melisende hasn't mentioned when she expects him to return. He's only been gone a little over a month. I doubt we will see him before mid-November, if then. Why do you ask?"

"It's more exciting with the dancing and music when he's in residence. He also seemed more at ease during this stay compared to other times."

"What do you mean by that?"

Emma flushed and drew back. "I'm sorry. It's not my place to speculate on the King's son."

Alix waved it away. "I'm curious as to what you meant by 'at ease'?"

Emma seemed to consider the question. "The last several visits, he was very solemn and preoccupied. He never stayed in the dining hall very long and there was very little entertainment."

"He was putting down rebellions. I'm sure that weighed heavily on his mind." Alix was quick to point out Richard's responsibilities, not knowing if the kitchen staff would be aware of his more political tasks. "But I do agree with you. I miss the dancing and the liveliness of the dining hall, too."

"I'm sure you miss the Duke, as well." Emma sent a knowing glance toward Alix.

"I do, but *que sera sera*." Alix shrugged her shoulders. Emma looked curiously at her, and Alix translated, "Whatever will be will be."

"The Duke's mood changed this last visit. And for the better. I've never seen him...enjoy his time here. I daresay, your arrival had much to do with that." Emma's lips curved in an impish grin. Alix's heart leapt at her words, wondering if she really had such an effect on Richard.

"Emma, more work, less talk." Marie stood with a wooden spoon in her hand t-sking the girl. They turned back to their chores with sly but guilty smirks.

Once the lanterns were polished and hung, Alix returned to her chambers. Melisende motioned to her to join them by the fire. "The girls have received some letters, and I would love to hear the gossip from the other courts. Come, join us." Alix curled up in a chair.

One of the girls had just opened her letter and read it silently.

"That's Gwyn. Her cousin is a lady-in-waiting to Queen Marguerite, the Young King's wife," Sybilla explained. "We hear of all the scandalous events in the Parisian court from her."

Gwyn finished the letter and regaled the girls with the news. "The Young King Henry and Queen Marguerite arrived in Paris a couple of weeks ago with a large entourage of knights and minstrels."

"How unfortunate that they lost their young son only days after he was born, and she hasn't fallen pregnant since," remarked one of the other girls. A collective sigh of sympathy wove its way through the group, while heads nodded in agreement. Once a king, or in this case the anointed king, married, everyone waited on tenterhooks for the first-born child to arrive, praying it would be a son.

"Oh no! She writes that King Henry expects all of his family to attend his Christ's Mass court." Gwyn looked up in dismay at Melisende. "If the Duke isn't going to be here, are we still going to celebrate the Holy Days?"

The girls looked at each other with sadness in their eyes. A few cries of denial even arose from the din of soft grumblings.

"Most assuredly we will." Melisende used a soothing voice, but there was no hiding her disappointment. "It just won't be as extravagant this year."

In an instant Sybilla turned toward Alix. "Did you know about the Duke attending his father's court?"

"Me? No, how would I know?"

"Perhaps he mentioned it to you while you were together?"

"No, we never discussed it."

Sybilla gasped. "That means Rob won't spend Christ's Mass here, either. What if they don't return at all and go directly to join his father?"

"Richard told me he would return," Alix said, "and I believe he will try to, unless something very important arises."

"I hope you're right. Why did I have to fall in love with a squire? Why couldn't I fall in love with a simple man who doesn't leave for months on end?" Her voice trembled and the frustration that had been building erupted. "This is your fault, Alix!"

Alix's back stiffened and she lifted her chin. "My fault? How is this my fault?"

"If you hadn't made him dance with me, my heart wouldn't be aching."

"You were quite happy to dance with him."

They glared at each other and Sybilla turned her back, sulking. Alix shook her head, annoyed that her closest friend was taking her heartache out on Alix. She rose, walked to her pallet and knelt by her coffer to get her cloak. Maybe a stroll before dinner would surely help to cool the fire that burned inside her.

When she pulled out the wrap, the brooch fell from her pouch and onto the floor. She froze.

Would it work this time? She hesitated to pick it up because she didn't want to find out. Instead she wrapped her hand in the cloak and used it to put the brooch back in the pouch. Emptiness engulfed her and suddenly all she wanted to do was climb into bed and shut the world away. She knew she could rise above what seemed like a petty argument between friends, but without Richard the loneliness shredded her soul into ribbons.

Alix carefully replaced her cloak, shut the lid, and lay down on her pallet wondering again if her friends and family knew she was missing. The low murmurs of voices in the room lulled her to sleep.

She woke several hours later and found herself alone. She hurried downstairs and entered the dining hall, relieved that she hadn't missed supper. Alix began to make her way to where Maud sat, then came to a standstill.

Several knights and squires were walking throughout the hall. Her heart stopped. Alix practically ran to Maud.

"Some of Richard's men are here. Has he returned?" Alix grasped the young girl's arm.

Maud looked up at her. "I knew it. You're in love with the Duke. I've never seen you act in such a way, Alix." Maud giggled. "But to answer your question, a few of the men have. Rob is here, so Sybilla's very happy, but the Duke didn't come with them."

Her heart sank and Alix plopped down on the bench.

"I'm sorry. I know you miss him."

Filling a plate with food, Alix forced herself to try to eat, but her appetite had vanished, and she pushed it away.

Sybilla sat down next to Alix, glowing with happiness. "Oh. Alix, it was wrong of me to be angry with you, and I'm so sorry we argued."

"Me, too. I heard Rob has returned. Do you know why they've come back?"

"The Duke was concerned about Queen Eleanor's palace being unprotected so he sent some knights to safeguard it."

"Oh. Did Rob say anything else?"

"No, nothing more."

Alix tried to hide her crestfallen look. She assumed Richard sent his men because he feared his disgruntled lords might attempt an attack on an unprotected palace, which meant things were not going any better between him and Hal. No matter the reason, she wished he had returned as well.

Melisende bustled about the hall, making sure the men had everything to their liking, since their arrival had been unexpected. "Alix, can you please help me?"

"Yes, of course, what can I do?"

"I'm unprepared for our guests. Would you please go up and check the Duke's chambers? I haven't cleaned them since he left and I don't know what state they're in."

Alix headed upstairs, wondering if she would run into some of Richard's men, but the upper floor seemed deserted. Her knock on the chamber door went unanswered. When she entered the room, she found it cold and dark, and she hastened to find a lantern. As she put fire to the wick, shadows cast upon the tapestried walls and memories surrounded her.

She envisioned Richard sitting on the window seat, drinking from a cup of wine and laughing at something clever she'd said. Or standing at the table, studying the architectural drawings of the damn castle he just had to build. She drew a shaky breath, looked around the outer room, and decided it was clean enough for his men.

Turning away from the window, she faced the door to his personal chamber. Drowning in memories, she forced herself to open it, trying her best to keep her emotions in check. Mentally, she shook herself, but her breath caught at the sight of his shirt folded neatly on the bed, as if waiting for her.

She picked it up and smoothed her hand over the cool fabric. He'd left this for her. If only she had come in here a month ago, she might have spared herself weeks of heartache. She laughed at herself and hurried out of the bedroom, the shirt in her arms, and shut the door behind her.

"Alix!"

She turned. "Rob!" She crossed her arms to hide the shirt. "How are you?"

"I'm faring well." He studied her with concern in his eyes. "And you?"

"I'm fine. Melisende hasn't sent me away yet." She laughed.

He smiled. "Richard sends his regards. He would have liked to join us, but he had some new ideas to protect and strengthen the defenses of Clairvaux."

"Yes, the new castle, always the new castle," she groused.

"He will come back." Rob's assuring tone did not ease her sadness. "Soon."

"I won't hold my breath."

Rob frowned at her. "Alix, please understand, Richard must travel constantly to maintain order in the realm, especially with his barons rebelling at every opportunity."

She nodded and felt a flush of heat on her cheeks. "I know it's impossible for him to stay in one place too long. I'm being uncharitable. I'm glad you're back and I daresay Sybilla is beyond excited."

Rob's smile lit his face like the sun bursting from behind a dark cloud. "I didn't realize how much she meant to me until I left. I have to say; I'm pleased to hear she feels the same way about me."

"I am happy for both of you. Now, I'd better go. Please tell the men that Richard's apartments are ready for them."

Rob nodded to her and Alix continued to the servants' quarters. When she entered, Sybilla was sitting on her pallet, beaming as she related details of her reunion with Rob to Maud. Alix joined them, smiling at the appropriate moments, doing her best to banish the green-eyed monster lurking within her. Failing miserably at this task, she decided to take a quick sponge bath in the hopes that the girls' conversation would have ended before she returned. Carrying Richard's shirt, she entered the bathing area and ran into Beatrice.

"Oh, Alix, you must be devastated that Richard didn't come back with the others."

"I can't imagine you care about my feelings. What do you want?"

Beatrice's demeanor instantly changed to cold and calculating. "You never could have had a relationship with him."

"And why is that? Do you think he would have gone back to you?"

"Certainly not, you stupid girl." Alix flushed in anger at Beatrice's words but remained silent. "He is in love with the unattainable."

"What are you talking about?"

"You mean *who* am I talking about. I'm sure he mentioned his son Philip to you." Alix nodded, cold fingers of dread rising within her as Beatrice continued. "Did he mention the boy's mother?"

"Yes. He said she lives in Mirebeau with his son, and he continues to care for their well-being."

"Ah, he told you that." Beatrice's voice dripped with compassion.

"What do you mean?"

"She's the only woman he's ever truly loved. She's married now so they can't be together, but every opportunity he has, he goes to visit them."

"If she's married, I can't imagine her husband would allow Richard to visit her."

"Dearest Alix, don't you know anything about court life? Her husband is quite a bit older than she, and they most likely won't have any children. However, with Richard as the boy's father, they can depend upon Philip inheriting land or making an advantageous marriage. It will be a boon for them, since I believe they are peasants." Beatrice's lip curled distastefully.

Alix stared at the floor and dug her nails into her trembling hands. Beatrice's words rang true. Richard had already stated that he wanted what was best for his son. He'd also said he had no feelings for the mother, but what if that was for Alix's benefit? He wouldn't be the first man to neglect to mention his attachment to another woman.

"You didn't think that he truly cared for you, did you?" Beatrice's short laugh echoed in the small room. "You are just a passing fancy. Like so many girls before you, his interest will fade and you'll find yourself back on the street where you came from. Neither of us ever had a chance with him, really, but at least now you know the truth."

The vindictive look in Beatrice's eyes as she turned and left punched Alix so hard in the midsection she almost choked. Humiliation and hurt flowed through her and hot tears threatened. How could she have been so naive? She'd only been a momentary distraction for him. That is why he hadn't returned.

He'd traveled to Mirebeau. Rob either was sworn to secrecy or didn't have the heart to tell her the truth. She sank to the cold floor and drew her knees up, wrapping her arms around them. Now, Alix knew how her mother had felt when she learned her husband had a lover.

During the time she had spent with Richard, she'd allowed herself to believe that the man she had started to care for felt the same way about her. Instead, she now forced herself to face reality. What if he had lost interest in her? Her safety in this time was dependent upon him. What would happen to her if he turned her out? Tears spilled down her cheeks and she swiped them, angry with her situation.

"Why am I letting that witch get to me?" Her mutter was louder than she anticipated and she looked around hoping no one had heard her. Historically, nothing was known of Philip's mother – not her name or who she even was. Alix had always assumed she'd been a peasant or prostitute, sparked by historians' insinuations that Richard had cared nothing for the women he took to his bed.

What if history and her own preconceived notions about him were wrong? Yes, men in Richard's time had dalliances, it was accepted. It hadn't been necessary for Richard to arrange intimate dinners for the two of them or go out of his way to converse with her, almost as if he were wooing her. Being a man of his time, and used to getting what he wanted, sleeping chastely next to each other was most likely not what he had planned for their first nights alone, but he hadn't pressured her for more.

He seemed to be genuinely interested in her, if Emma and Melisende were to be believed, and they had no reason to lead her astray. Richard lived centuries ago and everything known about him came from chroniclers who had their own biases concerning rulers. She was guilty of believing their writings as gospel, but now, with the man himself within her reach, she had the incredible opportunity to learn the truth.

I won't listen to Beatrice's lies. Alix sat on the floor, repeating that mantra, until the cold emanating from the stone seeped into her bones and drove her to her feet. The water in the tub needed to be heated, but after Beatrice's revelation Alix was beyond caring. She splashed icy water on her face and took a quick, sponge bath, unable to erase the seed of doubt Beatrice had planted. What if the witch was telling the truth?

Alix forced the disturbing thought from her mind and pulled the soft shirt on. As she did, she inhaled the scent that was quintessentially Richard, and dug her nails into her hands, fighting the urge to cry. She missed him more than she thought possible. How would she cope when she returned to her time without him?

~ *Chapter 13* ~

BEAMS OF PALE MORNING sunlight poured through the windows. Alix stretched and rubbed her eyes, still exhausted from her fitful sleep. The feel of Richard's shirt against her skin brought mixed feelings of longing and doubt.

She rose and dressed, then folded the shirt and tucked it under the silk fabric in her coffer where it would never see the light of day. If one piece of clothing could bring her so much heartache, she'd never wear it again. Her fingers brushed the pouch, and she stilled.

The lure of experiencing history had eclipsed the fact that she wasn't from this century. Even if Richard did have feelings for her, she didn't belong in this time. Would today be the day she'd try to make the brooch work again? She drew a shaky breath and closed the lid, hoping to banish the brooch, and what she must do, from her mind. But not today.

Sybilla tentatively wished her a good morning.

Alix forced a bright smile before responding in like.

"I'm glad you appear more like yourself this morning." Sybilla sighed, then wrapped her woolen cloak around herself.

On the way to the chapel, they made casual conversation. Alix was careful with her words, and she suspected Sybilla was doing the same. During Matins, Rob and Sybilla exchanged covert glances and it took all of Alix's willpower not to run out of the chapel. *Oh God, please give me the strength to get through this,* she prayed.

Once the service was over, Alix hurried outside, but Maud caught up to her.

"Alix, remember when you told me about what you call Halloween, and the traditions you have back home? All Hallows Eve is only a couple of weeks away. Do you think we could celebrate?"

"I think that would be fun, actually." Alix's spirit ticked up a notch. "We can carve gourds or whatever root vegetables are available and tell scary stories at night."

"Stories about what?"

"Ghosts, witches, and things that go bump in the night."

Maud's eyes widened in fear and excitement. "It sounds wonderful! Please, let's do it, Alix. Even with some of the knights here, it's still dull."

"I agree. I'll ask if we can decorate and then go from there."

After breakfast, Alix tracked down Melisende. "Melisende, do you celebrate Samhain, the day before All Hallows Eve?"

"No. I've heard of it, but we don't celebrate it in Aquitaine. We are Christians and it's a pagan celebration, isn't it?"

Samhain was a pagan-based holiday which marked the end of harvest season and the beginning of winter, or the dark half of the year. Sensing that she was not going to be amenable to the idea, Alix searched her mind for a plausible explanation. "Originally it was. Now, where I'm from, it's more like a festival to remember loved ones who have passed on. Children dress up and we carve gourds or turnips to decorate as offerings to the deceased. And there are games, such as bobbing for apples."

Melisende furrowed her brow. "And you wish to do that here?"

"Since most of the knights are still away, there's not much entertainment in the evenings. I thought the other girls and I could carve some turnips and maybe tell a few stories. It would only be for one night." Alix hoped her explanation and innocent smile would win the housekeeper over.

Melisende considered for a moment, then nodded. "I don't see the harm in it, so I will think on it and let you know."

Maud ran up to Alix after Melisende walked away, hopping around like a jackrabbit. "What did she say?"

"She's going to think about it."

"Oh, this will be so much fun. I can't wait!"

"I'm looking forward to it, too." For the first time since Richard left, Alix felt excited about something.

The days passed by uneventfully. The knights remained at the palace and Richard stayed away. Rob and Sybilla were inseparable. And although Alix didn't begrudge them their happiness, seeing them together reminded her of what she didn't have, so she concentrated on planning for Halloween. Melisende had agreed they could celebrate "within reason" and allowed Alix to take Maud into town to buy some gourds or other vegetables they could carve.

"I haven't been to town in so long. I am looking forward to visiting the vendors' carts!" Maud smiled up at Alix, enthused.

"We can't spend any money on ourselves," Alix warned her, although she intended to look for a shop or vendor that sold laces. As they reached the main street, Alix smiled at Maud's wide-eyed expression as she took in the sights and was grateful Richard had asked Melisende to find a position for her, or she wouldn't have met Sybilla and Maud, two girls for whom she was developing a deep affection.

"Maud, we'll shop later. First, I want you to meet someone." Alix glanced ahead at a wooden sign with a painted white stag's head in the distance. When she reached to open the door, Maud hung back.

"We can't go in there, Alix. That's for men only."

"I know the couple who run it. We will be fine." She dragged Maud inside the dimly-lit tavern. As before, the men turned to stare as they entered, but when the two girls approached a long table and Alix called out the tavern owner's name, they turned their attention back to their drinks.

"Petronilla, I hope you are doing well?"

Petronilla hurried over and gave Alix a quick hug.

"I'm fine, and how are you, dear? I have often wondered how you were faring in the Duke's palace."

"Very well, thank you. He found a position for me as a household servant. I would like you to meet Maud, a good friend of mine. Maud, this is Petronilla. She saved me when I first arrived."

The older woman waved away the compliment. "I was all too pleased to help you out and you did me a great service, as well." She leaned forward to wipe spilled ale off the table and stacked used mugs on her tray, then motioned for the girls to sit. "I want to hear everything, but first, can I get you anything to eat or drink?"

"We've eaten, but wine would be perfect."

"So, you're used to drinking wine now?"

Alix nodded and turned up one corner of her mouth. "I am, but I still can't drink it with breakfast."

Petronilla returned soon with the wine and they spent some time catching up with stories of court and tavern life.

"It all sounds very exciting." Petronilla sighed. "But I heard the Duke left some time ago. When does he return?"

Alix shrugged. "Some of his knights have returned, but no one quite knows when he will make a reappearance."

When Maud excused herself to use the outdoor privy, Petronilla demanded to know what was going on between Alix and Richard.

"Picked up on that did you? I feel so foolish. We spent time together and I began to care for him, but one of the other girls told me that he's – well, he's in love with another woman. I don't want to believe it, but the longer he stays away, I worry it might be true."

"Oh, dearie, I'm so sorry, but I'm surprised there is someone else. When he came to the tavern to find you, it was clear to me that he only had eyes for you."

"What do they say? A sailor has a girl in every port? I'm beginning to fear I was just another woman."

Maud returned a moment later and they rose to continue their quest for Halloween supplies.

"I'm so glad you came by to visit. You must let me know what happens, Alix." Petronilla stood and gave her a hug.

"I will, I promise. Take care, and I'll stop by again soon."

They made their way outside, then headed up the crowded street to the produce stalls, and brightly-painted caravans. All manner of vendors lined the street, selling vegetables, fruits, dried game, and other edibles Alix had never seen before. Merchants sold wool, silk and muslin, in all colors, as well as pre-made garments for wealthier folk.

Finding no pumpkins, Alix decided they could use turnips instead, and after buying six, they continued through the market.

"Look at these!" Maud exclaimed, pausing at a vendor selling exquisite lace, ribbons for the hair, and ties for dresses. Maud picked up a delicate lace shawl, admiring the handiwork, while Alix browsed through the myriad of colored ties.

"Can I help you find something special, miss?" A painfully thin girl of no more than nine was working this particular stall.

"These ties are beautiful." Alix held up ones in gray, blue, and russet.

"How many would you like?" Hope sparkled in the girl's eyes.

Alix sighed. "All of them, but unfortunately, I can only choose a few."

"The russet and blue would go with your dresses, but you said we couldn't spend money on ourselves." At Maud's nudge, Alix shushed her, noting the merchant girl's threadbare dress, which had been let out as much as possible and mended many times.

"I can give you a good price, miss."

"They are beautiful, but I only have this amount." Alix held out the coins in the palm of her hand.

The girl's eyes widened. "It's more than enough, miss." She quickly took the money.

"You are not very good at bargaining, Alix," Maud laughed as they left with the purchase.

"I know I paid too much, but she needed the money more than I do."

On the way back, they chatted about the dresses they would buy if they had the coin, and what designs they would carve for Halloween. As they entered the palace foyer and passed by the dining hall, voices and laughter indicated supper had just begun.

"Maud, let me take the purchases upstairs and I'll be back down shortly."

Alix stowed the vegetables in a drawer in the study and returned to the dining hall.

As she slid onto the long bench, she overheard Maud talking to Sybilla and some of the younger girls about what was for sale in the market and their plans for Halloween.

Lost in her own musings, Alix was only half-listening when Maud began talking about going to the tavern. She tried to intervene but it was too late.

"You went into a tavern?" One of the girls screeched.

"Yes, but we were perfectly safe. Alix worked there before she came here." The girls looked at Maud in awe.

"Ladies aren't allowed in taverns." Gwyn looked at Alix as if she'd committed a carnal sin.

"That's more of a guideline than a hard and fast rule, but Maud is correct. I knew the owners, so we were safe."

The girls stared in amazement, and behind them, Beatrice listened in, a smug and satisfied look on her face. Alix knew it was only a matter of time before Melisende found out what they did.

Sure enough, on her way back upstairs Melisende confronted her. "Alix, meet me in the study immediately." Alix entered and Melisende shut the door behind her. "What were you thinking going to a tavern, let alone taking a child into such an establishment?"

"I was working there when the Duke found me. I am friends with the owners, and I hadn't seen them since I came here. I didn't think it would be a problem to visit."

"Even though the Duke isn't in residence, that doesn't give you the right to do as you please. Ladies do not frequent such places, and being in his employ, you are expected to hold higher standards. If you continue in this vein, I will have no choice but to inform him of your activities. In fact, I have half a mind to reconsider allowing this little gathering you are planning for All Hallows Eve."

"Oh, please don't cancel it due to my poor judgment! The girls are so looking forward to it."

Melisende crossed her arms over her chest and tapped her foot. "Very well, but don't make me regret finding a position for you. Do I make myself clear?" Melisende scolded, her eyes hard.

Alix bit her tongue to hold back her retort. Although Richard had the last say in whom he employed, the housekeeper could make Alix's life unpleasant if she continued to cause a disturbance in the order of the household.

"I apologize. I acted foolishly. I won't take Maud or any other girl into such a place again." She looked at the floor, hiding her annoyance at how little freedom women had in this time.

"See to it that you don't." Melisende stalked out, her staccato footsteps fading down the hallway.

Alix went to the window and stared out, furious that Beatrice had tattled on her. How was she going to survive living there, shackled by the constraints of Medieval society? She was an independent twenty-first century woman, not used to answering to anyone. But if she pushed Melisende too far, she might inform Richard.

In light of Beatrice's revelation, Alix worried that Richard had lost interest in her, especially after she had so willingly fallen into bed with him. From the moment she'd arrived at the palace, she'd been under Richard's protection. What if he decided she was too troublesome and she found herself out on the streets? The cold truth snaked through her. This wasn't her time or her life. If Richard turned his back on her, she had few resources to call upon.

Back in the room, Alix assured Maud and Sybilla that she'd apologized and smoothed things over with Melisende. She smiled at the relief on their faces.

"Alix, Rob received correspondence from Richard today." The excitement in Sybilla's voice brought a twinge of hope to Alix's deflated mood.

"I'm surprised he had time to write."

Sybilla tilted her head. "Aren't you the least bit curious as to what he wrote?" Alix merely shrugged. "Well, if you're not interested…" Sybilla trailed off.

"No, I am, please. What did he say?"

"He enquired after his household and said he expects to arrive in two or three weeks." Alix's heart palpitated but she wasn't sure if it was happiness, apprehension, or a mix of both. Sybilla blinked her eyes but said nothing.

Alix formulated a response. She needed to play it cool. "It will be nice to have him back. I daresay the entertainment will be much improved."

"What's happened, Alix? You've been acting strangely this last week. Have your feelings for Richard changed so quickly?"

Alix sank onto her pallet, raking her hand through her hair.

"Please tell me what's bothering you."

Needing to confide in someone, Alix sighed and repeated what Beatrice had told her. "So, you see, it could be that I was reading too much into our time together. I was just a naive substitute, just someone to help pass the time and…" Alix looked around the room, making sure no one else was in earshot, "…sate his desires."

"You can't believe what Beatrice says. She's jealous that he's paid so much attention to you, which has caused you to become rivals. I must admit, I am surprised he has a son. This is the first I've heard of it. But I'm glad he takes responsibility for the boy's upbringing. Many men wouldn't do that."

"True." Alix knew that Richard did indeed provide for Philip, which was a gallant and loving thing to do in this day. He would arrange a good marriage for him when he got older, as well.

"Don't be too hasty in your judgment. Talk to him when he returns. This might be a complete fabrication or at least a greatly exaggerated relationship."

"You're right. I don't have enough proof either way. However, I should prepare myself for the worst-case scenario."

* ~ * ~ *

Melisende hadn't mentioned anything more about cancelling their Halloween celebration, so Alix proceeded with the plans. Sharpened knives in the Middle Ages differed from ones in her time. Turnips were also a much harder vegetable to cut than pumpkins, so instead of actually carving the turnip, she planned to scrape the skin to form faces. She'd appropriated a couple of knives from breakfast, and when they finally had a few hours to themselves before supper, went in search of Maud.

"I have turnips and some knives, so let's see what we can do with them."

"Where are we going to carve them? We can't do it here or in the dining hall."

"I have an idea. Follow me."

She led Maud to the wrought iron gate that led to the garden.

"This is magical!" Maud exclaimed. "I've never been in here before."

"I haven't either. Let's explore."

They passed underneath an archway and discovered a smaller garden planted with rose bushes. This section seemed to have a woman's feel to it and Alix wondered if Queen Eleanor had been the main contributor to the design. On the far side, another archway led to a labyrinth of little gardens, bordered by tall hedges, perfect for lovers' trysts. Continuing on, the two came upon an expansive rectangular grassy area lined with poplars on either side, which drew the visitor's eye to a large fountain surrounded by marble benches. They approached the fountain, but it looked like it hadn't worked in many years. The water had evaporated long ago, and rotten leaves and a thick layer of dark humus filled the basin.

"I can't believe this. I never knew it was here." Maud looked around her.

"We can carve the turnips here then, since no one will venture this far out." Alix brushed leaves and dirt off one of the benches and carefully sat down. She opened her sack and took out a knife and turnip. After butchering one turnip, while testing various ways to cut and scrape the hard flesh, Alix determined first of all, never try carving a turnip, and second, scraping the skin off was the easiest way to create designs. Luckily, she'd bought quite a few of the confounded vegetables and they managed to carve five turnips with differing faces.

Admiring their handiwork, they headed back so their absence wouldn't be noted.

Maud went to the dining hall, while Alix headed up to the study to put the turnips in a desk drawer next to the unused fireplace. Excitement for the imminent night overshadowed the hurt from Beatrice's story, at least for now.

* ~ * ~ *

Maud skipped over to Alix in excitement after the morning All Hallows Eve chapel service. "Are we still going to tell stories tonight?"

"Melisende hasn't withdrawn her approval for the celebration," Alix said.

"I can't wait!" Maud clasped her hands in anticipation. "Everyone is so excited."

"I'm looking forward to it as well."

The morning was cloudy and drizzly, and the fire in the girls' room offered little warmth as it sputtered in the frigid wind that swept down the chimney. The girls mended torn chemises and tunics amidst muted conversations. Alix concentrated on repairing a ragged hem on her dress but kept ripping out the uneven stitches. The afternoon dragged, made longer by the lack of light shining through the windows in their room, but finally it was suppertime, and Alix stuffed the unfinished garment into her coffer. After everyone else had gone downstairs, Alix went to the study to place the turnip carvings in visually arresting places such as the mantle above the fireplace and on the table. She would light lanterns later, and of course, there would be a fire. As she was leaving, the sound of rain pattered against the window, indicating a storm was blowing in. Perfect weather for ghost stories.

Downstairs, the girls chattered about the evening but Alix shushed them. She didn't want everyone to know what was going on. Some of the knights were eating at their table, but most were absent. With Richard away, she assumed they preferred to take advantage of the entertainment offered in town.

"Oh, I almost forgot." Sybilla smiled. "Rob received word that Richard is definitely due back within the next couple of weeks. You have to talk to him, Alix, and sort out this misunderstanding."

Alix nodded and shrugged, hoping Beatrice was being spiteful and spreading lies.

After supper, Maud came over with Gwyn and Sarah in tow.

"Sybilla, would you like to come with us, or do you have plans?" Alix asked as she stood.

Sybilla glanced at Rob, but he was deep in conversation with one of the other knights. "I would love to come with you. Otherwise, I fear I'll have a very lonely evening."

They trooped upstairs to the study, the younger girls giggling and whispering behind their hands in anticipation. Alix lit the lanterns and started a fire as the girls took their places on the settee and chairs.

Everyone marveled over the turnips. "How realistic!" Gwyn exclaimed. "They are like little malevolent beings."

The flames danced as gusts of wind blew through the spaces between the windows casting eerie shadows upon the walls.

"First," Alix said, "a history lesson. Halloween is what my country celebrates on October 31, but its origins are from Samhain, a Celtic festival that marked the end of the harvest season and the beginning of the dark time, or what we know as winter. Samhain is also known as the Festival of the Dead, for it is believed that this is when the veil that separates the world of the living from the underworld is at its thinnest, allowing spirits to pass through."

A few of the girls jumped and squealed as tree branches scraped and rattled against the windows like skeletal fingers knocking to come in. Alix smiled, thrilled that Mother Nature was putting on a good show. "Doorways to the fairy realm open on this day and fairies or elven folk come to our world along with the dead, as well. It is said that the fairies steal humans back to the other side for all eternity."

"How do people stop them?" Gwyn's eyes were huge in her round face.

"In order to satisfy the spirits, people hold festivals and offer food and drink. To protect one's home from these restless souls, vegetables such as turnips are carved with grotesque faces and placed on windowsills to ward off the evil spirits." The wind whistled eerily and the girls huddled closer to Alix. "If there are any spirits trying to come in, we have protection, so we are safe for at least this Samhain night. Now, are you too frightened to continue?"

The girls all shook their heads, but Alix paused a moment, gauging if they were telling the truth. She compiled all of her knowledge, along with bits and pieces of movies and fiction that she'd seen and read. Then she wove stories about ghosts that roamed this world, forever re-enacting the last scene of their lives, or ones with unfinished business trying to contact the living.

She told of humans who seemed normal, but when the moon was full, they turned into huge werewolves that would attack and kill any livestock or person unlucky enough to cross their path. Especially gruesome were her tales of vampires who wandered the night searching for human blood, sleeping in coffins during the day, and turning into bats at will in order to escape angry townsfolk at night.

Hours had passed. Alix didn't want to anger Melisende by keeping the girls up too late, so she told one last story of Hansel and Gretel and the evil witch that would lure children to her gingerbread house, fatten them up and devour them. The girls clung to each other and trembled. Even Sybilla looked nervous.

"Are there really witches that eat children?" Sarah crossed herself, as she waited expectantly for Alix's reply.

"Only in fairy tales. Most witches are benevolent."

"So, witches really exist?"

She smiled to calm the girls' apprehension. "I've been to many places in this world and I can say I've never come across a witch, except in tales." Sarah looked relieved, as did the others. "I believe we have had enough stories tonight. Sybilla, will you help me put out the fire?"

They left the study after Alix replaced the turnips in the drawer, intending to throw them out the next day, and returned to their room. Melisende merely glanced at them when they entered and continued reading a letter.

"Thank you for inviting me, Alix," Sybilla said, putting her arm around Alix's shoulder. "I know our friendship has been strained these last several days."

"It's my fault. With Beatrice's sniping, I haven't been the best of company. I have to admit I've also been a little jealous, seeing how happy you are with Rob. I will try harder to be more optimistic." Alix smiled, wanting to be able to deliver on her promise.

They finished their nightly routine and were ready for bed when Melisende approached. "I trust your celebration was a success?"

"Yes, it was. I think the girls enjoyed it. Thank you for allowing it."

"You're welcome. You'll be pleased to hear that I received a letter from the Duke, announcing his plan to return within the fortnight."

"Yes, Sybilla told me. I'm sure he can't wait to be back."

Melisende furrowed her brow. "I thought you would be happier about this."

"It'll be nice to see him again. At the very least, the entertainment will improve."

Melisende sighed and left, shaking her head.

"What happened to 'trying harder' Alix?" Sybilla chided.

"Tomorrow. I will try tomorrow."

~ *Chapter 14* ~

THE STORM THAT HAD blown in on Halloween night continued to rage the next morning. The girls' breaths misted in the frosty air of their quarters as the gale wind found its way through chinks between the windows and the stones. The remnants of autumn vanished as the howling wind stripped the last of the leaves from the skeletal branches and tossed them about. Even though a fire roared in the fireplace, the stone walls absorbed the cold from outside and did little to insulate the interior of the castle against the frigid temperature.

Unable to attend the morning service in the icy weather, the girls huddled around the fire, attempting to stay warm. The wind gusted and spattered rain against the window. Back home, Alix would have curled up in a chair with a good book in her warm living room and listened to the howling storm. Now she understood the phrase 'as drafty as an old castle' firsthand. Even seated next to the fire, she shivered as she worked her needle and thread on the sampler Sybilla had given her. Her fingers, numbed at the tips, fumbled as she attempted to push the needle through the cloth, and the thread had come out of the needle in her clumsy hands.

Her head ached as she strained to see the markings on the sampler in the flickering light. With nothing else to do to bide her time, she went to the window to look out into the empty courtyard. The weather was too miserable for the groomsmen to exercise the horses, so even that visual entertainment was absent.

These close quarters and limited activity thoroughly tested Alix's patience. The hours passed slowly, but each night brought Richard one day closer to returning. Not knowing the depth of feeling he might have for his son's mother, her apprehension grew. She feared Richard's interest in her had been nothing more than a game to alleviate his boredom, and when he kissed her, another woman was on his mind.

No, she wouldn't go down this dark path. From Richard's reaction during their lovemaking, she couldn't believe she was a mere substitute. She would ask him when he returned and uncover the truth.

Footsteps scuffed on the stone floor and a voice broke into her tortured thoughts.

"Alix, are you feeling well?"

She looked up. "Yes, Melisende. I'm fine."

"Something seems wrong. You haven't been yourself in days. Would you like to talk about it?"

Alix bit her tongue to keep from blurting out Richard's secret. "This weather is so depressing. And with the onset of this storm, I've had the worst headache."

"I have some herbs to brew a medicinal tea that might help. I keep them in the study." She led Alix to the room, opened the drawer to the desk and pulled out a small chest.

Alix peered over her shoulder as she unlocked it and lifted the lid.

The supply was meager at best. "It looks like you need to re-stock before the winter. This is the time of year when people suffer from the fl... I mean the ague." Alix caught herself in time. Although influenza was common, that term wasn't. "There could be illnesses in the palace. I've had instruction in the use of medicinal herbs. If you would like, I can go into town and get supplies from the apothecary." Alix hoped the day trip would give her some much needed respite from the gloom. Although Melisende hadn't said any more on the subject of Alix's poor behavior, this task presented a way to stay on her good side.

"That would be very helpful, Alix. Let me know what you believe we'll need, and I'll give you some coin to cover the expenses."

Alix attempted to conjure up the course on Medieval medicine she'd taken while getting her masters. Colds and influenza were rampant this time of year. Black elderberry was used to treat the flu and bring down fevers, as well as feverfew, coriander, and boneset, although she didn't think she could find the latter. Yarrow was used to relieve headaches, but Alix doubted it would help all that much and preferred to rely on the modern miracle drug, ibuprofen. Chamomile and peppermint relieved stomach ailments, and hyssop and goldenseal could treat coughs.

When she'd finished her list, she wanted to ask Melisende if she'd missed anything. Melisende sat near the fireplace, so Alix had to pass Beatrice on the way.

"How are you faring, Alix, now that Richard is soon to return? I thought it prudent to tell you the truth before you gave your heart to him. It would be horrible to wonder why he didn't reciprocate your sentiment."

"You just want to rekindle your own affair with him. Go ahead. He's all yours. If he still wants you, that is." She hurried on, hoping her words appeased Beatrice's need to get the upper hand. Alix would like nothing more than to rid herself of the spiteful girl for good.

Melisende agreed with Alix's list of herbs and added fenugreek, which was helpful in the first stages of pneumonia.

"This should be enough." Melisende gave her a small bag of coins. "Are you sure you want to go today? The weather outside is miserable."

"It's stopped raining and I think the exercise will help cure my headache."

"Be quick about it, then. The days are getting shorter and I don't want you to get caught in the dark."

Alix was putting on her cloak at the top of the stairs when Rob stopped her.

"Where are you going in this weather?"

"If you must know, I need to go into town."

"I'll come with you, then. You oughtn't go alone." His voice echoed off the stone walls.

"I'll be fine, but thank you." She started down the stairs.

"Sybilla told me that you took Maud into town and Melisende was none too pleased." Rob's sharp tone stopped Alix in her tracks. "If you'd asked me, I would've been more than happy to accompany you. Poitiers is one of the safer towns in Aquitaine, namely because Richard resides here, but one can't be too careful. Especially a woman on her own. If anything should happen to you, Ri..."

"I'm sure Richard doesn't care what I do," Alix interrupted. "In fact, if something were to happen to me, he might even think it a blessing in disguise." She marched to the door that led to the courtyard and pushed her way through.

The sky was a steely gray and the wind bitingly cold. Her cloak offered little protection, but she refused to admit defeat, and continued through the wooden gates and down the path leading to town. After a while, she slowed her pace, and heard footsteps crunching in the icy gravel behind her.

Whirling around, she confronted her shadow. "Why are you following me, Rob? I can take care of myself!"

Rob regarded her with care. "And why would you think Richard would welcome something dangerous befalling you?"

"If it did, he wouldn't have to deal with me and he could be with..." She stopped abruptly.

"Be with whom?" Rob questioned.

She shrugged, turned her back on him and trudged ahead.

He grabbed her arm. "Stop! Explain what you are talking about."

"It's not important. Whatever happened between Richard and me is in the past. It is better if it stays there. Now, if you are going to force your company on me, I want to hear no more talk of him. If you can't abide by that, then stay here."

Rob laughed. "I can see why he's intrigued by you. You definitely present a challenge, and he needs someone who can stand up to him."

"What did I say?"

"Very well, no more talk of Richard. What are you looking for in town?"

"I have to find an apothecary and replenish the herb supply, and afterward I want to visit a friend."

"I am guessing the friend is the one who owns the tavern?"

"How do you know that?" Alix narrowed her eyes.

"You took Maud to a tavern. I assumed you must know the owner, or you wouldn't have put her in that situation."

"Situation? We were fine. I've been to many a tavern and never had any problems."

"In your country, it might be acceptable, but here, a woman is only looking for one thing if she enters that type of establishment without a chaperone."

"And what would that be?" she teased him.

Rob blushed. "Er." It was comical that a grown man would be ashamed to speak of such things to another adult. "You know, the kind of thing that a woman looks for if she's not very respectable."

"Oh, you mean only harlots frequent taverns alone, looking for paying customers?"

"Alix!"

"I'm sorry, I couldn't help it. You looked so embarrassed. Yes, I probably shouldn't have taken Maud with me, but I did, and you are more than welcome to join me if you dare." She grinned at him.

"Let us go." He gallantly offered his arm.

They ambled down the muddy street, picking their way over puddles where icy rinds had formed around the edges. The apothecary was in a dark, twisting street off the main path. Entering the low-ceilinged shop, Alix was surprised at how many fresh herbs hung on hooks suspended from the ceiling beams. She inhaled deeply but was unable to pick out any one particular scent. She was amazed at the number of jars filled with dried herbs that lined the shelves.

The owner approached from behind a high counter. "Good afternoon. May I help you find something?"

"Yes, I'm looking for these herbs, do you have them available?" Alix relayed the memorized herbs by rote. He nodded, then busied himself locating the various herbs. Alix wandered around the shop looking at jars filled with herbs and leaves of different shapes and colors, wondering what people used them for since many had unfamiliar names on the labels. On a small table near the back, she found some oils in small vials. Opening them to smell the scents, she was thrilled to find sandalwood and vanilla.

"How did you come by these particular oils?" she asked the shop owner, as he approached her.

"A merchant traveling from the Middle East. He traded them for some herbs."

Experimenting, she put a couple of drops of vanilla on the inside of each wrist followed by a drop of sandalwood and then rubbed them together. She inhaled the warm scent of vanilla tempered by the spicy sandalwood.

"If you like those oils, I will include them in your purchase."

Alix shook her head, smiled, and replaced the vials. The oils were exotic and would undoubtedly cost more than she could afford. "No, I only came to buy the herbs."

"You are the first customer to have shown any interest and I would like them gone. I need the space." He flicked his hand in the direction of his shelves filled to capacity with jars.

Alix laughed. "In that case, thank you. Were you able to find all the herbs I listed?"

"The only one I don't have is boneset? I'm unfamiliar with it."

"You might know it as herbe à fièvre."

"Ah, yes, that name I know. Unfortunately, I have none."

Alix completed her purchase and turned to Rob. "I've finished what I needed to do. You can go back if you like. I'm only going to be a little while longer."

"I'm feeling a bit parched, actually. I believe a tankard of ale is required."

"Where do you have in mind? I'm sure you know the best taverns in Poitiers."

"Lady's choice."

Alix laughed. "Fine, let's go then."

Rob pulled open the door to the tavern to allow Alix entrance first. After a cursory glance, the patrons ignored them for the most part. Of course, they would pay her no mind. She was with a man.

"Alix, my dear! What can I get for you and your fine friend?" Petronilla's eyes traveled up and down Rob's physique.

"Petronilla, this is Rob, one of Richard's squires, and we'll each have an ale please."

Petronilla placed two tankards in front of them. Alix took a tentative sip of the amber brew, amazed at how good it was. "Now this is what should be served at supper. It's much better than the wine."

Rob laughed. "Don't tell that to Richard. He's very proud of Aquitaine's wines and never touches ale unless he has to."

"What a pity. I like a man who drinks beer, or ale as you call it."

Rob lifted his mug and clinked it with hers. "Santé."

They talked with Petronilla for some time, and when some men entered that Rob knew, he went to converse with them.

"Tell me, Alix, is this a new man? What happened with Richard?"

Alix gazed back at the younger man. "Rob is just a friend. He actually is besotted with one of the girls I work with. Richard will return soon, but I don't know how I feel about that."

"I still can't believe he's interested in another woman." Petronilla frowned as she refilled Alix's tankard.

Alix shrugged. "It's possible the person who told me was being spiteful and malicious, but I need to prepare myself in case it is true." Alix stared into the golden liquid.

"You won't find your answers in that tankard, dear." Petronilla patted her hand in sympathy then turned away, overcome by a paroxysm of coughing.

"Petronilla, are you coming down with something?"

"No. Well, it's possible. Many of the patrons have been sick and I might have caught whatever they had."

"I just purchased herbs for the palace supply. Do you have a cup I can use?" Alix measured some elderberry and handed it to her. "Make a tea out of this and drink it two or three times a day. It will ease your cough."

"I can't afford to get sick, or Gerard will be completely overwhelmed."

Rob made his way back to Alix and Petronilla. "Alix, it's getting late. We need to return or Melisende will be worried."

"Of course." Alix nodded to him before turning to Petronilla. "Don't forget to drink the tea. I will come back as soon as I can to check on you." Alix gave Petronilla a hug and flung her cloak over her shoulders before she and Rob headed into the gathering dusk.

The wind had died down but the air was frosty and their labored breath made icy puffs of condensation in front of them as they trudged up the hill. When they returned, Alix made her way upstairs while Rob went off to the stables to make sure the stable boys were taking proper care of the horses.

She put her purchases, except for the oils, in the medicine chest and went to the room to tell Melisende of her success and give her back what little money remained. Pulling her cloak off, she continued to shiver, and moved to stand in front of the fire.

Sybilla came over. "I saw you return from town with Rob."

"Yes, I think he was afraid I would get into trouble if I went by myself. He insisted on acting as my chaperone."

"Did he say anything of your concerns?"

"No. I didn't think it prudent to discuss Richard's personal life with one of his men. If he knows anything about it, he didn't mention it."

They went down for supper, and as usual, Emma brought Alix her water. The girl's cheeks were flushed. "Emma, are you feeling well?"

"No. I feel hot but I keep shivering and my entire body aches." Emma massaged her neck as she spoke.

Alix exchanged looks with Sybilla, both girls arriving at the same conclusion. Alix stood and pressed the inside of her wrist to the ailing girl's forehead. "You feel like you might have a fever. I have some herbs upstairs that can help to lower it. Let me get them."

Sybilla followed her upstairs to the study. "Do you think it's catarrh or the ague? The season for it is beginning."

Alix nodded as she lifted the chest out of the drawer. "Yes, she has a fever and she feels achy. Those are classic symptoms. The sooner she starts taking the herbs, the better." Opening the chest, she took out some elderberry and some feverfew in case the fever progressed. She muttered, "I wish I had some ibuprofen."

"What is i-bu-pro-fen?"

"Nothing. I'm just trying to think of any other herbs that will help. I think these should suffice."

Alix went to the kitchen to give Emma the herbs with instructions on making the tea, told her to drink plenty of fluids and eat to maintain her strength, then demanded she go home. The cook glared at her audacity but seeing how ill Emma looked, she agreed with Alix's diagnosis and suggestion for Emma to rest. After Emma left, Alix cautioned the rest of the staff about a possible flu outbreak and instructed them on how to help avoid the contagious disease before she headed back upstairs.

"Do you think Emma will recover?" Sybilla asked.

"I don't see why not. She's young and healthy and the herbs will lower her fever." Privately, Alix didn't know what would happen, but hoped for the best. She was used to being able to go to a doctor and get real medicine for the flu. She prayed the concern on her face didn't show. Influenza outbreaks in this age could take the lives of hundreds.

~~*

The next morning her hopes fell, as several of the girls awoke complaining of chills.

"Alix." Maud's whine beckoned her to the girl's pallet. Alix pushed her damp, blonde ringlets aside, and put the back of her hand to Maud's forehead. She was hot.

"Alix, you bought enough herbs, didn't you?" Melisende came over, wringing her hands in front of her.

"I did. Can you give me a count of how many are sick, so I can start making tea?" Another consideration struck her. "Melisende, the sick girls need to be quarantined. The last thing we want is for all the rest to be exposed and we'd have an epidemic on our hands."

"I agree, but where should we put them?"

"A place that's comfortable and warm. I think the study would work."

"This is your fault! If you hadn't gone to town you wouldn't have brought the illness back with you." The blame in Beatrice's tone irked Alix to no end.

"It's not my fault, and you know it. Besides, I'm perfectly fine, so I couldn't have gotten the others sick." Alix glared at Beatrice, daring her to back down.

"Girls! We have bigger problems and I don't need you two bickering. Alix, go and make some tea. Beatrice, find out how many girls are feeling unwell."

Alix retrieved the herbs and went down to the kitchen, where she found a skeleton crew working. "Where is everyone?"

Jeanne was busy cutting vegetables but looked up at Alix's question. "Many of the servants are sick."

"How are you feeling? Any muscle aches or a fever?"

"I'm fine. Someone had to come in to prepare the meals."

"May I boil some water for tea? Some of the girls upstairs are feeling poorly."

Jeanne gave her a large, iron pot, which she hung from a hook in the immense fireplace. Soon, she had the elderberry leaves steepening, the pungent, sweet scent filling the air. She left some tea with Jeanne as a precaution and took the rest upstairs.

"Melisende, here is the tea. Should we move the girls to the study now?"

"That would be a good idea," Melisende agreed. "I've set up some pallets so they're not sleeping on the floor. Let me get the girls."

Melisende returned with the girls in tow and Alix handed out the tisanes.

"Maud, drink this, it will help with your fever."

"I feel so ill. Beatrice said it was because we went into town. Do you think that's true?"

"No. I think one of the kitchen servants likely brought it into the palace. Since it's very contagious, it spreads quickly." Maud grimaced at the bitter taste of the elderberry tea. "Keep drinking. I know it tastes awful but it will help."

"Melisende, the girls need to stay hydrated. I'm going back to the kitchen to get water for them to drink. Can you watch them?"

"Certainly. If you need anything from downstairs, let me know. I'll get one of the servants to help out."

Waiting for the boiled water to cool, Alix went outside. The palace felt oppressive and suffocating. The cool air provided a welcome break. She wrapped her arms around herself as she shivered. Taking a deep breath of fresh air, she wandered into the courtyard.

One of the knights approached her. "Miss?"

"Yes?"

"We've heard that there is sickness here. Is it true?" the man inquired, worry laced in his voice.

Not wanting to terrify him, she candy-coated the truth. "Some of the girls are sick, but they are being treated and should recover quite soon."

"I heard it was smallpox. Isn't that a death knell?"

"No, it is most definitely not smallpox. I believe it's catarrh and most people recover from that." The man looked very much relieved, nodded to her and hurried off, she surmised, to inform his compatriots.

Melisende was still in the room making sure the girls were comfortable and warm when Alix returned with flagons of water.

"Melisende, I can manage this and if I need anything, I'll let you know."

"Be careful. You could get sick too, Alix." She looked around the room. "I feel guilty about leaving the girls."

"I will handle everything here. You need to keep the household running smoothly." Alix hoped that the flu shots she'd had in the past had built up enough antibodies in her system to protect her against this. They could all perish, if not properly taken care of.

Melisende looked at her doubtfully but left, only after Alix promised she would alert her if the girls' symptoms worsened. Handing out cups of water, she noticed that Maud was the only one whose fever seemed higher.

Hours later, Alix felt out of her element as Maud's fever spiked and the other girls complained of body aches. She went downstairs to find Melisende and to ask for guidance. The older woman was sitting next to Beatrice, but when Alix entered, she stood the girl up and walked her over. "Beatrice feels ill as well. Can you please take her upstairs?"

"Yes, and the girls should eat something to keep up their strength. Could you bring some toasted bread and butter when you get a chance? Come, Beatrice, I will find room for you."

"You are relishing this aren't you?" Beatrice's lips twisted in disgust as she followed her upstairs.

"What are you talking about? I wouldn't wish this illness on my worst enemy." Alix glared at Beatrice, who looked abashed but recovered quickly.

"I heard from one of the knights last night that Clairvaux is quite dull and the men are eager to return home. I wonder why Richard is staying away so long. Something… or someone must have captured his interest. I think a letter should be sent to Richard. He will be furious if he's not told about what is happening here." Beatrice regarded her. "This is his household, or have you forgotten that? You seem to relish playing the lady of the house."

Alix gaped at her. "Certainly, I haven't forgotten. Melisende is the one who oversees everything, not me. The decision to tell Richard is hers alone. I only have knowledge of herbs, so this is one of the few ways I can be useful."

"All I know is that things have changed since you arrived, and not in a positive way."

Alix left Beatrice in the study and went to get her bedding, fuming over the conversation. Sybilla had told her Rob was grateful to be home since Clairvaux was so uncomfortable. Why was Richard staying away? What if there was more truth to Beatrice's revelation than she wanted to admit. Surely, he had deeper feelings for the mother of his child than some woman he found in a forest and hardly knew?

Alix found fresh linens and headed down the hall, cursing Beatrice for instilling more doubt. Returning to the study, Alix checked again on the girls, then went to sit by the window and stared into the gray sky. Maybe she should encourage Melisende to write to Richard, but what good would that do? If he returned early, there was the real possibility he or his men would fall ill, as well. Tending to an ill Richard was an unpleasant idea. It was better he did not know, and when he arrived, God willing, everyone would have recovered by then.

The next day passed the same as the first. Maud and now Beatrice were still feverish, but the other two girls' symptoms were improving. Melisende relieved Alix so she could rest and eat since she had been too busy to go to breakfast and hadn't slept much the night before.

"Alix, you ought to let the doctors tend the girls," Sybilla reproached gently as they ate supper. "You're exhausted and if you don't take care of yourself, you're going to collapse."

"I'm fine, really. If the girls worsen, I'll let Melisende send for them."

Sybilla gave her a doubtful look, and Alix concentrated on tearing apart a piece of chicken on her plate to hide the worry in her eyes.

Later that night, one of the girl's coughing fits woke Alix out of a restless sleep on the settee. Lighting the lantern, she looked around the room for the source. Beatrice coughed again and Alix went over to her. "How are you feeling?"

"My chest hurts when I breathe or cough," Beatrice whimpered, as she tried to draw shallow breaths to mitigate the pain. Alix felt her forehead. She was burning up.

"Drink the rest of the tea." Alix helped her sit and sip the tisane, trying to think of what to do. She could put her in a bath to bring the fever down, but decided to try some cool compresses first.

She hurried to the servants' chamber and found Melisende sitting by the fire.

"Beatrice has gotten worse." Alix raked her hand through her hair. "Her fever is higher, and now she's coughing. I need real medicine, not useless herbs."

"Alix, are you coming down with it, too? You are not making sense, dear." Alix saw fear in the older woman's brown eyes.

"I've tried all the remedies I know. Do you have any suggestions of different herbs that might work?"

Melisende furrowed her brow, and then shook her head. "You've tried elderberry, but we can brew a tisane of coriander. On second thought, feverfew might be best."

Alix nodded, downcast. "I'm going to wet some cloths. As they cool, they might bring her fever down."

She went to her coffer and pulled out the lightweight fabric that hadn't been used to make dresses. She grabbed the linen, tore it into long strips and went into the changing area to soak it in water. Returning to the study, she pulled down Beatrice's sheet, found she was drenched in sweat and still burning hot to the touch. Alix removed her tunic followed by her chemise, but Beatrice didn't notice and only shifted uneasily. Covering her with the cool cloths, she prayed as she had never prayed before for God to help her.

Beatrice winced and hunched her shoulders to try to alleviate her chest pain as a paroxysm of coughing wracked her body. She slumped against her pillow, struggling to draw breath. Alix brushed back Beatrice's blonde, sweat-soaked hair and wiped her brow with a cool cloth, then went to the fireplace to check the small metal pot of water that was simmering. She carefully lifted it with a cloth wrapped around the handle and carried it back, then poured some of the steaming water in a cup to steep the feverfew leaves.

Alix helped Beatrice sit up against the pillow and draped a clean cloth tent-like over her head. "Breathe deeply." She held the pot under the cloth close enough for the steam to rise, but far enough away to not burn her. Beatrice's shallow breaths became deeper as the steam opened her bronchial tubes and her breathing eased. Her face was still flushed and she shivered with chills. Alix managed to get her to take some tea and piled warm blankets on her to try to stop her teeth-chattering. Finally, Beatrice settled and fell into a fitful sleep. Alix wiped her brow and face again with a cool cloth then pulled a chair next to her pallet to monitor her through the night.

Birds chirped outside the window and woke Alix. She pushed her tousled, copper hair out of her eyes and blinked in the bright sun that lit the room, as she slowly became cognizant of her surroundings. Beatrice slept soundly. Pressing the inside of her wrist to the girl's forehead, Alix breathed out a sigh of relief, feeling cooler skin under her touch.

As Alix changed the drenched sheets, Beatrice stirred, then whispered, her voice raspy. "You stayed here all night?"

"Yes. I wanted to make sure you were comfortable."

Beatrice looked at her in surprise, then gratification. "Thank you. I'm sure you didn't want to…"

"Whatever– differences we have, I've never wished you any ill will." Alix went to check on Maud and was disappointed to see there was no change in the small girl's condition. Her cheeks were still aflame and her fever remained.

"Alix, will Beatrice recover? Her cough sounds terrible and she's been rambling in her sleep."

"She's better today. I'm sure she will recover, Maud." She tried to allay Maud's fears, and if she were honest, her own as well.

"It is not just catarrh, is it?"

"No, I think it has gone into pneumonia. But one can recover from it," Alix added quickly, as Maud's eyes widened.

"Sit with me, Alix, please. I'm scared." Maud clutched Alix's hand tightly.

"For certes, I will." Alix patted the girl's hand reassuringly and stayed with her until she fell asleep.

"How is Maud doing?" Melisende's quiet approach from behind startled Alix.

"Oh, Melisende! I'm so glad you're here." Alix drew her to the window, away from others. "There's no change. I fear Beatrice has pneumonia and I don't have the skills to cure her."

"I believe I should send word to the Duke and let him know what is happening."

Alix shook her head. "He can't help. If he and his men return now, they could fall ill, too. These girls are still contagious. Let's try to manage this ourselves. If the girls worsen, we can send someone for the doctor."

"You might be right. Go take some time for yourself and rest, dear while I watch the girls."

Alix nodded, left the stuffy room, and breathed deeply of the fresher air in the hallway. The servants' quarters were empty and she sighed in relief, glad she didn't have to answer questions about the girls' health. She went to her pallet, pulled her cloak from her coffer and went down the back stairs. Once outside, she meandered along the path to the courtyard and up to the copse of trees. The air was bitterly cold but the sun shone down in warm rays.

She lifted her face to the warmth, and the tension of the last few days slowly slipped away. The sun felt like an old friend in this cold world. She closed her eyes and swayed to the sound of the breeze whistling quietly amongst the bare branches of the naked trees that surrounded her. Calmed by the Zen of nature, she found the strength to return. She'd stayed away longer than intended and quickened her pace.

Opening the door to the sickroom, she came to a standstill. A middle aged doctor was within, bent over a table arranging a metal bowl and small items that looked like scalpels.

"What the hell do you think you are doing?" she yelled at him. He looked up shocked. "Get out of here, you bastard! Leave now!"

The doctor frowned at her with his bushy black eyebrows, his lips curling back in disgust. "Being a servant," he sneered, "you know nothing of medicine. This young woman is very ill. Go away and let me do my job!" He turned back to the table and continued to prep the instruments.

Alix stomped over, shouting words that would make a hardened sailor take notice, grabbed the man's arm, and forced him out of the room before she slammed the door behind him.

Checking on Beatrice, Alix sighed, relieved he hadn't started yet. The last thing the girl needed was a doctor bleeding her. Not for the first time, Alix was amazed that with the archaic ideas people had in the Middle Ages, it was a wonder the Europeans even survived.

Melisende rushed in, glowering at Alix. "What have you done? I called for the doctor since there was little improvement. How dare you send him away!"

"Melisende, he was going to bleed her. Although I know it's a common practice, the last thing a sick person needs is to be further weakened. Besides, her fever is down and I think she is on the mend. Bleeding her could cause a major setback. I believe this practice can do more harm than good."

"I disagree with your opinion, Alix. You have until tomorrow. If she doesn't improve you will be relieved of your duties and the doctor will take care of her!" Melisende stated and left.

Shaking her head in exasperation, Alix went to check on Maud. "Are you feeling any better?"

"Some, but I still feel warm."

Alix pressed the inside of her wrist to her forehead. "You're still feverish, but you are cooler than you were, so the herbs are helping. I need to go to the kitchen to make more tea, but I will be back soon."

When Alix reached the kitchen, a sense of sadness filled the room. Some of the servants were weeping.

"What has happened?" Dread crept over her.

"A couple of the servants have died from the illness." Marie, the portly cook, gave a solemn answer.

Coldness gathered in her. "Who... who were they?" she whispered, thinking about Emma.

"Jeanne fell ill a couple of days ago, and we got word this evening that she had passed, and another died yesterday morning." Tears flowed down Marie's chubby cheeks.

"Was it... Emma who passed?" At the cook's negative headshake, Alix exhaled in relief. "I am so very sorry," Alix stammered, feeling the sentiment inadequate for the situation.

The cook nodded as she wiped her eyes then returned to her tasks. Alix finished making the tea and fled back upstairs. In the hallway, she was unable to control her emotions. Her breathing faltered. Choking back sobs, she ran to the only place she felt safe, Richard's chambers. She never made it inside. Her knees hit the cold stone floor in front of the door. Tears pricked behind her eyes, then streamed down her cheeks as if a dam had opened. She had seen Jeanne only a few days ago. How could she have died from the flu so suddenly?

Just as Alix let out a stifled sob, Melisende reached the top of the stairs, and rushed over. "Alix? What has happened?"

"I can't do this anymore. I can't be here; I want to go home." Alix wiped her nose on her sleeve as she sobbed.

Melisende knelt and patted her shoulder. "I know you're having a hard time, but I'm truly glad you are here. Your duties were never meant to include taking care of the girls, but bless you for doing it." Melisende squeezed Alix's hand and smiled. "I'm sure the girls, especially Maud, feel more comfortable with you than the doctor."

"I feel useless though. I don't know how to help anymore. Two of the kitchen servants have died from this illness. I am honestly afraid."

"Take your time. I will check on the girls."

Alix remained on the floor until her tears ended, then wiped her eyes, and went back to the study once she had composed herself.

"There is no further change in Beatrice, but Maud's fever has broken. The other two girls seem much better." Melisende's brightened tone encouraged her.

"That's wonderful news." Hurrying over to Maud to see for herself, Alix placed the back of her hand on the girl's forehead. Her fever had indeed broken.

"Do you think you can manage to eat something, Maud? You've eaten hardly anything in four days."

"I do have a bit of an appetite; toast perhaps?"

"Of course, let me get some."

"I'll bring up some food," Melisende offered and strode out of the room.

"Beatrice isn't doing any better, is she?" Maud asked.

Alix shook her head. "There has been no change. Her fever and chills come and go and she's still coughing. But I am hopeful. There's no reason why she couldn't make a complete recovery. Now rest until Melisende comes back. I don't want you to relapse."

Alix went over to Beatrice and hope faded as she touched her flushed skin. She lifted Beatrice's head to help her drink some tea, but as soon as she moved, a paroxysm of coughing creased her chest. Settling back against the pillow, Beatrice struggled to draw breath. Alix's glance lingered on the other girls in the room, aware of how contagious certain types of bacterial pneumonia were.

Melisende returned with the toast and Alix steered her toward the window where they could talk in private.

"The other girls are beginning to recover and Maud is on the mend as well, but I fear for them if they stay near Beatrice, for she has not. I'm worried that she's developed a type of illness beyond the ague, so perhaps it would be best for them to go back with the others now?"

"Certainly, I'll take care of it."

Alix stayed with Beatrice all night, nervously listening to her fast, shallow breathing. The rattling in her chest was constant, but Alix was terrified when it ceased, and silence filled the room. Leaning over, she was relieved at the rise and fall of Beatrice's chest as she finally seemed to be breathing clearly. The next morning her fever seemed lower, but she was still short of breath and her skin was hot and dry. Alix was about to go downstairs to make some more tea, when the sound of harsh coughing sent her hurrying to Beatrice's side. Wiping Beatrice's mouth with a towel, she gasped at the smear of blood. "Oh, my God!" she panicked. "What do I do now?"

~ *Chapter 15* ~

THE COLD WIND GUSTED over the flat plain and whistled through the bare trees of the forest that skirted Poitiers, shaking the naked branches. The sun was on its downward arc, painting the sky in streaks of red and orange. Richard had sent one of his knights ahead to alert the gatekeeper of their imminent arrival and was riding next to André.

"Your mood is improving the closer we get to Poitiers, and the palace, my dear cousin." André shivered in his cloak and pulled it closer. "Any particular reason why?"

Richard laughed. "It will be nice to return to some luxuries. Clairvaux is a bit lacking at the moment for my taste."

"And there is no other reason?"

Richard raised his brow at him. "What are you implying?"

"It's no secret that before we left, your nights were spent entertaining a particular young woman. I imagine you wish to continue your pursuit?"

Richard smiled as he averted his eyes from his cousin's knowing look. Usually, after successfully wooing a woman into his bed, ennui set in and he began to look elsewhere.

To his great surprise, after leaving Poitiers, he hadn't been able to put Alix out of his mind. Nor did he want to. He missed their conversations and bantering– and their last night together, and the morning that followed had never left his mind. His body tightened with renewed tension, anticipating feeling her warm, curvaceous body in his arms and his bed. The pleasure she had found with him filled him with pride– her body's response to his caresses were unlike anything he had witnessed. "Alix fascinates me. She's captured my interest like no other woman ever has."

André glanced at him, and his eyebrows arched. "Well, cousin, what a welcome surprise." The men chuckled, then turned as they heard hoof beats sound in the distance. "I wonder why the rider is in such a hurry?"

The knight that Richard sent ahead to alert the gatemen they were arriving, came to a stop in front of them. "Your Grace! There is smoke in Poitiers! I returned immediately, so I don't know if there has been an attack."

"God's blood!" Richard swore. He and his knights raced to the gate to see what had happened. They entered and looked around, expecting to see devastation. Instead, piles of bedding lay burning in front of several homes.

"What has happened here?" Richard demanded of the gatekeeper.

"Your Grace, there has been illness throughout the town."

"Which disease?"

"Catarrh. There have been quite a few deaths."

"Has it reached the palace?"

"I don't know, Your Grace, but I expect so."

The blood drained from Richard's face. He turned and spurred his horse, leaving his men behind.

* ~ * ~ *

Alix paced, her footsteps shuffling on the floor as she debated whether to ask the doctor to return. Voices, metallic ringing, and chaotic hoof beats echoed up to her from outside the window. The study overlooked a portion of the courtyard and she rushed to the window. Men scrambled, leading horses to the stables while the knights oversaw squires as they unloaded trunks from the carts.

"It looks like Richard has arrived." Alix turned to tell the others and was surprised to see alarm on Beatrice's face. "What is it, Beatrice?"

"Please come here." Alix rushed to Beatrice and placed the back of her hand on the girl's forehead. "I'm not improving, am I?" Beatrice whispered in a raspy voice.

"Nonsense, of course you are. You were affected by the illness more than the others. It's just taking longer for you to recover. Can I get you some tea or toast?"

She shook her head weakly. "Alix, I haven't been entirely truthful with you about Richard. Can you ever forgive me?"

Alix looked at her in shock. "Why would I forgive you?"

Beatrice looked hurt. "I guess I shouldn't expect you to." She began to cough again, and Alix reached over and put a cup of tea to her lips.

"Drink this, it will help calm your cough. You told me what I needed to know about Richard, so no, you have done nothing that needs to be forgiven."

Beatrice looked like she wanted to say more, but her coughing spasm grew violent and she fought to get what little air she could get into her lungs. Alix wiped her brow and did her best to make her comfortable. "Beatrice," Alix whispered, but she had fallen into a fitful sleep. Beatrice's complexion was ashen, her shallow breaths rattling in her chest again.

~~*

Richard stormed into the hallway and started up the stairs but stopped as Melisende rushed down to meet him.

"Your Grace! Thank God you have arrived."

"What is going on and why wasn't I informed about this?" Richard demanded.

"We've had some sickness, and a few of the girls have been quite ill, but they are recovering. There have been two deaths, but no new cases in days, so I think the worst has passed."

His heart dropped and cold sweat broke out on his brow. "Deaths?" he asked tightly.

"A couple of the kitchen servants succumbed to the illness, but no one in the palace."

Melisende motioned toward the dining hall. "Please, eat and rest. I need to take some food upstairs, but then I will tell you everything."

He hastened into the dining hall. "Rob, what in God's name is going on? I can't get Melisende to tell me anything useful!"

"Obviously, you know that there has been illness here, but I think all but one has recovered. Alix is upstairs, but from what Sybilla has told me, it doesn't sound promising."

Richard's chest tightened and he paled. "Alix is ill? Has a doctor been sent for?"

"Oh, no, Alix is not the one ill. She's been taking care of the other girls."

"Why is everyone trying to put me in an early grave? Where is the doctor? We have some of the best available."

Rob grinned at him. "Alix banned him from the sickroom."

"What are you talking about?"

"Apparently, he was trying to bleed her patient and she took issue and threw him out. The words she used, well, let's just say most men wouldn't dare utter." Rob laughed.

"What did she say?" Richard demanded. Rob leaned in close to repeat them and both men laughed aloud after Rob told him. "I can't even imagine my father saying that."

"I'm impressed," André admitted. "I wouldn't have thought it. A woman who can out-curse you, Richard! If you can't handle her, I will gladly take her off your hands."

"You might be my cousin but take what belongs to me and I will easily forget we are related." André raised his hands in mock apology. Richard poured himself some wine, and took a long drink, wondering how long it would be until he could see Alix.

*　~　*　~　*

Dark, purple circles marred the delicate skin underneath Beatrice's eyes. Her ashen skin and bluish lips made her look as if she had already succumbed to Charon. Her fever had spiked again and her body shook with chills. Alix knew she ought to call a priest to read her the last rites, but that felt like pronouncing a death knell upon her. She helped her to drink some tea, and smoothed her pale brow with a cool cloth, not knowing what else to do for her.

"Beatrice, I'm going to call for the doctor."

Beatrice reached out her hand to stop her. "No don't leave me, I have need of confession."

"You need a priest for that. Let me find one." Alix tried to keep fear from her voice.

Beatrice grabbed her hand again. "Stay. Please. I hated you when you first came here because Richard had brought you," Beatrice whispered with as much force as she could, yet Alix still had to lean close to hear. "He was different around you. I wanted to hurt you." She coughed violently, and Alix held a handkerchief to her lips, then helped her lay back against the pillow. Alix folded the white cloth hastily, hiding the bright smear of blood.

"Alix, he does care about you, more than he ever did for me."

Alix looked at her in shock. "Why are you telling me this now?"

"You stayed with me. You didn't have to, especially after the way I treated you. You've been very kind to me, and I don't deserve it. Don't leave me Alix, I'm so scared..." Beatrice whispered, her voice failing.

She looked into Beatrice's watery eyes and knew what she had to do. "Let me summon a priest for you." If Beatrice heard her, she didn't acknowledge it. Alix sat cross-legged on the floor until Beatrice fell asleep. Laying Beatrice's hand down gently, she stood stiffly, her knees aching from her cramped position, smoothed her wrinkled dress, then set on her trek to find a priest. She watched her feet as she plodded along and listened to the soft click of her shoes against the stone hallway echo throughout the cavernous space.

When she looked up, she spied Gwyn coming up the stairs. She approached at Alix's beckoning. "Please go now and find a priest. Hurry, there may not be much time." Gwyn's eyes widened in alarm. Nodding emphatically to convey her understanding, Gwyn's hurried footsteps faded as she retraced her steps and ran down the stairs.

Alix returned to Beatrice's side and took her hand, trying to think of some type of prayer that would offer comfort. The only one she knew was the Lord's Prayer and she recited it, as tears ran down her face. When she had finished, she kept a hold of Beatrice's hand hoping the contact of another human might keep death locked in Hades.

As time crept by, Alix wondered where the damn priest was. For what seemed like an eternity, she watched the faint rise and fall of Beatrice's chest with each shallow breath until her body lay peaceful and still upon her pallet. Alix covered Beatrice with the sheet and stood numbly by her side. Unbidden tears flowed down her cheeks, streaking clean tracks down her weary face. She wiped at them with fingers that had toiled tirelessly to save the life of this woman who lay before her. Melisende. She needed to find Melisende. Her steps were heavy as she moved to the door and reached to open it with a shaking hand but stopped when she heard voices on the other side.

"Lady Melisende!" Richard called. "We need to talk. You will tell me what has been going on and why I wasn't informed."

"Certainly, Your Grace, and I have some things I need to tell you as well, but first I need to check on Beatrice."

"It's Beatrice who is ill?"

"You didn't know?"

Just as Alix put her hand on the doorknob, it turned and the door swung open. She was face to face with Richard.

"Alix, you look positively sick."

Richard's observation only furthered Alix's moment of sorrow, for she knew it was true. "Melisende." Her voice was low and humble as she averted her eyes from his. "I'm sorry. I tried everything but there was nothing more I could do."

Melisende gasped. "Oh, my poor girl."

"Someone needs to tend to her body. I just can't." Alix's voice broke.

"We will, don't worry, dear."

Alix passed by and as Richard moved to intercept her, she threw up her arm to ward him off, not seeing the distress on his face. Melisende's faint words carried down the hall as she walked away. "Will you let her go, Your Grace?" Melisende suggested gently. "She's been caring for the girls since they became ill and she needs some time to herself."

Outside, Alix turned toward the gardens. She would have to explain her actions but right now, all she wanted was the solitude and blamelessness of nature.

She walked past the fountain and continued deeper into an area she had never visited before. Finding a bench, she lay down and stared up at the sky, wondering for the first time since she was a child whether or not there was anything after death. She had never experienced death first hand and was devastated that she couldn't do anything to save Beatrice. The last thing she wanted to do right now was deal with the ramifications that would occur once she faced Richard and Melisende, so she lay on the bench while the sun sank lower on the horizon and the temperature dropped.

* ~ * ~ *

The priest had finally arrived, and although too late to hear confession, he said prayers over Beatrice. A tearful Melisende went to the chapel to pray and Richard returned to his chambers. This was not the homecoming he'd envisioned. He ordered his pages to unpack his trunks, and as they did so, he stalked the length and breadth of his chambers as he tried to curb his exasperation. Alix had put her own health at risk by taking care of the girls herself, and he was furious. As selfless an act as it was, what if she had become ill herself and succumbed? Shocked by his own epiphany, he sank into a chair and tried to reconcile his feelings. What was happening to him?

As dusk fell, he headed downstairs to find her. The mood was somber in the dining hall. Most of the ladies were crying at the loss of their friend.

"Sybilla, have you seen Alix?" Richard's deep voice rang through the hall, breaking through the soft, feminine weeping like a knife.

"Your Grace." Sybilla greeted him and curtsied at his approach. "No, I haven't. Let me look upstairs." She stood and padded out of the room.

Richard paced, bereft in his anxiety over Alix's state. Was she sick herself by now? Was she distraught in her own sorrow? Soon, Sybilla returned. "I checked the servants' room, but it was empty.

"Where would she go?"

"You might try the gardens."

Standing at the mouth of the garden's entry, he was at a loss as to where to begin his search in the vast maze of foliage ahead. Knowing Alix, she had probably traipsed aimlessly amongst the shrubbery, so after ordering his squires to fan out and help search, he followed suit, cursing this waste of good hunting land. Darkness was soon upon him, and he used the moon's dim light as a guide as he trudged into areas he was unaware even existed.

*　~　*　~　*

Alix took a deep breath, preparing herself to return to the castle and face the wretched scene she had fled from when an angry oath rang out in Richard's unmistakably deep voice. She prayed he wouldn't see her, but as luck would have it, he marched into the little garden where the shadows weren't dark enough to hide her.

"Richard, what are you doing out here?"

"God's legs, Alix! I have been looking for you all over this accursed place!" She bent her head and bit her bottom lip to stop from laughing at his rudimentary use of the Lord's name. Richard took a deep breath. "My sincere apologies. I didn't mean to shout. I know this has been a difficult time for you."

The stress of the last week, doubting that Richard cared for her, the girls' illnesses and Beatrice's death had stretched her to the limit. Even though Alix had detested her, Beatrice had apologized for her behavior in the end, and her death was hard to accept. Alix tried to contain her laughter, but soon it bubbled up from within, and she dissolved into tears. Richard stared at her and shifted his weight as tears streamed unchecked down her face.

Richard sat next to her and put his hand over hers. He had always had a soothing effect on her, and the ache in her heart calmed. She raised her chin to face him. "I'm sorry. I'm fine now." She sniffled and wiped her eyes. He looked slightly ill at ease, and she tried to assuage the situation. "Your little oath, it was kind of funny. Do people take you seriously when you say it?" He grabbed her arm and dragged her up. She realized immediately that she had made a grievous mistake by mocking him.

"I don't know why I wasted my time coming here." His icy tone chilled her spirit and she shivered.

"Tell me, why are you here, then? Surely, you didn't tire of the female company you kept on your journey?"

He looked at her with disdain. "What in God's name are you referring to?"

Wisely, she held her tongue not wanting to anger him further. "Never mind. I appreciate your coming out here, but I can find my way back." She tried to pull her arm away but he held it in a vice-like grip.

"You are not going anywhere until you explain what you meant." The wind picked up and she shivered in the cold, night air. He touched her cheek and relented. "You're freezing. Come, let's get you back."

She didn't argue and followed him as he led the way. When she had fled the study after Beatrice's death, she didn't think about her destination, or what she would need when she arrived there, just that she needed to escape. Not grabbing her cloak on the way out was becoming a bad habit.

As the wind rose, she grew colder by the minute until she couldn't stop shivering. Bone-tired and hungry from her long hours at Beatrice's bedside, she could only concentrate on moving one foot in front of the other and had no energy left to rub her own arms for warmth.

Her teeth chattered so loud that she was sure even the dead could hear them. Richard picked her up and tucked her head under his chin. "You're going to freeze to death, woman!" He nestled her close to his body.

She put her arms around his neck and let out a shaky sigh, clenching her teeth together tight, working her jaw muscles to keep teeth firmly pressed together. The last thing she needed was to chip a tooth. "You're so warm," she whispered into his neck.

* ～ * ～ *

Desire shot through him as her breath warmed his skin. He tightened his arms about her and she cuddled closer. "Wench, move again and I will either drop you, or take you on the ground," he warned, and ruefully shook his head. God, he had missed her more than he expected. Reaching the palace, he carried her upstairs to his chambers. Some of his men were sitting at the table conversing and drinking. "Send in my pages to draw a hot bath." The men stared at him as he held a shivering Alix in his arms. "Now! And make haste!"

They scurried from the room, shouting orders down the hall. He set her down and she wobbled toward the fireplace. She held her hands out over the warmth and rubbed them together. Minutes later, a knock on the door startled her.

"Enter!"

Three pages carrying buckets of steaming water clambered to the bedchamber. They prepared the tub, stoked the fire to a roar and proceeded to leave. "I want that tub full to the top," Richard ordered. "Another run of hot water." They nodded and left, the door clicking shut behind them.

"Would you like food, wine?"

She shook her head. "I'm so exhausted, I don't think I have the energy to eat." She swayed and rubbed her eyes. Richard picked her up, brought her to the bedchamber and lay her on the bed. Her heavy eyelids fluttered closed.

"Stay awake, Alix. You need to warm and nourish your body, lest you fall ill."

The pages returned carrying only two more buckets between the three of them. "What's the meaning of this?"

The oldest page winced at Richard's ire. "That's all of the ready hot water in the castle, Your Grace."

Richard grunted. "Very well. Pour it in the tub and leave us."

They did as commanded and as the door clicked shut behind them, Richard turned Alix to her side and pulled her laces loose, tugging her soiled dress to the floor. "Alix, you're as cold as ice!" Her teeth chattered as her body shivered uncontrollably.

For the first time, Richard saw her naked body as something to be adored instead of conquered and wanted nothing more than to get her warm and comfortable. He walked to the tub and tested the water, then picked her up. "Into the bath you go." Her body seemed so small in his arms. He carefully placed her in the water and her eyes flew open.

"That's hot!"

He chuckled. "Not to worry, I tested it. You're just so cold, it feels hot. I assure you it will warm you through and through without burning."

She put her feet down and tried to stand up.

"Down with you, love." He wrapped his arms around her shoulders and pushed her into the tub.

The water encompassed her shoulders. She tipped her head back and closed her eyes.

Richard stroked her arm and felt her shaking body relax. According to Melisende, Alix had watched over the sick girls for over a week without a break. Richard gazed on this woman and a swelling in his chest grew tight. He would never let anything happen to her again.

Soap in hand, he began rubbing her body with his lathered palms.

She sighed. "That feels nice, Richard."

He knew she wouldn't be able to stay awake much longer, so he didn't hesitate and made sure he cleansed every bit of her, including her hair. The water cooling and her body scrubbed clean, he pulled her from the water, wrapped her in a rough towel and lay her on the bed. "Alix, I left my shirt for you. Where is it?"

She opened her luminous, hazel eyes and smiled at him. "In my coffer. I slept in it while you were gone."

Pleased, he rummaged through one of the trunks his squires delivered to his quarters earlier and found a clean shirt to put on her. He smiled at her as she sat on the edge of his bed, hair still damp from the bath and clad only in his shirt. "I've never seen you look more beautiful, Alix. Now, under the pelts."

For once, she did as she was told.

Richard went to the main chamber and grabbed some bread and wine. Alix was dozing when he returned, but he knew she needed nourishment. He sat on the edge of the bed, slid his arm under her shoulders and sat her up. "Drink." Woozy, but awake, she sipped from the goblet he put to her mouth.

"Will you feed me, too, Your Grace?"

Richard smiled at Alix's sleepy voice. "It would be my pleasure." He ripped off a small chunk of the dark, crusty bread and placed it in her mouth.

She chewed, her eyes closing. "Another drink and then you can sleep here tonight. Tomorrow we will talk."

"Whatever you say." She took one last sip from the cup he offered and slid down under the furs; her wet, bronze hair splayed out on the pillow like an angel's.

He returned to the main room, closing the bedchamber door behind him, poured some wine and slumped onto the window seat, not wishing to disturb her. He sighed and sipped his wine.

With Alix tucked in his bed, his thoughts turned to his brother. Hal's treachery in attempting to lure his barons weighed on his mind. Surely,

Geoffrey would support whoever had a better chance of winning. Now, Richard had domestic concerns as well. He had to contend with Melisende's displeasure, which most likely concerned Alix. He was beginning to understand why his father's decisions were as changeable as the wind. He had to put out fires quickly before they spread. Bone-weary, with a headache coming on, he rubbed his temples, leaned back against the wall, and soon fell asleep. The fire sputtered out sometime in the early morning hours, and the cold seeping in from the window woke Richard. He stood shivering, still half-asleep, and went to rebuild the fire. He laid down on the too-small settee and bent his long legs, hoping morning would come soon.

Richard stirred again as the sun peeked over the horizon, coloring the sky in orange and pink. He stretched, grimacing from his cramped position and swore he would not spend another night there again. Alix remained fast asleep. He repositioned the furs over her shoulders and stroked her hair. "Sleep, my love. I have to find Melisende to discover what mischief you've caused in my absence."

"Lady Melisende, I would like to speak with you."

"Yes, of course." She followed him into the study and closed the door.

"What has been going on here? Why wasn't I informed about the epidemic?"

Melisende shifted uneasily. "We decided that it was better for us to handle the illness on our own rather than exposing you and your men, Your Grace."

"Who is 'we'?"

"Myself and Alix."

"Hence, Alix was involved?"

"Yes, but when we learned that you were returning within the week, she suggested that we take care of the sick oursel..." She paused and looked at Richard with fearful eyes.

"Alix chose not to tell me right away, and you followed her suggestion?" His voice shook with rage and high color flared in his cheeks. "Why is Alix making decisions that concern me and my domain?"

"She thought it prudent to wait until your return. She worried that you or your knights could become ill as well if you were exposed. We were dealing with the ague and pneumonia, Your Grace, two very contagious illnesses. She seems to have a certain knowledge about these things. I trust her judgment." To Richard's surprise, Melisende was steadfast in her confidence of Alix's abilities.

"I understand her logic, but I should have been told. From now on, you will apprise me of everything significant that is going on here, regardless of what you think I need to know."

"Yes, I'm sorry, but please don't blame Alix. She was only acting in your best interest."

"Only I will decide what is in my best interest, Melisende, and I will speak to Alix about that later. Last night, you mentioned other things I ought to know?"

She gazed up at the Duke with guilty eyes. "Alix wanted to celebrate Halloween, a holiday tradition from her country. It seemed harmless enough. She and several of the girls carved gourds and she told stories of witches and spirits from the underworld. Alix also went to a tavern, apparently to visit a friend, and took Maud with her, which I didn't approve of."

Melisende stood wide-eyed and stock-still as she waited for his wrath.

"Is that all she has done?"

"Yes. Isn't that enough?"

"Story-telling and visiting a tavern? Granted, those weren't the wisest choices she could have made, but I was expecting worse, to tell you the truth."

"You aren't vexed with her?"

"I wouldn't say that, but not as angry as I imagined I would be upon my return."

She sagged in relief. "What about her sending the doctor away?"

"Could he have helped Beatrice?" he asked quietly.

"I… I don't know. It's possible."

"I believe she acted in good faith when she sent him away, and as you said, she does seem to have a certain 'knowledge' about things. I don't think she had malicious intent." He turned away. This conversation was over. Now he had to go and deal with Alix herself.

When Richard arrived back at his chambers, Alix was still abed. After he commanded his page to stoke the fire, he poured some wine and considered what to do about her actions.

* ~ * ~ *

Alix burrowed deeper underneath the warm pelts that covered her. Soft strains of music from the next room vied with the singing of birds outside the window. Rubbing her eyes, she sat up, and looked around at her familiar surroundings. She fluffed her still damp hair and throwing the covers off, gasped as the chilly air hit her skin. Richard's shirt provided little protection against the cold, but her heart filled with warmth as she remembered how he took care of her the night before. She also recalled his anger and wanted to put off the inevitable argument for as long as possible. She went into the bathing room and brushed her hair, but looking in the highly polished, silver metal mirror, she sighed. All she was doing was delaying. It was time to face him.

She cracked open the door and peeked out. Richard relaxed on the window seat, playing the lute. She stood and listened to the melody, until he looked up and smiled as if embarrassed.

"Continue, please. I like it." She perched on a chair at the table as far away from him as she could. It was futile, no amount of distance would keep the inevitable conversation at bay, but putting a table, settee and chair between them felt safe.

He played for a while longer then placed the instrument aside. He stood and looked her in the eye. At this moment, she knew she wasn't facing Richard, but the Duke, and that her reckoning was at hand.

"I know you are…" she began.

"Silence." His demand was direct. "Whose decision was it to keep me uninformed about what was going on in my realm?"

She forced her eyes to meet his. "The decision was mine, Your Grace, but you already knew that."

His countenance darkened. "I did. I wanted to see if you would admit it. What was the basis for your reasoning?"

"There wasn't anything you could have done. There was illness among the townspeople and here in the castle. If you and your knights had arrived earlier there was a chance that some of you would have fallen sick, as well."

He couldn't fault her rationale, but he would be damned if he would admit it. "I should have been informed by the individual who is overseeing my household's upkeep while I am away, and that person is not you."

Heat rose in her cheeks. "I thought it was for the best. I was mistaken." She stood. "It won't happen again." She stalked to the door, forgetting she was only wearing his shirt.

"I have not dismissed you!" he shouted. She had rarely heard him raise his voice, but she refused to let him see her shock as she turned to face him.

"What more do you require, Your Grace? I'm sorry, but I made a decision that I believed to be right at the time. And I would do it again." Her chin rose and fists clenched as she challenged him.

"God's bones, woman, why must you always question my authority?"

"I don't, but you weren't here!"

"You knew where I was. Clairvaux is not even a day's ride. You could have sent a squire in the morning and we would have been back by nightfall."

Alix shrugged her shoulders. "I didn't want to bother you if you had other things, or people, on your mind."

"What exactly are you insinuating?"

In response, she crossed her arms and glared at him.

He strode over to her. "Tell me!"

Her emotions warred with each other. Richard's protectiveness last night proved he cared for her, but Beatrice's sly remarks concerning his feelings for Philip's mother continued to plague her. They shared a child together–a bond that would always connect them. A bond that likely far outweighed any feelings Richard might have for her. Still emotionally drained from Beatrice's death, the hurt she had tried to suppress during Richard's absence surged inside her. Hot tears pricked her eyes and her throat tightened with stifled sobs.

Richard stared at her; his brows drawn together. Angry that he was privy to her show of weakness, she was unable to curb her outburst. "Did you think I wouldn't find out, Richard? Oh, I know you told me part of the truth, but you were probably laughing at me thinking how gullible I was. I must admit, you were very believable, but now I know."

"Is this what you were rambling about in the gardens? If so, then enlighten me since I have no idea what you are referring to."

"No. I refuse to listen to any more of your lies." Turning, she reached for the door.

"Either tell me what I've done to wrong you, or this conversation is finished."

She whirled back to face him. "Go back to your lover! I don't care. She can have you. I'm done."

Anger flamed in the depth of his eyes, and his lips thinned. Richard stalked toward Alix, his face inches from hers. "Who are you talking about? *Mon Dieu*, I shouldn't have to explain myself to you!"

Towering over her, he gripped her upper arms so tight he lifted her on her toes.

Pure fear paralyzed her as she stared into his stormy eyes.

Her legs shook, and her heart hammered like a wild bird trying to escape its cage. No, she would never be a victim again. "Take your hands off me!"

~ *Chapter 16* ~

HE IMMEDIATELY RELEASED HER. She stumbled backwards her eyes wide with fear. He stomped to the table, poured wine and gulped it, hoping it would dull his senses enough to cool down his searing anger. Someone had struck her in the past. He'd seen it before. He could imagine why it might have happened. Alix could vex a saint and had a stubborn streak that rivalled his own, but no woman deserved to be beaten. Or worse. He chanced a glance in her direction and caught her rubbing her arms, taking shaky breaths. He was sure that she would have his hand marks bruised into her shoulders by the next day. He poured her a cup, left it on the table, and went to sit in the window seat.

"I apologize. I didn't mean to get so angry with you, but, Alix, you sorely test me."

For a second, she waited by the door, then walked to the table and picked up her wine. She flashed a glance in his direction like a hunted animal, then chose the chair closest to the door, looking as if she might flee at any moment, should his mood darken.

"What did you mean by my lover?"

She raised the cup to her lips and took a long swig before answering. "Someone told me that you were more attached to Philip's mother than you let on." She paused, and he motioned for her to continue. "They said that she was your true love, but you couldn't be together because she was married." She finished her wine and stood to pour some more, but then took the entire flagon with her.

His eyebrow arched. "If I had deep feelings for my son's mother, do you think a marriage would stop me from getting what I wanted?"

Alix tilted her head considering. "Yes. Isn't adultery considered a sin in the eyes of the Church?"

"Being in my position, however, I could find a priest very willing to absolve me of all sins."

She appeared to relax, but only slightly. The wine on an empty stomach was having the intended effect. "So why aren't you with her?"

He looked at her bemused. "I don't have feelings for her, Alix."

"I don't believe you. I think you just won't admit it."

"Who told you this?"

She shrugged and looked away. "Someone. It's not important."

"Alix," he warned.

"Fine, it was Beatrice."

"Beatrice. And you believed her?"

"Yes, it sounded plausible." She forced herself to look up at him.

"I have never lied to you, Alix. I get enough deception and lies from my own family. I would rather keep that out of my personal life." He stood, carefully gauging her reaction. He would never tell her of the nameless women whom he had taken to bed in Clairvaux. His immediate lust had been sated, but afterward he was left unsatisfied and aching, finding little relief in wine as he tried not to think of a certain hazel-eyed woman with whom he had found so much pleasure.

He moved closer to her and held out his hand, but she jumped up and shied away. Her sudden movement caused the chair to teeter on its back legs until it crashed to the floor.

She took one step back as he approached. He reached out a hand caressed her cheek and drew her to him. "You're trembling. I'm so sorry Alix, I would never hurt you."

She nodded; her breath warm on his neck as he held her. His remorse turned to desire as she became calm in his arms and his body throbbed with a sudden, aching need for her; to feel her, to adore her, to make her feel safe, and... loved. Richard tilted her chin up and brushed his lips to hers. How could one woman be so soft, so gentle, yet so spirited at the same time?

He was prepared to release her if she asked, but she returned his light kisses while his hands skimmed down her body. He lifted the hem of her shirt, pulled it over her head, and threw it on the floor. His lips met hers again and she leaned against him as she lightly touched his lips with her tongue. His blood heated from the touch of her soft lips and his hands tangled in her hair as he lowered his head to crush his mouth upon hers.

Pent up anger from their quarrel proved to be a powerful aphrodisiac.

Having Alix surrender in his arms almost pushed him to the breaking point standing right there in the middle of the main chamber. The trust she must have in him to be so free and vulnerable surpassed his understanding. She looked into his eyes, their souls connecting as she pulled his shirt off then untied the drawstring on his pants, her hands sliding down his thighs as she pushed them to the floor. He shuddered as she caressed his inner thighs, then gripped him tightly. He gasped. "I can't wait, Alix. I must have you now." His husky whisper echoed in the silent room.

Lifting her, he carried her forward until her back pressed against the smooth wooden door. He hiked her up with one arm as he wrapped his other arm behind her back for support. Her legs tightened around him, and a low moan grumbled in her throat as he slowly entered her. She tried to match his thrusts but her hands kept slipping as she found no traction against the door. He lifted her higher and she clung to him, allowing him to guide her movements. Her soft cries increased in frequency and volume as she tightened her legs, drawing him deeper. Her body stiffened around him and she cried out, shaking, as she gave in to her climax. Already teetering on the edge, Richard's own release was swift and he held her tightly as they came together.

"I have missed you, Alix."

"I can tell." Her erratic breaths stirred his hair. She kissed his shoulder, neck and finally his lips. "Maybe you should go away more often."

"Perhaps I should, if I have homecomings like this to look forward to."

She trembled as she slid down his muscular length, his embrace keeping her from collapsing. He picked her up in his arms, carried her into the bedroom and placed her on the bed. As she nestled next to him, he was amazed at how his body had responded to her. His orgasms were always more intense with her than any other. There was something unique about this woman; something intriguing, something passionate, something he wanted to possess and not let go. It frightened him.

"I can clearly see how making up after an argument can prove quite beneficial," Richard jested with a chuckle. His fingertips feathered up and down her upper arm.

Alix smiled. "It does have its merits, but I don't recommend using it as foreplay."

He loosened his arm around her, touching the bluish bruises beginning to mar the pale, unblemished skin on her arm.

She sighed then brushed a lock of hair from his brow. "I'm fine, don't worry about it. Just promise me it won't happen again."

"I want you to know that I would never hurt you. Please believe me."

"I know you wouldn't." Kissing him, she rubbed her hand over his usually clean-shaven jaw. "You're all scruffy."

He ran his hand down her leg, rolled over and whispered in her ear, "I'll take care of it later." He caressed the inside of her thigh and she let out a soft moan and arched upward. "You are insatiable, Alix."

"Only with you, Richard." He smiled, then slowly trailed moist kisses down the sensitive skin on her neck. Her pulse raced underneath his lips. He caressed her soft, pale skin, moving downward to capture her breast in his mouth, teasing the nipple until it peaked. He pulled it with his teeth and she inhaled sharply. His roughened hands massaged her breasts as his warm lips caressed her stomach, teasing her with his tongue as he moved lower. She gasped when he kissed her inner thigh, the scruff on his jaw rasping her intimately and she gripped his shoulders as his warm lips trailed slowly upward. He tormented her with his tongue, carefully avoiding her sensitive flesh and she pressed upward, needing more.

"Please, oh, Richard, please…" Her whimper caused his royal member to harden as she tried to pull him to her. He smiled against her heated skin, then pushed his tongue forward, caressing and lathering her throbbing core. She tossed her head back, her hips bucking toward him. Her fingers kneaded his shoulders and she let out soft cries as he focused in on the sensitive area. Alix writhed beneath him as her climax peaked. "Ah, yes!" She pressed her hips upward as her body shuddered.

She sank back against the bed, her body trembling in the aftermath. Richard moved upward and kissed her, his hand caressing her hair as her breathing slowed. He rolled to his back and drew her to him, but when she trailed her hand down his stomach, he laughed and caught it in his, bringing it up to his chest.

"Unfortunately, men take longer to recover than women, especially when they are so thoroughly satisfied."

Alix pouted. "I suppose I must wait then." He gave her a sleepy smile and pulled her to him, until her head rested on his shoulder and her leg entwined with his. This was the homecoming he had desired.

* ~ * ~ *

Alix rolled over and reached for Richard but felt only blankets. She pulled his feather pillow to her and inhaled his scent, her body still humming with the passion of their multiple lovemaking sessions. No man had ever taken her to the heights of pleasure as Richard had. The connection she felt with him when they were together touched her very soul and she never wanted to lose that.

She swallowed the sudden lump in her throat. She didn't belong there. One day she would have to return home and leave the man who had stolen her heart. Drawing a shaky breath, she tried to force the painful thought away but icy fingers crept up her spine.

They had never taken precautions. What if she fell pregnant? She couldn't bear the thought of abandoning her child in the past, but could she deny Richard the opportunity to be a father again? Her mind spun with the possible ramifications. No, announcing she was pregnant wasn't a conversation she wanted to have, and she vowed to speak to Richard about being more careful.

Indistinct low voices murmured on the other side of the closed door, and she hoped that Richard had picked up their discarded clothes from the floor before he let the visitor enter. The chill of the bedroom stole over her as she tiptoed to the armoire, took out one of Richard's shirts and put it on. She pressed her ear to the door, but all was quiet, and she carefully opened it. To her relief, Richard was alone sitting at the table that was covered in food.

"Well, you have certainly been busy."

He turned, smiling. "You didn't want to eat last night, and I was famished."

"I haven't had food since, well, I can't remember. Days I think." Her gaze strayed over the floor. "Um… you did pick up our clothes, didn't you?"

"Your dress has been laundered, and yes, I did, lest your wanton behavior last night become court gossip." His soft laugh echoed in the room and happiness bubbled up inside her. She had missed his easy manner when they were together, his strong yet calming presence, the way he looked at her as if she were the only woman in the world.

He handed her a plate filled with chicken falling off the bone, boiled beans, and turnips. Alix smiled at the turnips, recalling how difficult they were to carve, took the plate and went to the window seat.

"I have a perfectly good table to eat on. That is its purpose."

"I know. I prefer it over here, but feel free to use it yourself." He gave her a calculating look, then joined her. Richard's goblet filled with spiced wine sat on the floor and Alix reached down to take a sip. Blood-red drops lingered on her lips and Richard leaned over to kiss them off. "I can get you some wine if you like, but I much prefer that you share mine," he murmured against her lips.

"Mmm, I do, too." She tipped the goblet to his lips so he could drink, then she kissed him, tasting the fragrant wine on his breath.

His husky laugh filled the room. "Eat, love. Or this meal will go to waste."

The food was delicious, and when Alix finished, she leaned back against the wall.

"That was perfect. I was beginning to feel faint from lack of sustenance."

"I must ask. How is it that you were nursing the ill servants?"

"What do you mean?"

"I employ one of the most qualified doctors available, but you refused to let him treat Beatrice."

Alix drew her brows together. "He was going to bleed her, which is the worst possible remedy for a sick person."

"She died, Alix. Perchance the doctor could have helped her."

"I don't think so. Bloodletting can help patients with certain illnesses, but with the ague, it would have weakened her severely. There was also a chance of developing an infection from the cut which would have been difficult to recover from." Alix wanted to tell Richard that in the 1800's physicians had determined that bleeding patients was more harmful than beneficial, but she held her tongue.

"You haven't answered my question. Why were you tending them? You could have fallen ill as well."

"I received many vaccines so I had a certain level of protection that others didn't."

"What is a vaccine?"

"Oh, shoot." Her murmured response didn't go unheard, as Richard's face contorted in curiosity and frustration. Now she had to offer some plausible explanation. "A vaccine is a type of medicine, which contains a small amount of the disease. When taken, the body destroys it to protect itself, which creates a resistance to it. If you happen to contract the illness after you have received the vaccine, either you don't get the illness at all, or if you do, the effects are much less severe." She stopped, seeing the confusion in his eyes.

"I have never heard of vaccines before. Is this a common practice where you're from?"

Tread carefully, she thought. "Yes, but it's still in the experimental phase so it hasn't been tested on many people yet." She jumped up and put her plate on the table.

"I wonder how long it would take until it became available to everyone." Richard's musing set off alarms in her mind. She needed to diffuse his line of thought, and fast.

"Years. Many years from now. What happened with Beatrice?"

"Her family is handling her interment."

She nodded. "Thank you again for taking care of her. I just couldn't be with her– after I tried so hard to save her." Worried that Melisende might tell Richard that Beatrice hadn't been shriven before her death, she decided it would be prudent of her to tell him first. "I called for a priest, but by the time he arrived it was too late."

"She didn't have her last rites read?"

"Not exactly."

"Alix! She wasn't able to confess and have her sins absolved?"

Alix didn't mention Beatrice asking for forgiveness from her. "I recited the Lord's Prayer. I didn't know what else to do, but it seemed to comfort her." She swung around to look at him. "You're religious, and believe in heaven, and I assume she did, as well. Do you think it was enough?"

"Enough for what?"

"To make her believe she would go to heaven?"

"Confessing her sins would have enabled her to go to heaven, and she was denied that."

"Is it enough to just confess your sins? In confession, doesn't the priest listen, then tell you to say five Hail Mary's and all is forgiven?"

"You shouldn't make light of this," he warned her.

"I'm sorry. I don't mean to, but it seems to me that people can break any commandment they want, and after confession, they are free to do it all over again."

"You have been to confession before, Alix. You know it's not that simple."

Her gaze slid to the floor.

"Are you even religious?" She was quiet, not sure how to answer that. "It's not a difficult question, Alix. Were you brought up in the Catholic faith?"

"I was baptized a Christian." She could never tell Richard her true belief lest she be labelled a heretic. As a young girl she'd believed in God, but as she grew older, she'd began to doubt His existence.

He relaxed, smiling. "Don't worry me like that again. Come here."

"Tell me, how did the fortification of your castle go?" Another subject change couldn't come soon enough.

His eyes lit up and he told her in great detail how the location would allow him to control the trade route through his barons, and how the walls could withstand any army that Hal could raise, describing it from a battlefield commander's perspective.

She fully appreciated what an accomplished soldier he was. "It sounds like a very advantageous castle. Unfortunately, I am sure your father will see it differently once he learns of it."

He regarded her evenly. "You are right about that. My father has asked all of us to his Christ's Mass court in Caen this year. I am sure it is a show of familial solidarity but there will be an underlying motive. There always is."

"Well, you must let me know what happens."

"In light of what went on this last time I left, I don't think I should leave you here."

"I will behave myself, I promise. I learned my lesson."

"I think you ought to join me in Caen. I would be interested to get your opinion about my unscrupulous brothers. My sister Matilda and her family are staying there, as well."

As much as she would love to meet the King of England, Henry's court was the last place Alix wanted to be. She was having a difficult enough time assimilating to this time period. Going with Richard would put her in the public eye, where every move she made would be scrutinized. "As tempting as it sounds to meet your brothers and the King, I will pass on the invitation."

"I am hopeful he will allow my mother out of her prison to join us. Surely you would want to meet her, Alix?"

"Do you really think he will?" Alix tried her best to appear curious, but she knew Eleanor wouldn't be in attendance.

Richard's brows drew down. "Father's moods are as mercurial as the wind. It depends on whether or not he is feeling magnanimous, I suppose."

"You would have received correspondence from her if she were to attend, would you not? Besides, taking a boat across the Channel this time of the year is quite dangerous, I've heard. In spite of your father holding her captive, I daresay he wouldn't want her to perish in a Channel crossing. Email her if you want, but I'm sure she'll tell you that she is to stay in England."

"I will write her. Wait, what did you say?"

"I said to write her."

"Those aren't the words you used."

Alix's heart pounded in her chest. Another slip up. How many more would it take before Richard became suspicious and realized that what she had told him concerning her life wasn't entirely true. "My apologies. I'm not familiar with your dialect. I'm still learning."

He nodded, appearing to accept her explanation, and she let out a soft sigh of relief. She got up and refilled their cups and settled back against the wall facing him.

"Consider attending the holiday festivities, Alix. If I know my father, he will spare no expense."

She nodded. "I'll think about it, but I can't promise anything." She sighed. "Everything will go back to normal tomorrow. With all that has gone on, I have been neglectful of my chores."

"And what constitutes normal?"

"Working for Melisende, morning services, daily life, you know 'normal' things." She grinned at him.

"Am I included in daily life?"

"You have returned, so yes, I imagine you would be."

"In what context would I be included?"

"I don't know, I haven't decided yet."

He took her hand and pulled her to him. "I'm not going to give you an opportunity to decide. I'm going to tell you."

"What if I do not wish to be told?"

"As your feudal Lord, I reserve the right to command you to do my bidding."

She giggled. "Ah, but, Richard, I am not your subject. You can't make me do anything I do not wish."

"Then I will persuade you." He drew her close and held her face in his hands. He kissed her, then sucked her bottom lip, his tongue tracing the inside of it. Her blood heated as he continued his slow exploration of her mouth. She reached up to tangle her hands in his thick hair, pulling him closer and kissing him thoroughly. When she released him, her head was spinning. Richard swayed where he stood, and she smiled to herself. His heavy breathing verified her effect on him.

~ *Chapter 17* ~

RICHARD WAS VERY GOOD at persuasion, as Alix was still floating from his kiss when she returned to the servants' quarters. She immediately went to see Maud and was relieved that the effects of the flu were fading.

Sybilla looked at Alix as she sank onto her pallet. "Maud is recovering. I was so worried about all of the girls. I'm glad the Duke has returned. I daresay you are as well." She turned to place a neatly folded dress in her coffer, then faced Alix again. "I know he was gone for weeks, but I hope Richard tried to be true to you."

Her matter-of–fact statement made Alix's stomach drop and she looked at Sybilla, confused. "What do you mean?"

Sybilla blanched and looked at the floor.

"Tell me!" Alix demanded.

Sybilla studied the ground. "My sincere apologies, I thought you knew. It's quite common when highborn men visit different towns, the local women offer their, um, wares to the men."

"That's a nice way of putting it." Alix did her best to calm her voice, hoping not to scare Sybilla into silence. "Did Rob say anything to you?"

"No! He said nothing. Even if the Duke did stray, Alix, it won't change anything. He's back now, so let it be."

"I was so consumed at the thought of his relationship with Philip's mother, that the likelihood of other women sharing his bed never entered my mind. When I confronted him about his lover, he made it sound like there had been no women. How could I have been so naïve?" She'd come to care for Richard and the revelation hurt. The first magical night they'd spent together was imprinted on her heart. The feel of his hands teasing her and his body thrusting against hers had ignited her desire to a level she had never experienced before. As they lay entwined, she felt a warmth and intimacy she'd never expected.

"He has feelings for you, Alix. He was very worried when he found out you were tending to the girls, and he searched for you after Beatrice's death. It's expected that men in his position sate their urges when they are separated for lengthy periods of time from their women. If he was with other women, I'm sure they meant nothing to him."

Alix's lips tightened. "I'm unused to the cavalier attitude men have toward fidelity. How would you feel if Rob was with another woman?"

Sybilla looked at her surprised. "His feelings for me haven't changed. I'm not happy with the thought of him being untrue, but as long as he returns to me, it's something that I must accept."

"Well, back home, a woman doesn't turn a blind eye to a man's infidelity. On the contrary, infidelity usually means that the bond is broken and the relationship doesn't progress. This 'wandering' is not what I'm used to." If she wanted to stay with Richard, she might have to *accept* this unfaithfulness and she didn't like that one bit.

Thankfully, Melisende approached, saving Alix from any more of this painful conversation. "Alix, with all the illness we had, we have run low on medicinal herbs. Would you mind going into town and replenishing our supply?"

A chance to get out of the palace was just what she needed. "No, not at all."

"Now hurry back." Melisende handed her some coins. "There are many chores to do now that the men have returned."

The day was slow to warm and the air still held a hint of the night-time chill. Alix walked briskly to town, and by the time she arrived, had slung her too-warm cloak over her arm. She went directly to the apothecary shop and gathered what she needed. With hours of daylight left, she decided to stop in the tavern and update Petronilla on what had happened in the last several days.

She found an empty space at the trestle table near the window and smiled when the owner approached. "Good afternoon, Petronilla. You look so much better than the last time I saw you. I wanted to come and check on you before, but several of the girls at the palace were sick, and I didn't have the opportunity. Did you avoid becoming ill?"

"I didn't, but the tea you gave me worked like a charm. I see the Duke has returned." Petronilla smiled knowingly and handed Alix a cup of wine.

"How do you know? Is there talk in town?"

Petronilla laughed. "No, he's over there with some of his men."

"Seriously?" Alix looked carefully over her shoulder. His back was to her, as he conversed with André and other men, she didn't recognize.

"Tell me what happened when he returned. You told me you thought he had another woman. Did you discover the truth about that?"

"Yes. Apparently, it was a fabrication, so that's a good thing." Alix decided not to mention the other townswomen he might have been with during his time away. What a mess that conversation could cause with him sitting merely feet away.

Petronilla looked over her shoulder. "Alix, Richard and his men are on the move."

"I hope he didn't see me come in." Alix hunched her shoulders, fighting the urge to glance backward. "I'm not supposed to be here, but I had to come into town anyway, and I couldn't resist a quick visit to see how you were feeling. Have they gone yet?"

"No, they haven't." A deep voice resonated from behind her.

"Great," she mouthed. "That's my cue to leave. Petronilla, it was wonderful seeing you. I'm so glad you're feeling better and I'm glad the herbs I gave you helped. I will stop by another time." Alix slid off the bench and stood. "Your Grace." She nodded at him and hurried out of the tavern with him at her heels. Why did she have to run into the one person she didn't want to see?

"I thought you weren't supposed to frequent the tavern, Alix."

"Melisende told me not to bring other girls, but she didn't exactly say I was forbidden." She whirled around to face him. "Petronilla was sick the last time I visited, and I gave her some herbs to ease her symptoms. I was just checking on her." Richard eyed her. "You won't tell Melisende I was here, will you? I think she's still upset with me."

Richard crossed his arms and raised his brow. "She did express her disapproval at your activities."

Alix tensed. "*My* activities?" she muttered under her breath, imagining how his time likely was spent at Clairvaux. "If you're referring to my storytelling, it was only a harmless bit of fun. As for going to the tavern, you said yourself the first day we met that it was one of the more reputable ones in town, so we were never in any danger." She glared at him. "I suppose you disapprove, as well?"

He remained silent and she looked down and focused on the small rocks embedded in the dirt at their feet. Her earlier bravado vanished as she wondered what penance she would have to pay.

"Alix, I'm not angry with you."

She looked up. "You're not going to punish me?"

He fought to cover his smile. "No, although I have half a mind to order you to learn Latin, since you are uneducated in that language. I also think you should attend evening services as well as the morning ones in order to become more fluent."

Alix huffed at the glint in his eyes. She knew him well enough to recognize when he was teasing her. "I can think of more pleasurable things to do on my knees than pray, but if that's your wish..." She gave him a coquettish half-smile then burst out laughing at his astonished look.

"Minx," he growled. "I won't tell Melisende you were here. Your secret is safe with me, but you had best return soon."

Alix turned and strode toward the road that led to the castle. Moments later hoof beats sounded behind her.

"Allow me to give you a ride back, or you will be late." Not waiting for her answer, Richard dismounted.

His hands were warm around her waist and as her eyes met his, her heart lurched. Richard was the man she'd always dreamt about, the legend come to life. He exuded power and confidence, but he also was generous, caring and affectionate. He filled the emptiness and longing within her soul that she hadn't known existed. She had fallen for this man and didn't want to be with anyone else.

Alix drew a shaky breath and concentrated on hitching up her skirts. Richard helped her into the saddle, covering her legs carefully with the fabric, his hand resting on her knee a bit longer than necessary. He swung up behind her and put his arm around her as his horse stamped restlessly at the shift in weight. The familiar flutters churned in her stomach at his touch. She experienced a sense of déjà vu recalling the day when he'd first brought her to Poitiers Palace, but this time, as they passed townspeople, she held her head high, proud to be seen with Richard.

A cool breeze rustled the leaves on the trees and she shivered. Richard wrapped his cloak around her and drew her back against his warmth. "I can't believe it will be winter soon." She sighed. "Does it snow here?"

"No, not often, but it will be cold."

"I wish it would snow and we could have a white Christmas. It never snows back home. Come to think of it, it never really gets that cold, either."

"Where is home?" His casual tone didn't fool her.

"You know, England."

"Yes, so you say, but somehow I don't truly believe that." They rode into the courtyard and a groomsman ran to take the reins that Richard tossed at him. He dismounted, and then helped Alix down.

"I appreciate the ride."

"You're very welcome but go inside. You're shivering."

She went upstairs and warmed herself by the fireplace in the servants' quarters. Nearby, Maud worked on embellishing a dress with delicate embroidery, her brows knit in concentration.

"Your stitches are so intricate and meticulous." Alix peered over her shoulder, trying to understand how one could make something so complicated. "You must have started at an early age."

"I did. My mother taught me to sew and embroider. I remember sitting beside her near the fire as she mended our clothes with the most delicate of stitches. I also learned how to manage a household, for when I get married."

"Manage a household?"

"Yes, balance the ledgers and supervise the cleaning and cooking. Obviously, I can sew clothes for my family and myself. My father will arrange a marriage for me in the next few years. I can only hope my husband is a good man." Worry shadowed Maud's gentle blue eyes.

Alix nodded, not knowing what to say to allay her fears. Women had very little freedom in these times. They were raised to be good wives and provide a satisfying home life for their husbands, who were chosen for them, with little concern for their own happiness.

"I am surprised that the Duke isn't married yet. His betrothal to the French king's daughter Alys was arranged years ago. If I were she, I would be either very angry, or mortified that it hasn't happened yet." Maud gave Alix a sly look.

"I see what you mean. I suppose one ought to feel sorry for her, but... wait, are you suggesting his not marrying her has something to do with me?" Alix planted a hand on her hip.

"Don't you think he would marry her if you weren't here?"

"No, I don't. As you pointed out, he has had years to marry her. I have only been here a couple of months. I think he has no interest in marriage at the moment."

"You might be right about that. I do dread his bringing a wife here though, as it will change everything."

"True. A girl marrying the son of a king would be considered almost royalty. She would bring many of her own ladies." Seeing alarm in the other girl's eyes, Alix back pedaled. "At least as of now, Richard has shown no signs of marrying." She turned back to the fire and murmured under her breath. "And he won't for a long time."

* ~ * ~ *

Now that Richard and his knights were in residence, the entertainment and the food vastly improved. Alix began to feel like herself again, but she still hadn't recovered from Beatrice and Jeanne's deaths. The other girls appeared to have accepted these tragedies and moved on, but death was a common occurrence in this age, so most of them had no doubt faced it before. After the evening meal, the music began, and Alix found herself alone since Sybilla and Rob had joined the other dancers on the floor. Maud was busy gossiping with Gwyn and Sarah. Alix sat alone at the table, bored. She glanced at Richard, but he was engaged with the same group of men he'd been with earlier that day at the tavern.

Feeling restless, she left and went upstairs to get her cloak, determined not to forget it this time, and went down the back stairs. The thick, woolen fabric provided enough protection against the cold air this particular evening, but she knew that it would get colder yet as the weeks passed. She paced along the path to the entrance into the gardens, a half-moon illuminating the way, and headed back to the fountain. The familiar, marble bench beckoned her and she lay upon it and marveled at the blanket of stars in the night sky.

She could see more stars than she ever had back home. Even on the clearest of nights, the Austin city light pollution was enough to hide the stars from view. For the first time, she truly understood how ancient astronomers viewed the heavens, and were able to create pictures in the night.

The bench grew colder as the temperature fell, so she sat up and wrapped her arms around her legs and sighed. "I don't know if I want to go home," she whispered into the night. She did miss her friends and family, and with the holidays fast approaching, homesickness caught her off guard often. Once again, she wondered if they knew she was missing and if they were searching for her. Maybe time had frozen or slowed down so much that the months here were measured in mere minutes back home.

The thought of leaving Richard cut her to the core. The longer she stayed, the more involved in his life she would become. Her greatest fear was that she could unintentionally alter history just by her mere presence. So far, nothing had happened that was likely to affect history in any way. She was a very small cog in the wheel of time. She wasn't supposed to have even met Richard, but as long as he continued doing what he was meant to do, everything should sort itself out in the end.

One thing was certain. She needed to stay in Poitiers if she could, and not insert herself in other parts of history. That meant not going to the King's Christmas court in Caen.

Her logical mind still warred with the historian in her. It seemed like an easy decision. Don't go. But this would be her only opportunity to meet some of history's greatest figures.

As she debated between staying or going, the temperature continued to drop, so she headed back, her footsteps crunching on the dried leaves that covered the path. The night was crisp and pleasant and Alix opted for a longer walk around the perimeter of the building.

Glancing up at Richard's windows, warm light shone through the panes, and shadows moved past the windows. Recalling his involvement with the men at supper, it was best not to visit, in case urgent matters occupied him.

"What are you doing back here?" Cold hands grasped her shoulders tightly.

Automatically, she reacted to the attack. Years of studying martial arts finally became useful. She elbowed her attacker hard in the solar plexus, then planting her leg behind his, she grabbed his arm and twisted her body to unbalance him and push him on the ground. In a second, she was standing over him with her foot on his throat.

"Who are you and why did you grab me?" Alix demanded furiously. The man looked helplessly at her. "Well? I asked you a question!"

Unable to answer, he motioned to his neck. Cautiously, she stepped back. "Stand up slowly and don't even think of trying that again!"

The man nodded, stood, then dusted himself off.

"Now, who are you and why did you attack me?"

"Why are you wandering around at night, miss?"

"I'm the one asking the questions! Answer me, who are you?"

* ~ * ~ *

Richard was in his chambers with André and Rob, gambling and joking about how poor a card player Rob was. After five rounds, the young squire was down to his last few coins. Hearing a disturbance outside, they rushed to look out the window, straining to see in the inky darkness.

"Jesu, what has Alix done now?" André asked.

Richard burst out laughing as he saw Alix confronting his knight, her hands balled into fists. "André, go save Georges before Alix kills him for accosting her." André nodded and hurried out. Richard glanced at Rob and arched his brow. "I'm glad she has no knowledge of my activities at Clairvaux. I will sleep easier knowing her anger isn't directed toward me."

"You'd best stay on her good side then, Your Grace," Rob laughed.

"I plan to."

* ~ * ~ *

Alix was still glaring at the man when André appeared around the corner. "Alix, please don't attack Georges."

"He's one of Richard's? I should have known."

"You can leave now, Georges, I'll sort this out." André tried to hide a smile as Georges walked past, rubbing his neck.

"You'll 'sort this out'? He attacked me first!"

"Why were you wandering around in the dark?" André crossed his arms.

"It was a nice night and… Wait, how dare you put this on me!" Alix's cheeks flamed at the look of shock on André's face. She had seen Richard's cousin at meals and at Mass, but had never spoken to him, and now her first words to this historical person were ones of accusation.

He smiled. "You're forgiven, but please refrain from hurting Richard's men."

"I'll try, but they ought to learn how to fight. When a man can be bested by a woman…" Alix shook her head and chuckled under her breath. It had been fun taking down Georges. The look of bewilderment on the man's face had been priceless.

They began walking back to the palace. "Where did you learn to fight like that?"

"Back home. When I was younger, I took self-protection classes. I ended up enjoying them immensely, so I continued taking them for quite some time."

"Self-protection. What is that?"

"We call it martial arts. It is a type of fighting that you can use as offense, but also to defend yourself. With rebels and thieves marauding the towns and villages, it's always good to be able to fight them off, if necessary." Alix was pleased with her fabricated explanation. "Who was that man anyway? I have never seen him or any of the other men that Richard was speaking with at supper." She changed the topic before André asked questions she wasn't willing or able to answer.

"That was Georges. He and the others were overseeing Clairvaux, but Richard called them here. When Richard goes to Caen to meet with his father, he wants all of his knights with him. You know of the antagonism between Richard and his father, and now with his brother Hal plotting against him, he doesn't want to put himself in a position where he's at a disadvantage."

"True, he needs to go to defend his duchy, or his father could very well take any one of his castles scattered throughout Aquitaine and give them to his brothers."

They entered the palace and André headed to the dining hall. "Alix, Richard will surely demand an explanation as to how a female defeated one of his highly-trained knights. You'd best make an appearance in his quarters."

Alix nodded, knowing André was right. She climbed the stairs, wondering what would happen next. She stood outside his door for quite some time mustering up her courage and resolve. She took a deep breath and blew it out hard before knocking.

"Enter!"

She was surprised to find him alone and crossed the room to the window seat, sat down and waited for his questions.

"Care to explain?"

She wanted Richard to know something about her past. Maybe it was for the best to come out with her story, hoping it would help him have a better understanding of who she is. It would also explain, with perfect clarity, why she attacked Georges outside. "When I was younger, I was returning home when a man attempted to rob me." Alix glanced at Richard. "I tried to fight back, but he was too strong. He struck me, and I fell to the ground. I'd never felt so helpless. After that, I learned how to protect myself so I wouldn't be a victim again."

Richard's face was in profile but disgust flared in his eyes before he turned toward the fireplace. "What happened to the bastard?" he ground out.

Alix's eyes narrowed and she dug her nails into her palms. "They never caught him. My father was furious at what had happened to me. If he had the chance, he would have killed the man."

"God's bones, Alix! I would have done the same thing!"

Alix smiled at his protectiveness. "I was terrified to venture outside and became a bit of a recluse for some time."

"Was it this event that led to your father's infidelity?"

Alix pursed her lips, surprised he had remembered that long-ago conversation. "There was already a rift in my parents' marriage, and I felt my attack exacerbated it. I think they both blamed themselves and each other for not being stricter in my upbringing. I had quite a bit of freedom. I'm sure they thought that led to the assault. My mother felt guilty and my father began to work longer hours until he stopped coming home altogether."

Richard was silent, an inscrutable look filling his eyes. "No woman should ever be subjected to that." The window seat cushion shifted under his weight as he joined her and took her hands.

"I agree, but you've committed worse acts. I know you've raped women in the past." She could never forget or forgive that part of his history.

He looked at her startled. "What do you know of that?"

"It doesn't matter. You stand accused of that crime do you not?"

"Yes," he admitted carefully. "But you don't understand the circumstances. My nobles rebelled. It was in retaliation. I needed to remind them that I am their feudal overlord and they answer to me. After battle, the spoils are claimed by the victors."

"Women are considered spoils? Why didn't you just strip the rebels of their castles or titles? It was unnecessary to rape helpless women then pass them on to your soldiers, as if they were chattel."

He stared at her. "I am their duke, Alix. These people belong to me."

"No, they don't 'belong' to you. You have sovereignty over them and they answer to you, but you don't own them or their loyalty. That is earned."

He glared at her. "It's the way my father has always treated his subjects, although I detest the practice. I wish there was another way, but it's proved to be an effective method to control my barons."

"Stripping an innocent girl of her virtue, or raping a woman and destroying her trust in men and possibly her marriage is how to control a man?" She knew she needed to approach him delicately and softly. She placed her hand gently on his knee. "You're right. I might not know how to control your barons, but if you were less heavy-handed and used more diplomacy in your dealings with them, I daresay you would find them more receptive to you. Aquitaine's problems will not be solved overnight but think on what I said. This is your chance to change things, especially now that Hal is trying to coerce your noblemen to his side." She stroked his face then kissed him, relieved when he pulled her closer and wrapped her in his arms. "I'm going to bed." She stood and headed to his bedchamber, then stopped. "I'm sorry, I should have asked if I could stay with you."

He laughed under his breath. "*Mon amor*, by now you should know that you have no need to ask."

She smiled at him and headed to his bedchamber, her heart racing at his term of endearment.

~~*

Once Alix had retired, Richard sighed and rose to pour some wine. He took a long drink and contemplated what she'd said. Her insight into how he ruled was accurate, but he and his father were of the same mindset when it came to the rights of a ruler.

Seeing how Henry had managed to keep peace with the way he chose to rule, Richard didn't see any reason to change. Alix would discourage him from ruling in this manner should he allow her to continue talking about politics, but he wanted and respected her advice on all matters. No other woman had made him question himself, his values and motives.

For some unknown reason, Alix's opinion was very important and he couldn't stomach the thought of her being disappointed in him. His pulse quickened and his hand tightened on his cup as he drained it. For the first time he was thinking of a woman in future terms.

He undressed and got into bed next to her. She turned to him. "I didn't mean to tell you how to run your kingdom."

"My duchy," he corrected her, and pulled the furs closer about them. "You had some valid points that I would do well to consider. Have you given more thought to joining me in Caen for my father's court?"

"I've thought on it, but I still don't think it's a good idea. I'm sure your family won't want to meet your bedmate."

Richard stilled. "I have never thought of you in those terms, Alix. You know that. If you were merely my bedmate, I wouldn't ask you to come with me. I want you with me because I suspect that my father has a hidden agenda, and I would like your input on the matter. You inexplicably know things about myself and my family, which is an asset, although I am not sure I want to know how you are privy to the information and knowledge you seem to possess."

"Well, whatever I am, I don't feel comfortable accompanying you as your unmentionable, with your brothers and their wives there. I don't think you ought to throw a monkey wrench into the situation by including me. Translated, that means I don't want to shake things up."

He laughed. "I have to admit; you would definitely enliven the festivities."

"Oh, so, I'd be the entertainment for the court and fodder for gossip? How could I possibly pass that up?"

"I'm sure I can change your mind." He ran his hand down her thigh, indicating which direction his thoughts were heading, prepared to stop if she was unwilling; always prepared to stop, now that he knew more of her past and how she felt about his former forceful liaisons. She shifted under the covers. "Alix, do you want me to continue?" His desire for her felt different now, pure, considerate, and his apprehension that she might refuse him cut.

"Let's see how persuasive you can be." Her whispered words tickled the hairs on his chest and she drew a line from his nipple to his hip with her fingernail.

His abdomen muscles tensed from the rake of her nail. Richard was amazed at how this woman could arouse him with one suggestive gesture of what was to come. She reached down and grasped him. His breath hitched but he never took his eyes from her. Her movements were delicate. Her hand warm and smooth.

Her eyes darkened as she parted her lips and took in a wisp of air. The fingers around him tightened with the first stroke, the motion slow. Then she increased the speed. Richard arched his neck and buried the back of his head into the pillow, sucking in air. His breathing became shallow. He lifted his head and his muscles clenched at the possessive look in her eyes.

The steady motion of Alix's hand continued until his body convulsed. His self-control almost shattered. "Jesu, love, I can't take much more," he choked out, desperate for relief.

He took deep breaths to regain control of his body. Alix shifted position and he turned toward her. With a quick motion she pushed him against the mattress, then sat back on her knees to study him. The pit of his stomach stirred. He wanted her, but this time he'd enjoy her depths.

She lowered her head and looked up through long lashes while her fingertips followed the curve of her breast, and then the outline of her waist until they reached the bottom of the soft, cotton shirt. Her lips curved in a smile and she grasped the hem and pulled the shirt over her head.

He marveled at the creaminess of her skin and her full breasts, which swung as she straddled him. He reached out to touch her, but she gripped his wrists and pinned them on either side of his head.

"I'm the one with power tonight, my dear Duke. You obey my commands…" She cleared her throat, "…My Lord."

Richard smiled, but did as he was told. "Absolutely, My Lady." Throbbing and desperate to bury himself deep inside, he lifted his hips off of the bed but she shifted away, not allowing him to penetrate her.

"My Lord, you forget yourself."

"Alix, I'm begging you."

She beamed at his supplication, sank down onto him and began to move, tormenting him. He stroked her thighs then moved his hands up to cup her breasts. She moaned as his touch traveled over her body. When he grazed her nipple with his thumb, she bent over him to allow him to capture her breast in his mouth.

His tongue swirled over the sensitive peak and she gasped and trembled above him. A groan vibrated in his throat, his body jerking in response. Suddenly, she pulled him to a sitting position. He grasped her in his arms and moved slowly at first then faster, but it wasn't enough. He hadn't penetrated her to the core and he needed more. Richard pushed Alix back against the bed and lifted her hips. To his surprise, Alix put her legs over his shoulders. He couldn't help but grin.

This, this right here, is what he wanted. His growl echoed in the room as he penetrated her fully, thrusting deeper than he ever had before, her tightness gripping him. All rational thought vanished, replaced by pure pleasure, as every muscle in his body clenched in preparation for a monumental climax. His cry of release filled the room before he collapsed on top of her, darkness swirling about him.

Moments later, when he came to, Alix's arms were around him.

"Welcome back." Her soft breath stirred his hair.

"Jesu." He struggled to think. "That's never happened before. No one has ever brought me pleasure like you." He searched for her lips and kissed her, then nestled back, wrapped in her warm embrace. He'd never possessed a woman so thoroughly. "Did I hurt you? It wasn't my intention to take you in that way…"

"You didn't hurt me. I know you would never hurt me. I trust you, always."

He rolled to his back and drew her to him. Her simple words were a balm to his soul, solidifying the intimate bond he felt with her.

"Somehow you were more persuasive than I," he murmured.

"Mmm, I was, wasn't I?"

"We'll continue this tomorrow then."

"I look forward to it."

~ *Chapter 18* ~

ALIX TURNED OVER, CAREFUL not to wake Richard. She had awakened in the middle of the night and had thought of nothing other than the Christmas court, for what seemed like hours now. Why was she even debating going? It would be a huge mistake. What would his family think of her? She already knew the answer and it wasn't pretty. Even if Richard considered her more than a bedmate, his brothers Hal and Geoffrey wouldn't see her that way, and their wives, Marguerite and Constance would definitely disapprove of her. Marguerite, would resent her, since her sister Alys was Richard's betrothed. Alix's presence would be a reminder of how well that union hadn't progressed.

God what a cliché. The master of the house, or palace in this case, sleeping with the help. The reality was, she had no true place in this time, and she needed to return home. As much as she wanted to stay with Richard and journey with him to meet his legendary family, the fewer ripples she made in the tapestry of his life, the better. "No, I'm definitely not going," she whispered, hoping that if she made her declaration aloud it would help to solidify her resolve. Soon she fell into a troubled sleep.

With everyone in service readying the palace for the long winter, the next several weeks passed quickly. Melisende kept Alix and the other household servants busy making candles, polishing lanterns, and gathering fresh rushes to put on the floor as insulation against the cold. Fortunately, the food stores were stocked and ready for the barren season. Very few vendors had goods to sell in the market now that the harvest was over, and what vegetables and meat were available were only fit to use in stews. Chores and gossip occupied Alix's days, and she spent her nights with Richard. As long as she went to Matins and did her duties, Melisende didn't complain. No more mention was made of her going to Caen, and Alix assumed Richard had decided that her prediction about a potential disaster was accurate and the invitation had been rescinded.

That morning had begun gray and cold, clouds obscuring the weak winter sun, as they had many a day before. If Alix had been in her time, tomorrow would've been Thanksgiving. Trying to survive in the Middle Ages consumed her every waking hour, leaving little time to think of home, but a twinge of homesickness trickled in as she pictured her family celebrating without her.

"Are you feeling poorly, Alix? I hope you aren't falling ill." Maud knit her brows as she concentrated on embroidering an intricate pattern on one of her dresses.

"Oh no, it's more homesickness than anything."

Maud smiled in sympathy. "I know how you feel. It does pass."

The thunder of hooves and voices just outside the window caused the girls to gather and peer out.

"Who are they?" Gwyn's question unsettled Alix as the girls watched men dismount in the courtyard below. If they were unfamiliar to her, then they were most likely unwelcome.

Melisende came over to see what the commotion was. "I wasn't informed we were to have guests. I will go find out."

The girls began speculating on who the visitors could be. "It's not the Young King. He would have arrived with much more fanfare." Gwyn was correct. Hal wouldn't travel with only a few men.

"It's most likely a noble or baron." Maud's yellow ringlets bounced as she walked back to her sewing.

"Hopefully, whoever it is will have some news about the court in Paris. I haven't heard from my cousin in a while and I don't know any of the new gossip." Ever the busybody, Gwyn seemed to have little concern about the benevolent or malicious intent of these strange visitors.

The men headed toward the palace, their voices fading in the distance. "Supper will be served soon. I imagine we'll find out who they are then." Alix turned from the window, just as curious about the newcomers as the rest of the girls.

* ~ * ~ *

Richard stood in the entryway talking to a tall, fair-haired man, with penetrating, blue eyes, and motioned to Melisende as she approached.

"Lady Melisende, my brother Geoff and his men have arrived. Prepare accommodations for them and make room in the dining hall as well."

"Of course, Your Grace." She curtsied to Richard, then to his half-brother Geoff, one of King Henry's base-born sons.

"Come, Brother, tell me what's going on at Father's court. Do you have any news from the French court in Paris? I'm sure King Philippe is up to his neck in treachery." Richard clapped his brother on the back as he led Geoff upstairs to his chambers.

Geoff closed the chamber door behind him and wasted no time. "When are you coming to Caen?"

"Can I offer you some wine before you start your inquisition?" Richard laughed, and motioned for him to take a seat.

Geoff had the good grace to look abashed, accepting the cup. "Father sent me. He has heard nothing from you on this topic and he is getting impatient."

"I'm sure he is. He likes to play the puppeteer and have all of us jump at his beck and call. I haven't decided when or even if I will attend court this year."

"I suggest you do. There have been some developments which I'm sure would interest you."

"By that, I take it you mean Hal's newfound loyalty to Philippe?"

"Ah, you know of that?"

Richard nodded.

"He and your brother Geoffrey have been in close communication with Philippe. I don't trust our brothers, and I think that is why Father called us all to his court. I'm sure he has a proposition for each of you." He steepled his fingers and shifted in his seat.

Richard took a long pull of wine from his goblet and strode to lean against one of the two chairs sitting near the fireplace. "I agree with that assessment. Father does have a plan, and it would be the perfect time to alert him to Hal's scheming with my barons, if he's not already aware of it. Perchance it is high time I make an appearance. It's beginning to look as though there is the potential for a very interesting Christ's Mass. I received a letter from my mother. Are you aware that she is to stay in England?"

Richard paced a few steps, his fingers whitening on his goblet. "He prefers to keep her imprisoned on that accursed island where she has few allies. He's allowed her to attend his other holiday courts, but not this one. I would like to know why she was left out of this particular family reunion." Richard was sure

Geoff noticed the bitter bite in his voice. "Come, I'm sure you and your men must be hungry." Richard beckoned Geoff to follow him downstairs.

"Why have you been staying here of all places, Richard? Granted, it's luxurious, and the town has some entertainment to offer, but for God's sakes, it's quite dull compared to Chinon, which has some of the best hunting lands in our father's kingdom."

"Poitiers is Mother's favorite city in Aquitaine and as Duke I've spent most of my time here. It feels more like home than Father's castles in Chinon or Caen. I also don't wish to be in proximity to my brothers." They took their places at the high table where their knights had already gathered, the new arrivals relaying news from the courts.

Geoff's gaze roamed over the room. "I see you have quite a few comely ladies in residence." Richard watched as Geoff admired several younger, shapely girls. "Mayhap one of them is your reason for staying?"

Richard feigned a small smile. "I prefer other diversions such as hunting. Speaking of which, I have a new gyrfalcon I'm training. We should go out tomorrow so I can show her off."

Just then, Alix entered with Sybilla, both of them ignoring their men. Geoff observed her closely. "Well, well, now she's a beauty, isn't she? Is she unmarried?"

"Yes, I believe so." Richard's tone betrayed nothing.

"Geoff! I heard you had honored us with your presence."

André gave Geoff's shoulder a firm slap as a form of greeting.

"André, it's good to see you, it's been far too long."

"What are you doing here? Don't tell me you've grown bored at King Henry's court?"

Geoff laughed. "Not at all. I was sent to discover whether or not Richard will attend Henry's Christ's Mass court next month. There are issues that need to be addressed."

"I think he should go. At least he can make his grievance against Hal's duplicity known."

"In case you hadn't noticed," Richard chimed in after having his fill of the conversation, "I'm sitting right here, and perfectly capable of making my own decisions."

Geoff laughed aloud. "Yes, you are known for your decisiveness on the battlefield, usually to the detriment of the enemy." He took a deep drink of wine then grew serious. "I believe your brothers, Hal and Geoffrey have made a pact with Philippe against you, Richard, and you need to quell it immediately lest you face a rebellion by your own nobles."

Richard narrowed his eyes. "I've never trusted either of my brothers, especially Hal. He's gullible. He can be swayed by the simplest of suggestions. I have no doubt he's scheming with Philippe, but I guarantee you that Philippe is the one leading him by the nose. On the subject of Father's court, at the moment, I have more pressing matters to worry about. You can relay that message to him."

"I will, but I do hope you decide to attend." Geoff raised his goblet. "Now, what about some good wine and entertainment? I wish to be impressed."

Richard looked over the hall and his gaze fell on Alix. It was as if she sensed it, and she glanced up at that moment and gave him a small smile. This was not lost upon Geoff and Richard knew it.

"Tell me, what is she to you, Brother?"

His interest in Alix brought out a strange, carnal feeling in Richard.

"Somehow you can't keep your eyes off of her."

Richard was silent. He preferred to keep his affairs private and Geoff was notorious for being loose-lipped, especially when deep in his cups.

Geoff clapped him on the shoulder laughing. "You wouldn't be the first to fall under the spell of a servant girl."

Richard's first thought was to protect Alix from potential gossip. "She is merely in my employ."

"Fair enough, but a girl that comely doesn't sleep alone, and most likely won't tonight."

Geoff was baiting him, but Richard hid a frown. The only indication that the taunt had hit a nerve was his hand tightening on his wine cup.

∼∼*

"Sybilla, who is that man with Richard?" Alix stole only fleeting glances at the Duke's table.

"It's his half-brother Geoff, from one of his father's extra-marital relationships."

Alix had heard of Geoff from her history studies, but her knowledge of him was limited. He would be named Archbishop of York by Richard after he became king. "I wonder what he's doing here? I hope he didn't bring unwelcome news."

"Concerning what, Alix?"

"Oh, I was just thinking aloud."

"It's a good thing you're smart and a good friend, because honestly, Alix, sometimes I simply don't understand you."

Alix laughed. "I sometimes forget my idioms are foreign to you. I'm glad we're friends too."

Rob's appearance to occupy Sybilla the rest of the evening cut the conversation short.

Seconds after Sybilla vacated her seat, Maud slipped in next to Alix.

"This is becoming a habit. You don't have to entertain me, Maud."

Maud giggled. "If Richard were only a knight, I'm sure he would keep you company, but as a duke he has rules to follow."

"For someone so young, you're quite wise. Thank you for sitting with me." The music started and soon after, the floor filled with dancers.

"Alix, would you care to dance?"

She turned and looked up, surprised. "André, are you sure you are willing to risk it? I'm not that accomplished a dancer. I wouldn't want to embarrass you."

"You couldn't possibly."

"I appreciate your show of faith. I'm willing to give it a try if you are." She took his proffered arm and headed out to the floor. Fortunately, there weren't that many different dances, and in the last couple of months she had learned most of them by simply watching, so when the music began, she was able to execute the steps.

"You are quite good, Alix."

"Thank you." She turned her eyes to the head table. "So that is Geoff, Richard's half-brother?"

"Yes." His smile faded as he glanced at the man seated next to Richard.

"What has he done to make you dislike him so?"

André gradually moved them away from the other couples before answering. "It's no secret that Henry has plans for Geoff, but in the clergy, while Geoff's ambitions lean in a loftier direction."

Alix was puzzled at his words. "Henry wouldn't possibly name him his successor. He's illegitimate."

"True, but Geoff hopes that he will be given a prominent position at court. Henry is shrewd. If Geoff is given a position in the Church, his claim to the throne, however tenuous, is erased."

"What is he doing *here*?" Alix turned away to touch the hand of the dancer opposite her.

André lowered his voice and continued as she rejoined him. "Geoff's loyalties lie with Henry. I believe he's attempting to determine who else will support Henry. Geoff has nothing to fear from Hal, but Richard is a formidable adversary. Richard and Geoff barely tolerate each other, but if Henry offers his support to Richard, you can be sure that Geoff will too. Caen will prove to be quite interesting during the Christ's Mass court." André's eyes hardened as he looked in Geoff's direction. "Have you decided to attend?" he asked, and then laughed at her surprised expression. "Richard told me he invited you. At first I was against the idea."

"I don't think it would be wise for me to go."

"Richard thinks enough of you to extend the invitation. Not to mention, you would be a welcome ally. Once you see the animosity between Henry's sons, you will better understand why Richard fears the possibility of his father taking valuable lands within his duchy and giving them to one of his brothers. It might help you to better understand him."

"I would undoubtedly cause a stir. That couldn't be good for Richard in any way."

André's brows raised seeming to consider Alix's comment. The music ended, they made their bows and curtsies and André went to join the other knights. Alix returned to her seat, still undecided about whether to attend the Christmas court or not.

Richard rose and strode to the door followed by Geoff. He turned to allow his brother to leave first, and catching Alix's eye, gave an imperceptible headshake. She lowered her eyes, indicating she understood that he didn't want her company tonight.

Soon after, she made her excuses to Maud and returned to her room. With time on her hands she decided to take a bath. Heating the water was a monumental task not to mention lugging the heavy buckets. "I would give anything for inside plumbing and hot water," she muttered as she emptied the bucket into the tub. When she sank down into the warm water fragranced with the vanilla oil she'd purchased from the apothecary, she leaned her head back with a satisfied sigh.

The idea of joining Richard in Caen and meeting his family thrilled her, but she worried that she would prove to be one more complication in an already volatile situation. All too soon, her bath water cooled, so she dressed hastily in the cold room. Voices echoed in the hall outside of the quarters as the girls made their way up the stairs.

"Alix?" Sybilla seemed surprised to see her. "Aren't you staying with Richard tonight?" Alix appreciated the low tone of Sybilla's voice, so others didn't overhear.

"He's entertaining Geoff so I'm here for as long as he stays, I suppose."

"I won't complain," Sybilla said with a smile. "I've missed our talks."

"So have I. Was there any news from the guests?"

"No. They are going to Caen for the Christ's Mass court, since King Henry asked his family to be there, but we already knew that."

"I'm sure Richard will take his men with him, since his brothers will be there. He won't want to be vulnerable. We can still make the holiday festive even with them away." Alix tried to offer an encouraging tone, but it fell flat and both girls knew why.

"How?"

"We can dress in our finery. I'm sure there will be music. The cooks will most likely prepare a special feast, and we can decorate."

"You still have the beautiful silk that Richard gave you. We can make you a dress from that. Do you think you'll go with him to Caen?"

"Why ever would I go with him?" Alix scoffed, getting up to pull the gray silk out of the coffer at the foot of her bed.

"He might invite you."

"Right, he's going to bring his... bedmate to meet his family." Alix was almost going to say whore but quickly changed it.

"I'm sure he thinks of you as more than that. He spends a lot of time with you, so he must enjoy your company."

"It's one thing to be with him here, where he's in charge and no one would dare say anything to him; it's quite another to be in his father's court, where his brothers and their wives would definitely have an opinion about me. Surely, it would be a low opinion." She smoothed her hand over the silk. "Sybilla, why don't you take the silk to make a dress for yourself? I won't have any use for it and I would hate for the material to go to waste." She held it up. "The dark gray would set off your coloring beautifully."

"Oh, I couldn't possibly! Richard gave it to you. He would be wroth if I took it."

"It was a gift to me and is now mine to do with as I wish, and I wish to give it to you."

Sybilla took the rich fabric and brushed her fingers over the shiny surface. "It is so beautiful. Are you sure?" When Alix nodded, she beamed. "Thank you. I've never had such fine fabric before."

"Wonderful, now it will be used by someone who will appreciate it."

"I will indeed." Sybilla placed the silk reverently in her coffer, then settled on her pallet as Melisende called lights out.

~ *Chapter 19* ~

ALIX STAYED UNDER THE covers as long as possible to escape the chill of the room, but eventually she had to get dressed. The sun peeked through the windowpane, diffusing golden beams of light that spread across the floor as she hastily pulled on her clothes. She went over to the window, the rising sun warming her as she watched the world wake up.

Deep voices and laughter emanated from the stables. Saddled horses stamped restlessly, their metal bridles jangling. Geoff and some of his men were in the courtyard and she wondered if they were leaving, but then a groomsman led Richard's steed out as well. Richard appeared with a falcon on his arm and handed the bird of prey to his squire, the boy's forearm protected by a covering. Richard laughed at something Geoff said, and clapped him on the shoulder. The men mounted their horses and rode off. *Happy hunting.*

Melisende sent Alix to the kitchen to polish the lanterns since they were entertaining royal guests. The cooks gossiped and chattered while they prepared venison, chicken, and vegetables.

"I've heard that the Duke might leave for the King's Christ's Mass court. Is this true?" Emma asked as she expertly chopped legumes.

Alix nodded as she scrubbed a discolored mark on the lantern. "He is expected to attend, and I doubt his father would accept his refusal."

"How exciting it will be! I'm sure they'll have music, dancing, and feasting. I would love to see the ladies in their finest dresses and beautiful jewels."

Emma's wistful tone echoed Alix's sentiments. Richard had offered her the opportunity to meet his father, the King of England, and his rebellious brothers, Geoffrey and Hal. Every fiber of her being pulled at her to go, but her presence at Richard's side would draw notice. This Christ's Mass court would prove to be a pivotal event in Richard's life. He could ill afford to divide his attention between shielding her from unwanted gossip and his father's agenda. She wouldn't risk it.

Alix wiped sweat from her brow as the heat in the kitchen rose. The strong odor of the gritty polish permeated the room and mixed unpleasantly with the aroma of food cooking. She hastened to finish her chores and once done headed outside to get some fresh air.

The soft breeze caressed her skin and starlings flitted from branch to branch as she took the path to the copse of trees on the hill, which afforded her a view of the town. This particular spot was also in direct view of the path Richard would take back to the palace. She leaned against a tree and looked past the town to where the vast forest merged with misty green hills rising in the distance. Her gaze was captured by a small dark smudge cresting a hill. The mass grew nearer, and she could make out figures on horseback. Hoofbeats thundering on the path echoed louder. As the men passed below, Richard talked and gestured animatedly with Geoff, indicating a fruitful hunting expedition.

After they entered the courtyard, she stood and collected her cloak from the ground. Shaking off the dirt and leaves, she wrapped it around her shoulders, then headed down the hill and turned the opposite way.

She had rounded the bend on the far side of the building when footsteps crunched on the gravel path behind her. "Richard what...?" He pulled her to him and kissed her.

"What did I do to deserve this?"

He laughed. "Do I need a reason?"

"Being the Duke, I suppose not. How did you know I was here?"

"I like to keep an eye on you to make sure you're not getting into trouble."

"Well, that doesn't sound stalkerish at all." He looked at her quizzically. "Never mind. I'd better get back. Don't you have guests to entertain?"

He nodded. "Geoff, one of my father's products from an illegitimate encounter."

"That's not a very kind description. It's not as though Henry was married to your mother at the time Geoff was born. Why do you dislike him so?"

"It's more distrust than anything. Being the son of a king, even though illegitimate, has many benefits. He has always supported our father and he's very ambitious."

"He doesn't seem to plan rebellions against you like your full brothers."

"True, but he schemes in other ways." Richard caressed Alix's cheek and tucked her hair behind her ear. "He came with a message from Father regarding Caen. Have you given any more thought to joining me?"

She gave him a steady look. "I've thought on it, and I really don't think I should. You're already at odds with your family. Gossip concerning your relationship with me and the speculation of what I am, or am not to you, will spread like wildfire. I don't want you caught in the fall-out. Surely, my presence would anger Hal's wife, as you are betrothed to her sister. You don't need any additional problems."

"Alix, we've discussed this. I'm assuming you think I consider you my whore, but I've never thought of you in those terms." The curl of his lip told her he wasn't pleased with her obviously thinking of herself as so lowly, yet again.

"You might not, but everyone else will. Most already do, but I endure it here because there are those that know we are genuinely fond of each other, so it's tolerable. In Caen, I will be a novelty, a worthy subject for malicious slander. I don't expect you to understand. I just can't accept being thought of only as your bedmate."

He swore under his breath, turned and left, his swift retreating footsteps crunching on the gravel path.

He'd offered her the opportunity of a lifetime, but at what cost? She was certain that the historians would note her presence and write her into the annals of history. Her stomach clenched in shame as she imagined people would know her only as Richard's whore, but her greatest fear was that she would change history.

Her heart ached at the thought of leaving Richard, but once again she was forced to face the truth. She didn't belong there. Could she return to her own time and live a life without him? A cold gust of wind made her shiver and she was shocked to see that the sun was much lower in the sky than she had anticipated. Shadows from the trees stretched long and tall across the path.

"Why must you always antagonize him, Alix?"

She whirled around to see André.

"Well, hello to you, too. Where did you come from?"

"When Richard returned angry, I came to see what the cause was, and I found you."

"You always assume I'm the one at fault," she chided him. "I don't want to put you in the middle of our problems."

"Normally I would agree, but not in this case. He's furious with you. What happened?"

She shrugged. "I told him I wouldn't accompany him to Caen on the grounds that his family wouldn't want to meet his whore."

André looked at her shocked. "You're nothing of the sort, Alix. Don't you know that?"

She raised her eyebrow. "There's no suitable label for what I am to him, so 'whore' is going to be the term others rest upon, and you know it. Richard ought to attend with someone who is more fitting than I. Maybe he should have gotten off his arse and married Alys. Then he wouldn't have this problem."

"Jesu, that's the last thing he needs." André smiled. "I'm not going to tell you what to do, but I have seen a difference in him for the better since you've been here. I think you ought to reconsider and I suggest you do so soon. This is not an invitation Richard extended lightly." Alix shot him a skeptical glare and let out a frustrated sigh.

"I see that my words have fallen on deaf ears. You're an impossible woman." Shaking his head, André turned and strode off.

She shuffled back to the castle, deep in thought over André's words and found herself at the top of the stairs, peering down the hallway toward Richard's chambers. She began to doubt the wisdom of André's advice. Even if she didn't travel to Caen, she still needed to make amends with Richard. She knocked on his door and held her breath, praying he wasn't within.

"Enter."

She moved past the squire and met Richard's gaze. He looked at her in cold silence and crossed his arms, as he waited for her to speak.

"I can't do this anymore, Richard. I'm tired of always fighting with you. I apologize for my earlier words."

He inclined his head indicating his acceptance, his eyes still hard.

"I'm sure at times you wish I was someone who was more compliant and less antagonistic." Alix looked past him toward the windows and waited for him to agree.

"God's bones, Alix, do you think that's what I want? A woman who doesn't speak her mind, who never takes me to task for things I've done, and generally makes life less interesting?"

"You must get tired of all the bickering. You have enough family issues without my adding to them."

"I have to admit I've never argued so much with a woman in my life, except possibly my mother."

Alix smiled wryly. "I'm not very good at keeping my opinions to myself."

"Nor do I want you to. You challenge me and make me view things differently. God knows I'm not the easiest person to be with."

"I am in complete agreement with you there."

His guffaw echoed in the room. "Truce?"

She wanted nothing more than to be by his side at his father's court, but it could be treacherous for both of them. "So where does that leave us? Does the invitation to Caen still stand?" Her tone was cautious, on one hand hoping he had changed his mind and on the other hand praying he still wanted her to go.

"Yes, most assuredly it does."

She took a deep breath and looked him in the eye. "Then, it would be my honor to accompany you."

"Was it that difficult to make this decision?"

"To be with you, no. To be subject to what your family will think of me, yes. To them I will merely be your servant who happens to be intimate with you."

"I've always kept my affairs private. My family doesn't even know who my son's mother is. The fact that I invited you should tell you something. The only person who is troubled by this is you."

A knock sounded on the door and a squire opened it to allow the servants entrance. Richard motioned for them to place the dishes on the table, then after he dismissed them, he filled two plates and carried them to the window seat.

"You have a perfectly good table, you know. Why don't we use that?" she teased.

He chuckled. "I prefer sitting over here actually. It is more comfortable."

"Tell me about the hunt. Were you successful?"

"You should have seen it." His face lit up. "My gyrfalcon is still young, but she is strong and fast. When she attacked the dove, it was a perfect kill."

Alix nodded, not sure what to say. She wasn't an enthusiastic fan of hunting and setting a bird to kill another seemed more like cannibalism than true sport. It was a raptor's method of hunting.

"You don't seem too impressed. Have you ever seen a gyrfalcon chase its prey? It's quite a magnificent sight."

"They are beautiful birds and I would like to see yours someday."

"Good, you need to become more knowledgeable about court life."

"Why is that, exactly? Does everything about me shout commoner?"

"Your speech is unusual, to say the least. It has its charm, and I quite like it, but you must not draw attention to yourself. You must realize that life here is very different from my father's court. There will be many highborn guests in attendance. How you behave will be a direct reflection on me."

"If it's going to be that much of an issue, I can stay here."

"Alix, hear me out before you jump to conclusions. Jesu, you're almost as bad as Hal in that respect! You two should get along very well."

She sighed. "What must I do?"

"First of all, behave as if you are a lady. Don't associate with the servants, as they are beneath you."

"But I am a servant."

Richard blew out a long sigh. "Second, and more important, never wander off on your own. I don't trust my brothers, or anyone else in that court. If they find you alone, who knows what lies they will tell or what you might say in return."

"True. I might divulge more information than I ought to. This is a bit overwhelming." She slumped back against the wall.

He put his plate aside and leaned forward to wrap his arms around her. "You'll be fine. Just stay close to me and I will not let anything happen to you, I promise."

* ~ * ~ *

The next day, Geoff and his men continued on their way to Caen. Alix was amused to see relief on Melisende's face as she sent the girls upstairs. Although entertaining royalty was an honor, it must also be exhausting. Alix went to her pallet and opened her coffer to pull out the fabrics that Richard had given her to see if there was anything suitable for a royal court. Finding only wool and linen, she closed the lid and collapsed despondently on it.

"Richard informed me that you'll spend Christmas with him in Caen. I can't even begin to imagine what festivities and entertainment will be offered." Melisende sat next to her. "You should be more excited, as this is an incredible opportunity to visit King Henry's court and meet the King himself."

Alix nodded and pursed her lips, wishing she hadn't agreed to this debacle. "They're going to detest me, Melisende." Alix moaned and put her head on Melisende's shoulder. "They will see me only as Richard's bedmate."

"Don't think that way. He invited you. He would never do that if you were merely his bedmate."

"He keeps telling me that, but I have misgivings. I know I will act inappropriately and embarrass him. I should stay here."

"Nonsense. Now show me what dresses and fabrics you have."

Alix laid out every item of clothing she possessed, and Melisende frowned, looking at the pile of material on the bed. "Didn't you have some silk? That would be perfect for the court."

"I gave it to Sybilla."

"Whatever for?"

"I wasn't planning on using it, and I figured she would get more out of it than I would."

"We will need to purchase more silk to make a dress, and we can embroider your other dresses to embellish them. Knowing Richard, he and his men are going to ride fast and make few stops, so you will need a riding dress. I think we can convert your original dress and perhaps one other."

Recalling her first ride to the town of Poitiers with Rob, Alix opened her coffer and pulled out her leggings and Richard's shirt. "Will these do? I can wear the leggings and the shirt is long enough to cover my legs to mid-thigh."

Melisende looked shocked. "Why on earth do you have one of Richard's shirts? And what on earth is that other material? Oh, never mind, I don't want to know." Alix grinned at Sybilla who had come over in time to hear Melisende's words. "That isn't proper, Alix. A lady never shows her legs to a gentleman!"

Alix sank down on the bed, her face in her hands. "God, this is a mistake. I'm going to tell him I'm staying here."

"Don't worry, dear, we'll figure out something."

"I'll return the silk to you, Alix, and we can make a dress from it." Sybilla's offer was sweet, but Alix heard the reluctance in her voice.

"No, that belongs to you now. I wouldn't dream of taking it back." Sybilla gave her a grateful smile. "Let's not talk about this anymore. I will tell Richard tonight that I am unable to join him, end of story."

Melisende looked disappointed. "Are you positive?"

"Yes, it's for the best. I'm sure he will be fine with my decision."

Alix refolded the clothes and placed them back in her coffer. Her pouch lay nearby and she frowned at the thought of the brooch within. Maybe her choice to stay in Poitiers was a blessing in disguise. She could work on figuring out how to return home. If she succeeded in Richard's absence, her disappearance most likely wouldn't be remarked upon. She only hoped Richard would accept her decision.

* ~ * ~ *

"I've decided to stay in Poitiers when you travel to Caen." Alix tipped up her chin, announcing confidently from her seat next to Richard on the settee in his chambers.

He glared at her. "What is your basis for this change?"

"You're going to have too many conflicts to handle and the last thing you need is to worry about whether or not I'm behaving properly."

"That's the reason? Your concern for my state of mind?"

She shrugged and nodded. "There's no other reason?" She shook her head looking everywhere except at him.

"Alix, tell me what it is that's truly bothering you this time."

She sighed. "I don't have anything to wear that is suitable for court."

He stared at her in astonishment. "You don't wish to go because you have nothing to wear? God's bones, I will never understand women! I gave you fabrics. You should have plenty of choices."

"But the court ladies will be impeccably dressed, especially your brothers' wives, and they will know that I'm not of their social class merely by how I'm dressed. My fear of them thinking I'm beneath them will be magnified if I show up wearing one of my woolen dresses."

He laughed. "I believe that will be the least of your worries."

"What is that supposed to mean?"

He held his hands up in apology. "I just meant that, knowing you, my family dynamics will be more of a concern than fashion."

"You obviously don't understand women and fashion, Richard. We dress to impress other women."

"This is why I never get involved with women. Your gender is too difficult to comprehend."

"*My* gender?" Alix pressed her hand to her chest. "With that attitude, however is it you are still unmarried, Your Grace?"

He laughed at her sarcasm. "I don't think I would excel at marriage. I'm not very good at compromise."

"You don't say."

He poured some wine for them and handed her a cup. "What do you need in order to feel presentable at court?"

"I need some nice fabric. I used the linen you gifted me to make cold compresses for the girls when they were sick. All I have left is the wool and that isn't luxurious enough."

"I remember gifting you some silk."

"Oh, right." She had hoped he had forgotten that.

"What do you mean by that?"

"I gave it to someone else."

He choked on his wine. "You gave it away? That was for your own use."

"I wasn't planning on using it, and it was mine to give away." He looked at her speechlessly. "I'm sorry, I didn't think it would be an issue."

"Alix, that material wasn't inexpensive. May I ask to whom you gave it?"

"It's none of your concern, but it was Sybilla, if you must know."

He sighed heavily. "Hence, you need more silk. Anything else?"

"I was thinking about the journey. You and your men will probably make very few stops on the ride to Caen. I don't wish to be a burden and slow you down. I thought if I modified my clothing it would make it easier for me to ride."

He nodded. "Let me know what you require and I will procure it."

"It would be easier if I took care of it myself, since I know what I'm looking for."

He gave her a measured look. "This requires money, I presume?"

"Of course. Nothing is ever free." She smirked.

"I'll instruct Melisende to give you enough on the morrow. I plan to leave within a fortnight."

"How long does it take to get there?"

"Most likely a half week of hard riding. We're traveling light, so don't bring every article of clothing you own."

"I only have three dresses as it is." Her Faire costume was much too thin to wear in the wintertime. She wore her woolen dresses almost daily, but the forest green dress Richard had gifted her was far too extravagant for common use. "You are sure you want me to come with you? I am fine staying here."

"We have spent too much time arguing about this. You are coming with me." The look on his face made it clear this was the last time they would discuss this.

She nodded in assent. "I hope you don't regret this."

He leveled a look at her. "Don't make me."

A few days later, she entered her room to find some beautiful crimson silk neatly folded on her bed. Sybilla was bouncing up and down waiting for her to see it.

"Alix, look what Richard gave you! It's exquisite. This will be lovely on you!"

"Ask and you shall receive." Alix picked up the shimmering fabric. Only royalty and the very wealthy wore crimson, since the dye to produce the color was expensive. The underlying meaning behind Richard's extravagant gift was one she couldn't ignore. "Will you help me make a dress that will rival the court women, Sybilla?"

"Yes. Maud can help, and I promise no one will be able to take their eyes off you."

"Excellent." Alix smiled. "Since we're riding to Caen, I need to pack light."

"Alix, don't forget, the style of the court also requires that you wear a veil," Sybilla pointed out.

"I'm aware of that, but I will be the only female going on this excursion, and I don't want to be a burden. I wish to be as inconspicuous as possible."

"What will you wear for traveling?"

"I have already sorted that out. God, Sybilla, I can't believe I agreed to this. Do you think it's a mistake?"

"Not at all. Obviously, he wants you with him. It's so romantic."

"I don't think romance is the reason. I think he wants to prove he's my liege and order me around."

"At least you get to spend Christ's Mass with him." A shadow crossed Sybilla's face.

"I'm so sorry." Of course, Rob would go to Caen as well. "Perhaps Richard will leave a few men behind to protect the palace."

"I hope so. Let's begin work on this dress." Sybilla took the silk from Alix. "We don't have much time."

The next two weeks passed in a whirlwind of activity. Alix located a seamstress in town and, after showing her the leggings, which earned her wide-eyed glances and mutterings, she ordered two more pairs made of wool, as well as some shirts. She also commissioned a cobbler to make her some calf-high leather boots, so she would have sturdy footwear instead of the flimsy shoes she wore daily.

It occurred to Alix that she would probably ride on her own. Although she had ridden quite a bit when younger, it had been years and she wasn't sure if she was proficient enough for a long trip. Not willing to burden Richard with another problem, she sought out Rob instead. After several days of refresher courses, she was confident she could make the journey without too much trouble, although she would never gain the riding proficiency of the knights.

She gasped with delight when Sybilla and Maud showed her the finished silk dress. The crimson hue caught the flickering light from the fire, reflecting the rich reds and purples from the flames. They'd worked their magic, embroidering the bodice and bottom of the skirt with intricate designs in gold thread. The sleeves were long, fitted at the elbow and flared gently at her wrists.

"Oh, my goodness, this is so beautiful. I have never seen anything like it. Thank you so much," she exclaimed hugging them both.

"You will be the most beautiful lady there," Maud beamed.

"Perhaps not, but at least I will have the most exquisite dress. I don't know how to thank you."

The girls smiled, pleased, and soon their talk turned to the court and what the other ladies might wear, especially the Young King's wife.

"I've heard that Marguerite is quite pretty and the Young King is the fairest of all the brothers." The starry-eyed look on Maud's face was endearing.

"Then he must be very striking indeed, to outshine the Duke." The first time she'd crossed paths with Richard, he seemed every bit as handsome and powerful as Thor, the Norse god of thunder.

The chatter continued, and Alix chimed in on occasion, but the mention of Hal reminded her of what Richard would face in Caen. The bubbly lightness faded and her chest constricted until she couldn't draw a full breath.

Trying to hide her apprehension, she sorted through the clothing piled on her pallet. The amount of material that encompassed the crimson silk, the green dress, and her indigo blue woolen dress wouldn't fit into anything but a large suitcase. She sank to the floor, unwilling to wrinkle the garments on the bed, and continued to stare at them as if by magic they would fold and fit into a small rucksack.

Sybilla appeared behind her. "May I help?"

"Can you make this shrink or magically ship it to Caen?" Alix waved her hand over the pile.

Sybilla laughed. "This is not impossible. Come. First, fold the clothes."

"How do people travel by horse and manage to take any belongings with them?"

"We use carts, especially when women are traveling," Sybilla explained. "But in this case, traveling with a band of only men, I wouldn't imagine they will bring one."

"I have one bag that I can cram some dresses in, but I need more."

"Let's ask the girls. I'm sure someone must have something you can use." They borrowed another bag and soon, all her clothes were packed, although a bit crushed.

The night before departing, Alix declined to stay with Richard, wanting to spend time with Maud and Sybilla before she left. They made her promise to write them with all the news of court.

"I can't imagine we'll be gone all that long, possibly only two weeks. You won't even have time to miss me."

"Alix, you will be gone for at least a month, if not longer, depending on whether Richard decides to return here or not." Maud nodded in agreement. "You didn't realize that?"

"No. Truly? I don't want to be gone for too long. I suppose I can come back if he and his men go elsewhere."

Sybilla gave her a troubled look. "You can't travel by yourself. You must be accompanied by a chaperone, preferably a man."

"It's not safe for anyone to ride alone, especially a woman." Maud circled a finger around one of her blonde ringlets.

"I guess I'll have to see what happens. I hate being dependent on others," Alix said.

"There are worse people to be dependent upon." Melisende arrived just in time to hear Alix's words.

"Are there? I highly doubt that."

Melisende shook her head. "To bed with you all. It's late and Alix needs her sleep."

"Yes, Mother." Alix smiled, and Melisende playfully swatted at her.

∼∼*

Sleep proved elusive. Her mind spun with the excitement of the trip, but she managed to nod off for a couple of hours before the sun rose. After the morning service, she changed into a wool shirt and her original pair of leggings, to save the newer ones for the arrival in Caen. She pulled on her boots, and asked Sybilla's opinion.

Sybilla studied her. "I don't know what to say. You look unusual, but it suits you. Whatever you call those," she gestured to her snug leggings, "are flattering on you. Most pants are loose fitting, but the style you created with those new ones accentuates your figure. I also like your knee-high boots. They are definitely a change from the ankle boots we normally wear."

"No man, or woman for that matter, will be able to take their eyes off of you." Maud crossed her arms. With eyebrows raised, she studied Alix's outfit. "You look very dashing, if that term can be applied to a woman."

Alix smiled and picked up her cloak. She carefully stowed her pouch containing the brooch into one of the sacks. She wished she could leave the piece of jewelry behind, but one day she would have to return to her own time and she dared not leave it unprotected.

Voices echoed from the courtyard below and she hurried to the window to peer out. Groomsmen readied the steeds, and pageboys and squires hurried about stowing sacks on packhorses.

"I guess I'd better go down or Richard will leave me behind." Alix grabbed one sack of clothes and Sybilla took the other, ostensibly to help, but Alix knew she wanted to say goodbye to Rob. Maud joined them as they descended the stairs. When would she return if ever? The thought of never seeing her friends again sent a twinge of sadness through her, and she resolved that she must return with or without Richard.

Alix peered over the crowd of squires and knights readying their horses, searching for Richard. The girls followed but stopped as Richard approached.

"Have you changed your mind?" he demanded.

"No, I'm ready to go." Alix frowned, confused by his accusation.

"Then where are your trunks?"

"I don't have any. Here, catch!" She tossed him her sack, followed soon after by the one Sybilla had carried down. He caught both and stared in astonishment at them.

"All of your clothes are in here?"

"I don't have the luxury of traveling like royalty. I packed light," Alix teased.

With one sack in each arm he heaved them up much like a weightlifter might do. "I must admit, I'm impressed. Some of my knights have more belongings than you do." He handed her bags to his page who tied them to one of the packhorses' saddles as she turned to say goodbye to Maud.

"I'm going to miss you so much, Alix. Please don't stay away too long," Maud sniffed.

"I'll try not to. Hopefully, we will return soon after the New Year." She hugged her friend tightly.

Melisende appeared behind her. "Have a good journey, Alix, and don't get into trouble." Her admonishment rang true, as this very subject had been on Alix's mind frequently since she'd agreed to attend the Christ's Mass court.

Laughing, Alix hugged her. "I will be on my best behavior, I promise."

"I am going to miss you, girl." Melisende discreetly wiped at her eyes.

"Now, don't cry or I'll follow suit."

Sybilla had said her goodbyes to Rob and came over to hug Alix. "I can't believe you're leaving. I already miss you."

"Me, too. Take care of yourself and I'll see you soon."

Richard gave last minute instructions to Melisende and Alix didn't want to intrude on their conversation, so she went to where Richard's horse stood. She scratched the horse's forehead and he nuzzled her affectionately.

Richard nodded to Melisende and strode to her. "Alix, this is Estèla. She is an excellent horse. Calm, yet fast." Richard stroked the horse's nose as he explained and Estèla nickered.

"Let me help you up."

She removed her cloak and held it out. "Hold this."

"My God, woman! Put some more clothes on!" At his outburst, the knights and squires within hearing distance all turned to see what the commotion was.

"What?" Alix shrugged. "I have clothes on."

Richard's eyes narrowed. His jaw clenched. "Alix, go upstairs and change immediately!"

"I think she looks fine," André stated as he came up behind Richard. "Let her wear it. I would much rather look at her than the dull scenery."

"That's what I am worried about." Richard's snarl made André chuckle.

"This is comfortable. How am I supposed to ride hard in a dress?" She raised her arms wide and turned toward the others near her. "Do any of you here have a problem with me dressed in this manner?" The multitude of expressions on their faces was priceless. "Well?" Alix glanced around. "I'm waiting for an answer." One by one the men shook their heads. Many tried to hide their amusement by covering their mouths.

"There. It's decided. If I'm not an embarrassment to your men, then I shouldn't be to you. Besides," she lowered her voice, "you have seen much more than this before." She batted her eyelashes.

He came closer, and his warm breath stirred her hair. "You can keep that on. Just be mindful that you look very desirable in those clothes and I don't want my men getting any ideas about you."

"I think I've proven I can protect myself."

"You have indeed." Richard chuckled. "Here." He stooped in front of her, lacing his fingers together to give her a boost up. Once she was astride her horse, he handed her cloak back. She draped it over her shoulders, took the reins in her hands, and sat straight in the saddle, thankful that women rode astride and not side-saddle.

~ *Chapter 20* ~

THE MID-MORNING AIR WAS cool, but the sun burned brightly and the wind was still, creating a perfect day. They made quite good time on the well-traveled road, accompanied by the rhythmic clumping of hooves, jangle of metal, and men's low voices. Richard stopped after several hours on the pretense of resting the horses, but Alix knew better.

She dismounted and joined him where he was tending his horse. "Don't stop on my account. I don't expect any favoritism."

"I didn't stop for you."

She rolled her eyes at his unconvincing reply. "I'm fine. If I need to rest, I'll tell you. You make me feel like a weak woman who can't keep up with the men." Alix tethered Estèla next to Richard's steed, relieved to be able to stretch her legs but she'd never let Richard know that.

"Alix, these men live in the saddle. They are used to long hours of riding and you are not. I'm trying to make this journey easier for you."

"I understand, but I am stronger than I look. Are we camping out tonight?"

"Yes, then tomorrow we'll stay in Saumur. My father has a castle there. It's too far a ride for your first day."

"What time will we make camp?"

"About an hour before nightfall."

Alix moved closer. "I do appreciate your concern, but if we keep stopping, we won't make Saumur by tomorrow night." She lowered her head and grasped his arm. "Do you agree?"

He covered her hand with his and nodded.

"Good. If I need to rest, I promise I'll tell you."

Richard stared off into the distance but the pressure on her hand from his told her he understood.

After watering the horses and allowing them to graze, they ate a quick lunch of cold meat and bread, then continued. The sun slowly sank toward the horizon streaking the cloudy sky in orange and red. Long shadows stretched across the road and Alix shivered in her cloak, as the wind picked up and the temperature fell.

Before it became too dark to see, Richard ordered his men to halt and make camp. Most of the men opted to sleep on blankets on the ground, but the Duke instructed his squires to set up his tent. A campfire barely kept the cold at bay, and after a quick meal, Richard sent Alix into the tent. Exhausted and chilled she pulled the fur blankets over her and in minutes was asleep.

* ~ * ~ *

Men's voices awakened Alix and she rolled over, grimacing as she massaged her aching back. She stood and stretched to increase the blood flow into her muscles. She had no intention of letting anyone know the degree of soreness her screaming body was experiencing. At the entrance to the tent she stretched one more time and pasted on a brilliant smile. With one yank she lifted the tent flap and stepped out.

After breaking their fast with bread and cheese, they continued on their journey. Hours later the winding, tree-lined dirt road curved sharply and the town of Saumur appeared in the distance. The chateau stood high up on a hill, and Alix stared in awe as they rode closer. The massive, square building had four octagonal towers, one forming each corner, and rose high above the stone wall that surrounded it.

"Your father has excellent taste in castles. It looks like something out of a dream."

Richard looked at her in agreement. "Father's castles are magnificent. Does my mother's palace in Poitiers pale in comparison, then?"

"Not at all. I do love that palace; they are just so different architecturally."

They rode to the tall, wooden outer wall, which protected the inner yard and castle. The gatemen recognized the Duke's standard and let them in immediately. The castellan appeared and apologized that they hadn't prepared accommodations, as they weren't aware of the Duke's visit.

Richard waved away his apology. "Whatever is available will suffice. We are only staying the night. All I require is someone to tend the horses, food for me and my men and a place to sleep."

"That can be arranged, Your Grace. Please follow me."

The men dismounted and gave their horses to the castle groomsmen. Alix followed suit and trailed Richard into the castle. As she did, the castellan looked shocked.

"Your Grace, we don't have rooms ready for your, er, lady."

"She will stay in my chambers." The corner of Richard's mouth pulled up in a smirk in response to the surprise in the castellan's eyes.

"Must you initiate gossip the minute we arrive?" Alix grumbled.

Richard laughed. "I like to make an entrance, and I want him to know that you are with me and will accordingly be treated with courtesy."

Alix found it hard to keep up with Richard. Several times she stopped to admire the interior architecture and had to run to catch up. The chamber door that Richard stopped in front of swung open to reveal a small but comfortable room. "Do I have time to bathe or is it too inconvenient?" She opened her bags to choose a dress.

"I'll have my page prepare it. I might join you if you don't mind?" A wicked smile pulled up the corner of his mouth.

"As tempting as that sounds, I fear we would never make it to supper. I would feel guilty if you starved on my account. Care to postpone it?"

"That probably would be for the best." He went to the door to call the boy while she gathered her clothes.

In the dining hall, Alix found herself between Richard and Georges. She wrung her hands and shifted in her seat. Ever since the incident, she'd felt uncomfortable around him. "I never had the chance to apologize for that night. I, uh…"

"The night you bested me?"

Alix laughed. "Yes, I overreacted. I know you were only doing your job, and I'm sorry." He nodded in acceptance. She sighed, feeling more relaxed now that she had cleared the air between them.

The servants carried out platters of food and filled the tables with various dishes. The cooks had done their best with no warning and Alix was surprised with the outcome, although in truth she was hungry enough to eat anything. Richard had been conversing with André, but once the platters were before them, he made sure she had the choicest morsels. It felt strange being at Richard's side, for this was the first time they'd ever sat together in public.

"Miss?" Georges addressed her in a muffled tone. "How did you manage to overcome me that night?"

"I was taught a special type of fighting. When you grabbed me, I was able to get you off balance by forcing you to use one leg and then it was easy to throw you to the ground."

"Do people use this to fight? It doesn't seem very practical."

"Not really. In ancient times, samurai warriors from Asia used this style in combat. Now there are students of the martial arts and they learn different moves to attain higher levels of proficiency."

"So, this fighting technique is more suited to hand-to-hand combat?" Richard asked, his voice filled with interest.

"Yes," Alix replied, turning toward him, unaware he had been listening to the conversation. "Or combat where short weapons are used. It wouldn't be useful against a knight, of course, because knights fight with swords, but if the knight were unhorsed and weaponless, it would be a very effective way to defeat your opponent."

"Perhaps you might show me some of the techniques?" Georges asked.

"Only if you show me how to handle a sword." The thought of learning the art of sword fighting from an actual Medieval knight sent chills down her spine.

Richard laughed. "I don't think that's a good idea."

"Why not? Do you think I am incapable of holding a sword?"

"Not at all. You have already proven yourself a good fighter. I'm protecting my men."

Georges sputtered, his mouth full of food, and almost choked in the process. Once he finished swallowing, his howl of laughter echoed off the stone walls.

Richard had a point, but she didn't want to lose the chance to learn to fight from one of 'King Richard's knights of the realm'.

She waved Richard away. "Don't mind him, Georges. I still wish to learn."

"Well, Your Grace? I'm happy to teach her, but it's your decision." Richard agreed by way of a non-committal shoulder shrug.

"It's decided then!" Alix beamed.

When the tables had been cleared, Alix sensed the men's desire to relax and flirt with the serving girls. She didn't want her presence to put a damper on the potential entertainment for the evening, so she turned and bid Richard good night.

"You're leaving?" he asked in surprise.

"Yes. I'm exhausted and I'm sure we will be off early tomorrow." She bid Georges good night and as soon as she stood all of the men rose. She curtsied and nodded. As she passed André, he held out his hand to stop her. "You did very well the last two days." His compliment warmed her heart. She respected André's opinion and was relieved she hadn't been a burden to the men.

"Thank you." She nodded and then continued on her way. She hurried to prepare for bed. The day's ride had tired her more than she had expected, and although she would never admit it to Richard, her already sore muscles were beginning to tighten and ache more. She knew the following day's journey wouldn't be pleasant.

* ~ * ~ *

Sitting up in bed, she bit her lip as her muscles screamed in protest. What she wouldn't give for two Tylenol. She always carried Tylenol so, why did she pick the day of Nottingham Faire to break her pattern? That small bottle would've easily fit in the pouch.

"Good morrow. I trust you slept well?" Richard stood, looking at a map spread out on the table.

"Morning. Whether or not it's good remains to be seen." She got out of bed and slowly made her way to her bags.

He glanced up at her, attempting to hide his grin. "I can ask the castellan if he has any salve for sore muscles."

"Go to hell. I will be fine."

"Alix, this is what I was trying to spare you, but you were so obstinate you couldn't see it."

"I hate it when you are right. Fortunately, that doesn't happen often." She took her clothes into the bathing room to change. Her abused muscles had stiffened during the night, and as she raised her arms to put her shirt on, her shoulders and back throbbed in protest. She carefully pulled on her leggings and grimaced as twinges in her lower back reminded her of the muscles she rarely used in such a manner.

"Where are we journeying to today?" She re-entered the room, kneading her shoulder.

"Tonight we'll stay in Le Mans, and the following night in Falaise. From there it's only nineteen miles to Caen."

"That sounds doable." She moved to the window to look out at the Loire River winding its way through the city, and the expanse of green forest and countryside that lay beyond. She could definitely get used to the views there, but was excited to see Caen, which helped motivate her for the long day ahead.

After a simple meal, the knights were ready to depart. As they rode out of the bailey, Alix gave one last longing glance back at the castle, wishing she had a camera to capture this moment that might never come again.

"I wish we could have stayed longer." Rob rode up next to her. "I'm sure you aren't in the best condition to travel today."

"I'm fine, really. Just a little sore." She tried to downplay her discomfort, but her wince as she shifted in her saddle surely gave her away. "I was admiring the architecture. I adore castles."

Rob snorted. "Most women do. Perhaps Richard will build you one."

"I should ask him. He built Clairvaux, so now he has experience. What's one more? He could hide me away in my very own castle and visit whenever he pleases."

Not a cloud marred the brilliant, blue sky, and the warmth from the sun held the cold at bay. Another perfect riding day. The calls of birds echoed through forests thick with evergreens and skeletal trees. Branches creaked and rubbed against each other in the wind, in a macabre dance. The road was wide and well-maintained, and Alix could enjoy the scenery instead of concentrating on her horse's footing.

When they reached Falaise two days later, she took care with her bath. She requested that her water was heated extra hot to help soothe her sore muscles and cleanse the dust that was caked on her skin and in her hair from the dusty ride. Richard's men had been vocal in discussing the beautiful women they expected to see in Caen when they arrived the next day, and she wanted to make a good impression. As she scoured dust and dirt from her skin with a cake of soap, she envisioned the people who would be at King Henry's court.

Butterflies fluttered in her stomach. The slightest mistake concerning her actions from tomorrow forward could have grievous consequences. She doubted as to whether she should attend, over and over in her mind, but it was too late now. In Poitiers, her relationship with Richard raised a brow or two, but was hardly tabloid fodder. Henry's court would be much different. She'd read accounts of this particular Christmas court and events that had occurred. Eyes would be upon her, and there was a real chance that her presence could be recorded by historians.

She stepped out of the bath and rubbed herself dry with a coarse towel. Picking up her clean shirt she put it on and hoped that when they arrived in Caen, she wouldn't smell like leather mixed with horses. Richard's invitation hadn't been extended lightly since he would be scrutinized by all who attended.

Those butterflies gave a little flutter and she began mentally preparing to keep herself in check and act like a lady from this moment on.

She dressed carefully the following morning, braiding her thick hair, which now hung well below her shoulders, and tugged on her new wool leggings and beige shirt.

The dense forest that had been their constant companion when they departed Falaise thinned until they were riding through the countryside dotted with small, wooden houses and patchwork fields. Warblers and sparrows flitted by as the entourage rode past low bushes. As they approached the bustling city of Caen, Alix's heart pounded and her hands trembled. Her thighs tensed and Estèla skittered sideways at the change in pressure. The town looked much like Poitiers, although much larger. The aroma of wood fires mixed with animal offal permeated the air. Single-story wooden structures lined the dirt roads and townspeople perused the vendors' carts positioned near the heavily trafficked road that entered the town. Her breathing quickened as Richard led the way to the castle that was visible on its vantage point high above the city, and she blew out hard to help relieve the building stress.

Rob had ridden next to her most of the journey, but Richard slowed down and motioned for Rob to go ahead. She knew all too well that Richard should be in the lead as they entered the town. She appreciated his gallant gesture and tried to relax the death-grip she had on the reins.

"We're almost there," he encouraged her.

The closer they rode, the faster her heart pounded. She brushed wind-blown hair out of her eyes and focused her attention on the path. Secretly she wished they were still in Poitiers, where life had become comfortable and familiar.

Before them was a long, wooden bridge crossing the moat that surrounded the outermost wall of the castle. The horses' hooves clattered on the wooden planks as they crossed the sluggish, dark water. A rotten stench wafted from the murky depths and Alix wrinkled her nose. They rode through a large gate into the courtyard and Alix's mouth fell open as she gaped at the imposing Norman tower dominating the interior. Groomsmen appeared to take the horses' reins, and the squires removed their belongings. Richard wrapped his hands gently around Alix's waist and carefully helped her down. He put his hands on her shoulders. "Are you ready?" She inhaled and nodded.

They made their way toward a large, rectangular stone building. Her heart hammered and her stomach churned as she prepared to meet the most famous figures in Medieval history.

~ *Chapter 21* ~

ONE OF THE KNIGHTS pushed open the heavy, wooden door and held it for Richard and Alix. Richard placed his hand on the small of her back and guided her in. All eyes turned toward them, and the deafening noise of voices talking over each other grew silent. As they ventured further into the hall, murmuring began anew.

Alix looked around the massive entry that was filled with what seemed like hundreds of people. The roar of the fire at the end of the room amplified the warmth of the bodies all around her, chasing away the damp chill of their long journey. Knights, lords, and ladies stood in groups or lined the long trestle tables that filled the room. Lanterns hung from the rafters and flames flickering in wall sconces provided light as the darkness outside grew.

"God's bones, Richard," she whispered. "What have you gotten me into now?"

"Come." Richard offered her his hand and she grabbed it as if it were a lifeline. Her nails dug into his palm and he winced in pain.

"I'm so sorry." She relaxed her grip. He lifted her hand to his lips, and Alix overheard one of the ladies murmur to another about how chivalrous and handsome the Duke was.

He led her down the center of the hall toward the high table where his family, with the exception of Henry's queen, Eleanor, waited. Hurrying to keep up with his long stride, her cloak billowed out behind her. The men looked at her in appreciation while the women glared. She fixed her gaze on the floor and only looked up when Richard stopped.

He first greeted his sister Matilda, a very slender woman with long, red-gold hair like Richard's and her husband Heinrich, a bear of a man with dark hair and neatly-trimmed beard. Richard announced their names for Alix's benefit, then motioned to a small girl of about nine and a boy several years younger who crouched in an alcove, their dark heads bent close together.

"Those are Matilda's children, Richenza and Otto." He then acknowledged Constance, Geoffrey's wife and Marguerite, Hal's queen. The latter looked at Alix then glanced quickly away, her eyes moving to a tall man with golden hair and an air of self-assurance. Richard turned to the handsome man and greeted his brother without enthusiasm. "Hal."

"Richard." The tone of his response was flat, as he sat at the table next to his blonde, blue-eyed wife.

Richard spoke in a precise manner to Geoffrey, who stood near the window with his wife Constance, whose long, brunette hair hung well past her waist. Her dark eyes narrowed as she stared at Alix. Geoffrey nodded to Richard and brushed his dark-blond hair out of his eyes as he appraised Alix.

Alix curtsied to his brothers, openly returned Geoffrey's curious gaze, and then turned her attention to the stocky red-haired man seated in front of her.

"Father, I wish to present Alixandra."

She curtsied deeply to him. "Your Grace."

If her arrival surprised the King, he masked it well. "Alixandra, welcome." Henry's piercing blue stare fixed upon her, and then he motioned to some empty seats.

"I'm surprised you made the time to join us," Hal said, his sneer and disdainful glance alighting on Alix.

Richard looked at his brother. Alix sensed that a scathing remark was on the tip of his tongue. The last thing she wanted was for a scene to erupt so soon after their arrival, so she put a deterring hand on his arm and shook her head. Alix was aware that Geoffrey had been following their exchange, and when Richard remained silent, the weight of his attentive gaze focused upon her.

"We haven't had time to change from our journey, and I daresay Alix would like to rest," Richard announced.

Alix gave him a vexed look, annoyed that he was using her as an excuse to postpone the interaction with his family.

"I expect to see you at supper." Henry's growl chilled Alix's blood. He dismissed them.

As they made their way to the door, Richard's half-brother Geoff moved forward to greet them.

"I'm glad you changed your mind and decided to come," he addressed Alix. "I don't believe we've been properly introduced."

"Geoff, this is Alixandra."

"I recall seeing you at Poitiers. Welcome." Geoff inclined his head.

"Thank you." She curtsied, unhappy that he remembered she was in Richard's employ.

"I trust we will see you downstairs again tonight?"

"I wouldn't dream of missing this familial show of solidarity." Richard looked Geoff in the eye, and steered Alix past him.

"You didn't have to be so short with him, Richard. I think you're as much at fault as Geoff for your poor relationship."

He pretended to be affronted. "Can you blame me for wanting to be alone with you, without being surrounded by my men?"

"Flattery will get you—"

"Everywhere I hope," Richard interrupted her.

Her heart flip-flopped at the suggestive look in his eyes. "That remains to be seen."

He laughed and slung his arm around her shoulders.

As they took their leave, the women's whispering echoed off the stone walls. The gossip had begun.

Their chambers were luxurious, and much like Richard's in Poitiers, there was a large wooden table surrounded by carved chairs. A fireplace took up most of one wall, and tapestries detailing intricate hunting scenes hung on the others. She entered the bedroom where a tall, ornate armoire stood next to the window. Warm fur blankets covered a curtained four-poster bed. Their bags had been stowed in a corner of the room next to the armoire.

Alix began to unpack, while Richard ordered his page to light a fire then prepare a bath. She carefully lifted out the crimson silk dress, shook out the wrinkles and hung it in the armoire, then unpacked and hung her green and indigo blue dresses, and the shirts and leggings she had brought with her.

Once his orders were carried out, Richard dismissed the boy, who bowed and left the room, closing the door behind him.

Richard pulled his shirt off and crossed to the steaming tub. Alix stared at his physique, relishing the fact that he was hers, at least for the time being. She gave him enough time to get into the bath, then she wandered over and stood in the doorway watching him.

"Are you going to just stand there, or make yourself useful?"

"I'm debating what I want to do to you." Fortunately, she was wearing her leggings and shirt so she managed to get undressed without help, and joined him in the bath. She sighed as she sank into the warm water. Although her muscles were not as sore as the first day, the dull aches reminded her of how much she had abused them.

"Turn around," she instructed him. Rubbing the soap briskly in her hands, she began to wash his back.

"I am capable of doing this myself."

"Fine then, if you want me to stop…"

"Pray, continue." His contented sigh filled the small chamber. As she lathered his chest, he caught her hands and pulled her to him, his desire obvious as he captured her lips with his.

* ~ * ~ *

Geoffrey turned as Hal bore down upon him, and grimaced as he recognized the furious look in his older brother's eyes.

"How dare Richard bring his whore to Father's court!" Hal growled. "There are more than enough women here of proper station that he could bed." He glanced at Marguerite. "Now I'm going to have to deal with my wife who is understandably upset since it's her sister who's betrothed to that miscreant!"

Geoffrey looked at him, irritated. As usual, Hal didn't see the bigger picture, the potential implication of Richard bringing his bedmate to court. "Our brother isn't married yet, so your lovely wife shouldn't worry her pretty head. What should concern us is *why* he brought that woman here openly."

"How could his bedmate possibly affect us?"

God help us, this is the next King of the Angevin empire. Geoffrey sighed at the thought. "Richard doesn't suffer fools gladly and he's given to suspicion, so how did she worm her way into his inner circle? It's possible that she's his spy and is privy to secrets in the French court or in the household of one of Aquitaine's rebellious nobles. She obviously has his implicit trust, which coming from Richard is high praise indeed. Secrets are quite often shared in bed and I, for one, am very interested in what Richard and Alixandra know about our plans."

Geoffrey left with Constance soon after, but his gut was in a knot. Would his and Hal's well-devised plan come to fruition?

As soon as they were away from prying eyes, Constance began her questioning. "Why do you think Richard brought that woman here? She's quite beautiful, but he's never paraded his conquests before. This one has the ability to sway him."

"Ah, you noticed that interaction as well. I'm not sure, love, but knowing Richard, he has his reasons, and I fear we are not going to like them."

* ~ * ~ *

Alix leaned near a lantern and took one last look in her small compact mirror. Deciding that she was presentable for court without the magic of modern-day cosmetics, she reached into her pouch, pulled out the two vials of oil, and added some drops to the inside of her wrists, mixing the two scents. She inhaled.

"Think this will do for court?" She pirouetted for Richard's inspection. She wore the green dress that Maud had embellished for her with delicate embroidered accents in dark blue. The rich color complemented her pale skin and coppery hair and enhanced her hazel eyes. She had asked Maud to take it in a bit so it would pack easier, so it was a snug fit. A decorative belt lay low on her hips and the skirt clung to her when she moved, accentuating her slenderness.

Richard's glance appraised her from head to toe. "You will best any lady here."

Pleased, she smiled, as she took his proffered arm and they left the room. Once outside, the chill of the air shocked her, and she wished her cloak hadn't been so travel-stained. Richard placed his arm around her, holding her close to his warm body as they hurried to the great hall. As soon as they entered, the whispers began. She was proud to be with Richard, who cut a dashing figure in his blue mantle and snug chausses, so she ignored the prying eyes and glaring stares as well as she could manage.

They approached the raised platform at the end of the hall where the royal family overlooked the festivities. She curtsied to Henry, then to the rest of his family, took her seat next to Richard and looked around the crowded hall. There must have been well over one thousand knights, squires, pages, nobles, and their wives and ladies-in-waiting in attendance. The din was thunderous. Platters of food covered the tables and flagons of wine flowed freely. The dishes in northern France were quite different than the ones she was accustomed to at the palace. Richard's lips curled at her indecisiveness about the selection of dishes before them. He pointed out different items such as meat pies filled with capon, salted herring, mutton smothered in gravy, as well as root vegetables. Before he placed an item on her plate, he gave her the opportunity to accept or refuse.

$$* \sim * \sim *$$

Hal's prowess in the jousting ring prompted him to regale everyone with stories of his recent victories at various tournaments. As the stories rang through the air, Henry watched Richard, surprised that he was so attentive to this girl. At first, he'd thought it an act, and expected his third son to become bored and shift his attention elsewhere, but as dinner progressed, he noted that Richard's interest in her never flagged.

Alixandra leaned over to say something to Richard, making him laugh, which reminded Henry of how he and Eleanor had been in the first years of marriage, whispering to each other and sharing secrets. Henry nodded and smiled at the appropriate times, as Hal continued his stories, but he was preoccupied with who this Alixandra was and why Richard had brought her to court.

After servants cleared the supper dishes, minstrels began to play a tune and dancers lined up below the royals' table. The noblewomen were dressed in richly-colored silk, the shimmery fabric reflecting the light from the lanterns as they circled their partners. After the dance ended, Henry stood, and the dancers bowed and curtsied to him. He nodded in acceptance, then requested his family's presence in his private sitting room off his chambers.

$$* \sim * \sim *$$

Alix was surprised to find that Henry's chambers were rather stark compared to the one she shared with Richard. A small table and chairs occupied one corner of the room, while a cushioned chair with a foot-rest and a settee rested near the newly-lit fire. Without tapestries hanging upon the stone walls, or rushes on the floor, the room retained much of the night chill. Richard sat next to Alix on the settee, his arm draped over the back, his fingertips lightly grazing her shoulder as he made small talk with his father who stood near the fire. Hal, Geoffrey and their wives mingled at the table, and as Richard's gaze occasionally fell on them, Alix recognized loathing in his eyes. She remained silent, in awe that she was in the King of England's presence, listening to him discuss hunting techniques.

"Will you join me, Alixandra?" Matilda asked.

"Yes, certainly." Alix stood and smiled at Richard's sister, once more noting that she shared the same coloring as her brothers with her blue eyes and waist-length reddish-gold hair. She followed Matilda to the window seat and sat down, shivering a bit as a chilled wind blew through the spaces between the panes of glass and stone. She smoothed her skirt as she tried to think of something to converse about.

"How are you enjoying Caen, Alixandra? Have you visited before?"

"No, I haven't. The King's court is breathtaking. I'm amazed by how many of his nobles attended. Please call me Alix, as everyone else does."

Matilda gave a slight tilt of her head. "You may call me Tilda then. I'm surprised Richard invited you to court."

Heat crept up Alix's cheeks and she prayed that in the dim light, Matilda wouldn't notice. Alix focused on her clenched hands as her stomach roiled. Matilda must know that she was a servant in Richard's household.

Matilda placed her hand over Alix's. "The last few times I've seen him he has only brought his knights."

Alix exhaled in relief at her words. "I think he was unwilling to leave me on my own. I believe he thought I would destroy the palace or sell it off stone by stone."

Tilda's brows furrowed a bit.

"I wouldn't have destroyed it." Alix smirked and both women giggled.

Alix asked about Matilda's children who had traveled with them, and they were soon in deep discussion about the difficulties and gratification of rearing royal offspring. Matilda's warmth and pleasantness made Alix forget her nerves and she was enjoying herself when Richard brought up the topic of Queen Eleanor.

"I received a letter from Mother. Why was she left in England and not invited to this Christ's Mass court? Don't you think she would have welcomed the chance to see everyone? She hasn't seen Matilda or her grandchildren in years." His gruff tone silenced everyone in the room.

Henry sighed.

Geoffrey jumped in as well. "Why did you leave her in England? She must be miserable by herself."

"I thought it best since traveling would have been taxing this time of year." Anger laced Henry's voice.

"I'm sure she would have agreed to come had you asked," Richard pointed out. Henry's gaze fell on Alix, who was trying her best to shrink into her seat.

"I imagine *you* have knowledge of the history of our family. Would you care to weigh in on this subject as well?" Henry's rage landed on Alix. Richard tried to hide his smile at the first part of Henry's statement, but then his blazing eyes met Alix's. She knew what it meant.

"Um, no, I don't have an opinion on the matter."

"I highly doubt that, Alixandra. I would like to know what you think." The icy tone of Henry's voice sent her pulse racing. Her mouth went dry and she pressed her trembling lips together.

Alix's mind worked quickly, seeking out a response that would defuse the simmering hostility. "Such a knowledgeable leader as yourself, you surely weighed the pros and cons. A channel crossing this time of year is indeed dangerous, is it not? Of course, your children would want their mother with them at this special time, but to avoid a potential incident in her travels, it was a prudent decision. I'm sure everyone is grateful that the Queen wasn't placed in that sort of peril."

Henry regarded her but remained silent. Richard threw her a look of relief. The room had gone chilly with the mention of Eleanor, but Marguerite quickly provided a diversion.

"Alixandra, I heard there was sickness at the palace in Poitiers. I trust everyone has recuperated?"

Alix looked at her in surprise. How could she have possibly heard that? Then Alix remembered Gwyn's cousin was in her employ. "Yes, some of the servants came down with the ague. Unfortunately, there were several deaths, but the other girls recovered."

"Some of the finest doctors are in Poitiers," Henry offered.

"If Alix had let the doctor in the sick room to treat her patients, which she didn't." Richard gave her a hard look.

She shrugged. Which earned her another look from Richard, and a masked smile from Geoffrey.

"Your patients? You didn't let the doctor treat them?" The confusion on Constance's face was real. Richard should not have brought this up.

"No." Richard smiled. "Alix drove him out."

Hal studied her as if she were a guttersnipe in his path. "How did you manage that? Royal doctors usually don't take orders from bedmates."

Richard glared at him, and even Henry seemed taken aback. Alix narrowed her eyes. "I can be very persuasive when I choose to be."

"I don't think it was persuasion that was used," Richard chided her. "What were the words you used?" He glanced at her, a devilish look in his eye. She shook her head and silently mouthed "no" as she realized what he meant to do. "Ah yes, I believe it was… 'Get out of here, you bastard, followed by some more colorful words, best not repeated in mixed company." A smile played on his lips as heat suffused Alix's face. Geoffrey laughed aloud and Henry actually smiled.

"Truly, you said that?" Geoffrey's brows rose high on his forehead.

"Richard is paraphrasing, but that sounds about right." Alix rolled her eyes.

The atmosphere lightened considerably, but soon Richard stood to leave, nodding to his father. Alix bid Tilda good night, curtsied to Henry and the rest of his family, and retired with Richard to their chambers.

Once inside, she turned to him and poked him in the chest. "Why the hell did you bring up Eleanor? Are you trying to raise your father's ire?"

"You heard what he said. He didn't intend to invite her. It's another of his ploys to keep us in line."

"For certes it is, that's his leverage over you."

"I had no idea he would have brought you into the fray. I apologize." He strode to her and feathered her cheek. "Hal was completely out of line."

Alix shook her head. "I'm sure everyone thinks the same about what I am. I just didn't think anyone would announce it as such."

He led her to the settee in front of the fireplace, which one of the servants had lit in their absence. "Do you regret coming here?" His voice was soft. "You haven't been here a day and already you've been subjected to our family strife."

"No, not at all. I already knew your family's relationships were strained. It's not a surprise. I quite like Tilda, and Marguerite seems to be pleasant, considering the circumstance with her sister. Constance on the other hand, I'm not so sure about."

"Constance is as devious as her husband Geoffrey. They're a perfect match." His voice held a warning note.

"Geoffrey is definitely one to keep an eye on." Her assessment drew a surprised look from Richard. "He watches everyone like a hawk and appears to be an excellent judge of character. As such, I'd say he's very talented in manipulating people. Hal, on the other hand, doesn't like taking responsibility. He wants to be told what to do and let someone else deal with damage control. He's very unpredictable. He will gladly follow whoever can give him what he desires, specifically the chance to rule without your father keeping him in line. Hal might very well have come up with the idea of rebelling, but I think Geoffrey is making the decisions."

"You deduced all this from today?"

She shrugged. "I'm a pretty good judge of character myself." *Having the luxury of an extensive knowledge about the history of this family doesn't hurt either.*

"I, for certes, am glad you are on my side."

"I have always been, and always will be on your side, Richard, even though I don't always agree with you." She leaned forward to kiss him, then pulled back when footsteps and voices sounded outside the door.

"My squires and pages are staying with us." His tone brooked no argument. She nodded when there was a knock and Richard bade them enter.

~ *Chapter 22* ~

ALONE, HENRY STARED AT the crackling fire. A servant refilled his cup and then bent down to add some more logs to the smoldering inferno. Henry dismissed him and his thoughts turned to his sons. Richard was getting to be tiresome, mentioning Eleanor at every opportunity, and with Hal and even Geoffrey questioning his motives, he realized how much his wife held their sons' loyalty. Geoffrey, and especially Richard, had always belonged to Eleanor. Instead of reining Richard in, Eleanor's imprisonment was causing him to become more of a liability.

When Henry had first anointed Hal as the Young King, it was easy to manage him. Henry was more than willing to allow Hal to fight in tournaments. Through such, Hal had earned the respect of his peers and had gained followers from his many victories. Richard however, had begun to make a name for himself on the battlefield and Geoffrey had proven himself to be a very capable leader. Those two showed initiative and leadership.

When Hal realized that Henry viewed these as qualities in his brothers, he had begun to question why his father didn't allow him the same authority to rule his lands that he afforded to his younger siblings. These days, he was more distant and difficult to control, and Henry worried that he might have protected him too much, not allowing him to test his wings.

In an effort to quell the rising resentment between his sons, Henry planned to make Geoffrey and Richard pledge homage to Hal, but he feared Richard would protest this request. The presence of Alixandra proved an intriguing wrinkle. Richard listened to her. Alix could very well prove useful in aiding in this endeavor. Henry hoped that she would see the wisdom of his plan and help convince Richard to agree. If she proved difficult, he would have no qualms about forcing her. Henry wondered how deep her loyalty to Richard ran. She appeared to be a very astute young woman and had to know she would never be a permanent fixture in Richard's life.

If he pushed hard, would she support Richard or abandon him?

~~*

The day began cold and blustery. Alix had curled up on the settee and watched André and another knight play a game of chess. Richard sat near the fire conferring with his men. On occasion, she'd catch his gaze upon her.

Days had passed since they'd been intimate and sleeping chastely next to him was driving her crazy. Their bedchamber might be private but Alix didn't feel comfortable making love with a room full of men on the other side of the door.

Richard stood and fetched their cloaks. He motioned to Alix to join him. She had to force herself to walk in a dignified manner. The opportunity of being alone with him for even a few minutes had her envisioning what she could do to him.

"I'm surprised you didn't argue with me about leaving the room." He draped her cloak over her before they descended the narrow, winding staircase.

"It was getting claustrophobic in there and I haven't had you to myself in ages." She halted their descent by pushing him against the wall and kissing him hard on the mouth.

"Jesu, it's been too long." His husky whisper sent a shiver down her spine and he cupped her face in his hands.

"And, we're going to have to wait longer," Alix muttered and drew back as low voices echoed in the stairwell from the floor beneath them.

"What is it you always say? People are around twenty-four-seven?"

"Yes, aren't you tired of it?" She nudged him.

"I am. There has to be someplace we can go to be alone."

"I'm sure the chapel is free, except for the ever-present priest. Surely, he would understand carnal desire. On second thought," she looked up at him through her lashes and pressed closer to his muscular body. "Don't priests and the Pope give up worldly possessions and pledge themselves to be pious and celibate? Maybe that's why they teach us not to commit sins, so we are all as miserable as they are."

"Alix! You are incorrigible. What am I to do with you?"

"Anything you want." She kissed him again, and then turned and sashayed down the smooth, stone steps.

Outside the keep, she gasped as the frigid air hit her. She missed the mild winters back home in Austin. Although Alix didn't think Richard was going to take her up on her suggestion, they wandered along the path that led to the chapel. In the midst of their journey, they came across Hal and Geoffrey deep in conversation. The two cast glares at Richard.

"What schemes are being plotted now? Isn't one rebellion enough?" The ice in Richard's voice sent a different sort of shiver down Alix's spine.

"I don't know what you are alluding to." Hal raised his chin. "You're creating plots that don't exist, little brother."

Richard flushed in anger at the insult. "You're a very poor liar. I know that you've been to Limoges, attempting to lure my barons to your cause."

Hal's lip turned up in a sneer. "Perhaps if you weren't so cruel in your ruling, your barons wouldn't be so easy to influence."

Richard's eyes narrowed. He crossed his arms and firmed his stance. "If you used what little brains you have you would know you just admitted to trying to sway them. You should also know they are using you for their own interest. What did the rebels offer you? Knowing you, they didn't have to offer much."

Hal glared at him. "Are you suggesting they bought me? That's hypocritical coming from you. Knowing your penchant for whores how much did you pay for yours? Perhaps you should have saved your money and used it to buy loyalty from your barons."

Both readied themselves for an altercation as Geoffrey looked on, a self-satisfied look in his eyes.

Alix intervened. "Stop it, both of you! You're acting like children." She grabbed Richard's arm. "Please, leave it. He's not worth it." She succeeded at holding him in place only long enough for Geoffrey to stride to Hal's side and drag him away.

"This isn't over, Brother." Richard yelled after them, before stalking off in the opposite direction. Alix ran to keep up.

"Richard, stop please!"

He turned to look at her, still furious. "This was a mistake! I shouldn't have brought you here. God's bones, I shouldn't have come here myself!"

"You had to come. At the very least, to be able to air your grievances against Hal."

"Damn Hal. How like the coward to drag you into our quarrel."

She waved it away. "I ought to have asked him what the going rate is for a whore these days. Maybe you aren't paying me enough."

He gaped at her. "I'm glad you have a sense of humor about this, my dear Alix, but Hal was out of line."

"Don't worry about me. Keeping your duchy intact is more important. At least now you know for certain that Hal and Geoffrey are plotting together. You need to tell your father, Richard. He must be made aware of their treachery."

"I will, love. My brothers will regret making an enemy of me."

Immediately after returning to their chambers, Richard motioned to André to join him at the table and dismissed his squires. Alix made to follow them, assuming he wished her to leave as well when Richard surprised her by asking her to stay.

"Hal all but admitted that he has been coercing my barons to his side. I plan to hold him accountable for his actions. I will die before he wrests Aquitaine from me." He paced the length of the chamber, seething with anger.

"I'm sure Hal would gladly welcome that." André was quick to point out Hal's ultimate goal.

"But your father might not," Alix said. "Although you aren't his favorite son, Henry isn't going to stand idly by and watch while Hal and Geoffrey attempt to destroy you. Eleanor would be furious with him if he did. She still has powerful allies who would fight against him should she request it."

André nodded in agreement.

"I concur," Richard sighed. "Father will have to choose who he will support. I'm just not sure which son it will be."

Richard strode to the door to call in his squires and André leaned toward Alix.

"Have you considered how this rebellion would affect you if it goes against Richard?" André asked in a hushed tone.

"I'm not sure what you mean."

"You must be aware that if Hal were to oust Richard, he would eradicate anything and anyone important to him."

Alix lifted her hands and shrugged.

"Hal would make you pay for supporting Richard. No doubt he would detail Richard on how that payment would be exacted."

For a fleeting moment, Alix thought of being tortured, raped and thrown in a dungeon, all possibilities if Hal were to overthrow Richard. But she knew better. Richard would be king, and sooner than anyone realized. "Hal has much bigger worries than me. I am inconsequential to him."

André looked at her, vexed. "Alix, can you not understand how important you are to Richard? Everyone can see this, except you. Even if they call you his whore or his bedmate, which you are not, they can see the truth. He cares about you, he listens to you; thus, you can be used against him for others' advantage."

Alix frowned at his words, not seeing what André apparently did. Richard rejoined them, and she excused herself with the promise she would return before dinner.

Outside, she chose a random direction, and almost a half-mile from the castle's outer walls, found herself in front of St. George's church, a small stone building with delicately-carved arched windows. She pushed open the heavy, wooden door and shivered in the coolness of the dim interior. The scent of incense and candles from morning Matins still hung in the air, but the church appeared empty. She wandered in, thankful for the peace and quiet.

André's words haunted her. Alix hadn't even considered the idea that she could be used against Richard. Her mere presence could change things now that she was known to his family, and their using her against him was a real possibility. She'd only thought of herself when she agreed to come to Caen. She wanted to experience history and believed her presence would be insignificant in regard to what Richard must soon face. The subject of gossip was the only disturbance she thought she would make.

Shuffling footsteps and the swish of skirts interrupted her thoughts. An older woman approached; her eyes fixed upon Alix. Familiarity tugged at Alix, although the woman was unknown to her.

"Tread with caution," the woman stated. "One wrong step from you and history will be rewritten. It has been foretold."

Alix knit her brow. "Whatever do you mean? I don't have the power to change anything."

"Ah, but you do. Heed my warning. Events will occur, and through no true fault of your own, you will be instrumental in a momentous decision."

The words echoed in Alix's ears, reminding her of a similar prediction she had heard at Nottingham Faire. This woman reminded her of the shopkeeper. "Who are you? How do you know of this? You must be mistaken."

"For years, I have counseled the King and have never given wrong advice." The woman lifted her chin and although shorter than Alix, managed to stare her down.

"I can't be responsible for changing history." Alix's stomach knotted. "Tell me what I must do!"

"You have been cautioned, and that is all I can relay." The woman turned and melted into the shadows.

Alix stared at her retreating figure and tried to calm the hammering of her heart. Surely the woman's dire prediction was only that – a prediction? She couldn't truly know what the future held, could she?

The door scraped open upon the stone tiles and Alix turned, hopeful that the woman had returned.

"Alix, what are you doing here?"

"This is the only place I could find where it's quiet enough to think."

Geoffrey smiled. "I'm surprised Richard let you out of his sight. He has a very suspicious nature, as you must realize by now."

I would be suspicious too, if I had brothers like you. "Are you suggesting that I'm not safe here?"

"Not at all, but one never knows. Danger can be found lurking everywhere."

"Present company excluded."

Geoffrey held up his hands, as if in surrender. "For certes. I have no reason to harm you."

Alix arched an eyebrow. Geoffrey leaned against a wooden column and crossed his arms. "I admit, I'm surprised my brother brought you here. He has never been very forthcoming about his women. Wherever did he meet you?" His tone was tinged ever so lightly with disdain.

"He didn't find me in a brothel, if that is what you are suggesting."

Geoffrey gave her a half-smile. "Hal often speaks before thinking. I wasn't insinuating that at all. Richard is very careful about who his close associates are. He must hold you in high esteem, Alix."

"I appreciate that." She studied him, unsure of his motives.

"You haven't been long in his employ?" Geoffrey continued in an easy conversational manner.

She sensed he was hopeful she would make a careless remark that would indicate why she was here.

He approached her with slow, short steps. "It has been at least seven years since I last visited Poitiers, but I would have remembered you. When Richard began overseeing the ducal palace, he kept Mother's ladies-in-waiting and servants in the hopes that father would soon release her. I remember they were quite a bit older than you."

"Then you ought to visit more often. Richard let Queen Eleanor's ladies go and now you will find his employees are much changed."

"How did your paths cross? Somehow you don't strike me as a mere servant."

His fishing scheme was obvious. She raised her chin and clasped her hands. "We met in a tavern. Due to my… circumstances, he offered me a position."

His eyes narrowed. "Circumstances?"

Alix relied on the story she had told before. "I was hired to be a governess, but the master of the house and I had a difference of opinion."

"He would rather bed you?"

She nodded. "When your brother found me, I was low on funds and had no prospects. He was kind enough to offer me employment."

Skepticism flared in his eyes. A cloud passed over the sun, inking out the light streaming through the stained-glass windows. Aware they were the only two in the darkened chapel, she felt vulnerable.

"It's getting dark, so I must get back. If you will excuse me?" Alix stood and curtsied.

"Allow me to escort you to your chambers."

"Thank you." She led the way out of the church, a niggling suspicion in the back of her mind that he had sought her out to question her. She felt like Red Riding Hood in the presence of the wolf.

Leading them up the winding stairway that led to her chambers, they met Richard coming down. "You're late. Where have you been?" Then he spied Geoffrey. "What are you doing with *him*?"

"We ran into each other in the church. He was kind enough to escort me back."

Geoffrey smiled at Richard's obvious displeasure.

"Is that so? A chance meeting, how fortuitous." Richard narrowed his eyes.

Alix held her breath, praying Richard wouldn't lose his temper.

Geoffrey nodded to her. "I look forward to seeing you at dinner."

Richard said nothing until Geoffrey was well out of hearing range. He turned to face her. His tense stance told her he was furious. She braced herself.

"What did I tell you about going off on your own?"

"Why can't you trust me? I now know what your brothers are like, and I don't blame you for being suspicious of them, but please give me a little bit of credit."

Richard took a deep breath and relaxed. He put his hands on her shoulders. "I do trust you. It's everyone else I have to worry about."

~ *Chapter 23* ~

GEOFFREY OPENED THE DOOR to the room and Constance spun around at the sound. She dismissed her maid who had been brushing her long, dark hair. "Well, did you find Richard's bedmate?"

"It took some searching, but yes, I did." Geoffrey went to the table and poured some wine.

"What did you discover? How much does she know about the rebellion? Do you think she is his spy?" Her inquisition ended when Geoffrey handed her a cup of wine.

He poured his own cup, and took his time before answering, amusing himself at his wife's growing impatience. "Although it is evident Alix is hiding something, she is not a spy. If she knows anything of our plan, it is only what Richard has told her, which in itself is quite telling. He must trust her implicitly."

"How can you be so certain?"

"I have my own court spies, as you well know, and this girl is not in his pocket. She doesn't strike me as being duplicitous enough to play the role of spy."

Constance stood and approached the table. "So what possible reason would he have to bring her to court?" she mused, then her dark eyes widened. "You don't think…"

He drained his cup and dropped into a chair. "Richard actually likes the girl." He clearly remembered the look of relief in his brother's eyes when he met Alix in the stairwell.

Constance looked at him in doubt. "You must be jesting. He can barely be civil to his own betrothed. The only things Richard cares for are Aquitaine and glory on the battlefield."

"I thought so too, but we might very well be wrong." He rubbed the back of his neck then stroked his chin. "I don't know how much Richard knows about Hal's plans, but I hope to God Hal realizes he must be more careful. Too many times, I've feared he would slip and invite Richard to the rebellion."

"You need to keep your brother in line, Geoffrey. We have worked too hard to lose everything."

"I will make sure Hal stays the course." Geoffrey leaned his head back against the chair and rotated the empty goblet in his hands. "For too long I have waited for promises from Father that remain unfulfilled. I am more than ready to take what is owed us."

~~*

The sun, banished behind thick, gray clouds, allowed sleet to fall like shards of glass to the earth, forcing all of Henry's court guests to gather in the great hall. Henry and Richard were conversing, although to Alix it didn't look like either was enjoying it. Her seat between Richard and Matilda afforded Alix the opportunity to inquire about Richard's ailing nephew who had remained behind in Germany. There was a disturbance among the guests as an imposing dark-haired man made his way to the dais.

Alix leaned against Richard to get his attention. "Who is that man?"

"Will Marshal, one of Hal's knights."

Alix clutched Richard's arm. "Will Marshal? *The* Will Marshal?"

"Yes, why are you so surprised?"

"Oh my God, I have heard stories of him. He is one of the most renowned jousters in France."

Richard frowned at her. "He's well known even in England?"

"Yes! Never in my wildest dreams would I have thought I would see him."

Annoyance vibrated in his voice. "Many men joust, especially Hal, since he would prefer to play war than actually engage in it."

She stroked his arm. "You have no reason to be jealous. Your accomplishments will far overshadow Will's."

"Whatever are you talking about?"

"Nothing, I was just…"

"Your Grace, please hear me out." Everyone turned toward Will as he knelt before Hal who looked askance at this turn of events.

"Yes, Will, what is it?" Hal's dismissive tone disgusted Alix. Will Marshal would serve five kings and be eulogized as the 'greatest knight who ever lived'. He deserved the utmost respect from Hal instead of being spoken to with near contempt.

"I am innocent of the crime perpetrated, and I ask you to grant me a trial to clear my name." The crowd murmured at Will's plea.

Hal sighed as he looked around the room. Seeing curious faces focused on them, he glared at Will. "I have no idea what you are referring to and there will most certainly be no trial."

Hal lied. Alix knew well the 'crime' Will Marshal referred to. The rumor was that Will had seduced Hal's wife Marguerite, but it was thought to be a political ploy by his enemies to keep him from gaining more influence with the Young King.

"As you wish, my King. Then I ask that I be released from your service as I can't serve you in good conscience." He bowed, backed away and pushed his way through the crowd. The hall erupted as the guests speculated upon what had transpired. Hal looked shocked at Will's request and had no answer for the questions thrown at him from all sides.

"What the hell was that about?" Alix wasn't sure if she should answer Richard's rhetorical question, but he would find out soon anyway.

"Will was accused of having an affair with Marguerite."

Richard turned sharply to Alix. "That's a ridiculous notion. How do you know of this?"

She shrugged. "I hear things."

"Tell me how you came by this knowledge." His voice was deceptively calm.

"People ignore me when I'm on my own. Gossip abounds when they think no one of significance is listening." She thought her lie sounded very convincing. "I overheard two men talking about Will and Marguerite. I don't believe it. I think they are just stirring up a hornet's nest. Obviously, Will found out, and well, the rest is history, as they say."

"This is an interesting turn of events." Richard stroked his chin with his hand, his mouth twisted, his eyes calculating. "It might be to our advantage."

"How is that, may I ask?"

"It could very well cause discord between Hal and his knights who are loyal to Will. At the very least, he has another issue to focus on rather than a rebellion."

"I'm glad that I am useful, after all. Unfortunately, I happen to be the worst servant ever."

Richard's lips curled and his hand found her upper thigh. "I never thought you would be stellar in that role."

"Then why ever did you employ me?"

"A woman emerging from the forest miles from any town is not a common occurrence. I wanted to find out more about you."

"Really? More likely you were bored and I was a potential diversion." At his sheepish look, she gasped. "Am I still simply a means to pass your time?"

He leaned over to kiss her on the cheek. "If you were merely a distraction, you wouldn't be here."

"How did I ever get so lucky?"

* ~ * ~ *

The atmosphere in Henry's chambers that evening was lighter and more enjoyable than the past several nights, due to Hal's and Marguerite's absence. A large fire crackled in the fireplace, heating the room and filling the air with the aroma of wood smoke. Servants refilled cups and plates of sweet wafers before melting back into the shadows. Henry and Geoffrey were playing chess, Alix was conversing with Matilda and Richard was talking to Matilda's husband, Heinrich.

"I'm sure Father has grand plans for Christ's Mass Eve and the following day." Matilda looked enthused as she explained some of the details of the evening to Alix. "He has spared no expense. With the number of highborn lords and nobles in attendance, no one can doubt their loyalty to their king."

"I must say, I was astounded to see how many of the King's nobles were here. His influence indeed stretches far. I'm very pleased that Richard invited me."

Constance swiveled in her chair. She apparently had been eavesdropping. "You've never been to a royal court, have you, Alix? I'm sure all of this must be so... foreign to you." She waved her hand in the air.

"No, I haven't, but I'm enjoying it very much." Alix tried her best to keep the annoyance out of her voice as Constance smirked and looked down her nose at her. "I'm sure this Christ's Mass court will be discussed for many years to come."

~ *Chapter 24* ~

ALIX HURRIED INTO THEIR chambers, blowing warm air on her numb hands as she waited for a young page to stoke the fire. A leisurely Saturday morning breakfast had lasted well into the early afternoon. Henry had spent much of it conversing with his more illustrious nobles, and his family was obligated to stay until he left. The walk from the dining hall back to their room had been cold. The corridors were still chilly as icy drafts found their way in through the cracks around windows.

Today was Christmas Eve, and although she and Richard were expected to be in attendance, she didn't relish another evening spent with Richard's kin. Alix also missed her own family, especially on this night that they always celebrated together.

Richard paced, his boots crunching on the rushes that covered the stone floor. "Make haste with that fire," Richard growled.

The boy jumped, sending burning coals onto the rushes in front of the hearth. "God's bones! Leave the fire before you burn the place down." Tension radiated from Richard as he stomped out the smoking coals.

Alix put a steadying hand on the boy's shoulder as he stumbled into her. His eyes were bright with unshed tears. "He's like a bear when he gets angry, but this will pass," she murmured.

She'd never seen Richard quite so agitated and a plan to make him forget his troubles for a little while blossomed.

She pled a headache and ordered Richard out of the chambers so she could rest, then enlisted Richard's squires and Rob to help. Rob was to make sure Richard remained occupied and she monitored the squires as they set up the chambers to her specifications. She sent a pageboy to the kitchen, with a list of dishes for an intimate meal.

As dusk fell, she took the opportunity to change into her indigo dress. She smoothed the soft wool with her hands as nervous excitement grew within her. Forgoing her veil, she brushed her hair until the brunette strands cascaded like silk past her shoulders. After checking her appearance, she applied some scented oil to the inside of her wrists and took one last look in the mirror. Pleased with the arrangements in the main chamber, she sent the squires away.

Alix paced the length and breadth of the room, wondering when Richard would return. As a failsafe, she had asked Rob to send Richard back on the pretense that she had worsened, but he would return to change for the festivities or at least to check on her health, so she expected him soon.

She looked out the window at the gathering darkness and began having misgivings. What if he thought this whole idea was childish? Although he had been chivalrous toward her on the rare occasion, nothing in the history books led her to believe he had a romantic bone in his body. She slumped down on the window seat and leaned back against the wall, certain she had wasted her time, when voices echoed in the stairway. She stood and laced her fingers, waiting for the door to open. He was talking to someone in the hallway and when he opened the door, he stopped and looked about the room.

Platters of food covered the dining table, lanterns hung from the rafters and candles flickered on tables and the mantle. A fire roared in the fireplace, exuding a warm glow and scented the room with fragrant wood smoke. "I see you have recovered."

"Yes, I am markedly improved."

He entered and looked around. "You did this?"

"I had some help. You have done so much for me and I wanted to thank you. I know it's not much, but I hope it's acceptable to you."

He smiled at her. "Although our absence will be remarked upon, I would much rather spend tonight with you than with my family. You look beautiful, Alix."

"Thank you." Richard's hair shone gold in the fire and the shadows accentuated the strong planes of his face. She led him to the settee in front of the blaze and brought him some wine, then busied herself making a plate for him. "I didn't know what you wanted, so I requested everything."

"Alix, sit down. You don't have to serve me. My squires can do that."

"No, I will. Besides, I sent your men away." A smile played on her lips at his look. "I think we have at least four hours alone before they return." She prepared a plate for herself and joined him.

"Did anything exciting happen today?"

He laughed. "No. The day was fairly civil, although everyone was talking about Will and what caused him to leave."

"I feel sorry for Marguerite. She must know of the rumors swirling about her, and I'm sure she's unhappy with the situation."

Richard shrugged. "As long as it keeps Hal occupied, I am thankful to whomever started the rumors."

"As of now, no talk of rumors, rebellions, or anything involving your family." Alix took a bite of tender, roasted chicken. She licked her fingers one at a time, sucking on the last one as she looked up through her lashes at Richard.

He licked his lips and took a deep drink of wine. "Well then, what about your family?" he queried. "You must miss them. How do you celebrate Christ's Mass?"

Did he miss her attempt at seduction? Maybe she was losing her touch. "We put up a tree and decorate it with ornaments and candles. We hold a big supper on the evening before, and the next morning we open presents. I do miss my family, especially my niece. I love seeing how excited she gets opening her gifts." She looked at him. "I have a confession to make. One of the reasons I did this…" waving her hand at the room, "—is because I'm tired of sharing you with everyone and I want you to myself like back ho— I mean back in Poitiers."

He sighed. "I miss that, as well."

She leaned forward, kissing his lips. Familiar flutters tumbled about in her stomach. He ran his hands through her hair and pulled her closer as his kiss deepened.

Exercising all of her will power, Alix pulled back, she had other plans for him. "Not yet." She nipped his ear lobe, then stood, entwining her fingers in his and led him to the bedroom where more lanterns imbued the room with a soft, yellow glow. A roaring fire burned in the hearth warming the space. She pushed him back on the bed and laughed at his look of surprise.

"Tonight, I get to do what I want to you, and you have no say in the matter. Are we clear?" He narrowed his eyes at her. "I assure you Richard, you are in very capable hands."

"Of that, I have no doubt. I am yours." He sat up pulling her between his legs as she stood beside the bed.

She ran her hands through his hair, bending down to kiss the sensitive area behind his ear. He gasped as she exhaled on the area and his hands stole about her waist pulling her closer. She kissed his neck and grasped the bottom of his soft, wool shirt, slowly pulling it up, and tossed the garment aside. Her breath came faster at the feel of his skin beneath her fingers. He squeezed her hips and moved his hands up to the laces on her dress.

"I quite like this plan of yours." He deftly untied her dress and pushed it down until it pooled at her feet, then trailed moist kisses across her stomach.

She stepped back, a small smile curving her lips. "No, no, Your Grace. No touching." Alix pushed him back and positioned him on the bed until he lay across it. He watched her with heavy-lidded eyes as she skimmed her hands down his chest, then she captured his lips, and raised his arms over his head. She broke contact for a moment to reach into the drawer next to the bed and pulled out a couple of scarves. She looped a scarf around one wrist and tied it to the bedpost.

"What the hell are you doing?" He pulled at the scarf and tried to free his arm. "I demand you untie me at once!"

"Remember, this is my night. I thought you were more adventurous. Stop struggling and relax." Soon, the other arm was bound and she knelt beside him surveying her handiwork as he glowered at her. "I like you like this."

"Like what? Helpless?" he growled.

She walked her fingers up his chest. "Under my control." He tested his restraints but couldn't loosen them. "Do you trust me?" She brushed his hair from his forehead.

He nodded, his steady gaze never leaving hers. Straddling him, she touched her tongue to his lips, tasting him, but when he strained to touch her, she sat back, out of reach. He relaxed against the bed, and she bent down again, flicking her tongue over his lips, until he parted them and she explored his mouth. His thigh muscles tightened between her legs and he groaned as she shifted her position.

She kissed his neck, moving down to the hollow in his throat where his quickened pulse beat against her lips, and inhaled his scent, the faint smell of leather mixed with soap. He gasped and pulled at the restraints around his wrists.

"No, no. The more you struggle, the more I will torture you."

Leaning forward to nuzzle his neck, her breasts grazed his skin and desire flooded between her legs at the light touch. All she wanted was his lips and hands caressing her body, but this was his night. She kissed his chest and teased his nipple with her tongue, then caught it in her teeth as he lurched against her. She slowly trailed kisses down to his washboard stomach and he tensed when she stroked his thighs. Untying his pants, she divested him of them, his manhood freed.

The hammering of her heart increased as she studied her captive's magnificent form. Love swelled within her for his man, and she wished they weren't from different times and stations in life.

She knew how her story would end – in heartache and pain. The desire in his eyes refocused her. She ran her nails along his inner thighs and he shuddered in response.

He inhaled as she pressed her lips and tongue to his stomach, a promise of things to come. His muscles tightened and goosebumps erupted on his skin as she blew cool air on the moist areas. Moving lower, she caressed him with her tongue and his body jerked in response. Using her teeth, she grazed his manhood and his hips thrust upward. She placed her hand on his stomach to still his movements as she brought him to the precipice, then denied him his pleasure.

"God, Alix, please... I can't wait any longer..." His breath came out in ragged bursts and his muscles flexed as he pulled at the scarves, desperate for release. Gripping him she brought him to the edge once more but stopped when the sound of ripping startled her.

"Richard!"

Moments later, he was sitting up, his hands around her waist as he lifted her onto him.

"Your sweet torture is most pleasurable, but I'm desperate to hold you, *mon amor*."

The words warmed her heart and caused a surge of desire. She wrapped her legs around him, needing him inside her more than ever before. His mouth caressed her breast and she trembled as he teased her nipple. He reached between her legs, his clever fingers stroking her. Her hips moved of their own accord but as her cries intensified, he stopped.

"Look at me, Alix." She tried, but his fingers were pleasuring her again. All she wanted was to throw her head back and surrender. "Open your eyes."

She forced them open and met his stormy blues. He pulled her closer with one arm while he continued to tease her with his other hand. She shuddered and grasped his shoulders tighter as her climax neared.

"You're mine. Give yourself to me." Her lips parted as they stared into each other's eyes, then she cried out and convulsed against him, their eyes locked on each other. His own breath gusted out and he held her until her body calmed.

"Jesu, love," he whispered. He brushed her hair from her dewy brow and gently kissed her. She had never experienced such an intimate moment. His arms tightened around her and he lay back down with her atop him. Entwining her fingers with his, she straddled him, but he stopped her.

"Would you pleasure me like you did before I left for Clairvaux?"

She furrowed her brows, then she gave him a half-smile. "Nothing would please me more." Her heart melted as relief flashed in his eyes, as if he feared she would refuse him.

She inched backward, her tongue trailing slowly down his chest to his stomach. Gripping his hardened member in her hand she flicked her tongue over the sensitive tip. Richard gathered her hair in his hands and she glanced up to see him watching her, anticipation in his eyes. Keeping her eyes on his, she swirled her tongue, tasting him as she slid her lips up and down his length. His body jerked underneath her at her touch. Quickly stroking him with her hand, she increased the pressure of her mouth.

"Alix... I can't wait..." His body stiffened then he called out her name, spilling his seed. She kept her mouth around him until he was spent, his body still. He pulled her to him kissing her, their breath mingling.

"Was that what you had in mind, Richard?" She murmured against his lips.

"Ah, love, that was and so much more."

Tattered scarfs lay about them and she picked up the torn fabric. "I can't believe you broke free. You're no fun."

"I'll buy you more, if you let me use them on you."

"I hope I'm not corrupting you," she teased him.

"I don't know where you get these ideas, but I'm not complaining. You are the most exciting, intoxicating woman I've ever met."

She snuggled against him as the fire burned out and the air in the room cooled. "I'm glad you invited me to join you. Your father's court is incredible."

"You do know that you had no true choice in the matter? You were coming with me whether you wanted to or not." His deep, baritone laugh filled the room as she slapped his shoulder.

"What if I had refused? You would have tied me up and thrown me into a cart?"

"That wasn't quite the scenario I planned, but I do like the idea of you tied up." He nuzzled her neck, tickling her with his week's growth of beard.

She nuzzled closer. "I think that could be arranged."

~~*

The following morning, Alix found Richard gazing out the window, lost in thought. The platters of food from the night before had been cleared. She assumed the squires must have done it in the early hours.

"Happy Christ's Mass, Richard."

He jumped and smiled up at her. "Happy Christ's Mass, love." He held out his hand. Taking it, she sat down and leaned against him. "That was one of the most enjoyable and unexpected nights I have spent since we left Poitiers."

"It was enjoyable for me, as well." She wished there could be more nights like last night, but she knew her presence in his life was finite. He fell silent and she glanced up at his pensive face. "What is it? Has something happened?"

"Not yet, but it will." His gaze drifted to the window. "I'm going to demand an audience with Father and tell him of Hal's treachery."

"Good. He needs to know. He might offer a solution that would be acceptable to both of you."

"Do you truly believe that?" The skepticism in his voice disquieted her. How horrible to wonder if your own father would protect you against a scheming sibling or not.

"Anything is possible. Besides, you might as well hear what he has to say."

"I wish mother were here. I would value her counsel on this matter."

"It might be best that she's not, for you know whose side she would choose, and that could cause more friction. I wish things were different for you. Most families have their issues but can remain close. Yours is so fractured, I don't think anything could repair it. When do you plan on doing this?"

"Father's court is traveling south to Angers next week. I will do it there, where there will be fewer interested noblemen."

One of the main reasons why royalty traveled so often was the lack of sanitation in a castle. She wrinkled her nose at the thought of latrines and chamber pots being emptied into the moats or surrounding ditches. With over a thousand guests at Caen, she'd already experienced how unbearable the stench could be.

"I thought after the New Year, we would go back to Poitiers. How long will you remain at your father's court?"

"I'm not sure, but not too long, I expect. We'll return home soon, I promise."

"We? You want me to come with you, to Angers? I thought you just wanted me to join you here. I didn't think I was going elsewhere."

"For certes, you are to come with me. Would you prefer to return home?"

"Actually, yes. Your father's court is incredible with the lavish feasts, music and dancing, but I am tired of Hal insulting me at every turn. Constance is a bitch and I am always on guard around Geoffrey." Richard's poor attempt to stifle his smile irritated her even more. "Do my issues amuse you?"

"No, I agree with your assessment. You have voiced exactly how I feel about them as well."

"Why couldn't you have just been a commoner?"

Richard laughed. "If only my mother had had fewer sons."

"True enough. But of course, I will journey to Angers with you if you wish. I would go anywhere with you."

* ~ * ~ *

Christmas dinner was as extravagant as Matilda had predicted and Alix was amazed at the amount of effort that must have gone into its planning. Polished brass lanterns hung from the rafters and all the wall sconces were lit, their flickering light providing a warm ambiance. Tables literally bowed under the sheer weight of the platters that covered them. Musicians playing lutes and harps accompanied a troubadour singing of chivalry and courtly love, but the sound was almost lost amongst the din of conversations.

The golden thread Sybilla and Maud used to embroider the crimson silk of Alix's dress shimmered in the candlelight. As Richard escorted Alix into the great hall, the stunned looks on the women's faces weren't lost upon her. Passing by groups of ladies, snippets of conversation floated to her. "Did you see the shade she's wearing?" "The Duke must think very highly of her." "I wonder how long she will remain his favorite."

Richard lifted her hand to his lips and pressed a kiss in her palm, his eyes dancing. No doubt, he'd heard the whispers, too. Warmth from this public display filled her heart and for once, she felt worthy of being with Richard. His brothers' wives were impeccably dressed in richly-embellished silk gowns as befitted a future Queen and the Duchess of Brittany, but even they looked impressed when Alix joined them on the dais, although Constance hid it quickly.

"I heard you were feeling unwell last night. I trust you have recovered?"

Matilda looked concerned as Alix took the seat next to her, Richard on her other side.

"Oh yes, thank you. I am much better." Alix forced a straight face as Richard grinned at their exchange.

"Sometimes escaping from the bustle of court has its benefits." Matilda nodded with a knowing look.

"Yes, it does."

Minstrels entertained throughout dinner and after servants removed the dishes, many of the guests joined in the dancing. Behind Matilda, her daughter Richenza twirled in time to the music and watched the dancers wistfully. Hal and Marguerite led several of the dances and Alix had to admit that they were a very striking couple. Her heart saddened with the knowledge that their happiness would end in the next several months, with a failed rebellion and an unexpected death.

"Shall we?" Richard held his hand out to her.

"Oh, I don't know. I'm not that familiar with these dances. I wouldn't want to embarrass you."

"I watched you dance with André. You were exceptional."

Alix laughed. "That was back home. There is more pressure here."

He gave her a look and she grudgingly capitulated. She took his hand, grasping it with shaking fingers. She feared that she would forget the dance steps and embarrass Richard, but the warm feel of his hand on the small of her back reassured her as he escorted her to where the other dancers were lining up.

"You are the most beautiful woman here." His whisper tickled the hairs on her neck. He held her face in his hands and brushed his lips across hers before he took his place with the other men. She wasn't quite sure where to look. The other dancers' disapproval caused her cheeks to burn. Tonight, was the first time he had ever publicly displayed his affection. For however long it lasted, he was hers, and now everyone knew it.

The lilting strains of music began. He bowed and she curtsied, his gaze never leaving hers. They approached each other and clasped hands, circling in time to the music. Richard was an excellent partner and once she recognized the music, her confidence grew and she began to enjoy herself. Every time they circled back to each other, he squeezed her hand or caressed her lower back.

The whispers and looks followed them. Her love for this man, who cared more about her feelings than social etiquette, deepened. The music ended, and he pressed his lips to her hand before they returned to their table.

"I hope I didn't disappoint you."

"You never disappoint me. I have danced with you before. If I had doubts concerning your skill, I wouldn't have asked." His lips curved upward.

"That's right. I taught you the waltz soon after I arrived in Poitiers..." The night they shared their first kiss would stay with her forever.

He beamed as he watched her remember. "The first of many, very enjoyable nights."

~ *Chapter 25* ~

THE CASTLE BUSTLED WITH chaos the next few days as guests made ready to return home and Henry's household, clergy and invited nobles, as well as his sons' households prepared to travel to Angers. Feeling in the way, Alix wandered outside and around the grounds as much as possible, steering clear of the great hall and other areas where she might run into Richard's brothers. Finally, everyone was ready to leave. Alix was amazed at how many carts and pack animals were used to transport Hal and Marguerite's belongings, as well as the possessions of their knights, ladies, and other household servants.

Richard came to stand behind Alix as she watched the commotion in the bailey.

"How do they get anywhere in a timely fashion?"

Her amused query made Richard snicker. "I have no idea, but women seem to be the main cause of the chaos, present company excluded. Speaking of which, have you packed yet? If so, I'll have my squire take your belongings downstairs."

"Yes, I'm ready to go."

"Are you going to wear that?"

Alix glanced at her dress in confusion. "When we left Poitiers, you weren't happy with my attire, and now this doesn't please you, either? I have to wear something while I ride. Or, shall I mount my horse wearing only a smile and save you the trouble of making my wardrobe decisions?"

A deep guffaw rumbled in Richard's throat. "Although that is a tempting thought, Alix..." He eyed her up and down. "What you're wearing is perfectly acceptable. I wasn't sure if you would be comfortable riding in a dress or not. Our destination is some distance away, and you made it clear that a dress is not suitable for riding astride your steed." She shifted her glance and wrung her hands. He placed his hands on her shoulders. "Is something bothering you? You seem testy."

"I have a sense of foreboding about this journey. I don't know how to describe it." How could she possibly tell him that his father would make him give up Clairvaux and pay homage to the Young King? In turn, Hal would take advantage of the situation and revel in Richard's servitude. At first. Then, Hal would humiliate him by refusing to accept Richard's homage by proclaiming his word wasn't to be trusted.

Richard took her in his arms. "Ah, love, it will be fine. There's nothing to worry about." She nodded, but she knew her fears would come to fruition.

As Alix waited in the courtyard for the groom to bring her horse, Matilda approached her.

"Alix, would you like to join me and the children in the wagon? I'm not sure where we are stopping tonight, and this journey could be very tiring."

"I don't want to impose, but thank you for the offer."

"It's not an imposition. Although I love my children, sometimes I long for adult conversation."

Alix laughed. "In that case, I would be very pleased to join you."

A groomsman held the horses' reins, while another helped Matilda and Alix climb into the cart. Alix balanced on the small bench in the center of the cart, then moved out of the way as the children clambered in, trying to see who could win the coveted position of being in front.

"Otto, Richenza, be more careful!" Tilda admonished, but a smile curved her lips. "They are so energetic. I hope they calm down soon."

"They're being children. I remember traveling as a child. I couldn't sleep a wink the night before, being so excited. I'm sure they'll settle down as the ride becomes long."

The journey proved most enjoyable due to Matilda's company. Her stories of raising children and learning the hard way that no matter how long it takes to clean a room, children manage to destroy it in a matter of minutes, kept Alix laughing in amusement.

"Matilda, I trust you are comfortable? Alix, how are you faring?"

Alix turned, surprised to see Richard riding alongside their wagon. Although he directed his initial question to his sister, his gaze remained locked upon Alix.

"We're doing quite well, thank you," Matilda replied.

"Uncle Richard, when will we arrive? I can't wait to see Grandfather's castle!" Otto stood and balanced precariously in the swaying wagon.

"The journey will take several weeks. Longer if you fall out and we have to find a doctor to stitch your wounds." Richard laughed as Richenza pulled her brother down next to her, and Otto rolled his eyes at his over-protective sister.

Richard continued to ride next to them, answering Matilda's questions about how their mother was faring in captivity; a conversation they couldn't have in front of Henry. The flat plains began to give way to forests and Richard rode ahead to join his men. Alix knew of the potential for attacks by routiers or thieves hiding amongst the dense trees and appreciated the knights' keen awareness of their surroundings.

"Alix, you have effected a change in my brother. I have never seen him so relaxed, and I daresay, happy."

"I don't know about that. He always seems in good spirits in Poitiers."

Matilda smiled at her. "He appears to be quite taken with you. I can't imagine he would let you go after he's married…" She broke off and raised her hand to cover her mouth.

Alix shook her head. "All I can hope for is to have as much time as possible with him before that occurs."

Matilda placed her hand on Alix's arm. "The manner in which my brother treats you proves that he truly cares for you. I've seen the way you look at him as well. When a woman marries a nobleman or a royal, she knows infidelity is common and even expected. I'm sure Alys already knows that will be part of their life together."

Alix's heart dropped like a stone. "I'm not from your world. I refuse to be any man's mistress, whether he be a commoner, or the King himself." The firmness in her voice was sure to convince Matilda of her resolve in this matter. And herself. "My mother suffered greatly when my father took a mistress and I refuse to be the cause of another person's pain and anguish. Besides, I couldn't bear seeing him with someone else, knowing he would never be completely mine."

"You would willingly give him up, just like that?" Matilda seemed surprised.

"It wouldn't be easy, but yes I would. I believe marriage is between two people and no others."

* ~ * ~ *

Angers castle loomed ahead of them, a hulking stone building that cast an imposing shadow in the gathering dusk. The immense, high wall had rounded towers at varying intervals, built with alternating dark and light stones. A wide, curving moat, carved into the earth in the front of the castle, flowed into the river that bordered the side of the grounds. The carts creaked across the planks of the immense drawbridge leading under a huge wooden gate into the courtyard. Richard wasted no time ordering his squires to take their belongings to their chambers.

Alix supervised the unpacking while Richard conferred with André about the best course of action to take with his father. After Alix hung their clothes in the large, wooden armoire, she took a seat by the window, the men's voices a low hum in the background. Thoughts of what was to come during this visit spun in her mind.

"Well, what is your opinion? Alix?" Richard's voice sounded in her distracted ears.

"That sounds fair," she responded.

"You think my giving Aquitaine to Hal is a good idea considering he would make a much better ruler than I?"

"No. For certes not, unless that's your decision…"

Richard motioned to André to leave them, then went to Alix. "Do you want to tell me what is bothering you?"

"I'm fine." She dragged her gaze from the window. "Why do you ask?"

"I just told you I was giving Aquitaine to Hal and you were indifferent, so unless you have had a change of heart about him, I can only assume that something is worrying you."

Alix raked her hand through her hair. "I told you before we left. I have a feeling that something is going to happen, and it's going to affect you adversely."

"How do you know this?"

"I don't know." She wished she could just tell him the whole truth. "Call it a woman's intuition."

"Alix, don't…" He broke off, as there was a knock at the door.

"Your father has agreed to see you in his chambers immediately, Your Grace," a squire announced.

"Tell him I will be there shortly." The squire left to deliver the message and Richard turned to Alix. "You have no cause to worry. Once I tell Father about Hal's duplicity in trying to obtain my nobles' loyalty for himself, he will have no choice but to support me unless he wants another rebellion on his hands. This time, between Hal and myself."

She nodded. "Tread carefully and hear him out. You don't want to inadvertently push him to Hal's side."

"I'll be careful. I always am." Richard gave her a cheeky grin and left her with her fears.

* ~ * ~ *

Henry shifted in his chair next to the fire as Richard paced the length of his chamber, hands locked behind his back.

"This is completely intolerable! I will not give my allegiance to Hal!"

"Richard…" Henry began.

"No! As brothers, we are on equal footing. Hal has his future crown from you, and I have Aquitaine from Mother, or have you forgotten where much of your wealth came from?" Richard's sneer was not lost on the King.

"I have not. Why must you always defy me? Tell me why you refuse to do as I ask."

Richard stomped to the table and refilled his wine cup. "Hal has been meeting with my nobles…" he began, prepared to tell Henry about Hal's double-dealings, when Henry held up his hand stopping him.

"Are you suggesting that Hal is plotting rebellion?"

"Indeed." Venom dripped from Richard's words.

Henry's eyes narrowed. "What proof have you?"

"Not definite proof, but enough to warrant a closer look into Hal's activities in Aquitaine."

Henry stared into the fire. For the past four or five months, he had the niggling suspicion that Hal was planning something. Politics had never truly interested Hal, but recently he had expressed a deeper interest in the quarrels between the highborn Lords of Aquitaine and Richard and spent more time in the company of the French king, than attending the jousting tournaments he was so fond of.

Henry summoned his squire. After a few hushed words, the boy hurried out of the room.

"You're accusing Hal of a serious infraction and I want to hear both sides of this story." Richard looked at his father, his eyes full of wariness followed by anger.

"Richard, I know there's mistrust between you two, but I hope we can put this to rest once and for all."

Tense moments passed between father and son, then the door flung open and the perpetrator himself entered, color high in his cheeks. "What treachery is this?" Hal demanded. "What lies has he been telling you, Father?"

Henry looked at his sons as they glared at each other. "Your brother has been enlightening me as to your scheming activities regarding his nobles."

Richard stepped forward first, a cold smile on his lips. "As I was saying, Hal has been secretly rendezvousing with my noblemen, attempting to turn them to his side." His eyes met Hal's. "Geoffrey rules Brittany and I have Aquitaine. For too long you have stood in Father's shadow. An anointed king in name only, with no land or power, you have been waiting for your own opportunity. Now you have set your sights on my realm."

"Is it true, Hal? Can you explain this?" Henry was unwilling to believe it of his eldest son.

Hal nodded. "Yes, his nobles have approached me with their grievances, since they don't care for his heavy-handed ruling and his taking of their women. He has also been fortifying Clairvaux, which poses a direct threat to my future lands. In light of this, I have given my support to them."

Henry stared at his eldest in shock. "They support you?"

"As I said, they wish for a more lenient and fairer ruler, something Richard cannot hope to be."

"They want a weak-willed puppet they can manipulate to do their bidding!" Richard's voice echoed in the chamber. "Don't think that they don't have their own interests at heart."

"Father, I've listened to their complaints and I want to solve them as a future king should."

"Hal, you can't turn Richard's nobles to your side," Henry tried to reason.

"They approached me. You can lay all the blame at Richard's feet." Hal marched out of the room, a smile on his lips.

Richard stalked to the fireplace and stared into it, his jaw clenched. Henry knew he had to strengthen the bonds between his sons or shorten their leashes. Once he was gone, would they band together to create a strong government, and protect each other's realms if one were challenged, or would they rebel against each other, destroying his great empire and all he had achieved?

The only way he could see to avoid this now, was to make Geoffrey and Richard pay homage to Hal, acknowledging him as their liege lord and attempt to make peace between them, however tenuous. He didn't foresee a problem with Geoffrey, but Richard was another matter. Fortunately, Alix was still with him and as before, he considered using her in his plans.

* ~ * ~ *

"Enter!"

Richard did as was bid. "Father, what is it you wish to see me about?" It had been several days since Hal's treachery had been brought to light. Richard hoped that his father finally realized that his favorite son was not to be trusted.

"Have a seat. Wine?"

Richard shook his head and leaned against the table, preparing himself for what Henry was going to say. He knew this wasn't going to be an easy conversation.

"You've been less than forthcoming with your dalliances. I'm surprised you brought Alixandra to my court so openly. Where did you find her?" Henry settled into a chair near the fireplace.

Richard's senses put him on high alert. He was thrown by this unexpected topic, but only observed curiosity in his father's eyes. "I met her in Poitiers."

"And you immediately took her into your household?" Henry raised one eyebrow.

"Something like that." A small smile played on Richard's lips as he recalled their meeting in the forest.

"How fortunate that she should fall into your lap, so to speak."

Richard snorted. "Yes, you could say that." He became solemn. "You didn't ask me here to talk about whom I share my bed with, did you?"

"As Hal mentioned, you are fortifying Clairvaux." Richard inclined his head in acknowledgement. "May I inquire as to why?"

Richard shrugged. "You're aware the castle is located near Chatellerault, a major trade route. I will not tolerate my barons taking advantage of the merchants any longer. Strengthening the castle sends a message to them that I have the power to control them and their actions. They're less likely to attack a fortified castle filled with well-trained knights within."

"You understand why Hal is angry, as it borders his lands? In light of these new allegations toward him, I can only assume he fears an attack from you."

"Clairvaux was once part of Poitou, giving him no cause to complain."

Henry's stare remained fixed on his son. "If it were vice-versa wouldn't you accuse him of threatening your lands?"

As if his brother would have the stomach to fight him. "Just so. What do you propose we do about this? I thought—"

"Richard…" He held up his hand to interrupt. "Hal is in the wrong, especially in his dealings with your nobles, but you are not without fault yourself. I believe another reason you were fortifying Clairvaux was to anger your brother." Richard was silent, waiting. "I want you to hand over Clairvaux."

"No! I won't give it to Hal. I refuse to allow him the satisfaction."

"Give it to me. That way neither of you can have any claim to use it."

Richard rubbed his chin and considered the idea. It was an acceptable solution. "Very well." Richard knew it would placate his father for a while. "However, this doesn't discount Hal's activities. I will deal with my brother as I see fit, whether I have your support or not." Without being dismissed, he turned and walked toward the door, the heels of his boots echoing off the high ceiling of his father's chambers.

Richard strode into his chambers, gesturing for his squires and pages to leave. As they hurried to obey, André waited to hear what had occurred.

"Where's Alix?"

"She went out. What did Henry want?"

"He wants Clairvaux." Richard crossed the room to pour some wine. "Now that Father knows of Hal's dealings, I wonder what avenue he will take, since he is forced to choose between his favorite son and me."

They discussed how this revelation could change the future until the light began to fade and dusk stole in. Richard rose and paced to the window. "Where is Alix? She should be back by now." He drank the rest of his wine, then went to his bedchamber to ready for dinner fully expecting her return by the time he had finished dressing.

When he emerged from his bedroom, André was still the only one in the darkening room. Richard frowned. "Come. Hopefully we'll meet her on the way."

Voices and laughter rang up the staircase as they descended. Moments later, they ran into Rob and Alix. "Where have you been?" Richard demanded.

"I went with Rob to town." Alix's voice was innocent and matter-of-fact. "Were you looking for me?"

"I was, but it can wait." Richard's frustration that she wasn't listening to his warnings to stay close cooled, knowing she was under Rob's protection.

"No, tell me." Ascending the steps, she took his arm and pulled him back upstairs, as André and Rob exchanged grins.

She went into the bedchamber to change for dinner, but left the door cracked. "What happened with your father?" she called out to him.

He moved to the door and leaned against the wall. "He wished to speak with me about Clairvaux."

"What did he say?" Her dress pooled at her feet and she stepped out of it.

"He made me yield it to him."

She chose a new dress and pulled it over her shoulders. "What would he get out of taking it?"

"If I kept it, Hal would consider it a threat to his lands. If it was given to him, he would use it to his advantage. To neutralize the situation, Father decided to take it himself, therefore nobody wins."

"I suppose that's equitable. How unfortunate that you put so much time into building it and in the end you are left with nothing." Alix approached him and turned so he could tie her laces.

"Am I left with nothing? Although I do want to control the commerce traveling through the region, Hal now knows that I don't respect him as a ruler. I'd say that's a triumph."

* ~ * ~ *

Dinner was a forced affair, the atmosphere frosty between Hal and Richard. The trip into town with Rob had lifted Alix's spirits and she'd been able to forget her troubles for a while, but tonight Hal was in his element, monopolizing the conversation.

Alix was chatting with Matilda, when Richenza reached over the table for a piece of bread, and knocked over a flagon of wine. Matilda jumped up to avoid the flow of red wine toward her, while Alix comforted a sobbing Richenza.

Henry motioned to a servant to come and mop up the spill.

"Let Alix clean it up," Hal laughed loudly. "Isn't that one of her many duties?"

Henry frowned at his eldest. It appeared that even he was tiring of Hal's malicious comments.

Alix froze, then turned to face Hal.

Richard recognized the look in her eyes and put his hand on her arm and gripped it. "Alix, no, not here." His plea was urgent under his breath.

Tired of being the object of Hal's rude remarks and insinuations, Alix stared at Hal but managed to swallow the biting retort that hovered on her tongue. She fumed throughout dinner, focusing on her plate so she wouldn't have cause to meet Hal's eyes. At last, Henry rose, signaling dinner and the ordeal was over. Alix wanted nothing more than to escape to her room, but that hope was dashed when Henry requested everyone's presence in his chambers.

Alix threw Richard a despondent look. "Must I join you? I can't abide any more of Hal's taunts."

"You will attend, Alix. Surely you can put your animosity aside for a short time?"

"You have no idea what you are asking of me, but I'll try." They made their way to Henry's chambers, Alix praying that this night would end soon.

~ *Chapter 26* ~

MATILDA AND HER FAMILY left the King's chambers early since they were departing the next morning. Constance and Geoffrey sat together on the settee, and Richard played chess with Henry as Hal watched. Alix was conversing with Marguerite, who had proved to be more likeable than originally thought, although both women carefully avoided the subject of Alys.

Hal finished his wine and looked around as he held up his cup for more. He frowned as he strode to the table to pour it himself. "Father, your servants have a bad habit of disappearing when they're needed. It must be difficult to find good help, don't you agree, Richard?" Hal asked loud enough for everyone to hear. "You've never been known for having good taste or making wise decisions when it comes to… the class of women you seek out. However, in this case, I'm sure Alixandra does everything you require of her. In and out of the bedchamber."

Henry glared at his eldest son along with Richard. Alix had had enough. Hal insulting her was one thing, but she wouldn't let him belittle Richard. She stood and approached him, hatred pulsing through her veins.

"I am sick to death of your snide comments and blatant insults! Yes, I am in the employ of your brother, but I work for a living!" Her low, scathing tone was enough to chill. "What do you do? Your father anointed you king of England but in name only since he doesn't allow you the power to rule. He supports you monetarily, but that isn't enough for you, is it? You always want more."

Alix closed the gap between them. Her fist clenched. "More money and more lands, and when he refuses, you throw a tantrum and stage a rebellion! Grow up already! God help the Angevin empire should you become the true king." Richard's perplexed expression caught her eye and she realized what she just did. She held her breath. "Oh, God, now I've done it," she whispered. Over her shoulder she risked a peek at Henry, who sat back in his chair with a look of satisfaction on his face.

The enormity of what she had said set in and she trembled. She curtsied and with studied dignity, maintained a steady pace to the door and opened it. She stepped into the hall, the voices of those inside muffled through the cracked door. She hesitated to listen at what might be her fate.

"She certainly knows how to make an exit," Geoffrey guffawed.

"What did she say to me, Father? I know the bitch insulted me," Hal demanded.

"Not now, Hal. Richard, go see to Alixandra, I will deal with her later."

The soft thud of the door closing sounded like a death knell. Tendrils of fear snaked through her body and a cold sweat erupted on her skin. She gathered her skirts, raced down the stairs, and ran to Richard's chambers.

~~*

Richard left the room, aghast at what had taken place. He entered his chambers, expecting to find Alix curled up on the bed in tears, but instead he found her pacing.

"What happened in there? What did you say to Hal?"

"You heard me. Jesus Christ, everyone heard me!" She paced a hot trail on the floor, not looking at him.

"Stop! Just stop." He took her hands and forced her to sit down in a chair. "I didn't understand what you said to him."

"What do you mean? You were there!"

"You spoke in English, Alix, not French."

"I did?" She furrowed her brow. "It's possible I suppose, as it is my native language." She looked up at him as a wave of relief washed over her tense body. "In that case, no one understood me because none of you speak English. Thank God!"

"Father speaks it quite well, so he understood. Tell me what you said."

His face tightened as she told him.

"Alix, that is grounds for treason. Insulting the anointed king is one transgression that neither Hal nor Father will ever forget."

"Oh, God, what will Henry do to me?" Fear filled her eyes and Richard's heart sank.

He shook his head. Kings had doled out severe punishment for far less, and he was apprehensive of what his father would require to make atonement.

"I'm so sorry." Her voice wavered. "I should leave. In my absence, maybe this will be forgotten, and it won't bring any trouble on you." She stood and headed to the bedroom when there was a knock on the door. She turned to stare at Richard.

"Enter."

"Your Grace, the King wishes to see the lady." The same squire that summoned Richard to the King's chambers now summoned Alix. She gasped and paled.

Richard crossed to her and put his hands on her shoulders. "Come, let's not waste time. My father has forgiven those that have done worse to him, so there is hope." She nodded as they made their way to the door.

"The King asks for the lady only."

Alix looked at the squire in consternation. "Why only me? Can't the Duke accompany me?"

The squire looked at her and repeated, "He summoned you, and you alone."

Richard gave her a reassuring smile as she left the room, then crossed to the window and stared out into the darkness, coldness stealing over him. What punishment would his father exact?

* ~ * ~ *

Alix followed the squire up the stairs, her gasping breath drowning out their footsteps.

The warning of the old woman she'd met in the church had come true. History as she knew it stood on a knife-edge. One misstep and everything could change. She balled her trembling hands into fists and willed her pounding heart to calm. Flames flickered as she passed lit sconces, throwing their distorted, twisting shadows against the walls, and she imagined it was like being escorted into the depths of Dante's *Inferno*.

Entering Henry's chamber, she found him standing before the fire. When he turned to face her, his cold look stole her breath. She stood, shifting from one foot to the other, her stomach churning in anticipation of his anger, which was surely coming.

"Sit." He pointed to a chair by the fire. "You have been in the employ of my son for several months, have you not?"

She took her seat, wiping her sweat-slicked palms on her skirt. Sitting upright on the edge of the chair, she focused on the floor to avoid the venomous look in the King's icy blue glare. "Yes, Your Majesty, I have, since early October."

"I assume you've been sharing his bed for almost as long." Her face heated at his disdainful comment, not sure he really expected an answer. "I realize that you're not highborn, merely a commoner, but for some reason Richard holds you in high enough regard to bring you to my court. He doesn't trust easily, so he must see something in you that I do not."

"I believe he trusts me as much as any person can trust another." Her eyes met his, a touch of asperity lacing her tone.

Henry's lips thinned in disapproval at her impertinence. "I'm sure he has apprised you of Hal's doings in Aquitaine." She nodded, waiting. "I have spent the majority of my life strengthening and expanding my empire and I refuse to let it be destroyed by petty fights amongst my sons. As Hal is my heir and will be king, I am going to require Geoffrey and Richard to pay homage to him publicly."

She raised her brow. Did she dare to speak? She couldn't help herself. "You must know that Richard, being the Duke of Aquitaine, won't willingly give his allegiance to Hal?"

"I know. That is where you come into play."

"Me? What do I have to do with this?"

"My son respects and listens to you. You will convince him that it is in his best interest to agree to these terms."

"I hold no sway over Richard." Alix leaned forward gripping the arms of the chair.

"Silence!" he thundered. "You have insulted the anointed king, which is treason. I've decided not to pursue punishment for your treacherous tongue if you do as I say. If not, we'll have other matters to discuss, ones that won't be so amenable to you."

She ran through her options, seeing no way out. "What would you have me do?" She tried her best to keep her voice from trembling.

"I admit I admire your mettle. It puts me in mind of Eleanor." He gave her a calculating look as his words sank in.

Her heart raced faster, and her stomach plummeted as Alix thought of Eleanor's years of imprisonment. Pressing her shaking knees together, she fought to hide her fear and gazed at him.

"Convince Richard to do as I command, and when you return home, keep him on a short leash. I don't want to hear any hint of insurgency."

"Shouldn't you save that speech for Hal? He is the one stirring up Richard's nobles."

"I am well aware of my eldest son's scheming. I will take Hal to task myself." Henry glowered in her direction. "You will also publicly apologize to Hal. As of now, I alone know what you said in my chambers. Make amends with Hal, grovel if you must, and there will be no need to divulge your words."

Alix lifted her chin. "I will do everything I can to convince him." Historically, Richard did pay homage to Hal, although his scheming brother refused to accept it. Acquiescing to Henry's orders would have no bearing on history, and she could escape the King's wrath.

"Good." His eyes hardened. "But, if you don't, I will hold you accountable for treason and your fate will be the same as my wife's. However, I promise you I will be far less lenient with you."

She gasped. "You wouldn't!"

"Would I not?" Henry's growl sent a fresh wave of adrenaline pulsing through her veins. "Leave me, but think carefully on your decision." She rose and shuffled to the door, her body utterly spent from fear and the effort it took to control it in front of the king of England. "Alixandra, if you flee, I will find you and I will look upon it as an act of defiance towards me, your King. Richard will pay the price for your insubordination."

His words stopped her exit. She turned to face him. "You can't use me to punish him. I'm not that important to him."

"If you don't want him to lose Aquitaine, play your part and play it convincingly. I don't have to tell you this conversation never happened. If I should inform Richard that you tried to worm your way into my good graces to save your own neck, I can guarantee that he'll consider this arrangement an act of betrayal." He turned back to the fire and dismissed her with a wave of his hand.

As Alix rushed out of Henry's chambers, she almost ran over the squire cowering outside the door. Farther down the corridor, she stopped and tried to calm herself, but she gave in to the tears that had been threatening since her outburst. She sank to the ground against the outside wall, cursing herself, Henry and Hal.

~ *Chapter 27* ~

WHAT WAS SHE GOING to tell Richard? When she entered their chamber, his knights were sitting at the table, but Richard was absent.

"Where is the Duke?" Alix swayed where she stood, drained from emotion.

"His father summoned him to his rooms." Rob stood and took Alix's elbow to steady her.

"He's on a tear tonight." She crossed the room, poured some wine, and slumped in the window seat.

"What did Henry want with you?" Rob sat next to her.

"He demanded that I apologize publicly for insulting Hal, which he completely deserved," she said, leaving out his other demand.

Rob laughed. "Richard told us what you said to Hal. Was that the only thing Henry required of you?"

"Yes. I'm worth nothing to him, so I guess my humiliation is recompense enough."

The door opened. At the murderous look on Richard's face, his men stood and beat a hasty retreat. Alix attempted to follow suit.

"Alixandra, stay." Richard's voice was deceptively calm.

She turned, but remained by the door, wondering why he wanted her there. A sense of foreboding rumbled in her stomach. Perhaps he knew what Henry had required of her and he was going to take his anger out on her. She prepared herself, ready to flee if necessary.

"I've just come from seeing my father."

She rubbed sweaty palms on her skirt. "What did Henry want with you?"

"Father has asked, no, demanded that I pay homage to Hal. We are both nobles and equals, yet once again he is treating Aquitaine as a lesser realm in his empire."

"Of course, you refused."

He shrugged. "Most assuredly I did. This is another of his ploys to make me seem the lesser ruler."

"Richard, Hal is the anointed king. He will become King of England, Normandy, and Count of Anjou. Although Aquitaine is a very important and powerful duchy, his empire *is* greater than yours."

He stared at her with hard eyes. "How dare you believe I am subordinate to Hal."

"I'm not saying that. As of now, you are equals. His titles are merely conferred on him, and until Henry dies, that's all they are, just titles. But one day he will be king."

"Aquitaine is my inheritance, and it will go to my heirs. I will never give it to Hal!"

"Did your father ask you to do that?"

"No. He demands only that I pay homage."

"So, just give your allegiance to Hal and that way you are beholden to each other. Can't you see that?" He regarded her evenly. What could she possibly say to convince him? "If you pay Hal homage, then you are under his protection. In turn, he must respect your decisions concerning your rule in Aquitaine. When he's king, think of all the resources he will have at hand. If you war with him, I fear you could be on the losing side."

"Are you denouncing me as a poor battlefield commander?"

It tore at her heart to see the disbelief and look of disappointment in his eyes at her words.

"No! You could easily destroy any army you come up against, but with all the money that Hal will have at his disposal, he could raise an impressive army against you. Since your nobles have shown him newfound loyalty, your numbers are further weakened." He was silent. "Please, do this. I don't want to see you go to war with Hal." Sensing he was accepting her words as truth, she played the last card she had. Although she knew the outcome of the rebellion, she hated playing the part of a weak woman. She went to him and laid her hand against his cheek. "I couldn't bear it if you went to war and didn't return."

He looked down at her and sighed. "Although your argument has merit, I need to consider all the ramifications of Father's demands. What did he ask of you?"

She shrugged, looking at the fireplace. "He demanded that I apologize to Hal."

"That's all? Nothing more? Don't lie to me, Alix, for I well know what he is capable of." He gripped her arm, forcing her to face him.

It was on the tip of her tongue to tell him what Henry had ordered her to do, but that would further incense Richard and could potentially change his decision to pay homage. "He promised not to tell Hal what I said if I publicly apologize." She looked at him. "I have no desire to be thrown into a dungeon, so I agreed."

"I was afraid he would demand a greater atonement from you."

She tried to muster a brave smile but failed. "So was I. My knees were so weak from fear that I could hardly stand. Perhaps he thinks that demeaning me somehow demeans you, even though I assured him I'm not that important to you."

Richard stepped forward and cupped her face in the warmth of his strong hands. Gone was the stern ruler, replaced by the considerate lover she knew so well.

"You're more important than you realize."

* ~ * ~ *

The following night, she stood on the parapet overlooking the town. Clouds drifted by, hiding the moon from sight while the freezing wind cut through her clothes. Shivering, she drew her cloak about her and gazed at the windows of the houses below, lit from within by the hearth fires.

"You're a damned hard woman to find, Alixandra. What are you doing out here in the freezing cold? Did Richard throw you out?"

"No. I needed air. I find that being forced to do your bidding is quite stifling."

Henry's lip curled. "I assume you spoke to him."

"Yes. He hasn't agreed yet, but after consideration I believe he will pay homage to Hal, although unwillingly." Alix wished she had the luxury of not knowing the consequences of Henry's demands. She wanted to spare Richard the indignity of Hal's attempt to humiliate him, but doing so would change the outcome, and history.

"Good." Henry smiled, pleased. "Well done, Alixandra."

"Is my part over now? I have done what you required."

"For now, yes. I'm tiring of the arguing between my sons. Tomorrow, after Matins you will apologize and Richard will pay homage to Hal. I refuse to allow this to drag out any longer." Henry paused then fixed his gaze on Alix. "When you return to Poitiers make sure Richard continues to honor his agreement. As for Hal, he has stated that if Richard pays homage, he will accept that and won't pursue the act of treason against you."

"Your Grace, can you order Hal to recognize Richard and his heirs as rulers of Aquitaine for generations to come? That is Richard's stipulation." Richard had no knowledge that Alix would make this request on his behalf, but Alix hoped that it would protect his duchy. "If Hal doesn't agree to that demand, *I* will tell Richard about our arrangement."

"How dare you threaten me! You are in no position to demand anything," Henry hissed, glancing around to make sure they were alone.

She quailed at his anger, her hands gripped tightly, then gathered what little courage she had left to keep her voice from quivering. "If you don't want another rebellion on your hands, make sure that Hal does as Richard demands."

He looked at her with pure hatred, turned and left just as quietly as he'd arrived. She stood, trembling with fear, trying to calm herself. A light scuff on the parapet sounded behind her and her heart leapt in her throat. She whirled around, but it was only dead leaves rasping against the stone wall.

She exhaled and paced along the parapet. Her stomach knotted with guilt and apprehension. What had she agreed to? Possible scenarios raced through her mind. Historically, Hal refused to accept Richard's homage, but, if Henry spoke with Hal, it was possible that he could convince the Young King to change his mind. If that were to happen, the rebellion against Richard could be averted, men's lives would be spared, and a possible truce might be enacted between the brothers. Although history would change, it would be for the better. On the other hand, if Hal stayed his course and refused Richard, history would remain the same. She wished she could tell Richard what she'd been ordered to do but he wouldn't appreciate her meddling in political affairs. And he would question how she knew of events that hadn't even happened. It was best to stay silent.

* ~ * ~ *

A squire opened the door at Alix's knock and she entered Richard's chambers, the warmth of the crackling fire welcome against her chilled skin. Richard sat at the table, letters of correspondence spread out before him. His eyes met hers and her heart leapt as it always did.

"Where in God's name have you been?" He stood and crossed the room. Irritation and worry flashed in his eyes. "My father didn't send for you again, did he?"

Her throat tightened as he'd guessed the truth, but she managed a smile. "No, I just wanted some time to think about what will happen soon." Afraid he might see the despair in her eyes, she turned toward the fire.

"Ah, yes. Father's demand that I pay Hal homage." Bitterness laced his tone.

Alix spun to face him. "Richard, please…"

"As much as it galls me to bow before that miscreant, you were very persuasive." He smiled at her and placed his hands on her shoulders. "Protecting Aquitaine takes precedence over my feelings toward Hal. I'll take whatever steps necessary to ensure that he'll never lay claim to my duchy."

"I know this is the last thing you want, but I would not want to see you and Hal war over Aquitaine." Her stomach tightened at the thought of what would soon happen. She would have to apologize to Hal, then watch him publicly belittle Richard, and be powerless to stop it.

Richard caressed her cheek with his hand. "For certes, I don't trust my brother." He bent to kiss her. She wrapped her arms around him and kissed him back until he broke contact, his ragged breathing mirroring hers. "As much as I would like to continue this, I must meet with my father. My duchy is my legacy, and I won't lose it. I must admit I have doubts as to the outcome of this mummery, but you and I will face it together." He kissed her again. "I know I can trust you, love," he murmured against her lips.

Alix shook off the sudden fear that snaked through her body. He could never know what his father had forced her to do. She took his face in her hands, smoothing her hands over the bristles of his beard, her heart swelling at the look of tenderness and protection in his eyes.

She loved this man, although she'd never said those exact words to him, and she knew he cared for her. She had no idea how long she would be able to remain in the twelfth century, but she vowed to herself that she would stand by him and fight for him, no matter what happened. "You have my loyalty, Richard. Now and always. Whatever happens tomorrow with your father and Hal, and in the days after that, we will face it together."

~ *Author Biography* ~

PAMELA TODD-HUNTER SPENT HER early years in Houston, Texas where she developed her love of reading. As a teen she was fortunate to have been able to move to Europe and soon she discovered gothic romance and fantasy. While visiting England and France her fascination with history was sparked.

After returning to the States for high school, she pursued her graduate degree in Geology, but she never lost her passion for history or romance.

She now resides in Houston with her husband and three children. Still working as a Geologist, she writes historical romance novels in her free time.

CPSIA information can be obtained
at www.ICGtesting.com
Printed in the USA
FSHW021154111119
63968FS